Stanley John

and educated Church

College, Oxfo obtained a degree in modern history. He qualified as a barrister and was called to the bar by the Inner Temple in 1881. His income was so little that he wrote some short stories which were published in *The Cornhill Magazine*, as a result of which the editor suggested he wrote on a larger scale. His first full-length novel, *The House of The Wolf* was serialized in the *English Illustrated Magazine* during 1883 but a publisher was not found until 1890. *Sophia* first appeared in 1900 during his period of writing historical romances, which lasted until 1908. In 1919 he began writing again, in a more serious vein, and his later books include *Ovington's Bank* and *The Great House*.

Weyman travelled widely and was a great friend of the novelist Henry Seton Merriman. In France in 1885 he was arrested on suspicion of being a spy. While in Switzerland he was presented with a tribute for the historical accuracy of his romantic novels. For the last thirty years of his life he lived in Denbighshire, where he was chairman of the Magistrates Bench. He died in 1928.

By the same author in Pan Books

THE CASTLE INN

CHIPPINGE

A GENTLEMAN OF FRANCE

STANLEY J. WEYMAN

SOPHIA

UNABRIDGED

PAN BOOKS LTD : LONDON

First published 1900.
This edition published 1972 by Pan Books Ltd,
33 Tothill Street, London, SW1.

ISBN 0 330 02994 0

*Printed in Great Britain by
Richard Clay (The Chaucer Press), Ltd,
Bungay, Suffolk*

To the gracious memory of
JAMES PAYN

CONTENTS

CHAPTER I

A Little Toad

IN THE dining-room of a small house on the east side of Arlington Street, which at that period – 1742 – was the Ministerial street, Mr and Mrs Northey sat awaiting Sophia. The thin face of the honourable member for Aldbury wore the same look of severity which it had worn a few weeks earlier on the eventful night when he had found himself called upon to break the ties of years and vote in the final division against Sir Robert; his figure, as he sat stiffly expecting his sister-in-law, reflected the attitudes of the four crude portraits of dead Northeys that darkened the walls of the dull little room. Mrs Northey on the other hand sprawled in her chair with the carelessness of the fine lady fatigued; she yawned, inspected the lace of her negligée, and now held a loose end to the light, and now pondered the number of a lottery ticket. At length, out of patience, she called fretfully to Mr Northey to ring the bell. Fortunately, Sophia entered at that moment.

'In time, and no more, miss,' madam cried with temper. Then as the girl came forward timidly, 'I'll tell you what it is,' Mrs Northey continued, 'you'll wear red before you're twenty! You have no more colour than a china figure this morning! What's amiss with you?'

Sophia, flushing under her brother-in-law's eyes, pleaded a headache.

Her sister sniffed. 'Eighteen, and the vapours!' she cried scornfully. 'Lord, it is very evident raking don't suit you! But do you sit down now, and answer me, child. What did you say to Sir Hervey last night?'

'Nothing,' Sophia altered, her eyes on the floor.

'Oh, nothing!' Mrs Northey repeated, mimicking her. 'Nothing! And pray, Miss Modesty, what did he say to you?'

'Nothing; or – or at least, nothing of moment,' Sophia stammered.

'Of moment! Oh, you know what's of moment, do you? And whose fault was that, I'd like to know? Tell me that, miss!'

Sophia, seated stiffly on the chair, her sandalled feet drawn under her, looked downcast and a trifle sullen, but did not answer.

'I ask, whose fault was that?' Mrs Northey continued impatiently. 'Do you think to sit still all your life, looking at your toes, and waiting for the man to fall into your lap? Hang you for a natural, if you do! It is not that way husbands are got, miss!'

'I don't want a husband, ma'am!' Sophia cried, stung at length into speech by her sister's coarseness.

'Oh, don't you?' Mrs Northey retorted. 'Don't you, Miss Innocence? Let me tell you, I know what you want. You want to make a fool of yourself with that beggarly, grinning, broad-shouldered oaf of an Irishman, that's always at your skirts! That's what you want. And he wants your six thousand pounds. Oh, you don't throw dust into my eyes!' Mrs Northey continued viciously, 'I've seen you puling and pining and making Wortley eyes at him these three weeks. Ay, and half the town laughing at you. But I'd have you to know, miss, once for all, we are not going to suffer it!'

'My life, I thought we agreed that I should explain matters,' Mr Northey said gently.

'Oh, go on then!' madam cried, and threw herself back in her seat.

'Only because I think you go a little too far, my dear,' Mr Northey said, with a cough of warning; 'I am sure that we can count on Sophia's prudence. You are aware, child,' he continued, directly addressing himself to her, 'that your father's death has imposed on us the – the charge of your person, and the care of your interests. The house at Cuckfield being closed, and your brother wanting three years of full age, your home must necessarily be with us for a time, and we have a right to expect that you will be guided by us in such plans as are broached for your settlement. Now I think I am right in saying,' Mr Northey continued, in his best House of Commons manner, 'that your sister has communicated to you the very advantageous proposal with which my good friend and colleague at Aldbury, Sir Hervey Coke, has honoured us? Ahem! Sophia, that is so, is it not? Be good enough to answer me.'

'Yes, sir,' Sophia murmured, her eyes glued to the carpet.

'Very good. In that case I am sure that she has not failed to point out to you also that Sir Hervey is a baronet of an old and respectable family, and possessed of a competent estate. That, in a word, the alliance is everything for which we could look on your behalf.'

'Yes, sir,' Sophia whispered.

'Then, may I ask,' Mr Northey continued, setting a hand on each knee, and regarding her majestically, 'in what respect you find the match not to your taste? If that be so?'

The young girl slid her foot to and fro, and for a moment did not answer. Then, 'I – I do not wish to marry him,' she said, in a low voice.

'You do not wish?' Mrs Northey cried, unable to contain herself longer. '*You* do not wish? And why, pray?'

'He's – he's as old as Methuselah!' the girl answered with a sudden spirit of resentment; and she moved her foot more quickly to and fro.

'As old as Methuselah?' Mr Northey answered, staring at her in unfeigned astonishment; and then, in a tone of triumphant refutation, he continued, 'Why, child, what are you dreaming of? He is only thirty-four! and I am thirty-six.'

'Well, at any rate, he is old enough – he is nearly old enough to be my father!' Sophia muttered rebelliously.

Mrs Northey could no longer sit by and hear herself flouted. She knew very well what was intended. She was twenty-nine, Sophia's senior by eleven years, and she felt the imputation that bounded harmlessly off her husband's unconsciousness. 'You little toad!' she cried. 'Do you think I do not know what you mean? I tell you, miss, you would smart for it, if I were your mother! Thirty-four, indeed: and you call him as old as Methuselah! Oh, thank you for nothing, ma'am! I understand you.'

'He's twice as old as I am!' Sophia whimpered, bending before the storm. And in truth to eighteen thirty-four seems elderly; if not old.

'You! You're a baby!' Mrs Northey retorted, her face red with passion. 'How any man of sense can look at you or want you passes me! But he does, and if you think we are going to sit by and see our plans thwarted by a chit of a girl of your years, you are mistaken, miss. Sir Hervey's vote, joined to the two county votes which my lord commands, and to Mr Northey's seat, will gain my lord a step in the peerage; and when Coke is married to you, his vote will be ours. As for you, you white-faced puling thing, I should like to know who you are that you should not be glad of a good match when it is offered you? It is a very small thing to do for your family.'

'For *your* family!' Sophia involuntarily exclaimed; the next moment she could have bitten off her tongue.

Fortunately a glance from Mr Northey, who prided himself on his diplomacy, stayed the outburst that was on his wife's lips. 'Allow me, my dear,' he said. 'And do you listen to me, Sophia. Apart from his age, a ridiculous objection which could only come into the mind of a school-girl, is there anything else you have to urge against Sir Hervey?'

'He's as – as grave as death!' Sophia murmured tearfully.

Mr Northey shrugged his shoulders. 'Is that all?' he said.

'Yes, but – but—'

'But what? But what, Sophia?' Mr Northey repeated, with a fine show of fairness. 'I suppose you allow him to be in other respects a suitable match?'

'Yes, but – I do not wish to marry him, sir. That is all.'

'In that,' Mr Northey said firmly, 'you must be guided by us. We have your interests at heart, your best interests. And – and that should be enough for you.'

Sophia did not answer, but the manner in which she closed her lips, and kept her gaze fixed steadfastly on the floor, was far from boding acquiescence. Every feature indeed of her pale face – which only a mass of dark brown hair and a pair of the most brilliant and eloquent eyes redeemed from the common-place – expressed a settled determination. Mrs Northey, who knew something of her sister's disposition, which was also that of the family in general, discerned this, and could restrain herself no longer.

'You naughty girl!' she cried, with something approaching fury. 'Do you think that I don't know what is at the bottom of this? Do you think I don't know that you are pining and sulking for that hulking Irish rogue that's the laughing-stock of every company his great feet enter? Lord, miss, by your leave I'd have you to know we are neither fools nor blind. I've seen your sighings and oglings, your pinings and sinkings. And so has the town. Ay, you may blush' – in truth, Sophia's cheeks were dyed scarlet – 'my naughty madam! Blush you should, that can fancy a raw-boned, uncouth Teague a fine woman would be ashamed to have for a footman. But you shan't have him. You may trust me for that, as long as there are bars and bolts in this house, miss.'

'Sophia,' Mr Northey said in his coldest manner, 'I trust that there is nothing in this? I trust that your sister is misinformed?'

The girl, under the lash of her sister's tongue, had risen from her chair; she tried in vain to recover her composure.

'There was nothing, sir,' she cried hysterically. 'But after this – after the words which my sister has used to me, she has only herself to thank if – if I please myself, and take the gentleman she has named – or any other gentleman.'

'Ay, but softly,' Mr Northey rejoined, with a certain unpleasant chill in his tone. 'Softly, Sophia, if you please. Are you aware that if your brother marries under age and without his guardian's consent, he forfeits ten thousand pounds in your favour? And as much more to your sister? If not, let me tell you that it is so.'

Sophia stared at him. but did not answer.

'It is true,' Mr Northey continued, 'that your father's will contains no provisions for your punishment in the like case. But this clause proves that he expected his children to be guided by the advice of their natural guardians; and for my part, Sophia, I expect you to be so guided. In the meantime, and that there may be no mistake in the matter, understand, if you please, that I forbid you to hold from this moment any communication with the person who has been named. If I cannot prescribe a match for you, I can at least see that you do not disgrace your family.'

'Sir!' Sophia cried, her cheeks burning.

But Mr Northey, a man of slow pulse and the least possible imagination, returned her fiery look unmoved. 'I repeat it,' he said coldly. 'For that and nothing else an alliance with this – this person would entail. Let there be no misunderstanding on that point. You are innocent of the world, Sophia, and do not understand these distinctions. But I am within the truth when I say that Mr Hawkesworth is known to be a broken adventurer, moving upon sufferance among persons of condition, and owning a character and antecedents that would not for a moment sustain inquiry.'

'How can that be?' Sophia cried passionately. 'It is not known who he is.'

'He is not one of us,' Mr Northey answered with dignity. 'For the rest, you are right in saying that it is not known who he is. I am told that even the name he bears is not his own.'

'No, it is not!' Sophia retorted; and then stood blushing and convicted, albeit with an exultant light in her eyes. No, his name was not his own! She knew that from his own lips; and knew, too, from his own lips, in what a world of romance he moved, what a future he was preparing, what a triumph might be, nay, would be, his by-and-by – and might be hers! But her mouth was sealed; already, indeed, she had said more than she had the right to say. When Mr Northey, surprised by her acquiescence, asked with acerbity how she knew that Hawkesworth was not the man's name, and what the man's name was, she stood mute. Wild horses should not draw that from her.

But it was natural that her brother-in-law should draw his conclusions, and his brow grew darker. 'It is plain, at least, that you have admitted him to a degree of intimacy extremely improper,' he said, with more heat than he had yet exhibited. 'I fear, Sophia, that you are not so good a girl as I believed. However, from this moment you will see that you treat him as a stranger. Do you hear me?'

'Yes, sir. Then – then I am not to go with you this evening?'

'This evening! You mean to Vauxhall? And why not, pray?'

'Because – because, if I go, I must see him. And if I see him I – I must speak to him,' Sophia cried, her breast heaving with generous resentment. 'I will not pass him by, and let him think me – everything that is base!'

For a moment Mr Northey looked a little nonplussed. Then, 'Well, you can – you can bow to him,' he said, pluming himself on his discretion in leaving the rein a trifle slack to begin. 'If he force himself upon you, you will rid yourself of him with as little delay as possible. The mode I leave to you, Sophia; but speech with him I absolutely forbid. You will obey in that on pain of my most serious displeasure.'

'On pain of bread and water, miss!' her sister cried venomously. 'That will have more effect, I fancy. Lord, for my part, I should die of shame if I thought that I had encouraged a nameless Irish rogue not good enough to ride behind my coach. And all the town to know it.'

Rage dried the tears that hung on Sophia's lids. 'Is that all?' she asked, her head high. 'I should like to go if that is all you have to say to me?'

'I think that is all,' Mr Northey answered.

'Then – I may go?'

He appeared to hesitate. For the first time his manner betrayed doubt; he looked at his wife and opened his mouth, then closed it. At length, 'Yes, I think so,' he said pompously. 'And I trust you will regain our approbation by doing as we wish, Sophia. I am sorry to say that your brother's conduct at Cambridge has not been all that we could desire. I hope that you will see to it, and show yourself more circumspect. I truly hope that you will not disappoint us. Yes, you may go.'

Sophia waited for no second permission. Her heart bursting, her cheeks burning, she hurried from the room, and flew up the stairs to shut herself in her chamber. Here, on the second floor, in a room consecrated to thoughts of *him* and dreams of *him*, where in a secret nook behind the bow-fronted drawer of her toilet table lay the withered flower he had given her the day he stole her glove, she felt the full wretchedness of her lot. She would see him no more! Her tears gushed forth, her bosom heaved at the thought. She would see him no more! Or worse, she would see him only in public, at a distance; whence his eyes would stab her for a jilt, a flirt, a cold, heartless, worldly creature, unworthy to live in the same world, unworthy to breathe the same air with Constancy.

And he had been so good to her! He had been so watchful, so assiduous, so delicate, she had fondly, foolishly deemed his court a secret from all.

The way to her heart had not been difficult. Her father's death had cast her, a timid country girl, into the vortex of the town, where for a time she had shrunk from the whirl of routs and masquerades, the smirking beaux and loud-voiced misses, among whom she found herself. She had sat mum and abashed in companies where her coarser sister ruled and ranted; where one had shunned and another had flouted the silent, pale-faced girl, whose eyes and hair and tall slender shape just redeemed her from insignificance. Only Mr Hawkesworth, the Irishman, had discerned in her charms that in a remarkably short time won his regards and fixed his attentions. Only he, with the sensibility of an unspoiled Irish heart, had penetrated the secret of her loneliness; and in company had murmured sympathy in her ear, and at the opera, where he had not the entrée to her sister's box, had hung on her looks from afar, speaking more sweetly with his fine eyes than Monticelli or Amorevoli sang on the stage.

For Sir Hervey, his would-be rival, the taciturn, middle-aged man, who was Hervey to half the men about town, and Coke to three-fourths of the women; who gamed with the same nonchalance with which he made his court – he might be the pink of fashion in his dull mooning way, but he had nothing that caught her eighteen-year-old fancy. On the contrary he had a habit of watching her, when Hawkesworth was present, at the mere remembrance of which her cheek flamed. For that alone, and in any event, she hated him; and would never, never marry him. They might rob her of her dear Irishman; they might break her heart – so her thoughts ran to the tremolo of a passionate sob; they might throw her into a decline; but they should never, never compel her to take *him*! She would live on bread and water for a year first. She was fixed, fixed, fixed on that, and would ever remain so.

Meanwhile downstairs the two who remained in the room she had left kept silence until her footsteps ceased to sound on the stairs. Then Mr Northey permitted his discontent to appear. 'I wish, after all, I had told her,' he said, moving restlessly in his chair. 'Hang it, ma'am, do you hear?' he continued, looking irritably at his wife, 'I wish I had taken my own line, and that is a fact.'

'Then you wish you had been a fool, Mr Northey!' the lady answered with fine contempt. 'Do you think that this silly girl would rest content, or let us rest, until you had followed her dear brother Tom, and brought him back from his charmer? Not she! And for him, if you are thinking of him, he was always a rude cub, and bound for the dogs one day or other. What does it matter whether he is ruined before he is of age or after? Eh, Mr Northey?'

'It matters to us,' Mr Northey answered.

'It may matter ten thousand to us, if we mind our own business,' his wife answered coolly. 'So do you let him be for a day or two.'

'It matters as much to Sophia,' he said, trying to find excuses for himself and his inaction.

'And why not? There will be so much the more to bind Coke to us.'

'He has plenty now.'

'Much wants more, Mr Northey.'

'Of course the thing may be done already,' he argued, striving to convince himself. 'For all we know, the match is made, and 'tis too late to interfere. Your brother was always wilful; and it is not likely the woman would let him go for a word. On the other hand—'

'There is no other hand!' she cried, out of patience with his weakness. 'I tell you, let be. Let the boy marry whom he pleases, and when he pleases. 'Tis no matter of ours.'

'Still, I wish this tutor had not written to us.'

'If the knot was not tied yesterday, there are persons enough will tie it today for half a guinea!' she said. 'It is not as if you were his only guardian. His father chose another elsewhere. Let him look to it. The girl is charge enough for us; and, for her, she benefits as much as we do if he's foolish. I wish that were the worst of it. But I scent danger, Mr Northey. I am afraid of this great Teague of hers. He's no Irishman if he doesn't scent a fortune a mile off. And once let him learn that she is worth sixteen thousand pounds instead of six thousand, and he'll off with her from under our very noses.'

'It's that Irish Register has done the mischief!' Mr Northey cried, jumping up with an oath. 'She's in there, in print!'

'Under her own name?'

'To be sure, as a fortune. And her address.'

'Do you mean it, Mr Northey? Printed in the book, is it?'

'It is; as I say.'

'Hang their impudence!' his wife cried in astonishment. 'They ought to be pilloried! But there is just this, we can show the entry to the girl. And if it don't open her eyes, nothing will. Do you get a copy of the book, Mr Northey, and we'll show it to her tomorrow, and put her on the notion every Irishman has it by heart. And as soon as we can we must get her married to Coke. There'll be no certainty till she's wedded. 'Twould have been done this fortnight if he were not just such a mumchance fool as the girl herself. He may look very wise, and the town may think him so. But there's more than looking wanted with a woman, Mr Northey; and for what I see he's as big a fool as many that never saw Pall Mall.'

'I have never found him that,' Mr Northey answered with a dry cough. He spoke with reason, for he had more than once, as heir to a peerage, taken on himself to set Sir Hervey right; with so conspicuous a lack of success that he had begun to suspect that his brother member's silence was not dullness; nay, that he himself came late into that secret. Or why was Coke so well with that great wit and fashionable, Hambury Williams? With Henry Fox, and my lord Chesterfield? With young Lord Lincoln, the wary quarry of match-making mothers, no less than with Tom Hervey, against whom no young virgin, embarking on life, failed of a warning? Mr Northey knew that in the company of these, and their like, he was no favourite, while Coke was at home; and he hid with difficulty a sneaking fear of his colleague.

What a man so highly regarded and so well received saw in a girl who, in Mr Northey's eyes, appeared every way inferior to her loud, easy, fashionable sister, it passed the honourable member to conceive. But the thing was so. Sir Hervey had spoken the three or four words beyond which he seldom went – the venture had been made; and now if there was one thing upon which Mr Northey's dogged mind was firmly fixed, it was that an alliance so advantageous should not be lost to the family.

'But Sophia is prudent,' he said, combating his own fears. 'She has always been obedient and – and well-behaved. I am sure she's – she's a good girl, and will see what is right when it is explained to her.'

'If she does not, she will see sorrow!' his wife answered truculently. She had neither forgotten nor forgiven the sneer about Methuselah. 'I'll tell you what it is, Mr Northey,' madam continued, 'she takes you in with her pale, peaky face and her round eyes. But if ever there was a nasty, obstinate little toad, she is one. And you'll find it out by-and-by. And so will Coke to his cost some day.'

'Still you think – we can bend her this time?'

'Oh, she'll marry him!' Mrs Northey retorted confidently. 'I'll answer for that. But I would not be Coke afterwards.'

CHAPTER II

At Vauxhall

In a year when all the world was flocking to the new Rotunda in Ranelagh Gardens, Mrs Northey would be particular, and have her evening party to Vauxhall. Open air was the fashion of the time, and it was from her seat at the open window in Arlington Street that she welcomed her guests. Thence, as each new-comer appeared she shouted her greeting, often in terms that convulsed the chairmen at the corner; or now and again, hanging far out, she turned her attention and wit to the carpenters working late on Sir Robert's house next door, and stated in good round phrases her opinion of the noise they made. When nearly all her company were assembled, and the room was full of women languishing and swimming, and of men mincing and prattling, and tapping their snuff-boxes, Sophia stole in, and, creeping into a corner, hid herself behind two jolly nymphs, who, with hoops six feet wide and cheeks as handsome as crimson could make them, were bandying jokes and horse-play with a tall admirer. In this retreat Sophia fancied that she might hide her sad looks until the party set out; and great was her dismay, when, venturing at last to raise her eyes, she discovered that she had placed herself beside, nay, almost touching the man whom of all others she wished to avoid, the detested Coke; who, singularly enough, had sought the same retirement a few moments earlier.

In the confusion of the moment she recoiled a step; the events of the day had shaken her nerves. Then, 'I beg your pardon, sir, I did not see that you were there,' she stammered.

'No,' he said with a smile, 'I know you did not, child. Or you would have gone to the other end of the room. Now, confess. Is it not so?'

She shrugged her shoulders. 'As you please, sir,' she said, 'I would not venture to contradict you,' and curtseying satirically she turned away her face. At any rate he should lie in no doubt of her feelings.

He did not answer. And, welcome as his silence was, something like contempt of a suitor who aspired to have without daring to speak took possession of her. Under the influence of this feeling, embittered by the rating she had received that morning, she fell to considering him out of the tail of her eye, but, in spite of herself, she could not deny that he was personable; that his features, if a trifle set and lacking vivacity, were good, and his bearing that of a gentleman at ease in his company. Before she had well weighed him, however, or done more than compare him with the fop who stood before her, and whose muff and quilted coat, long queue and black leather stock were in the extreme of the fashion, Sir Hervey spoke again.

'Why does it not please you?' he asked, almost listlessly.

'To do what, sir?'

'To be beside me.'

'I did not say it did not,' she answered, looking stiffly the other way.

'But it does not,' he persisted. 'I suppose, child, your sister has told you what my views are?'

'Yes, sir.'

'And what did you say?' he murmured.

'That – that I am much obliged to you, but they are not mine!' Sophia answered, with a rush of words and colour; and, punished as she had been that morning, it must be confessed, she cruelly enjoyed the stroke.

For a moment only. Then to her astonishment and dismay Sir Hervey laughed. 'That is what you say now,' he answered lightly. 'What will you say if, by-and-by, when we know one another better, we get on as well together as – as Lady Sophia there, and—'

'And Lord Lincoln?' she cried, seeing that he hesitated. 'Never!'

'Indeed!' he retorted. 'But, pray, what do you know about Lord Lincoln?'

'I suppose you think I know no scandal?' she cried.

'I would prefer you to know as little as possible,' he answered coolly; in the tone she fancied which he would have used had she been already his property. 'And there is another thing I would also prefer you did not know,' he continued.

'Pray, what is that?' she cried, openly scornful; and she flirted her fan a little faster.

'Mr Hawkesworth.'

The blood rushed to her cheeks. This was too much. 'Are you jealous? or only impertinent?' she asked, her voice not less furious because it was low and guarded. 'How noble, how chivalrous, to say behind a gentleman's back what you would not dare to say to his face!'

Sir Hervey shrugged his shoulders. 'He is not a gentleman,' he said. 'He is not one of us, and he is not fit company for you. I do not know what story he has told you, nor what cards he has played, but I know that what I say is true. Be advised, child,' he continued earnestly, 'and look on him coldly when you see him next. Be sure if you do not—'

'You will speak to my sister?' she cried. 'If you have not done it already? Lord, sir, I congratulate you. I'm sure you have discovered quite a new style of wooing. Next, I suppose, you will have me sent to my room, and put on bread and water for a week? Or buried in a parsonage in the country with Tillotson's Sermons and the "Holy Living"?'

'I spoke to you as I should speak to my sister,' Sir Hervey said, with something akin to apology in his tone.

'Say, rather, as you would speak to your daughter!' she replied, quick as lightning; and, trembling with rage. she drove home the shaft with a low curtsey. 'To be sure, sir, now I think of it, the distance between us justifies you in giving me what advice you please.'

He winced at last, and was even a trifle out of countenance. But he did not answer, and she, furiously angry, turned her back on him, and looked the other way. Young as she was, all the woman in her rose in revolt against the humiliation of being advised in such a matter by a man. She could have struck him. She hated him. And they were all in the same story. They were all against her and her dear Irishman, who alone understood her. Tears rose in Sophia's eyes as she pictured her present loneliness and her happiness in the past; as she recalled the old home looking down the long avenue of chestnut trees, the dogs, the horses, the boisterous twin brother, and the father who by turns had coarsely chidden and fondly indulged her. In her loss of all this, in a change of life as complete as it was sudden, she had found one only to comfort her, one only who had not thought the whirl of strange pleasures a sufficient compensation for a home and a father. One only who had read her silence, and pitied her inexperience. And him they would snatch from her! Him they would—

But at this point her thoughts were interrupted by a general movement towards the door. Bent on an evening's frolic the party issued into Arlington Street with loud laughter and louder voices, and in a moment were gaily descending St James's Street. One or two of the elder ladies took chairs, but the greater part walked, the gentlemen with hats under their arms and canes dangling from their wrists, the more foppish with muffs. Passing down St James's, where Betty, the fruit woman, with a couple of baskets of fruit, was added to the company, they crossed the end of Pall Mall, now inviting a recruit, after the easy fashion of the day, and now hailing a friend on the farther side of the street. Thence, by the Mall and the Horse Guards, and so to the Whitehall Stairs, where boats were waiting for them on the grey evening surface of the broad river.

Sophia found herself compelled to go in the same boat with Sir Hervey, but she took good heed to ensconce herself at a distance from him; and, successful in this, sat at her end, moody, and careless of appearances. There was singing and a little romping in the stern of the boat, where the ladies principally sat, and where their hoops called for some arrangement. Presently a pert girl, Lady Betty Cochrane, out at sixteen, and bent on a husband before she was seventeen, marked Sophia's silence, nudged those about her, and took on herself to rally the girl.

'La, miss, you must have been at a Quakers' meeting!' she cried, simpering. 'It is easy to see where your thoughts are.'

'Where?' Sophia murmured, abashed by this public notice.

'I believe there is very good acting in – *Doblin!*' the provoking creature answered, with her head on one side, and a sentimental air; and the ladies tittered and the gentlemen smiled. 'Have you been to – Doblin, miss?' she continued, with a look that winged the innuendo.

Sophia, her face on fire, did not answer.

'Oh, la, miss, you are not offended, I hope!' the tormentor cried politely. 'Sure, I thought the gentleman had spoken, and all was arranged. To be sure—

'"O'Rourke's noble fare
Will ne'er be forgot
By those who were there,
And those who were not!"

And those who were not!' she hummed again, with a wink that drove the ladies to hide their mirth in their handkerchiefs. 'A fine man, O'Rourke, and I have heard that he was an actor in – Doblin!' the little tease continued.

Sophia, choking with rage, and no match for her town-bred antagonist, could find not a word to answer; and worse still, she knew not where to look. Another moment and she might even have burst into tears, a mishap which would have disgraced her for ever in that company. But at the critical instant a quiet voice at the stern was heard, quoting—

'Whom Simplicetta loves the town would know,
Mark well her knots, and name the happy beau!'

On which it was seen that it is one thing to tease and another to be teased. Lady Betty swung round in a rage, and without a word attacked Sir Hervey with her fan with a violence that came very near to upsetting the boat. 'How dare you, you horrid man?' she cried, when she thought she had beaten him enough. 'I wish there were no men in the world, I declare I do! It's a great story, you ugly thing! If Mr Hesketh says I gave him a knot, he is just a—'

A shout of laughter cut her short. Too late she saw that she had betrayed herself, and she stamped furiously on the bottom of the boat. 'He cut it off!' she shrieked, raising her voice above the laughter. 'He cut it off! He would cut it off! 'Tis a shame you will not believe me. I say—'

A fresh peal of laughter drowned her voice, and brought the boat to the landing-place.

'All the same, Lady Betty,' the nearest girl said as they prepared to step out, 'you'd better not let your mother hear, or you'll go milk cows, my dear, in the country! Lord, you little fool, the boy's not worth a groat, and should be at school by rights!'

Miss Betty did not answer, but cocking her chin with disdain, which made her look prettier than ever, stepped out, sulking. Sophia followed, her cheeks a trifle cooler than they had been; and the party, once more united, proceeded on foot from the river to the much-praised groves of Pleasure; where ten thousand lamps twinkled and glanced among the trees, or outlined the narrowing avenue that led to the glittering pavilion. In the wide and open space before this Palace of Aladdin a hundred gay and lively groups were moving to and fro to the strains of the band, or were standing to gaze at the occupants of the boxes; who, sheltered from the elements, and divided from the humbler visitors by little gardens, supped *al fresco*, their ears charmed by the music, and their eyes entertained by the ever-changing crowd that moved below them.

Two of the best boxes had been retained for Mrs Northey's party, but before they proceeded to them her company chose to stroll up and down a time or two, diverting themselves with the humours of the place and the evening. More than once Sophia's heart stood still as they walked. She fancied that she saw Hawkesworth approaching, that she distinguished his form, his height, his face amid the crowd; and conscious of the observant eyes around her, as well as of her sister's displeasure, she knew not where to look for embarrassment. On each occasion it turned out that she was mistaken, and to delicious tremors succeeded the chill of a disappointment almost worse to bear. After all, she reflected, if she must dismiss him, here were a hundred opportunities of doing so in greater freedom than she could command elsewhere. The turmoil of the press through which they moved, now in light and now in shadow, now on the skirts of the romantic, twilit grove, and now under the blaze of the pavilion lamps, favoured the stolen word, the kind glance, the quick-breathed sigh. But though he knew that she was to be there, though of late he had seldom failed her in such public resorts as this, he did not appear; and by-and-by her company left the parade, and, entering the boxes, fell to mincing chickens in china bowls, and cooking them with butter and water over a lamp, all with much romping and scolding, and some kissing and snatching of white fingers, and such a fire of jests and laughter as soon drew a crowd to the front of the box, and filled the little gardens on either side of them with staring groups.

Gayest, pertest, most reckless of all, Lady Betty was in her glory. Never was such a rattle as she showed herself. Her childish treble and shrill laugh, her pretty flushed face and tumbled hair were everywhere. Apparently bent on punishing Coke for his interference she never let him rest, with the result that Sophia, whose resentment still smouldered, was free to withdraw to the back of the box, and witness rather than share the sport that went forward. To this a new zest was given when Lord P—, who had been dining at a tavern on the river, arrived very drunk, and proceeded to harangue the crowd from the front of the box.

Sophia's seat at the back was beside the head of the half-dozen stairs that descended to the gardens. The door at her elbow was open. On a sudden, while the hubbub was at its height. and a good half of the party were on their feet before her – some encouraging his lordship to fresh vagaries, and others striving to soothe him – she heard a stealthy hist! hist! in the doorway beside her, as if someone sought to gain her attention. With Hawkesworth in her mind she peered that way in trembling apprehension; immediately a little white note dropped lightly at her feet, and she had a glimpse of a head and shoulders, withdrawn as soon as seen.

With a tumultuous feeling between shame and joy, Sophia, who, up to this moment, had had nothing clandestine on her conscience, slipped her foot over the note and glanced round to see if anyone had seen her. That moment an eager childish voice cried in her ear, 'Give me that! Give it me!' And then, more urgently, 'Do you hear? It is mine! Please give it me!'

The voice was Lady Betty's; and her flushed pleading face backed the appeal. At which, and all it meant, it is not to be denied that a little malice stirred in Sophia's breast. The chit had so tormented her an hour earlier, had so held her up to ridicule, so shamed her. It was no wonder she was inclined to punish her now. 'Yours, child,' she said, looking coldly at her. 'Impossible.'

'Yes, miss. Please – please give it me – at once, please, before it is too late.'

'I do not know that I shall,' Sophia answered virtuously, from the height of her eighteen years. 'Children have no right to receive notes. I ought to give it to your mother.' Then, with an unexpected movement, she stooped and possessed herself of the folded scrap of paper. 'I am not sure that I shall not,' she continued.

Lady Betty's face was piteous. 'If you do, I – shall be sent into the country,' she panted. 'I – I don't know what they'll do to me. Oh, please, please, will you give it me!'

Sophia had a kindly nature, and the girl's distress appealed to her. But it appealed in two ways.

'No, I shall not give it you,' she answered firmly. 'But I shall not tell your mother, either. I shall tear it up. You are too young, you little baby, to do this!' And suiting the action to the word, she tore the note into a dozen pieces and dropped them.

Lady Betty glared at her between relief and rage. At last 'Cat! Cat!' she whispered with childish spite. 'Thank you for nothing, ma'am. I'll pay you by-and-by, see if I don't!' And with a spring, she was back at the front of the box, her laugh the loudest, her voice the freshest, her wit the boldest and most impertinent of all. Sophia, who fancied that she had made an enemy, did not notice that more than once this madcap looked her way; nor that in the midst of the wildest outbusts she had an eye for what happened in her direction.

Sophia, indeed, had food for thought more important than Lady Betty, for the girl had scarcely left her side when Mrs Northey came to her, shook her roughly by the shoulder – they had direct ways in those days – and asked her in a fierce whisper if she were going to sulk there all the evening. Thus adjured, Sophia moved reluctantly to a front seat at the right-hand corner of the box. Lord P— had been suppressed, but broken knots of people still lingered before the garden of the box expecting a new escapade. To the right, in the open, fireworks were being let off, and the grounds in that direction were as light as in the day. Suddenly, Sophia's eyes, roving moodily hither and thither, became fixed. She rose to her feet with a cry of surprise, which must have been heard by her companions had they not been taken up at that moment with the arrest of a cut-purse by two thief-takers, a drama which was going forward on the left.

'There's – there's Tom!' she cried, her astonishment extreme, since Tom should have been at Cambridge. And raising her voice she shouted 'Tom! Tom!'

Her brother did not hear. He was moving across the open lighted space, some fifteen paces from the box; a handsome boy, foppishly dressed, moving with the affected indifference of a very young dandy. Sophia glanced round in an agony of impatience, and found that no one was paying any attention to her; there was no one she could send to call him. She saw that in a twinkling he would be lost in the crowd, and, acting on the impulse of the moment, she darted to the stairs, which were only two paces from her, and flew down them to overtake him. Unfortunately, she tripped at the bottom and almost fell, lost a precious instant, and lost Tom. When she reached the spot where she had last seen him, and looked round, her brother was not to be seen.

Or yes, there he was, in the act of vanishing down one of the dim alleys that led into the grove. Half laughing, half crying, innocently anticipating his surprise when he should see her, Sophia sped after him. He turned a corner—the place was a maze and dimly lighted – she followed him; she thought he met someone, she hurried on, and the next moment was all but in the arms of Hawkesworth.

'Sophia!' the Irishman cried, pressing his hat to his heart as he bowed before her. 'Oh, my angel, that I should be so blest! This is indeed a happy meeting.'

But she was far at the moment from thinking of him. Her brother occupied her whole mind. 'Where is he?' she cried, looking every way. 'Where is Tom? Mr Hawkesworth, you must have seen him. He must have passed you.'

'Seen whom, ma'am?' her admirer asked with eager devotion. He was tall, with a certain florid grace of carriage; and ready, for his hand was on his heart, and his eyes expressed the joy he felt, almost before she knew who stood before her. 'If it is any one I know, make me happy by commanding me. If he be at the ends of the earth, I will bring him back.'

'It is my brother!'

'Your brother?'

'Yes – but you would not know him,' she cried, stamping her foot with impatience. 'How annoying!'

'Not know him?' he answered gallantly. 'Oh, ma'am, how little you know me!' And Hawkesworth extended his arm with a gesture half despairing, half reproachful. 'How little you enter into my feelings if you think that I should not know *your* brother! My tongue I know is clumsy, and says little, but my eyes' – and certainly they dwelt boldly enough on her. blushing face, 'my eyes must inform you more correctly of my feelings.'

'Please, please do not talk like that!' she cried in a low voice, and she wrung her hands in distress. 'I saw my brother, and I came down to overtake him, and – and somehow I have missed him.'

'But I thought that he was at Cambridge?' he said.

'He should be,' she replied. 'But it was he. It was he indeed. I ran to catch him, and I have missed him, and I must go back at once. If you please, I must go back at once.'

'In one moment you shall,' he cried, barring the road, but with so eloquent a look and a tone so full of admiration that she could not resent the movement. 'In one moment you shall. But, my angel, heaven has sent you to my side, heaven has taken pity on my passion, and given me this moment of delight – will you be more cruel and snatch it from me? Nay, but, sweet,' he continued with ardour, making as if he would kneel, and take possession of her hand, 'sweetest one, say that you, too, are glad! Say—'

'Mr Hawkesworth, I am glad,' she murmured, trembling; while her face burned with blushes. 'For it gives me an opportunity I might otherwise have lacked of – of – oh, I don't know how I can say it!'

'Say what, madam?'

'How I can take – take leave of you,' she murmured, turning away her head.

'Take leave of me?' he cried. 'Take leave of me?'

'Yes, oh, yes! Believe me, Mr Hawkesworth,' Sophia continued, beginning to stammer in her confusion, 'I am not ungrateful for your attentions, I am not, indeed, ungrateful, but we – we must part.'

'Never!' he cried, rising and looking down at her. 'Never! It is not your heart that speaks now, or it speaks but a lesson it has learned.'

Sophia was silent.

'It is your friends who would part us,' he continued with stern and bitter emphasis. 'It is your cold-blooded, politic brother-in-law; it is your proud sister—'

'Stay, sir,' Sophia said unsteadily. 'She *is* my sister.'

'She is; but she would part us!' he retorted. 'Do you think that I do not understand that? Do you think that I do not know why, too? They see in me only a poor gentleman. I cannot go to them, and tell them what I have told you! I cannot,' he continued, with a gesture that in the daylight might have seemed a little theatrical, but in the dusk of the alley and to a girl's romantic perceptions commended itself gallantly enough, 'put my life in their hands as I have put it in yours! I cannot tell them that the day will come when Plomer Hawkesworth will stand on the steps of a throne and enjoy all that a king's gratitude can confer. When he who now runs daily, nightly, hourly the risk of Layer's fate, whose head may any morning rot on Temple Bar and his limbs on York Gates—'

Sophia interrupted him; she could bear no more. 'Oh, no, no!' she cried, shuddering and covering her eyes. 'God forbid! God forbid, sir! Rather—'

'Rather what, sweet?' he cried, and he caught her hand in rapture.

'Rather give up this – this dangerous life,' she sobbed, overcome by the horror of the things his words had conjured up. 'Let others tread such dangerous ways and run such risks. Give up the Jacobite cause, Mr Hawkesworth, if you love me as you say you do, and I—'

'Yes? Yes?' he cried; and across his handsome face, momentarily turned from her as if he would resist her pleading, there crept a look half of derision, half of triumph. 'What of you, sweet?'

But her reply was never spoken, for as he uttered the word the fireworks died down with startling abruptness, plunging the alley in which they stood into gloom. The change recalled the girl to a full and sudden sense of her position; to its risks and to its consequences, should her absence, even for a moment, be discovered. Wringing her hands in distress, in place of the words that had been on her lips, 'Oh, I must go!' she cried. 'I must get back at once!' And she looked for help to her lover.

He did not answer her, and she turned from him, fearing he might try to detain her. But she had not taken three steps before she paused in agitation, uncertain in the darkness which way she had come. A giggling, squealing girl ran by her into the grove, followed by a man; at the same moment a distant fanfare of French horns, with the confused noise of a multitude of feet trampling the earth at once, announced that the entertainment was over, and that the assembly was beginning to leave the gardens.

Sophia's heart stood still. What if she were missed? Worse still, what if she were left behind? 'Oh,' she cried, turning again to him, her hands outstretched, 'which is the way? Mr Hawkesworth, please, please show me the way! Please take me to them!'

But the Irishman did not move.

CHAPTER III

The Clock-maker

IT EVEN seemed to Sophia that his face, as he stood watching her, took on a smirk of satisfaction, faint, but odious; and in that moment, and for the moment, she came near to hating him. She knew that in the set in which she moved much might be overlooked, and daily and hourly was overlooked, in the right people. But to be lost at Vauxhall at midnight, in the company of an unauthorized lover – this had a horribly clandestine sound; this should be sufficient to blacken the fame of a poor maid – or her country education was at fault. And knowing this, and hearing the confused sounds of departure rise each moment louder and more importunate, the girl grew frantic with impatience.

'Which way? Which way?' she cried. 'Do you hear me? Which way are the boxes. Mr Hawkesworth? You know which way I came. Am I to think you a dolt, sir, or – or what?'

'Or what?' he repeated, grinning feebly. To be candid, the occasion had not been foreseen, and the Irishman, though of readiest wit, could not on the instant make up his mind how he would act.

'Or a villain?' she cried, with a furious glance. And in the effort to control herself, the ivory fan-sticks snapped in her small fingers as if they had been of glass. 'Take me back this instant, sir,' she continued, her head high, 'or never presume to speak to me again!'

What he would have said to this is uncertain, for the good reason that before he answered, two men appeared at the end of the alley. Catching the sheen of Sophia's hoop skirt, where it glimmered light against the dark of the trees, they espied the pair, took them for a pair of lovers, and with a whoop of drunken laughter came towards them. One was Lord P—, no soberer than before; the other a brother buck flushed with wine to the same pitch of insolence, and ready for any folly or mischief. Crying 'So ho! A petticoat! A petticoat!' the two Mohocks joined hands, and with a tipsy view-halloa! swept down the green walk, expecting to carry all before them.

But it was in such an emergency as this that the Irishman was at his best. Throwing himself between the shrinking, frightened girl and the onset of the drunken rakes, he raised his cane with an air so determined that the assailants thought better of their plan, and, pausing with a volley of drunken threats, parted hands and changed their scheme of attack. While one prepared to rush in and overturn the man, the other made a feint aside, and thrusting himself through the shrubs, sprang on the girl. Sophia screamed, and tried to free herself; but scream and effort were alike premature. With a rapid twirl Hawkesworth avoided my lord's rush, caught him by the wrist as he blundered by, and swinging him off his legs, flung him crashing among the undergrowth. Then, whipping out his sword, he pricked the other who had seized Sophia, in the fleshy part of the shoulder, and forced him to release her; after which, plying his point before the bully's eyes, he drove him slowly back and back. Now the man shrieked and flinched as the glittering steel menaced his face; now he poured forth a volley of threats and curses, as it was for a moment withdrawn. But Hawkesworth was unmoved by either, and at length the fellow, seeing that he was not to be intimidated either by his lordship's name or his own menaces, thought better of it – as these gentlemen commonly did when they were resisted; and springing back with a parting oath, he took to his heels, and saved himself down a by-path.

The Irishman, a little breathed by his victory, wasted no time in vaunting it. The girl had witnessed it with worshipping eyes; he could trust her to make the most of it. 'Quick,' he cried, 'or we shall be in trouble!' And sheathing his sword, he caught the trembling Sophia by the hand, and ran with her down the path. They turned a corner; a little way before her she saw lights, and the open space near the booths which she had seen her brother cross. But now Hawkesworth halted; his purpose was still fluid and uncertain. But the next moment a shrill childish voice cried, 'Here she is; I've found her!' and Lady Betty Cochrane flew towards them. A little behind her, approaching at a more leisurely pace, was Sir Hervey Coke.

Lady Betty stared at Hawkesworth with all her eyes, and giggled. 'Oh, lord, a man!' she cried, and veiled her face, pretending to be overcome.

'I saw my brother,' Sophia faltered, covered with confusion, 'and ran down – ran down to – to meet him.'

'Just so! But see here, *brother*!' Lady Betty answered with a wink. 'Go's the word, now, if you are not a fool.'

Hawkesworth hesitated an instant, looking from Sophia to Sir Hervey Coke; but he saw that nothing more could be done on the occasion, and muttering 'Another time,' he turned away, and in a moment was lost in the grove.

'She was with her brother,' Lady Betty cried, turning, and breathlessly explaining the matter to Coke, who had seen all. 'Think of that? She saw him, and followed him. That's all.

Lord, I wonder,' she continued, with a loud giggle, 'if they would make such a fuss if I were missing. I declare to goodness I'll try.' And, leaving Sophia to follow with Sir Hervey, she danced on in front until they met Mrs Northey, who, with her husband and several of her party, was following in search of the culprit. Seeing she was found, the gentlemen winked at one another behind backs, while the ladies drew down the corners of their mouths. One of the latter laughed, maliciously expecting the scene that would follow.

But Lady Betty had the first word, and kept it. 'Lord, ma'am, what ninnies we are!' she cried. 'She was with her brother. That's all!'

'Hee, hee!' the lady tittered who had laughed before. 'That's good! Her brother!'

'Yes, she was!' Betty cried, turning on her, a very spitfire. 'I suppose seeing's believing, ma'am, though one is only fifteen, and not forty. She saw her brother going by the – the corner there, and ran after him while we were watching – watching the— But oh, I beg your pardon, ma'am, you were otherwise engaged, I think!' with a derisive curtsey.

Unfortunately the lady who had laughed had a weakness for one of the gentlemen in company; which was so notorious that on this even her friends sniggered. With Mrs Northey, however, Lady Betty's advocacy was less effective. That pattern sister, from the moment she discovered Sophia's absence, and divined the cause of it, had been fit to burst with spleen. Fortunately, the coarse rating which she had prepared, and from which neither policy nor mercy could have persuaded her to refrain, died on her shrewish lips at the word 'brother.'

'Her brother?' she repeated mechanically, as she glowered at Lady Betty. 'Her brother here? What do you mean?'

'To be sure, ma'am, what I say. She saw him.'

'But how did she know—that he was in London?' Mrs Northey stammered, forgetting herself for the moment.

'She didn't know! That's the strange part of it!' Lady Betty replied volubly. 'She saw him, ma'am, and ran after him.'

'Well, anyway. you have given us enough trouble!' Mrs Northey retorted, addressing her sister; who stood before them trembling with excitement, and overcome by the varied emotions of the scene through which she had passed in the alley.

'Thank you for nothing, and Master Tom, too! Perhaps if you have quite done you'll come home. Sir Hervey, I'll trust her to you, if you'll be troubled with her. Now, if your ladyship will lead the way? I declare it's wondrous dark of a sudden.'

The party, taking the hint, turned, and quickly made its way along the deserted paths towards the entrance. As they trooped by twos and threes down the Avenue of Delight many of the lamps had flickered out, and others were guttering in the sockets, fit images of wit and merriment that had lost their sparkle, and fell dull on jaded ears. Coke walked in silence beside his companion until a little interval separated them from the others. Then, 'Child,' he said in a tone grave and almost severe, 'are you fixed to take no warning? Are you determined to throw away your life?'

It was his misfortune – and hers – that he chose his seasons ill. At that moment her heart was filled to overflowing with her lover, and her danger; his prowess, and his brave defence of her. Her eyes were hot with joyful happy tears hardly pent back. Her limbs trembled with a delicious agitation; all within her was a tumult of warm feelings of throbbing sensibilities.

For Sir Henry to oppose himself to her in that mood was to court defeat; it was to associate himself with the worldliness that to her in her rapture was the most hateful thing on earth; and he had his reward. 'Throw away my life,' she cried, curtly and contemptuously, ''tis just that, sir, I am determined not to do!'

'You are going the way to do it,' he retorted.

'I should be going the way – were I to entertain the suit of a spy!' she cried, her voice trembling as she hurled the insult at him. 'Were I to become the wife of a man who, even before he has a claim on me, dogs my footsteps, watches my actions, defames my friends! Believe me, sir, I thank you for nothing so much as for opening my eyes to your merits.'

'Oh, Lord!' he exclaimed in despair almost comic.

'Thank you,' she said. 'I see your conduct is of a piece, sir. From the first you treated me as a child; a chattel to be conveyed to you by my friends, with the least trouble to yourself. You scarcely stooped to speak to me until you found another in the field, and then 'twas only to backbite a gentleman whom you dared not accuse to his face!'

As she grew hotter he grew cool. 'Well, well,' he said, tapping his snuff-box, 'be easy; I shan't carry you off against your will.'

'No, you will not!' she cried. 'You will not! Don't think, if you please, that I am afraid of you. I am afraid of no one!'

And in the fervour of her love she felt that she spoke the truth. At that moment she was afraid of no one.

''Tis a happy state; I hope it may continue,' Coke answered placidly. 'You never had cause to fear me. After this you shall have no cause to reproach me. I ask only one thing in return.'

'You will have nothing.' she said rudely.

'You will grant me this, whether you will or no!'

'Never!'

'Yes,' he said, 'for it is but this, and you cannot help yourself. When you have been married to that man a month think of this moment and of me, and remember that I warned you.'

He spoke soberly, but he might have spoken to the winds for all the good he did. She was in air, picturing her lover's strength and prowess, his devotion, his gallantry. Once again she saw the drunken lord lifted and flung among the shrubs, and Hawkesworth's figure as he stood like Hector above his fallen foe. Again she saw the other bully flinching before his steel, cursing, reviling, and hiccoughing by turns, and Hawkesworth silent, inexorable, pressing on him. She forgot the preceding moment of dismay when she had turned to her lover for help, and read something less than respect in his eyes; that short moment during which he had hung in the wind uncertain what course he would take with her. She forgot this, for she was only eighteen, and the scene in which he had championed her had cast its glamour over her, distorting all that had gone before. He had defended her; he was her hero, she was his chosen. What girl of sensibility could doubt it?

Coke, who had left them at the door of the house in Arlington Street, finished the evening at White's where, playing deep for him, he won three hundred at hazard without speaking three unnecessary words. Returning home with the milk in the morning, he rubbed his eyes, surprised to find himself following Hawkesworth along Piccadilly. The Irishman had a companion, a young lad who reeled and hiccoughed in the cool morning air; who sung snatches of tipsy songs, and at the corner of Berkeley Street would have fought with a night chairman if the elder man had not dragged him on by force. The two turned up Dover Street, and Sir Hervey, after following them with his eyes, lost sight of them, and went on, wondering why a drunken boy's voice, heard at haphazard in the street, reminded him of Sophia.

He would have wondered less and known more had he followed them farther. At the bottom of Hay Hill the lad freed himself from his companion's arm, propped his shoulders against the wall of Berkeley Gardens, and with a drunken solemnity proceeded to argue a point. 'I don't understand,' he said. 'Why shouldn't I speak to S'phia, if I please? Eh? S'phia's devilish good girl, why do you go and drag her off? That's what I want to know.'

'My dear lad,' Hawkesworth answered with patience, 'if she saw you she'd blow the whole thing.'

'Not she!' the lad hiccoughed obstinately. 'She's a good little girl. She's my twin, I tell you.'

'But the others were with her.'

'What others?'

'Northey.'

'I shall kick Northey, when I am married,' the lad proclaimed with drunken solemnity. 'That's all.'

'Well, you'll be married tomorrow.'

'Why not today? That's what I want to know. Eh? Why not today?'

'Because the fair Oriana is at Ipswich, and you are here,' the Irishman answered with a trace of impatience in his tone. Then under his breath he added, 'D—n the jade! This is one of her tricks. She's never where she is wanted.'

In the meantime the lad had been set in motion again, and the two had reached the end of Davies Street at the north-west corner of the square. Here, perceiving the other mutter, Tom – for Sophia's brother, Tom, it was – stopped anew. 'Eh? What's that?' he said. 'What's that you are saying, old tulip?'

'I was saying you were a monstrous clever fellow to win her – today or tomorrow,' Hawkesworth answered coolly. 'And I'm hanged if I know how you did it. I can tell you a hundred gay fellows in the town are dying to marry her. And no flinchers, either.'

''Pon honour?'

'Ay, and a hundred more would give their ears for a kiss. But lord, out of all she must needs choose you! I vow, lad,' Hawkesworth continued with enthusiasm, 'it is the most extraordinary thing that ever was. The finest shape this side of Paris, eyes that would melt a stone, ankles like a gossamer, a toast wherever she goes, and the prettiest wit in the world; sink me, lad, she might have had the richest buck in town, and she chooses you.'

'Might she really? Honest now, might she?'

'That she might!'

Tom was so moved by this picture of his mistress's devotion and his own bliss that he found it necessary to weep a little, supporting himself by the huge link-extinguisher at the corner of Davies Street. His wig awry, and his hat clapped on the back of it, he looked as abandoned a young rake as the five o'clock sun ever shone upon; and yet under his maudlin tears lay a real if passing passion. 'She's an angel!' he sobbed presently, 'I shall never forget it! Never! And to think that but for you, if your chaise had not broken down at my elbow, just when you had picked her up after the accident at Trumpington, I should never have known her! And – and I might have been smugging at Cambridge now, instead of waiting to be made the happiest of men. Oriana,' he continued, clinging to the railings in a tipsy rhapsody, 'most beautiful of your sex, I vow—'

A couple of chairmen and a milk-girl were looking on grinning. 'There, bed's the word now!' Hawkesoworth cried, seizing him and dragging him on. 'Bed's the word! I said we would make a night of it, and we have. What's more, my lad,' he continued in a tone too low for Tom's ear, 'if you're not so cut tomorrow, you're glad to keep the house – I'm a Dutchman!'

This time his efforts were successful. His lodging, taken a week before in the name of Plomer, was only a few doors distant. In two minutes he had got Tom thither; in three, the lad, divested of his coat, boots, and neckcloth, was snoring heavily on the bed; while the Irishman, from an armchair on the hearth, kept dark watch over him. At length he too fell asleep, and slumbered as soundly as an innocent child, until a muffled hammering in the parlour roused him, and he stood up yawning and looked about him. The room, stiflingly close, lay in semi-darkness; on the bed sprawled the young runagate, dead asleep, his arms tossed wide. Hawkesworth stared awhile, still half asleep; at last, thirsting for small beer, he opened the door and went into the parlour. Here the windows were open: it was high noon. The noise the Irishman had heard was made by a man whose head and shoulders were plunged in a tall clock that stood in one corner. The man was kneeling at his task mending something in the works of the clock. The Irishman touched him roughly with his foot.

'Sink that coffin-making!' he cried coarsely. 'Do you hear? Get up!'

The clock-maker withdrew his head, looked up meekly to see who disturbed him, and – and swore. Simultaneously Hawkesworth drew back with a cry, and the two glared at one another. Then the man on the floor – he wore a paper cap, and below it his fat elderly face shone with sweat – rose quickly to his feet. 'You villain!' he cried, in a voice tremulous and scarcely articulate, so great was his passion. 'I have found you at last, have I? Where's my daughter?' and he stretched out his open hands, crook-fingered, and shook them in the younger man's face. 'Where is my daughter?'

'Lord, man, how do I know?' Hawkesworth answered. He tried to speak lightly, but with all his impudence he was taken aback, and showed it.

'How do you know?' the clock-maker retorted, again shaking his hands in his face. 'If you don't know, who should? Who should? By heaven, if you don't tell me, and truly, I'll rouse the house on you. Do you hear! I'll make you known here, you scoundrel, for what you are. This is a respectable house, and they'll have none of you. I'll so cry you, you shall trick no man of his daughter again. No, for I'll set the crowd on you, and mark you.'

'Hush, man, hush!' Hawkesworth answered, with an anxious glance at the door of the chamber he had left. 'You do yourself no good by this.'

'No; but by heaven I can do you harm!' the other replied, and nimbly stepping to the door that led to the stairs, he opened it and held it ajar. 'I can do you harm! A silver tankard and twenty-seven guineas she took with her, and I'll swear them to you. By God, I will!'

Hawkesworth's face turned a dull white. Unwelcome as the meeting and the recognition were, he had not realized his danger until now. The awkward circumstances connected with the tankard and the guineas had escaped his memory. Now it was clear he must temporize. 'You need not threaten,' he said doggedly. 'I'll tell you all I know. She's – she's not with me; she is on the stage. She's not in London.'

'She's not with you?'

'No.'

'You're a liar!' the clock-maker cried, brutally.

'I swear it is true!' Hawkesworth protested.

'She is not living with you?'

'No.'

'Did you marry her?'

'Ye – ye – No!' Hawkesworth answered, uncertain for a moment which reply would be the better taken. 'No; I – she left me, I tell you,' he continued hurriedly, 'and went on the stage against my will.'

The clock-maker laughed cunningly, and his face was not pleasant to see. 'She's not with you,' he said, 'she's not married to you, and she's not in London? You deceived her, my fine fellow, and left her. That's the story, is it? That's the story I've waited two years to hear.'

'She left me,' Hawkesworth answered. 'Against my will, I tell you.'

'Anyway she's gone, and 'twill make no difference to her what happens to you. So I'll hang you, you devil,' the old man continued, with a cold chuckling determination, that chilled Hawkesworth's blood. 'No, you don't,' he continued, withdrawing one half of his body through the doorway, as Hawkesworth took a step towards him. 'You don't pinch me that way: Another step, and I give the alarm.'

Hawkesworth recalled the opinion he had held of this grasping old curmudgeon, his former landlord – who had loved his gay, flirty daughter a little, and his paltry savings more; and his heart misgave him. The alarm once given, the neighbourhood roused, at the best, and if no worse thing befell him, he would be arrested. Arrest meant the ruin of his present schemes. 'Oh, come, Mr Grocott,' he faltered. 'You will not do it. You'll not be so foolish.'

'Why not?' the other snarled, in cruel enjoyment of his fears. 'Eh! Tell me that. Why not?'

But even as he spoke Hawkesworth saw the way out of his dilemma. 'Because you'll not do a thing you will repent all your life,' he said, his brazen assurance returning as quickly as it had departed. 'Because you'll not ruin your daughter. Have done, hold your hand, man, and in two days I'll make her a grand lady.'

'You'll marry her, I suppose,' old Grocott answered with a savage sneer.

'Yes, to a man of title and property.'

'You're a great liar.'

Hawkesworth spread out his hands in remonstrance. 'Judge for yourself,' he said. 'Have a little patience. Listen to me two minutes, my good fellow; and then say if you'll stand in your daughter's light.'

'Hang the drab! She's no daughter of mine,' the old man cried fiercely. Nevertheless he listened, and Hawkesworth, sinking his voice, proceeded to tell in tones, always earnest, and at times appealing, a story that little by little won the hearer's attention. First Grocott, albeit he listened with the same apparent incredulity, closed the door. Later, his interest growing, he advanced into the room. Then he began to breathe more quickly; at length, with an oath, he struck his hand on the table beside him.

'And you say the lad is here?' he cried.

'He is here.'

'Where?'

'In that room.'

'By gole, let me see him!'

'If he is asleep,' Hawkesworth answered, assenting with reluctance. He crossed the room and cautiously opened the door of the chamber in which Tom lay snoring. Beckoning the old man to be wary, he allowed him to peer in. Grocott looked and listened, stole forward, and, like some pale-faced ghoul, leant over the flushed features of the unconscious lad. Then he stealthily returned to the parlour, and the door between the two rooms was shut.

'Well,' the Irishman asked, 'are you satisfied?'

'What do you say his name is?'

'Maitland – Sir Thomas Maitland of Cuckfield.'

'She'll be Lady Maitland?'

'To be sure.'

'And what do you call – her now?' the clock-maker asked. He seemed to find a difficulty in pronouncing the last words.

'Clark – Mistress Oriana Clark,' Hawkesworth answered. 'She's at Ipswich, or was, and should be here tomorrow.'

Grocott's nose curled at the name. 'And what are you going to get out of this?' he continued, eyeing the other with intense suspicion.

The Irishman hesitated, but in the end determined to tell the truth, and trust to the other's self-interest. 'A wife, and a plum,' he said jauntily. 'There's a girl, his sister, I'm going to marry; she takes ten thousand out of his share if he marries without his guardian's consent. That's it.'

'Lord, you're a rascal!' Grocott ejaculated, and stared in admiration of the other's roguery. 'To take ten thousand of my son-in-law's money, and tell me of it to my face. By gole, you're a cool one!'

'You can choose between that and nothing.' Hawkesworth answered, confident in his recovered mastery. 'You can do nothing without me, you see. No more can Oriana.'

The old man winced. Somehow the name – her name had been Sarah – hurt him. 'What's the name of – of the other one?' he said. 'His sister – that you're going to marry?'

'Sophia,' the Irishman answered.

CHAPTER IV

A Discovery

THE SCENE in the gardens had moved Sophia's feelings so deeply that, notwithstanding the glamour Hawkesworth's exploit had cast over her, a word of kindness addressed to her on her arrival in Arlington Street might have had far-reaching results. Unfortunately her sister's temper and Mr Northey's dullness gave sweet reasonableness small place. Scarcely had the chairman been dismissed, the chairs carried out, and the door closed on them before Mr Northey's indignation found vent. 'Sophia, I am astonished!' he said in portentous tones; and, dull as he was, he *was* astonished. 'I could not have believed you would behave in this way!'

'The more fool you!' Mrs Northey snapped; while the girl, white and red by turns, too proud to fly, yet dreading what was to come, hung irresolute at the foot of the stairs, apparently fumbling with her hood, and really growing harder and harder with each reproach that was levelled at her.

'After all I said to you this morning!' Mr Northey continued, glaring at her as if he found disobedience to orders such as his a thing beyond belief. 'When I had prohibited in the most particular manner all communications with that person, to go and – and meet him in a place of all places the most scandalous in which to be alone with a man.'

'La, Northey, it was that made her do it!' his wife rejoined sourly. 'Go to bed, miss, and we will talk to you tomorrow. I suppose you thought we were taken in with your fine tale of your brother?'

'I never said it was my brother!' Sophia cried, hotly.

'Go to bed. Do you hear? I suppose you have sense enough to do that when you are told,' her sister rejoined. 'We will talk to you tomorrow.'

Sophia choked, but thought better of it, and turning away, crept upstairs. After all, she whispered, as her hands squeezed convulsively the poor hood that had not offended her, it mattered little. If he were good to her what recked it of others, their words, or their opinion? What had they ever done for her that she should be guided by them, or what, that she should resign the happiness of her life at their bidding? They had not real care for her. Here was no question of father or mother, or the respect due to their wishes; of kindness, love, or gratitude. Of her brother-in-law, who bullied her in his dull, frigid fashion, she knew little more than she knew of a man in the street; and her sister spared her at the best a cold selfish affection, the affection of the workman for the tools by which he hopes he may some day profit.

Naturally, her thoughts reverted to the lover who that evening had shown himself in his true colours, a hero worthy of any poor girl's affection. Sophia's eyes filled with tears, and her bosom rose and fell with soft emotion as she thought of him and pictured him; as she flushed anew beneath his ardent glances, as she recalled the past and painted a future in which she would lie safe in the haven of his love, secured from peril by the strength of his arm. What puny figures the beaux and bloods of town looked beside him! With what grace he moved among them, elbowing one and supplanting another. It was no wonder they gazed after him enviously, or behind his back vented their petty spite in sneers and innuendoes, called him Teague, and muttered of Murphies and the bog of Arran. The time would come – and oh, how she prayed it might come quickly – when the world would discover the part he had played; when, in a Stuart England, he would stand forward the friend of Cecil, the agent of Ormonde, and the town would recognize in the obscurity in which he now draped himself and at which they scoffed, the cloak of the most daring and loyal conspirator that ever wrought for the rightful king!

For this was the secret he had whispered in Sophia's ear; this was the explanation he had given of the cold looks men cast on him in public. Nor was it too incredible for the belief of a romantic girl. In that year, 1742, the air in London was full of such rumours, and London, rumour said, was full of such men. The close of Sir Robert Walpole's long and peaceful administration, and the imminence of war with France, had raised the hopes of the Jacobites to the highest pitch. Though the storm did not break in open war until three years later, it already darkened the sky, and filled the capital with its rumblings. Alike in the Cabinet, where changes were frequent and great men few, and in the country where people looked for something, they hardly knew what, unrest and uneasiness prevailed. Many a sturdy squire in Lancashire and Shropshire, many a member at Westminster, from Shippon and Sir Watkyn downwards, passed his glass over the water-jug as he drank the King; and if Sophia, as she drew her withered flower from its hiding-place, that it might lie beneath her pillow through the night, prayed for King James and his cause, she did only what many a pretty Jacobite, and some who passed for Whigs, were doing at the same hour.

In the meantime, and pending the triumph for which she

longed so passionately, her dear hero's pretensions helped her not a whit; on the contrary, were they known, or suspected, they would sink him lower than ever in the estimation of her family. This thought it was that, as she lay revolving matters, raised in her mind an increasing barrier between her and her sister. The Northeys were firm Whigs, pledged not less by interest than by tradition to the White Horse of Hanover. They had deserted Sir Robert at his utmost need, but merely to serve their own turn; because his faction was drooping, and another, equally Whiggish, was in the ascendant, certainly with no view to a Stuart Restoration. Her Hawkesworth's success, therefore, meant their defeat and downfall; his triumph must cost them dear. To abide by them, and abide by him, were as inconsistent as to serve God and Mammon.

Sophia, drawn to her lover by the strength of maiden fancy, saw this; she felt the interval between her and her family increase the longer she dwelt on the course to which her mind was being slowly moved. The consciousness that no compromise was possible had its effects upon her. When she was summoned to the parlour next day, a change had come over her; she went not shyly and shamefacedly, open to cajolery and kindness, as she had gone the previous day, when her opinion of her lover's merit had fallen short of the wrapt assurance that this morning uplifted her. On the contrary, she went armed with determination as solemn in her own sight as it was provoking in the eyes of older and more sagacious persons.

Mrs Northey discerned the change the moment Sophia entered the room; and she was proportionately exasperated. 'Oh, miss, so you'll follow Miss Howe, will you?' she sneered, alluding to a tale of scandal that still furnished the text for many a sermon to the young and flightly. 'You'll take no advice!'

'I hope I shall know how to conduct myself better, ma'am,' Sophia said proudly.

Mr Northey was less clear-sighted than his wife. He saw no change; he thought in all innocence that the matter was where he had left it. After clearing his throat, therefore, 'Sophia,' he said with much majesty, 'I hope you have recovered your senses, and that conduct such as that of which you were guilty last night will not be repeated while you are in our charge. Understand me; it must not be repeated. You are country bred, and do not understand that what you did is a very serious matter, and quite enough to compromise a young girl.'

Sophia, disdaining to answer, spent her gaze on the picture above his head. The withered flower was in her bosom; the heart that beat against it was full of wondering pity for her sister, who had been compelled to marry this man – this man, ugly, cold, stiff, with no romance in his life, no secret – this man, at the touch of whose hand she, Sophia, shuddered.

'I consider it so – so serious a transgression,' Mr Northey resumed pompously – little did he dream what she was thinking of him – 'that the only condition on which I can consent to overlook it is that you at once, Sophia, do your duty by accepting the husband on whom we have fixed for you.'

'No,' Sophia said, in a low but determined tone, 'I cannot do that!'

Mr Northey fancied that he had not heard aright. 'Eh,' he said, 'you—'

'I cannot do that, sir; my mind is quite made up,' she repeated.

From her chair Mrs Northey laughed scornfully at her husband's consternation. 'Are you blind?' she said. 'Cannot you see that the Irishman has turned the girl's head?'

'Impossible!' Mr Northey said.

'Don't you hear her say that her mind is made up?' Mrs Northey continued contemptuously. 'You may talk till you are hoarse, Northey, you'll get nothing; I know that. She's a pig when she likes.'

Mr Northey glowered at the girl as if she had already broken all bounds. 'But does she understand,' he said, breathing hard, 'that marriage with a person of – of that class, is impossible? And surely no modest girl would continue to encourage a person whom she cannot marry?'

Still Sophia remained silent, her eyes steadily fixed on the picture above his head.

'Speak, Sophia!' he cried imperatively. 'This is impertinence.'

'If I cannot marry him,' she said in a low voice, 'I shall marry no one!'

'If you cannot marry that – that Irish footman?' he gasped,

bursting into rage. 'A penniless adventurer, who has not even asked you.'

'He has asked me,' she retorted.

'Oh, by Gad, ma'am, I've done with you,' Mr Northey cried, striking his fist on the table; and he added an expletive or two. 'I hand you over to madam, there. Perhaps she can bring you to your senses. I might have known it,' he continued bitterly, addressing his wife. 'Like and like, madam! It's bred in the bone, I see!'

'I don't know what you mean, Northey,' his wife answered with a sneer of easy contempt. 'If you had left the matter to me from the beginning, 'twould have been done by now. Listen to me, Miss Obstinate. Is that the last word you'll give us?'

'Yes,' Sophia said, pluming herself a little on her victory.

'Then you'll go into the country tomorrow! That's all!' was Mrs Northey's reply. 'We'll see how you like that!'

The blow was unexpected. The girl's lips parted. and she looked wildly at her sister. 'Into the country?' she stammered.

'Ay, sure.'

'To – to Cuckfield?' she asked desperately. After all, were she sent to her old home all was not lost. He had heard her speak of it; he knew where it was; he could easily trace her thither.

'No, miss, not to Cuckfield,' her sister replied, triumphing cruelly, for she read the girl's thoughts. 'You'll go to Aunt Leah at Chalkhill, and I wish you joy of her tantrums and her scraping. You'll go early tomorrow; Mr Northery will take you; and until you are away from here I'll answer there shall be no note-palming. When you are in a better mind, and your Teague's in Bridewell, you may come back. I fancy you'll be tamed by that time. It will need mighty little persuasion, I'm thinking, to bring you to marry Sir Hervey when you've been at Aunt Leah's for three months.'

Sophia's lip began to tremble; her eyes roved piteously. Well might the prospect terrify her, for it meant not only exile from her lover, but an exile which she saw might be permanent. For how was he to find her? To Cuckfield, the family seat, he might trace her easily; but in the poor hamlet on the Sussex coast, where her aunt, who had tripped in her time and paid the penalty, dragged on a penurious existence as the widow of a hedge-parson, not so easily. There a poor girl might eat out her heart, even as her aunt had eaten out hers, and no redress and no chance of rescue. Even had she the opportunity of writing to her lover she did not – unhappy thought – know where he lived.

Mrs Northey read her dismay, saw the colour fade in her cheeks, and the tears gather in her eyes, and with remorseless determination, with cruel enjoyment, drove the nail home.

'There'll be no Vauxhall there,' she sneered, 'and mighty few drums or routs, my dear! It's likely your first masquerade will be your last; and for the wine-merchant actor that you were to see at Goodman's Fields tomorrow, you may whistle for him; and for your dear Amorevoli. It's to be hoped, Miss Lucy, you'll find your Thomas worth it,' she continued, alluding to the farce that held the town, 'when you get him.' And then, changing her ground, with no little skill, 'See here, child,' she said, in the tone of one willing to argue, 'are you going on with this silliness? Think, my dear, think, while it is time, for 'twill be too late at Chalkhill. You don't want to go and be buried in that hole till your brother comes of age?'

Sophia, resentful but terrified, subdued both by the prospect and by the appeal to her reasonableness, had hard work to refrain from tears as she uttered her negative. 'No, I – I don't want to go,' she stammered.

'I thought not; then you shall have one more chance,' Mrs Northey answered, with a fair show of good nature. 'If you'll give me your word not to write to him, you shall have a week to think of it before you go. But you'll keep your room – on that I must insist; there you'll have time to think, and I hope by the end of the week you'll have come to your senses, my dear. If not, you'll go to Aunt Leah.'

The mixture of severity and kindness was clever, and it had its effect upon poor Sophia, who stood weighing the alternatives with a rueful face. While she remained in town, if she might not see him, she was still near him, and he near her. She would not be lost to him nor he to her; and then, what might not happen in a week? 'I will promise,' she murmured, in a low uncertain tone.

'Good,' Mrs Northey answered; 'then you may go to your room.'

And to her room Sophia would have gone, in a mood fairly open to the influence of reason and solitude. But in an evil moment for himself Mr Northey, smarting under a defeat which his wife's victory rendered the more humiliating, thought he espied an opportunity of restoring his dignity.

'Yes, you may go,' he said sourly; 'but take this with you. You will see there,' he continued, fussily selecting a letter from a pile on the table, and handing it to her, 'what are the terms in which a gentleman seeks an alliance with a lady. It is from Sir Hervey, and I shall be much surprised if it does not produce a very different impression on you from that which that person has made.'

'I do not want it,' Sophia answered; and held out the letter between her finger and thumb, as if it had an evil odour.

'But I insist on your taking it,' Mr Northey replied with temper; and in spite of the warnings which his wife's contemptuous shrugs should have conveyed to him, he repeated the command.

'Then I will read it now,' the girl answered, standing very upright, 'if you order me to do so.'

'I do order you,' he said; and still holding the folded sheet a little from her, she opened it, and with a curling lip and half averted eye, began to read the contents. Suddenly Mrs Northey took fright; Mr Northey even was surprised by the change. For the girl's face grew red and redder; she stared at the letter, her lips parting widely, as in astonishment. At last, 'What? What is this?' she cried, 'Tom? Then it was – it was Tom I saw last night.'

'Tom!' Mr Northey exclaimed.

'Yes, it was Tom!' Sophia cried; 'and – oh, but this is dreadful! This must be – must be stopped at once!' she continued, looking from the paper to them and back again with distended eyes. 'He is mad to think of such a thing at his age; he is only a boy; he does not know what he is doing.' Her voice shook with agitation.

'What the deuce do you mean, miss?' her brother-in-law thundered, rising furious from his chair. 'Have you taken leave of your senses? What do you mean by this – this nonsense?'

'Mean?' his wife answered with bitter emphasis. 'She means that, instead of giving her Coke's letter, you have given her the

Cambridge letter; the letter from Tom's tutor. You have done it, like the fool you always are, Northey.'

Mr Northey swore violently. 'Give it me!' he cried harshly. 'Do you hear, girl? Give it me!' And he stretched out his hand to recover the letter.

But something in the excess of his chagrin, or in the words of the reproach Mrs Northey had flung at him roused suspicion in the girl's mind. She recoiled, holding the paper from him. 'It is five days old!' she gasped; 'you have had it four days – three at least; and you have said nothing about it. You have not told me! And you have done nothing!' she continued, her mind jumping instinctively to the truth, at which Mr Northey's guilty face hinted not obscurely. 'He is on the brink of ruining himself with this woman, and you stand by though you are told what she is, and were told three days ago. Why? Why?' Sophia cried, as Mr Northey, with an oath, snatched the letter from her. 'What does it mean?'

'Mean? Why, that one unruly child is enough to manage at a time!' Mrs Northey answered, rising to the occasion. She spoke with venom, and no wonder; her hands tingled for her husband's ears. He had improved matters with a vengeance. 'It's fine talking, you little toad,' she continued, with a show of reason; 'but if you don't listen to sense who are here, how are we to persuade him, and he not here? Tell me that, miss. A nice pattern of discretion and prudence you are to talk. Hang your impudence!'

'But you have done nothing,' Sophia wailed, her affection for her brother keeping her to the point. 'And I saw him last night; it was he whom I saw at Vauxhall. I could have spoken to him, and I am sure he would have listened to me.'

'Listened to his grandmother!' Mrs Northey retorted, with acrid contempt. 'We have done what we think right, and that is enough for you, you baby. A nasty disobedient little toad, running into the very same folly yourself, and then prating of us, and what we should do! Hang your fine talking; I've no patience with you, and so I tell you, miss.'

'But,' Sophia said slowly, her voice grown timid, 'I don't understand—'

'Who cares whether you understand!'

'Why – why you make so much of marrying me the way

you wish, and yet let him go his way? If he does this, you'll get some of his money I know, but it cannot be that. It couldn't be that. And yet – and yet—' she cried, with a sudden flush of generous indignation, as conviction was borne in upon her by Mr Northey's hang-dog face – 'yes, it is that! Oh, for shame! for shame! Are you his sister, and will ruin him? Will ruin him for the sake of – of money!'

'Silence, you minx!' Mrs Northey cried; and she rose, her face white with rage, and seizing her sister's arm, she shook her violently. 'How dare you say such things? Do you hear? Be silent!'

But Sophia was beside herself with passion, she would not be silent. Neither the dead Northeys on the walls, nor the living sister should stifle the expression of her feelings.

'I take back my promise,' she cried, panting with excitement; her words were scarcely coherent. 'Do you hear? Do you understand? I promise nothing after this. You may beat me if you like; you may lock me up, it will be all the same. I'll go into the country tomorrow, but I'll make no promise. I shall see Hawkesworth if I can! I shall run away to him if I can! I'd rather do anything – anything in the world after this, than go on living with you.'

'You'll not go on living with me!' Mrs Northey answered through pinched lips, and her eyes glittered after an ugly fashion. 'I'll see to that, you little scald-tongue! You'll go to Aunt Leah and feed pigs, and do plain-stitch; I hope it may agree with those dainty hands of yours. And you'll run away from there if you can. She'll see to that. I'll be bound she'll break some of that pretty spirit of yours, grand as you think yourself. So because your precious Tom chooses to take up with some drab or other, you put it on us, do you? Go, you little vixen,' Mrs Northey continued harshly, 'go to your room before I do you a mischief! You'll not promise, but the key shall. Up, miss, up, we will have no more of your tantrums!'

Reduced to tears, and broken down by the violence of her emotions, Sophia asked nothing better than to escape, and be alone with her misery. She turned, and as quickly as she could she hurried from the room. Fast as she went, however, Mrs Northey pushed after her, treading on her heels, and forcing her on. What passed between them Mr Northey could not hear, but in no long time Mrs Northey was down again, and flung a key on the table. 'There,' she cried, her nose twitching with the constraint she put upon her rage. 'And what do you think of your management now, Mr Imbecile?'

'I always said,' he answered sullenly, 'that we ought to tell her.'

'You always said.'

'Yes, I did.'

'*You* always said!' his wife cried, her eyes flashing with the scorn she made no attempt to hide. 'And was not that a very good reason for doing the other thing? Wasn't it, Mr Northey? Wasn't it? Oh, Lord! why did God give me a fool for a husband?'

CHAPTER V

The World Well Lost

MRS NORTHEY was no novice. She knew something of intrigue, something of her sex. Her first step was to discharge Sophia's woman, a village maid, who had come with her young mistress from the country. The key of the offender's chamber was then intrusted to madam's own woman, Mrs Martha, a sour spinster, matured not by years only, but by an unfortunate experience of the other sex, which secured her from the danger of erring on the side of leniency where they were concerned. Mr Northey could not immediately leave London, therefore it was necessary that arrangements for the culprit's transport to the surer custody of Aunt Leah at Chalkhill should be postponed, but all that Mrs Northey could do short of this she did. And these dispositions made, she prepared to await events with a mind tolerably at ease.

In every net, however, there are meshes, and small is the mesh through which a large fish cannot escape. It is probable that poor blubbering Dolly, the dismissed maid, innocent as she declared herself, was in somebody's pay, and knew where information could be sold. For before Sophia had been confined to her room for four hours, before the first passionate tears were dried on her cheeks, a clock-maker. who had come in to regulate the tall clock on the stairs, made the odd mistake of mounting, when no one was looking, to the second floor. A moment later a finger-nail scraped Sophia's door, a note was thrust under it, and deftly as he had come, the workman, a pale, fat, elderly man, crept down again. He made little noise, for, to save his honour's drugget, he had left his boots in the hall.

Sophia, recovering from a momentary astonishment, pounced on the note, opened it and read it; and, alas for her discretion, her eyes sparkled through her tears as she did so. Thus it ran:

'SWEETEST AND BEST BELOVED OF YOUR SEX,—

'The raptures of my heart when my eyes dwell on yours cannot be hidden, and must have convinced you that on you depends the life or death, happiness or misery, of your Hector. If you will, you can plunge me into an abyss of hopelessness, in which I must spend the rest of my existence; or if you will, you can make me in possessing you the happiest, as I am already in aspiring to you the boldest, of mankind. Oh, my Sophia, dare I call you that? Can such bliss be reserved for me? Can it be my lot to spend existence in the worship of those charms, for which the adoration of the longest life passed in thinking of you and serving you were an inadequate price! May I dream that I shall one day be the most enviable of men? If so, there is but one course to be taken. Fly, dearest, fly, your cruel relatives, who have already immured you, and will presently sacrifice you, innocent and spotless, on the vile altar of their ambition. Hold a white handkerchief against your window at six this evening, and the rest is easy. At dusk the day after tomorrow – so much time I need – I will find means to remove you. A few minutes later Dr Keith, of Mayfair Chapel, a reverend divine, who will be in waiting at my lodgings, will unite you in indissoluble bonds to one whose every thought thenceforth – not given to his King – will be consecrated to the happiness of his Sophia.

'Already my heart beats with rapture; I swoon at the

thought. The pen falls from the hand of your humble, adoring lover,

'HECTOR (COUNT PLOMER).'

Need we wonder that Sophia held the letter from her and held it to her, scanned it this way, and scanned it that way, kissed it, and kissed it again; finally, with a glance at the door, hid it jealously within her dress? She would have done these things had she been as much in the dark about Tom, and the machinations formed to rob him, as she had been when she rose that morning. But she would have halted there. She would have pardoned her lover his boldness, perhaps have liked him the better for it; but she would not have granted his prayer. Now, her one aspiration was for the moment when she might take the leap. Her one feeling was impatience for the hour when she might give the signal of surrender. The pillars of her house were shaken; her faith in her sister, in her friends, in her home was gone. Only her lover remained, and if he were not to be trusted she had no one. She did not tell herself that girls had done this thing before, maiden modesty notwithstanding, and had found no cause to repent their confidence; for her determination needed no buttressing. Her cheeks flamed, and she thrilled and trembled from head to foot as she pictured the life to which she was flying; but the cheek flamed as hotly when she painted the past and the intolerable craft and coldness of the world on which she turned her back.

The window of her room looked into Arlington Street. She stood at it gazing down on the stand of chairmen and sedans that stretched up to Portugal Street, a thoroughfare now part of Piccadilly. The end of the scaffolding outside Sir Robert Walpole's new house – the house next door – came within a few feet of the sill on which she leaned; the hoarse, beery voices of the workmen, and the clangour of the hammers, were destined to recall that day to her as long as she lived. Yet for the time she was scarcely conscious of the noise, so close was the attention with which she surveyed the street. Below, as on other days, beaux sauntered round the corner of Bennet Street on their way to White's, or stood to speak to a pretty woman in a chair. Country folk paused to look at Sir Bluestring's new house; a lad went up and down crying the *Evening Post*, and at the corner at the lower end of Arlington Street, then open at the south, a group of boys sat gambling for halfpence.

Sophia saw all this, but she saw no sign of him she sought, though St James's clock tolled the three quarters after five. Eagerly she looked everywhere, her heart beating quickly. Surely Hawkesworth would be there to see the signal, and to learn his happiness with his own eyes? She leaned forward, then on a sudden she recoiled; Sir Hervey Coke, passing on the other side, had looked up; he knew, then, that she was a prisoner! Her woman's pride rebelled at the thought, and hot with anger she stood awhile in the middle of the room. Whereon St James's clock struck six; it was the hour appointed. Without hesitation, without the loss of a moment, Sophia sprang to the window, and with a steady hand pressed her handkerchief to the pane. The die was cast.

She thought that on that something would happen; she felt sure that she would see him, would catch his eye, would receive some mark of his gratitude. But she was disappointed; and in a minute or two after gazing with a bold bashfulness this way and that, she went back into the room, her spirits feeling the reaction. For eight and forty hours from this she had naught to do but wait; for all that time she was doomed to inaction. It seemed scarcely possible that she could wait so long; scarcely possible that she could possess herself in patience. The first hour indeed tried her so sharply that when Mrs Martha brought her supper she was ready to be humble even to her, for the sake of five minutes' intercourse.

But Mrs Martha's conversation was as meagre as the meal she brought, and the girl had to pass the night as best she could. Next morning, however, when the woman – after jealously unlocking the door and securing it behind her after a fashion that shook the girl with rage – set down her breakfast, the crabbed old maid was more communicative.

'Thank the Lord, it is a'most the last time I shall have to climb those stairs,' she grumbled. 'Aye, you may look, miss' – for Sophia was gazing at her resentfully enough – 'and think yourself mighty clever! It's little you think of the trouble your fancies give such as me. There!' putting down the tray. 'You may take your fill of that and not burst either. Maybe 'taint delicate enough for your stomach, but 'twas none of my putting.'

Sophia was hungry, and the meal was scanty. but pride made her avert her eyes. 'Why is it almost the last time?' she asked sharply. 'If they think they can break my spirit by starving me—'

'Hoity-toity!' the woman said, with more than a smack of insolence. 'I'd keep my breath to cool my porridge if I were you! Lord, I wouldn't have your hot temper, miss, for something. But 'twon't help you much with your Aunt Leah, from all I hear. They say she was just such a one as you once, and wilful is no word for her.'

Sophia's heart began to beat. 'Am I to go to her?' she asked.

'Aye, that you are, and the sooner the better for my legs, miss!'

'When?' Sophia's voice was low.

'Tomorrow. No later. The chaise is ordered for six. His honour will take you himself, and I doubt you'll wish you'd brought your pigs to another market before you've been there many days. Leastways, from what I hear. 'Tis no place for a decent Christian, I'm told,' the woman continued, spitefully enjoying the dismay which Sophia could not conceal. 'Just thatch and hogs and mud to your knees, and never a wheeled thing, John says, in the place, nor a road, nor a mug of beer to be called beer. All poor as rats, and no one better than the other, as how should they be and six miles of a pack-road to the nearest highway? You'll whistle for your lover there, miss.'

Sophia swallowed her rage. 'Go down!' she said.

'Oh, la! I don't want to stay!' Mrs Martha cried, tossing her head. 'It's not for my own amusement I've stayed so long. And no thanks for my kindness, either! I've my own good dinner downstairs, and the longer I'm here the cooler it'll be. Which some people like their dinner hot and behave themselves accordingly. But I know my duty, and by your leave, miss, I shall do it.'

She bounced out of the room with that, and turned the key on the outside with a noisy care that hurt the ear if it did not wound the spirit. 'Nasty proud-stomached thing!' she muttered as she descended the stairs. 'I hope Madam Leah will teach her what's what! And for all she's monstrous high now, I warrant she'll come to eating breast of veal as well as another. And glad to get it. What Sir 'Ervey can see in her passes me, but men and fools are all one, and it takes mighty little to tickle them if it be red and white. For my part I'm glad to be rid of her. One's tantrums is as much as I can put up with, duty or no duty.'

Mrs Martha might have taken the matter more easily had she known what was passing in the locked room she had left. Sophia's indifference was gone; she paced the floor in a fever of uncertainty. How was she to communicate with her lover? How tell him that his plans were forestalled, and that on the morrow, hours before his arrangements were mature, she would be whisked away and buried in the depths of the country, in a spot the most remote from the world? True, at the foot of his letter was the address of his lodging – at Mr Wollenhope's in Davies Street, near Berkeley Square. And Dolly – though Sophia had never yet stooped to use her – might this evening have got a letter to him. But Dolly was gone; Dolly and all her friends were far away, and Mrs Martha was stone. Sophia wrung her hands as she walked feverishly from the door to window.

She knew nothing of the hundred channels through which a man of the world could trace her. To her eyes the door of Chalkhill bore the legend Dante had made famous. To her mind, to go to Aunt Leah was to be lost to her lover, to be lost to the world. And yet what chance of escape remained? Vainly thinking, vainly groping, she hung at the window tearing a handkerchief to pieces, while her eyes raked the street below for the least sign of him she sought. There were the same beaux strutting round the same corner, hanging on the same arms, bowing to the same chairs, ogled from the shelter of the same fans. The same hackney-coachmen quarrelled, the same boys gambled at the corner. Even Sir Hervey paused at the same hour of the afternoon, looked up as he had looked up yesterday, seemed to hesitate, finally went on. But Hawkesworth – Hawkesworth was nowhere.

Her eyes aching with long watching, the choke of coming tears in her throat, Sophia drew back at last, and was in the act of casting herself on her bed in a paroxysm of despair, when a shrill voice speaking outside her door reached her ears. The next moment she heard her name.

She sprang to the door, the weight lifted from her heart. Any happening was better than none. 'Here!' she cried. 'Here!' And she struck the panels with her hands.

'Where? Oh, I see,' the voice answered. Then 'Thank you, my good woman,' it went on, 'I'll trouble you no farther. I can open for myself. I see the key is in the lock.'

But on that Mrs Martha's voice was raised, loudly remonstrant. 'My lady,' she cried, 'you don't understand! I've the strictest orders—'

'To keep her in? Just so, you foolish thing. And so you shall. But not to keep me out. Still – just to be sure I'll take the key in with me!' On which Sophia heard the key turn sharply in the lock, the door flew open, and in bounced Lady Betty. To insert the key on the inside and secure the door behind her was the work of a moment. Then she dropped the astonished Sophia an exaggerated curtsey.

'La, miss, I crave your pardon, I'm sure,' she said, 'for calling your name so loud on the stairs, but that silly thing would do nothing but her orders. So as she would not show me the way, I ran up myself.'

'You're very kind!' Sophia said. And she stood, trembling, and feeling sudden shame of her position.

Lady Betty seemed to see this. 'La! is it true they won't let you out?' she said.

Sophia muttered that it was.

The visitor's eyes roved from the meagre remains of the midday meal to the torn shreds of handkerchief that strewed the floor. 'Then it's a shame! It's a black monstrous shame!' she cried, stamping on the floor. 'I know what I should do if they did it to me! I should break, I should burn, I should tear! I should tear that old fright's wig off to begin! But I suppose it's your sister?'

'Yes.'

Lady Betty made a face. 'Horrid thing!' she exclaimed. 'I never did like her! Is it because you won't – is it because you have a lover, miss?'

Sophia hesitated. 'La, don't mind me. I have five!' the child cried naïvely. 'I'll tell you their names if you like. They are nothing to me, the foolish things, but I should die if I hadn't as many as other girls. To see them glare at one another is the finest sport in the world.'

'But you love one of them?' Sophia said shyly.

'La, no, it's for them to love me!' Lady Betty cried, tossing her head. 'I *should* be a fool if I loved them!'

'But the letter – that I tore up?' Sophia ventured.

The child blushed, and with a queer laugh flung herself on the other's neck and kissed her. 'That was from a – a lover I ought not to have,' she said. 'If it had been found, I should have had my ears boxed, and been sent into the country. You saved me, you duck, and I'll never forget it!'

Sophia bent on the most serious imprudence could be wise for another. 'From a lover whom you ought not to have?' she said gravely. 'You'll not do it again, will you? You'll not receive a second?'

'La, no, I promise you,' Lady Betty cried, volubly insistent. 'He's – well, he's a nobody, but he writes such dear, darling, charming notes! There, now you know. Oh, yes, it was horrid of me. But I hate him. So that's enough.'

'You promise?' Sophia said, almost severely.

'I vow I do,' Lady Betty cried, hugging her. 'The creature's a wretch. Now tell me, you poor thing, all about *him*. I've told you my affair.'

Here was indeed a blind leader of the blind, but after a little hesitation Sophia told her story. She was too proud to plead the justification her sister's treatment of Tom supplied; nor was there need of this. Even in the bud, Lady Betty found the story beautiful; and when Sophia went on to her lover's letter, and blushing and faltering owned that he had pressed her to elope, the listener could contain herself no longer. 'Elope!' she cried, springing up with sparkling eyes. 'Oh, the dear bold man! Oh, how I envy you!'

'Envy me?'

'Yes! To be locked in your room and starved – I hope they starve you – and scolded and threatened and perhaps carried into the country. And all the time to be begged and prayed and entreated to elope, and the dear creature wailing and sighing and consuming below. Oh, you lucky, lucky, lucky girl!' And Lady Betty flung herself on Sophia's neck and embraced her again and again. 'You lucky thing! And then perhaps to be forced to escape down a ladder—'

'Escape?' Sophia said, shaking her head piteously. And she

explained how far she was from escaping. 'By this time tomorrow,' she continued, choked by the bitter feelings the thought of tomorrow begot, 'I shall be at Chalkhill!'

'No, you will not!' Lady Betty cried, her eyes sparkling. 'You will not!' she repeated. 'By good luck 'tis between lights. Put on your hoop and sacque. Take my hat and laced jacket. Bend your knees as you go down the stairs, you gawk, and no one will be a bit the wiser.'

Sophia stared at her. 'What do you mean?' she said.

'Northey's at the House, your sister's at Lady Paget's,' the girl explained breathlessly. 'There is only the old fright outside, and she's had a taste of my tongue and won't want another. You may walk straight out before they bring candles. I shall wait ten minutes until you are clear, and then, though they'll know it's a bite, they won't dare to stop my ladyship, and – oh, you darling, it will be the purest, purest fun. It will be all over the town tomorrow, and I shall be part of it!'

Sophia shuddered. 'Fun?' she said. 'Do you call it fun?'

'Why, of course it will be the purest, purest fun!' the other cried. 'The prettiest trick that ever was played! You darling, we shall be the talk of the town!' And in the gaiety of her heart, Lady Betty lifted her sacque, and danced two or three steps of a minuet. 'We shall – but how you look, miss! You are not going to disappoint me?'

Sophia stood silent. 'I am afraid,' she muttered.

'Afraid? Afraid of what?'

'I am afraid.'

'But you were going to him tomorrow?'

Sophia blushed deeply. 'He was coming for me,' she murmured.

'Well, and what is the difference?'

The elder girl did not answer, but her cheeks grew hotter and hotter. 'There is a difference,' she said.

'Then you'll go to Chalkhill!' Lady Betty cried in derision, her voice betraying her chagrin. 'La, miss, I vow I thought you'd more spirit! or I would not have troubled you!'

Sophia did not retort; indeed, she did not hear. In her heart was passing a struggle, the issue of which must decide her lot. And she knew this. She was young, but she knew that as her lover showed himself worthy or unworthy of her trust so must her fate be happy or most miserable, if she went to him. And she trembled under the knowledge. Chalkhill, even Chalkhill and Aunt Leah's stinging tongue and meagre commons, seemed preferable to a risk so great. But then she thought of Tom, and of the home that had grown cold; of the compensations for home in which others seemed to find pleasure, the flippant existence of drums and routs, the card-table, and the masquerade. And in dread, not of Chalkhill, but of a loveless life, in hope, not of her lover, but of love, she wrung her hands. 'I don't know!' she cried, the burden of decision forcing the words from her as from one in pain. 'I don't know!'

'What?'

'Whether I dare go!'

'Why,' Lady Betty asked eagerly, 'there is no risk.'

'Child! child, you don't understand,' poor Sophia wailed. 'Oh, what, oh, what am I to do? If I go it is for life. Don't you understand?' she added feverishly. 'Cannot you see that? It is for life!'

Lady Betty, startled by the other's passion, could only answer, 'But you were going tomorrow, miss? If you were not afraid to go tomorrow—'

'Why today?' Sophia asked bitterly. 'If I could trust him tomorrow, why not today? Because – because – oh, I cannot tell you!' And she covered her face with her hands.

The other saw that she was shaking from head to foot, and reluctantly accepted a situation she only partly understood. 'Then you won't go?' she said.

The word 'No' trembled on Sophia's lips. But then she saw as in a glass the life to which she condemned herself if she pronounced it; the coldness, the worldliness, the lovelessness, the solitude in a crowd, all depicted, not with the compensating lights and shadows which experience finds in them, but in crude lines such as they wear in a young girl's fancy. In the past was nothing to retain her; in the future her lover beckoned; only maiden modesty and dread of she knew not what withstood a natural impulse. She would and she would not. Painfully she twisted and untwisted her fingers, while Lady Betty waited and looked.

On a sudden in Arlington Street a small-coalman raised his shrill cry; she had heard it a score of times in the last two days; now she felt that she could not bear to hear it again. It was a small thing, but her gorge rose against it. 'I will go!' she cried hoarsely. 'Give me the clothes.'

Lady Betty clapped her hands like a child at a play. 'You will? Oh, brave!' she cried. 'Then there's not a minute to be lost, miss. Take my laced jacket and hat. But stay – you must put on your sacque and hoop. Where are they? Let me help you. And won't you want to take some – la, you'll have nothing but what you stand up in!'

Sophia winced, but pursued her preparations as if she had not heard. In feverish haste she dragged out what she wanted, and in five minutes stood in the middle of the room, arrayed in Lady Betty's jacket and hat, which, notwithstanding the difference in height, gave her such a passing resemblance to the younger girl as might deceive a person in a half light.

'You'll do!' Lady Betty cried; all to her was sport. 'And you'll just take my chair: it's a hack, but they know me. Mutter "home," and stop 'em where you like – and take another! D'you see?'

The two girls – their united ages barely made up thirty-four – flung themselves into one another's arms. Held thus. the younger felt the wild beating of Sophia's heart, and put her from her and looked at her with a sudden qualm of doubt and fear and perception.

'Oh,' she cried, 'if he is not good to you! If he – don't don't!' she continued, trembling herself in every limb. 'Let me take off your things. Let me! Don't go!'

But Sophia's mind was now made up. 'No,' she said firmly; and then, looking into the other's eyes, 'Only speak of me kindly, child, if – if they say things.'

And before Lady Betty, left standing in the middle of the darkened room – where the reflection of the oil lamps in the street below was beginning to dance and flicker on the ceiling – had found words to answer, Sophia was half-way down the stairs. The staircase was darker than the room, and detection, as Lady Betty had foreseen, was almost impossible. Mrs Martha, waiting spitefully outside her mistress's door on the first landing, saw as she thought, 'that little baggage of a ladyship' go down; and she followed her muttering, but with no intention of intercepting her. John in the hall, too, saw her coming, and threw wide the door, then flew to open the waiting chair. 'Home, my lady?' he asked obsequiously, and passed the word; finally, when the chair moved off, he looked up and down, and came in slowly, whistling. Another second, and the door of the house in Arlington Street slammed on Sophia.

'And a good riddance!' muttered Mrs Martha, looking over the balusters. 'I never could abear her!'

CHAPTER VI

A Chair and a Coach

THE GLASSES of the chair, which had been standing some time at the door, were dimmed by moisture, and in the dusk of the evening its trembling occupant had no cause to fear recognition. But as the men lifted and bore her from the door, every blurred light that peeped in on her, and in an instant was gone, every smoking shop-lamp that glimmered a moment through the mist, and betrayed the moving forms that walked the sideway, was, to Sophia, an eye noting and condemning her. As the chairmen swung into Portugal Street, and, turning eastwards, skirted the long stand of coaches and the group of linkmen that waited before Burlington House, she felt that all eyes were upon her, and she shrank farther and farther into the recesses of the chair.

A bare-footed orange girl, who ran beside the window waving ballads or bills of the play, a coach rattling up behind and bespattering the glass as it passed, a link-boy peering in and whining to be hired, caused her a succession of panics. On top of these, the fluttering alarms of the moment, pressed the consciousness of a step taken that could never be retraced; nor was it until the chairmen, leaving Piccadilly behind them, had entered the comparative quiet of Air Street, and a real difficulty rose before her, that she rallied her faculties.

The men were making for Soho, and if left to take their course, would, in a quarter of an hour set her down at the door of Lady Betty's home in King's Square. That would not do. But to stay them, and to vary the order from 'Home' to Mr Wollenhope's house in Davies Street, where her lover lodged, did not now seem the simple and easy step it had appeared a few minutes earlier, when the immediate difficulty was to escape from the house. Lady Betty had said that the men knew her. In that case, as soon as Sophia spoke to them they would scent something wrong, and, apprised of the change of fares, might wish to know more. They might even decline to take her whither she bade them!

The difficulty was real, but for that very reason Sophia's courage rose to meet it. At present she knew where she was; a minute or two later she might not know. The sooner she took the route into her own hands, therefore, the better it would be; and as the men turned from the narrow street of Air into Brewer Street and swung to the right towards Soho, she tapped the glass. The chair moved on. With impatience, natural in the circumstances, Sophia tapped again and more sharply. This time the front bearer heard, and gave the word. The chair was set down, and the man, wiping his brow, raised the lid.

'What is it, my lady?' he said, with a rich Irish accent. 'Shure, and isn't it right ye are? If we went by Windmill Street, which some would be for going, there's a sight of coaches that way.'

'I don't want to go to King's Square,' Sophia answered firmly.

'Eh, my lady, no? But you said "Home."'

'I want to go to the West End again,' Sophia said. 'I've remembered something; I want to go to Davies Street.'

'Faith, but it's a fine trate your ladyship's had,' the Irishman cried good-humouredly, 'and finely I should be scolded if his noble lordship your father knew 'twas with us you went; but it's home now you must go; you've played traunt long enough, my lady! And – holy Mother!' – with a sudden exclamation – ''tis not your ladyship! Oh, the saints, Micky, she's changed!'

The second chairman came round the chair, stared, and rubbed his head; and the two gazed in perplexity at poor Sophia, whose face alone appeared above the side of the conveyance. 'Take me to Davies Street by Berkeley Square,' she commanded, tapping the front impatiently. 'To Mr Wollenhope's house. What does it matter to you where I go?'

'To Davies Street?'

'Yes; cannot you hear?'

'Faith, and I hear,' the Irishman answered, staring. 'But then, the saints help us, 'tis not yourself. 'Twas her ladyship hired me to go to Arlington Street, and to take her home, and it's not leaving her I'll be!'

'But her ladyship lent me the chair!' Sophia cried desperately. 'She'll take another. Cannot you understand? She knows all about it. Now take me to Davies Street.'

Her voice trembled with anxiety, for at any moment she might be seen and recognized. A lamp in an oilman's window, one of the few lights that at long intervals broke the dull gloom of Brewer Street, shone on the group. Already a couple of chairs had swung by, the carriers casting, as they passed, a curious look at the stationary chair; and now a coach, approaching from the Soho direction, was near at hand. Every second she delayed there was a second on the rack. What would Sir Hervey or Lord Lincoln, what would any of the hundred acquaintances she had made since she came to town, say of a girl found unprotected, after nightfall, astray in the public streets?

Alas, the men still hesitated, and while they stood staring the coach came up. Before Sophia could add reproaches to her commands, it was checked opposite the group. The coachman leant down, and in a tone of disappointment – as if it were only then he saw that the chair was occupied – 'You've a fare, have you?' he said. 'You can't take a lady to Crown Court, King Street?'

Before the Irishman could answer, 'Here my man,' a woman's voice cried from the coach, 'I want to go to Crown Court, St James's, and the coach can't enter. Double fare if you are quick! Here, let me out!'

'But, faith, ma'am, I've a fare,' Mick cried.

'They've a fare,' the coachman explained, leaning down anew.

'The fare can take my coach,' the voice answered imperiously; and in a twinkling, a smartly dressed woman, wearing red and white and plenty of both, yet handsome after a fashion, had pushed first her hoop and then herself out of the coach. 'See here, ma'am,' she cried, seeing Sophia's scared face, 'the coach is paid, and will take you anywhere in reason. 'Twill make no difference to you and all to me, and a mite of good nature is never thrown away! I've to go where a coach cannot go. Up a court, you understand.'

Sophia hesitated. Why did not the lady, whose bold eyes did not much commend her, pursue her way to Portugal Street, and descend there, where chairs might be had in plenty? Or why, again, was she in such a clamourous hurry and so importunate? On the other hand, if all were right, nothing could have fallen out more happily for herself; it was no wonder that, after a momentary hesitation, she gave a grudging assent. One of the chairmen, who seemed willing enough to make the change, opened the door; she stepped out and mechanically climbed into the coach. 'To Davies Street, Mayfair,' she said, sinking back. 'To Mr Wollenhope's, if you please.'

Quickly as she took her part, the strange lady was quicker; in a second she was in the chair and the chair was gone. It seemed to vanish. A moment and the coach also started, and lumbered westwards along Brewer Street. Now at last Sophia was at liberty to consider – with no obstacle short of Mr Wollenhope's door – how she should present herself to her lover, and how it behoved him to receive her.

She found it more easy to answer the second question than the first. Well indeed she knew how it became him to receive her. If in men survived any delicacy, any reverence, any gratitude, these were her due who came to him thus; these must appear in his greeting, or the worst guided, the most hapless of maids, was happy beside her. He must show himself lover, brother, parent, friend, in his one person; for he was her all. The tenderest homage, the most delicate respect, a tact that fore-ran offence, a punctilio that saw it everywhere, the devotion of a Craven, the gratitude of a Peterborough, were her right who came to him thus, a maiden trusting in his honour. She was clear on this; and not once or twice, but many times, many times, as she pressed one hand on the other and swallowed the tell-tale lump that rose and rose in her throat, she swore that if she did not meet with these, if he did not greet her with them, plain in eye and lip – aye, and with a thousand dainty flowers of love, a thousand tender thoughts and imaginings, not of her, but for her – she had better have been the mud through which the wheels of her coach rolled!

It was natural enough that, so near, so very near the crisis, she should feel misgiving. The halt in the dark street, the chill of the night air, had left her shivering; had left her with an overwhelming sense of loneliness and homelessness. The question was no longer how to escape from a prison, but how, having escaped, she would be received by him, who must be her all. The dice were on the table, the throw had been made, and made for life; it remained only to lift the box. For a little, a very little while, since a matter of minutes only divided her from Davies Street, she hung between the old life and the new, her heart panting vaguely for the sympathy that had been lacking in the old life, for the love that the new life had in store. Would she find them? Child as she was, she trembled now that she stood on the brink. A few minutes and she would know. A few minutes, and—

The coach stopped suddenly, with a jerk that flung her forward. She looked out, her heart beating. She was ready to descend. But surely this was not Davies Street? The road was very dark. On the left, the side on which the door opened, a dead wall, overhung by high trees, confronted her.

'Where am I?' she cried, her hand on the fastening of the door, her voice quivering with sudden fright. 'We are not there?'

'You are as far as you'll go, mistress,' a rough voice answered from the darkness. 'Sorry to alter your plans. A fine long chase you've given us.' And from the gloom at the horses' heads, two men advanced to the door of the coach.

She took them for footpads. The dead wall had much the appearance of the wall of Burlington Gardens, where it bounds Glasshouse Street; at that spot, she remembered, a coach had been robbed the week before. She prepared to give up her money, and was groping with a trembling hand for a little knitted purse, when the men, still grumbling, opened the door.

'I suppose you know what's what,' the foremost said. 'At suit of Margott's of Paul's Churchyard. You'll go to my house, I take it? You'll be more genteel there.'

'I don't understand,' Sophia muttered, her heart sinking.

'Oh, don't come the innocent over us!' the man answered coarsely. 'Here's the *capias*. Forty-eight, seven, six, debt and costs. It's my house or the Marshalsea. One or the other, and be quick about it. If you've the cash you'd better come to me.'

'There's some mistake,' Sophia gasped, involuntarily retreating into the farthest corner of the coach. 'You take me for someone else.'

The bailiffs – for such they were – laughed at the joke. 'I take you for Mrs Clark, alias Grocott, alias anything else you please,' the spokesman answered. 'Come, no nonsense, mistress; it's not the first time you've been behind bars. I warrant with that face you'll soon find someone to open the door for you.'

'But I'm not Mrs Clark,' Sophia protested. 'I'm not indeed.'

'Pooh, pooh!'

'I tell you I am not Mrs Clark!' she cried. 'Indeed, indeed, I am not! It has nothing to do with me,' she continued desperately. 'Please let me go on.' And in great distress she tried to close the door on them.

The bailiff prevented her. 'Come, no nonsense, mistress,' he repeated. 'These tricks won't serve you. We were waiting for you at the Ipswich stage; you got the start there, and very cleverly, I will allow. But my mate got the number of the coach, and if we had not overtaken you here we'd have nabbed you in Davies Street. You see we know all about you, and where you were bound. Now where is to be?'

Sophia, at the mention of Davies Street, began to doubt her own identity; but still repeated, with the fierceness of despair, that she was not the person they sought. 'I am not Mrs Clark!' she cried. 'I only took this coach in Brewer Street. You can ask the coachman.'

'Ah, I might, but I shouldn't get the truth!'

'But it is the truth!' Sophia cried piteously; truly punishment had fallen on her quickly! 'It is the truth! It is indeed!'

The bailiff seemed to be a little shaken by her earnestness. He exchanged a few words with his fellow. Then, 'We'll take the risk,' he said. 'Will you come out, ma'am, or shall I come in?'

Sophia trembled. 'Where are you going to take me?' she faltered.

'To my house, where it's ten shillings a day and as genteel company as you'd find in St James's!' the fellow answered. 'S'help me, you'll be at home in an hour! I've known many go in all of a shake, that with a glass of mulled wine and cheerful company were as jolly by nightfall as Miss at a fair!' And without waiting for more, the man climbed into the coach and plumped down beside her.

Sophia recoiled with a cry of alarm. 'La!' he said, with clumsy good nature, 'you need not be afraid. I'm a married man. You sit in your corner, ma'am, and I'll sit in mine. Bless you, I'm sworn to do my duty. Up you get, Trigg!'

The second bailiff mounted beside the coachman, the coach was turned, and in a trice Sophia was once more trundling eastwards through the streets. But in what a condition!

In the power of a vulgar catchpoll, on her way to a low sponging house, she saw herself borne helpless past the house that, until today, she had called her home! True, she had only to prove who she was in order to be released. She had only to bid them turn aside and stop at Mr Northey's mansion, and a single question and answer would set her free. But at what a cost! Overwhelmed and terrified, at her wits' end how to bear herself, she yet shrank from such a return as that!

Gladly would she have covered her face with her hands and wept tears of bitter mortification. But the crisis was too sharp, the difficulty too urgent for tears. What was she to do? Allow herself to be carried to her destination, and there incarcerated with vile persons in a prison which her ignorance painted in the darkest colours? Or avow the truth, bid them take her back to her brother-in-law's, and there drain the cup of ignominy to the dregs? In either case decision must be speedy. Already Arlington Street lay behind them; they were approaching St James's Church. They were passing it. Another minute and they would reach the end of the Haymarket.

Suddenly she clapped her hands. 'Stop!' she cried. 'Tell him to stop! There's Lane's. They know me there. They'll tell you that I am not the person you think. Please stop!'

The bailiff nodded, put out his head, and gave the order. Then, as the coach drew up to the shop, he opened the door, 'Now, no tricks! ma'am,' he said. 'If you go a yard from me I nab you. Smooth's my name when I'm well treated; but if Mr

Lane knows you I'll take his word and ask your pardon. I'm not unreasonable.'

Sophia did not pause to reply, but descended, and with hot cheeks hurried across the roadway into the well-known silk-mercer's. Fortunately, the shop, at certain times of the day the resort of Piccadilly bloods, was deserted at this late hour. All the lamps but one were extinguished, and by the light of this one, Mr Lane and two apprentices were stowing goods under the counter. A third young man stood looking on and idly swinging a cane; but to Sophia's relief he retired through the open door at the back, which revealed the cosy lights of a comfortable parlour.

The tradesman advanced, bowing and rubbing his hands. 'Dear me,' he said, 'you are rather late, ma'am, but anything we can do – William, relight the lamps.'

'No,' Sophia cried. 'I do not want anything. I only – Mr Lane,' she continued, blushing deeply, 'will you be good enough to tell this person who I am.'

'Dear, dear, my lady,' Mr Lane exclaimed, becoming in a moment a very Hector, 'you don't mean that – what is this, my man, what does it mean? Let me tell you I've several stout fellows on the premises, and—'

'No need,' the bailiff answered gruffly. 'I only want to know who the – who the lady is.' He looked crestfallen already. He saw by the lamplight that his prisoner was too young; a mere girl in her teens. And his heart misgave him.

'This is Miss Maitland, sister-in-law to the honourable Mr Northey, of Arlington Street, and the House,' the tradesman answered majestically. 'Now, my man, what is it?'

'You are sure that she is not a – a Mrs Oriana Clark?' the bailiff asked, consulting his writ for the name.

'No more than I am!' Mr Lane retorted, sniffing contemptuously. 'What do you mean by such nonsense?'

'Nothing now,' the discomfited bailiff answered; and muttering 'I am sure I beg her ladyship's pardon! Beg her pardon! No offence!' he bent his head with ready presence of mind and hurried out of the shop; his retreat facilitated by the fact that Sophia, overcome by her sudden release, was seized with a fit of giddiness, which compelled her to cling to the shop-board.

In a moment the good Lane was all solicitude. He placed a

chair for her, called for volatile salts, and bade them close the door into the street. Sending the staring apprentices about their business, he bustled out to procure some water; but in this he was anticipated by the young man whom she had seen in the shop when she entered. Too faint at the moment to remark from what hand she took it, Sophia drank, and returned the glass. Then, a little revived by the draught, and sensible of the absurdity of the position, she tried to rise, with a smile at her weakness. But the young man who had brought the water, and who had something of the air of a gentleman, foppishly and effeminately dressed, implored her to sit awhile.

'Sure, ma'am, you can't be rested yet!' he cried, hanging over her with a solicitude that seemed a little excessive. 'Such an outrage on divine beauty merits – stap me! the severest punishment. I shall not fail, ma'am, to seek out the low beast and chastise him as he deserves.'

'There is no need,' Sophia answered, looking at the spark with mild surprise; she was still too faint to resent his manner. 'I am better now, I thank you, sir. I will be going.'

'Stap me, not yet!' he cried effusively. 'A little air, ma'am?' and he fell to fanning her with his hat, while his black eyes languished on hers. ''Twill bring back the colour, ma'am. Has your ladyship ever tried Florence water in these attacks? It is a monstrous fine specific, I am told.'

'I am not subject to them,' Sophia answered, forced to avert her eyes. This movement, as it happened, brought her gaze to the open door of the parlour; where, to her astonishment, she espied Mr Lane, standing, as it were, in ambush, dwelling on the scene in the shop with a face of childish pleasure. Now he softly rubbed his hands; now he nodded his head in an ecstasy. A moment Sophia watched him, her own face in shadow; then she rose a little displeased, and more puzzled.

'I must go now,' she said, bowing stiffly. 'Be good enough to see if my coach is there.'

The beau, taken aback by her manner, turned to the silk mercer, who came slowly forward. 'Is her ladyship's coach there?' the young gentleman cried with great stateliness.

Mr Lane hurried obsequiously to the door, looked out, and returned. 'Dear, dear, ma'am,' he said, 'I fear those wretches took it. But I can send for a chair.'

'Call one, call one!' the gentleman commanded. 'I shall see the lady to her door.'

'Oh, no, no!' Sophia answered quickly. 'It is not necessary.'

'It is very necessary at this hour,' Mr Lane interposed; and then apologized for his intervention by rubbing his hands. 'I could not think of – of letting you go from here, ma'am, without an escort!' he continued, with another low bow. 'And this gentleman, Mr—'

'Fanshaw, man, Fanshaw,' the young spark said, stroking his cravat and turning his head with an absurd air of importance. 'Your humble servant to command, ma'am. Richard Fanshaw, Esquire, of Warwickshire. 'Tis certain I must attend you so far; and – and oh, hang this!' he continued, breaking off in a sudden fit of rage. For in the act of bowing to her, he had entangled his sword in a roll of Lyons that stood behind him. 'Fellow, what the deuce do you mean by leaving rubbish in a gentleman's way?' and he struggled furiously with it.

Sophia could scarcely forbear a smile as Mr Lane ran to the rescue. Yet with all his efforts

The bold knight was red
And the good stuff was shred

before the little beau was freed. He cursed all tailors, and, to hide his confusion, hastened rather clumsily to hand her to the chair.

She was in a new difficulty. Lane would give the order 'Arlington Street'; Mr Fanshaw, smirking and tip-tapping at the side, would insist on seeing her home. And she herself for an instant, as the cold night air met her on the threshold of the oil-lit street, and she shivered under its touch, hesitated. For an instant her fears pleaded with her, bade her take warning from the thing that had already befallen her, whispered 'Home!' At that hour the future, mirrored on the gloomy surface of the night-street, on the brink of which she stood, seemed dark, forlorn, uncertain.

But her pride was not yet conquered; and without a vast sacrifice of pride she could not return. Her escapade would be remembered against her; she would be condemned for the attempt, and despised for its failure. Home, in her case, meant no loving mother longing to forgive, no fond tears, no kisses mingled with reproaches; but sneers and stinging words, disgrace and exile, a child's punishment. Little wonder that she grew hard again since, on the other side, a girl's first fancy beckoned roseate; or that, when she announced with an easy air that she had to go to Davies Street, Mr Lane detected nothing suspicious in her tone.

'Dear, dear, ma'am, it's rather late,' he said. 'And the streets not too secure. But Rich— Mr Fanshaw will see you safe. Much honoured. Oh, much honoured, I am sure, ma'am. Delighted to be of service. My humble obedience to your sister and Mr Northey.'

A last backward glance as she was lifted and borne from the door showed her Mr Lane standing in his shop-entrance. He was looking after her with the same face of foolish admiration which she had before surprised; and she wondered afresh what it meant. Soon, however, her thoughts passed from him to the over-dressed little fop who had added himself to her train, and whose absurd attempts to communicate with her as he strutted beside the glass, his sword under his arm and his laced hat cocked, were almost as amusing as the air of superb protection which he assumed when he caught her eye. Really, he was too ridiculous. Moreover, she did not want him. His presence was uncalled for now; and when she reached Davies Street, might involve her in new embarrassments. She would have dismissed him, but she doubted if he would go; and to open the glass and make the attempt might only incite him to greater freedoms. Sophia bit her lip to repress a smile; the little beau took the smile for encouragement, and kissed his hand through the glass.

CHAPTER VII

In Davies Street

THE CHAIRMEN pushed on briskly through Piccadilly and Portugal Street until they reached the turnpike on the skirts of the town. There, turning to the right by Berkeley Row, they reached Berkeley Square, at that time a wide, unplanted space, surrounded on three sides by new mansions, and on the fourth by the dead wall of Berkeley House. For lack of lighting, or perhaps by reason of the convenience the building operations afforded, it was a favourite haunt of footpads. Sophia was a prey to anxieties that left no room in her mind for terrors of this class; and neither the dark lane, shadowed by the dead wall of Berkeley Gardens nor the gloomy waste of the square, held any tremors for her; but the chairmen hastened over this part of their journey, and for a time her attendant squire was so little in evidence that in the agitation into which the prospect of arrival at her lover's threw her, she forgot his presence. She strained her eyes through the darkness to distinguish the opening of Davies Street, and at once longed and feared to see it. When at last the chair halted, and, pressing her hand to her heart to still the tumult that almost stifled her, she prepared to descend, it was with a kind of shock that she discovered the little dandy mincing and bowing on the pavement, his hand extended to aid her in stepping from the chair.

The vexation she had suppressed before broke out at the sight. She bowed slightly and avoided his hand. 'I am obliged to you, sir,' she said ungraciously; 'I won't trouble you farther. Goodnight, sir.'

'But – I shall see you back to Arlington Street, ma'am?' he lisped. 'Surely at this hour an escort is more than ever necessary. I declare it is past eight, ma'am.'

It was; but the fact put in words stung her like a whip. She winced under all that the lateness of the hour implied. It seemed intolerable that in a crisis in which her whole life lay in the balance, in which her being was on the rack until she found the reception that should right her, coverting her boldness into constancy, her forwardness into courage – when she trembled on the verge of the moment in which her lover's eye should tell her all – it was intolerable that she should be harassed by this prating dandy. 'I shall find an escort here,' she cried harshly. 'I need you no longer, sir. Goodnight.'

'Oh, but ma'am,' he protested, bowing like a Chinese mandarin, 'it is impossible I should leave you so. Surely, there is something I can do for your ladyship.'

'You can pay the chairman!' she cried contemptuously; and

turning from him to the door before which the chair had halted, she found it half open. In the doorway a woman, her back to the light, stood blocking the passage. Doubtless, she had heard what had passed.

Sophia's temper died down on the instant. 'Is this Mr Wollenhope's?' she faltered.

'Yes, ma'am.'

An hour before it had seemed simple to ask for her lover. Now the moment was come she could not do it. 'May I come in?' she muttered, to gain time.

'You wish to see me?'

'Yes.'

'Is the chair to wait, ma'am?'

Sophia trembled. It was a moment before she could find her voice. Then, 'No,' she answered faintly.

The woman looked hard at her, and having the light at her back, had the advantage. 'Oh!' she said at last, addressing the men, 'I think you had better wait a minute.' And grudgingly making way for Sophia to enter, she closed the door. 'Now, ma'am, what is it?' she said, standing four-square to the visitor. She was a stout, elderly woman, with a bluff but not unkindly face.

'Mr Hawkesworth lodges here?'

'He does, ma'am.'

'Is he at home?' Sophia faltered. Under this woman's gaze she felt a sudden overpowering shame. She was pale and red by turns. Her eyes dropped, her confusion was not to be overlooked.

'He is not at home,' the woman said shortly. And her look, hostile before, grew harder.

Sophia caught her breath. She had not thought of this, and for a moment she was so overpowered by the intelligence, that she had to support herself against the wall. 'When will he return, if you please?' she asked at length, her lip quivering.

'I'm sure I couldn't say. I couldn't say at all,' Mrs Wollenhope answered curtly. 'All I know is he went out with the young gentleman at five, and as like as not he won't be home till morning.'

Sophia had much ado not to burst into tears. Apparently the woman perceived this, and felt a touch of pity for her, for, in an altered tone, 'It is possible,' she asked, 'you're the young lady he's to marry tomorrow?'

The words were balm to the girl's heart. Here was sure footing at last; here was something to go upon. 'Yes,' she said, more boldly. 'I am.'

'Oh!' Mrs Wollenhope ejaculated. 'Oh!' After which she stared at the girl, as if she found a difficulty in fitting her in with notions previously formed. At last, 'Well, miss,' she said, 'I think if you could call tomorrow?' with a dry cough. 'If you are to be married tomorrow – it seems to me it might be better.'

Sophia shivered. 'I cannot wait,' she said desperately. 'I must see him. Something has happened which he does not know, and I must see him, I must indeed. Can I wait here? I have nowhere to go.'

'Well, you can wait here till nine o'clock,' Mrs Wollenhope answered less dryly. 'We shut up at nine.' Then, after glancing behind her, she laid her hand on Sophia's sleeve. 'My dear,' she said, lowering her voice, 'begging pardon for the liberty, for I see you are a lady, which I did not expect – if you'll take my advice you'll go back. You will indeed. I am sure your father and mother—'

'I have neither!' Sophia said.

'Oh, dear, dear! Still, I can see you've friends, and if you'll take my advice—'

She was cut short. 'There you are again, Eliza!' cried a loud voice, apparently from an inner room. 'Always your advice! Always your advice! Have done meddling, will you, and show the lady upstairs.'

Mrs Wellenhope shrugged her shoulders as if the interruption were no uncommon occurrence. 'Very well,' she said curtly; and turning, led the way along the passage. Sophia followed, uncertain whether to be glad or sorry that the good woman's warning had been cut short. As she passed the open door of a room at the foot of the stairs she had a glimpse of a cheery sea-coal fire, and a bald-headed man in his shirt sleeves, who was sitting on a settee beside it, a glass of punch in his hand. He rose and muttered, 'Your servant, ma'am!' as she passed; and she went on and saw him no more. But the vision of the snug back-parlour, with its fire and lights, and a red curtain hanging before the window, remained with her, a picture of comfort and quiet, as far as possible removed from the suspence and agitation in which she had passed the last two hours.

And in which she still found herself, for as she mounted the stairs her knees quaked under her. She was ashamed, she was frightened. At the head of the flight, when the woman opened the door of the room and by a gesture bade her enter, she paused and felt she could sink into the ground. For the veriest trifle she would have gone down again. But behind her – behind her, lay nothing that had power to draw her; to return was to meet abuse and ridicule and shame, and that not in Arlington Street only, for the story would be over the town. Lane the mercer, whose shop was a hotbed of gossip, the little dandy who had thrust himself into her company, and tracked her hither, the coachman who had witnessed the arrest, even her own friend Lady Betty – all would publish the tale. Girls whom she knew, and from whose plain-spoken gossip she had turned a prudish ear, would sneer in her face. Men like Lord Lincoln would treat her with the easy familiarity she had seen them extend to Lady Vane, or Miss Edwards. Women she respected. Lady Pomfret, the duchess, would freeze her with a look. Girls, good girls like Lady Sophia, or little Miss Hamilton – no longer would these be her company.

So, she had gone too far; it was too late to turn back; yet she felt, as she crossed the threshold, it was the one thing she longed to do. Though Mrs Wollenhope hastened to light two candles that stood on a table, the parlour and the shapes of the furniture swam before Sophia's eyes. The two candles seemed to be four, six, eight; nay, the room was all candles, dancing before her. She had to lean on a chair to steady herself.

By-and-by Mrs Wollenhope's voice, for a time heard droning dully, became clear. 'He was up above,' the good woman was saying. 'But he's not here much. He lives at the taverns of the quality, mostly. 'Twas but yesterday he told me, ma'am, he was going to be married. You can wait here till nine, and I'll come and fetch you then, if he has not come in. But you'd best be thinking, if you'll take my advice, what you'll do.'

'Now, Eliza!' Mr Wollenhope roared from below; to judge from the sound of his voice he had come to the foot of the stairs. 'Advising again, I'm bound. Always advising! Some day your tongue will get you into trouble, my woman. You come down and leave the young lady to herself.'

'Oh, very well.' Mrs Wollenhope muttered, tossing her head impatiently. 'I'm coming. Coming!' And shielding her light with her hand, she went out and left Sophia alone.

The girl remained where she had paused on entering, a little within the door, her hand resting on a chair. And presently, as she looked about her, the colour began to creep into her face. This was his home, and at the thought she forgot the past; she dreamed of the future. His home! Here he had sat thinking of her. Here he had written the letter! Here, perhaps in that cupboard set low in the wainscot beside the fire, lay the secret papers of which he had told her, the Jacobite lists that held a life in every signature, the Ormonde letters, the plans for the Scotch rising, the cipher promises from France! Here, surrounded by perils, he wrote and studied far into the night, the pistol beside the pen, the door locked, the keyhole stopped. Here he had lain safe and busy, while the hated Whig approvers drew their nets elsewhere. Sophia breathed more quickly as she pictured these things; as she told herself the story Othello told the Venetian maid. The attraction of the man, the magic of the lover, dormant during the stress she had suffered since she left Arlington Street, revived; the girl's eyes grew soft, blushes mantled over her cheeks. She looked round timidly, almost reverently, not daring to advance, not daring to touch anything.

The room, which was not large, was wainscotted from ceiling to floor with spacious panels, divided one from the other by fluted pillars in shadow relief, after the fashion of that day. The two windows were high, narrow, and round-headed, deeply sunk in the panelling. The fireplace, in which a few embers smouldered, was of Dutch tiles. On the square oak table in the middle of the floor, a pack of cards lay beside the snuffer tray, between the tall pewter candlesticks.

She noted these things greedily, and then, alas, she fell from the clouds. Mrs Wollenhope had said that he had lived in the rooms above until lately! Still, he had sat here, and these were his belongings, which she saw strewn here and there. The book laid open on the high-backed settle that flanked one side of the hearth, and masked the door of an inner room, had been laid there by his hand. The cloak that hung across the back of one of the heavy Cromwell chairs was his. The papers and ink-horn, pushed carelessly aside on one of the plain wooden window-seats, had been placed there by him. His were the black riding-wig, the whip, and spurs, and tasselled cane, that hung on a hook in a corner, and the wig-case that stood on a table against the wall alongside a crumpled cravat, and a jug and two mugs. All these – doubtless all these were his. Sophia, flustered and softened, her heart beating quick with a delicious emotion, half hope, half fear, sat down on the chair by the door and gazed at them.

He was more to her now, while she sat in his room and looked at these things, than he had ever been; and though the moment was at hand when his reception of her must tell her all, her distrust of him had never been less. If he did not love her with the love she pictured, why had he chosen her? He whose career promised so much, who under the cloak of frivolity pursued aims so high, amid perils so real. He must love her! He must love her! She thought this almost aloud, and seeing the wicks of the candles growing long, rose and snuffed them; and in the performance of this simple act of ownership, experienced a strange thrill of pleasure.

After that she waited awhile on her feet, looking about her shyly, and listening. Presently, hearing no sound, she stepped timidly and on tip-toe to the side-table, and lifting the crumpled cravat, smoothed it, then, with caressing fingers, folded it neatly and laid it back. Again she listened, wondering how long she had waited. No, that was not a step on the stairs; and thereat her heart began to sink. The reaction of hope deferred began to be felt. What if he did not come? What if she waited, and nine found her still waiting – waiting vainly in this quiet room where the lights twinkled in the polished panels, and now and again the ash of the coal fell softly to the hearth? It might – it might be almost nine already!

She began to succumb to a new fever of suspense, and looked about for something to divert her thoughts. Her eyes fell on the book that lay open on the seat of the settle. Thinking, 'He has read this today – his was the last hand that touched it – on this page his eyes rested,' Sophia stooped for it, and holding it carefully that she might keep the place for him, reverently, for it was his, she carried it to the light. The title at the head of the page was *The Irish Register*. The name smacked so little of diversion, she thought it a political tract – for the book was thin, no more than fifty pages or so; and she was setting it back on the table when her eye, in the very act of leaving the page, caught the glint, as it were, of a name. Beside the name, on the margin, were a few pencilled words and figures; but these, faintly scrawled, she did not heed at the moment.

'Cochrane, the Lady Elizabeth?' she muttered, repeating the name that had caught her eye. 'How strange! What can the book have to do with Lady Betty? It must be some kind of peerage. But she is not Irish!'

To settle the question, she raised the book anew to the light, and saw that it consisted of a list of persons' names arranged in order of rank. Only – which seemed odd – all the names were ladies' names. Above Cochrane, the Lady Elizabeth, appeared Cochrane, the Lady Anne; below came Coke, the Lady Catherine, and after each name the address of the lady followed if she were a widow, of her parents or guardians if she were unmarried.

Sophia wondered idly what it meant, and with half her mind bent on the matter, the other half intent on the coming of a footstep, she turned back to the title-page of the book. She found that the fuller description there printed ran *The Irish Register, or a list of the Duchess Dowagers, Countesses, Widow Ladies, Maiden Ladies, Widows, and Misses of Great Fortunes in England, as registered by the Dublin Society.*

Even then she was very, very far from understanding. But the baldness of the description sent a chill through her. Misses of large fortunes in England! As fortunes went, she was a miss of large fortune. Perhaps that was why the words grated upon her; why her heart sank, and the room seemed to grow darker. Turning to look at the cover of the book, she saw a slip of paper inserted towards the end to keep a place. It projected only an eighth of an inch, but she marked it, and turned to it; something or other – it may have been only the position of the paper in that part of the book, it may have been the presence of the book in her lover's room – forewarning her; for in the act of turning the leaves, and before she came to the marker, she knew what she would find.

And she found it. First, her name, 'Maitland, Miss Sophia, at the Hon. Mr Northey's in Arlington Street.' Then – yes, then, for that was not all or the worst – down the narrow margin, starting at her name. ran a note, written faintly, in a hand she knew; the same hand that had penned her one love letter, the hand from which the quill had fallen in the rapture of anticipation, the hand of her 'humble, adoring lover, Hector, Count Plomer'!

She knew that the note would tell her all, and for a moment her courage failed her; she dared not read it. Her averted eyes sought instead the cupboard in the lower wainscot, which she had fancied the hiding place of the Jacobite cipher, the muniment chest where lay, intrusted to his honour, the lives and fortunes of the Beauforts and Ormondes, and Wynns and Cottons and Cecils. Was the cupboard that indeed? Or – what was it? The light reflected from the surface of the panels told her nothing, and she lowered the book and stood pondering. If the note proved to be that which she still shrank from believing it, what had she done? Or rather, what had she not done? What warnings had she not despised, what knowledge had she not sighted, what experience had she not overridden? How madly, how viciously, in the face of advice, in the face of remonstrance, in modesty's own despite, had she wrought her confusion, had she flung herself into the arms of this man! This man who – but that was the question!

She asked herself trembling, was he what this book seemed to indicate, or was he what she had thought him? Was he villain, or hero? Fortune-hunter, or her true lover? The meanest of tricksters, or the high-spirited chivalrous gentleman, laughing at danger and smiling at death, in whom great names and a great cause were content to place their trust?

At last she nerved herself to learn the answer to the question. The wicks of the candles were burning long; she snuffed them anew, and holding the book close to the light, read the words that were delicately traced beside her name.

'Has 6000 guineas charged on T.M.'s estates. If T.M. marries without consent of guardians has £10,000 more. Mrs N. the

same. T. is at Cambridge, aged eighteen. To make all sure, T. must be married first – query Oriana, if she can be found? Or Lucy Slee – but boys like riper women. Not clinch with S.M. until T. is mated, nor at all if the little Cochrane romp (page 7) can be brought to hand. But I doubt that, and S.M. is an easy miss, and swallows all. A perfect goose.'

Sophia sat awhile in a chair and shivered, her face white, her head burning. The words were so clear that, the intials notwithstanding, it was not possible to misinterpret them; or to set on them any construction save one. They cut her as the lash of a whip cuts the bare flesh. It was for this – thing that she had laid aside her maiden pride, had risked her good name, had scorned her nearest, had thrown away all in life that was worth keeping! It was for this creature, this thing in the shape of man, that she had over-leapt the bounds, had left her home, had risked the perils of the streets, and the greater perils of his company. For this – but she had not words adequate to the loathing of her soul. Outraged womanhood, wounded pride, contemned affection, which she had fancied love, seared her very soul. She could have seen him killed, she could have killed him with her own hand – or she thought she could; so completely in a moment was her liking changed to hatred, so completely destroyed on the instant was the trust she had placed in him.

'And S.M. is an easy miss, and swallows all. A perfect goose!' Those words cut more deeply than all into her vanity. She winced, nay, she writhed under them. Nor was that all. They had a clever, dreadful smartness that told her they were no mere memorandum, but had served in a letter, and tickled at once a man's conceit, and a woman's ears. Her own ears burned at the thought. *'S.M. is an easy miss, and swallows all. A perfect goose!'* Oh, she would never recover it! She would never regain her self-respect!

The last embers had grown grey behind the bars; the last ash had fallen from the grate while she sat. The room was silent save for her breathing, that now came in quick spasms as she thought of the false lover, and now was slow and deep as she sat sunk in a shamed reverie. On a sudden the cooling fireplace cracked. The sound roused her. She sprang up and gazed about her in affright. remembering that she had no longer any business there, nay, that in no room in the world had she less business.

In the terror of the moment she flew to the door; she must go, but whither? More than ever, now that she recognized her folly, she shrank from her sister's scornful eyes, from Mr Northey's disapproving stare, from the grins of the servants, the witticisms of her friends. The part she had played, seen as she now saw it would make her the laughing-stock of the town. It was the silliest, the most romantic; a school-girl would cry fie on it. Sophia's cheek burned at the thought of facing a single person who had ever known her; much more at the thought of meeting her sister or Mrs Martha, or the laced bumpkins past whom she had flitted in that ill-omened hour. She could not go back to Arlington Street. But then – whither could she go?

Whither indeed? It was nine o'clock; night had fallen. At such an hour the streets were unsafe for a woman without escort, much more for a girl of gentility. Drunken roysterers on their way from tavern to tavern, ripe for any frolic, formed a peril worse than footpads; and she had neither chair not link-boys, servants nor coach, without one or other of which she had never passed through the streets in her life. Yet she could not stay where she was; rather would she lie without covering in the wildest corner of the adjacent parks, or on the lonely edge of Rosamond's pond! The mere thought that she lingered there was enough; she shuddered with loathing, grew hot with rage. And the impulse that had hastened her to the door returning, she hurried out and was half-way down the stairs, when the sound of a man's voice, uplifted in the passage below, brought her up short where she stood.

An instant only she heard it clearly. Then the tramp of feet along the passage masked the voice. But she had heard enough – it was Hawkesworth's – and her eyes grew wide with terror. She should die of shame if he found her there! If he learned, not by hearsay, but eye to eye, that she had come of her own motion, poor, silly dupe of his blandishments, to throw herself into his arms! That were too much; she turned to fly.

Her first thought was to take refuge on the upper floor until he had gone into his room and closed the door; two bounds carried her to the landing she had left. But here she found an unexpected obstacle in a wicket, set at the foot of the upper flight of stairs; one of those wickets that are still to be seen in old houses, in the neighbourhood of the nursery. By the light that issued from the half-open doorway of the room, Sophia tugged at it furiously, but seeking the latch at the end of the gate where the hinges were, she lost a precious moment. When she found the fastening, the steps of the man she had fancied she loved, and now knew she hated, were on the stairs. And the gate would not yield! Penned on the narrow landing, with discovery tapping her on the shoulder, she fumbled desperately with the latch, even, in despair, flung her weight against the wicket. It held; in another second, if she persisted, she would be seen.

With a moan of anguish she turned and darted into Hawkesworth's room, and sprang to the table where the candles stood. Her thought was to blow them out, then to take her chance of passing the man before they were relighted. But as she gained the table and stooped to extinguish them, she heard his step so near the door that she knew the sudden extinction of the light must be seen; and her eyes at the same moment alighting on the high-backed settle, in an instant she was behind it.

It was a step she would not have taken had she acted on anything but the blind, unthinking impulse to hide herself. For here retreat was cut off: she was now between her enemy and the inner room. She dared not move, and in a few minutes at most must be discovered. But the thing was done; there was no time to alter it. As her hoop slipped from sight behind the wooden seat, the Irishman entered, and with a laugh flung his hat and cane on the table. A second person appeared to cross the threshhold after him; and crouching lower, her heart beating as if it would choke her, Sophia heard the door flung to behind them.

CHAPTER VIII

Unmasked

THERE ARE men who find as much pleasure in the intrigue as in the fruits of the intrigue; who take huge credit for their own finesse and others' folly, and find a chief part of their good in watching, as from a raised seat. the movements of their dupes, astray in a maze of their planting. The more ingenious the machination they have contrived, the nicer the calculations and the more narrow the point on which success turns, the sweeter is the sop to their vanity. To receive Lisette and Fifine in the same apartment within the hour; to divide the rebel and the minister by a door; to turn the scruple of one person to the hurt of another, and know both to be ignorant – these are feats on which they hug themselves as fondly as on the substantial rewards which crown their manoeuvres.

Hawkesworth was of this class; and it was with feelings such as these that he saw his nicely jointed plans revolving to the end he desired. To mould the fate of Tom Maitland at Cambridge. and of Sophia in town, and both to his own profit, fulfilled his sense of power. To time the weddings as nearly as possible, to match the one at noon and to marry the other at night, gratified his vanity at the same time that it tickled his humour. But the more delicate the machinery, the smaller is the atom, and the slighter the jar that suffices to throw all out of gear. For a time, Oriana's absence, at a moment when every instant was of price, and the interference of Tom's friends was hourly possible, threatened to ruin all. It was in the enjoyment of the relief, which the news of her arrival afforded, that he returned to his lodgings this evening. He was in his most rollicking humour, and overflowed with spirits; Tom's innocence and his own sagacity providing him with ever fresh and more lively cause for merriment.

Nor was the lad's presence any check on his mood. Hawkesworth's joviality, darkling and satirical as it was, passed with Tom for lightness of heart. What he did not understand, he set down for Irish, and dubbed his companion the prince of good fellows. As they climbed the stairs, he was trying with after-supper effusiveness to impress this on his host. 'I swear you are the best friend man ever had,' he cried, his voice full of gratitude. 'I vow you are.'

Hawkesworth laughed, as he threw his hat and cane on the table, and proceeded to take off his sword that he might be more at ease. His laughter was a little louder than the other's statement seemed to justify; but Tom was in no critical mood, and Hawkesworth's easy answer. 'You'll say so when you know all, my lad,' satisfied the boy.

'I do say it,' he repeated earnestly, as he threw himself on the settle, and, taking the poker, stirred the embers to see if a spark survived. 'I do say it.'

'And I say, well you may,' Hawkesworth retorted, with a sneer from which he could not refrain. 'What do you think, dear lad, would have happened, if I'd tried for the prize myself?' he continued. 'If I'd struck in for your pretty bit of red and white on my own account? Do you remember Trumpington, and our first meeting? I'd the start of you then, though you are going to be her husband.'

'Twenty minutes' start,' Tom answered.

Hawkesworth averted his face to hide a grin. 'Twenty minutes?' he said. 'Lord, so it was! Twenty minutes!'

The boy reddened. 'Why do you laugh?' he asked.

'Why? Why, because twenty minutes is a long time – sometimes,' Hawkesworth answered. 'But there, be easy, lad,' he continued, seeing that he was going too far, 'be easy – no need to be jealous of me – and I'll brew you some punch. There is one thing certain,' he continued, producing a squat Dutch bottle and some glasses from a cupboard by the door. 'You have me to thank for her! There is no doubt about that.'

'It's what I've always said,' Tom answered. He was easily appeased. 'If you'd not asked my help when your chaise broke down at Trumpington – you'd just picked her up, you remember? – I should never have known her! Think of that!' he continued, his eyes shining with a lover's enthusiasm; and he rose and trod the floor this way and that. 'Never to have known her, Hawkesworth!'

'Whom to know was to love,' the Irishman murmured, with thinly veiled irony.

'Right! Right, indeed!'

'And to love was to know – eh?'

'Right! Right, again!' poor Tom cried, striking the table.

For a moment Hawkesworth contemplated him with amusement. Then – 'Well, here's to her!' he cried, raising his glass. 'The finest woman in the world!'

'And the best! And the best!' Tom answered.

'And the best! The toast is worthy the best of liquor,' Hawkesworth continued, pushing over the other's glass; 'but you'll have to drink it cold, for the fire is out.'

'The finest woman in the world, and the best!' the lad cried; his eyes glowed as he stood up reverently, his glass in his hand. 'She is that, isn't she, Hawkesworth?'

'She is all that, I'll answer for it!' the Irishman replied, with a stifled laugh. Lord! what fools there were in the world! 'By this time tomorrow she'll be yours! Think of it, lad!' he continued, with an ugly-sounding, ugly-meaning laugh; at which one of his listeners shuddered.

But Tom, in the lover's seventh heaven, was not that one. His Oriana, who to others was a handsome woman, bold-eyed and free-tongued, was a goddess to him. He saw her through that glamour of first love that blesses no man twice. He felt no doubt, harboured no suspicion, knew no fear; he gave scarce one thought to her past. He was content to take for gospel all she told him, and to seek no more. That he – he should have gained the heart of this queen among women seemed so wonderful, so amazing, that nothing else seemed wonderful at all.

'You think she'll not fail?' he cried, presently, as he set down his glass. 'It's a week since I saw her, and – and you don't think she'll have changed her mind, do you?'

'Not she!' Hawkesworth answered.

'She'll come, you are certain?'

'As certain,' Hawkesworth cried gaily, 'as that Dr Keith will be ready at the chapel at twelve to the minute, dear lad. And, by the way, here's his health! Dr Keith, and long may he live to bless the single and crown the virtuous! To give to him that hath not, and from her that hath to take away! To be the plague of all sour guardians, lockers-up of maidens, and such as would cheat Cupid; and the guardian-angel of all Nugents, Husseys, and bold fellows! Here's to the pride of Mayfair, the curse of Chancery, and the godfather of many a pretty couple – Dr Keith!'

'Here's to him!' Tom cried, with ready enthusiasm. And then more quietly as he set down his glass, 'There's one thing I'd like, to be perfectly happy, Hawkesworth, only one. I wish it were possible, but I suppose it isn't.'

'What is it, lad?'

'If Sophia, my sister, could be there. They'll be sisters, you see, and – and, of course, Sophia's a girl, but there are only the two of us, for Madam Northey doesn't count. But I suppose it is not possible, she should be told?'

'Quite impossible!' Hawkesworth answered with decision; and he stooped a hide a smile. The humour of the situation suited him. 'Quite impossible! Ten to one she'd peach! No, no, we must not initiate her too soon, my boy; though it is likely enough she'll have her own business with Dr Keith one of these days!'

The boy stared at him. 'My sister?' he said slowly, his face growing red. 'With Dr Keith? What business could she have with him?'

'With Dr Keith?' Hawkesworth asked lightly. 'Why not the same as yours, dear boy?'

'The same as mine?'

'Yes, to be sure. Why not? Eh, why not?'

'Why not? Because she's a Maitland!' the lad answered, and his eyes flashed. 'Our women don't marry that way, I'd have you to know! Why, I'd – I'd rather see her buried.'

'But you're going to marry that way yourself!' Hawkesworth reasoned. The boy's innocence surrprised him a little and amused him more.

'I? But I'm a man,' Tom answered with dignity. 'I'm different. And – and Oriana,' he continued, plunging on a sudden into dreadful confusion and redness of face, 'is – is different of course, because, because – well, because if we are not married in this way, my brother Northey would interfere, and we could not be married at all. Oriana is an angel, and – and because she loves me, is willing to be married in this way. That's all, you see.'

'I see. But you would not like your sister to be married on the quiet?'

Tom glared at him. 'No,' he said curtly. 'And for the why, it is my business.'

'To be sure it is! Of course it is. And yet, Sir Tom,' Hawkesworth continued, his tone provoking, 'I would not mind wagering you a hundred it is the way she will be married, when her time comes.'

'My sister?'

'Yes.'

'Done with you!' the lad cried.

'Nay, I don't mind going farther,' Hawkesworth continued. 'I'll wager you the same sum that she does it within the year.'

'This year?'

'A year from today.'

Tom jumped up in heat. 'What the devil do you mean?' he cried. Then he sat down again. 'But what matter!' he said, 'I'll take you.'

Hawkesworth as he pulled out his betting book turned his head aside to hide a smile. 'I note it,' he said. '"P. H. bets Sir Thomas Maitland a hundred that Miss Sophia Maitland is married at Dr Keith's chapel; and another hundred that the marriage is within the year."'

'Right!' Tom said, glowering at him. His boyish estimate of the importance of his family, and of the sacredness of his womankind, sucked the flavour from the bet; ordinarily the young scapegrace loved a wager.

Hawkesworth put up his book again. 'Good,' he said. 'You'll see that that will be two hundred in my pocket some day.'

'Not it!' Tom answered, rudely. 'My sister is not that sort! And perhaps the sooner you know it, the better,' he added, aggressively.

'Why, lad, what do you mean?'

'Just what I said!' Tom answered shortly. 'It was English. When my sister is to be married, we shall make a marriage for her. She's not – but the less said the better,' he concluded. breaking off with a frown.

Hawkesworth knew that it would be prudent to quit the subject, but his love of teasing, or his sense of the humour of the situation, would not let him be silent. 'She's not for such as me, you mean?' he said, with a mocking laugh.

'You can put it that way if you choose!'

'And yet, I think – if I were to try?'

'What?'

'I say, if I were to try?'

Sir Tom scowled across the table. 'Look here!' he said, striking it heavily with his hand, 'I don't like this sort of talk. I don't suppose you wish to be offensive; and we'll end it, if you please.'

Hawkesworth shrugged his shoulders. 'Oh, by all means, if you feel that way,' he said. 'Only it looks a little as if you feared for your charming sister. After all, women are women. Even Miss Sophia Maitland is a woman, and no exception to the rule, I presume?'

'Oh, hang you!' the boy cried, in a fury; and again struck his hand on the table. 'Will you leave my sister's name alone? Cannot you understand – what a gentleman feels about it?'

'He cannot!'

The words came from behind Sir Tom, who forthwith sprang a yard from the settle, and stood gaping; while Hawkesworth, his glass going to shivers on the floor, clutched the table as he rose. Both stood staring, both stood amazed, and scarce believed their eyes, when Sophia, stepping from the shelter of the settle, stood before them.

'He cannot!' she repeated, with a gesture, a look, an accent that should have withered the man. 'He cannot! For he does not know what a gentleman feels about anything. He does not know what a gentleman is. Look at him! Look at him!' she continued, her face white with scorn; and she fixed the astonished Irishman with an outstretched finger that could scarce have confounded him more had it been a loaded pistol set to his head. 'A gentleman!' she went on passionately. 'That a gentleman? Why, the air he breathes pollutes us! To be in one room with him disgraces us! That such an one should have tricked us will shame us all our lives!'

Hawkesworth tried to speak, tried to carry off the surprise; but a feeble smile was all he could compass. Even Irish wit, even native impudence were unequal to this emergency. The blow was so sudden, so unexpected, he could not in a moment arrange his thoughts, or discern his position. He saw that for some reason or other she had come to him before the time; but he could not on the instant remember how far he had disclosed his hand before her, or what she had learned from him while she lay hidden.

Naturally Tom was the quicker to recover himself. His first thought on seeing his sister was that she had got wind of his plans, and was here to prevent his marriage. And it was in this sense that he interpreted her opening words. But before she had ceased to speak, the passion which she threw into her denunciation of Hawkesworth, turned his thoughts into a new and fiercer channel. With an oath, 'Never mind him!' he cried, and stepping forward gripped her, almost brutally, by the wrist. 'I'll talk with him afterwards. First, miss, what the devil are you doing here?'

'Ask him,' she answered; and again pointed her finger at Hawkesworth. 'Or no, I will tell you, Tom. That man, the man who calls himself your friend, and called himself my lover, has plotted to ruin us. He has schemed to get us into his net. Tomorrow he would have married you to – to, I know not whom. And when he had seen you married, and knew you had forfeited a fortune to me, then – then I should have been a fit match for him! I! I! And in the evening he would have married me! Oh, shame, shame on us, Tom, that we should have let ourselves be so deluded!'

'He would have married you!' Tom cried, dropping her hand in sheer astonishment.

'The same day!'

'Hawkesworth? This man here? He would have married you?'

'You may well say, he!' she answered, a wave of crimson flooding her cheeks and throat. 'The thought kills me.'

Tom looked from one to the other. 'But I can't understand,' he said. 'I didn't know – that he knew you, even.'

'And I didn't know that he knew you!' she answered bitterly. 'He is a villain, and that was his plan. We were not to know.'

Tom turned to the Irishman; and the latter's deprecatory shrug was vain. 'What have you to say?' Tom cried in a voice almost terrible.

But Hawkesworth, who did not lack courage, was himself again, easy, alert, plausible. 'Much,' he said coolly. 'Much, dear lad. The whole thing is a mistake. I loved your sister' – he bowed gravely in her direction, and stole a glance as he did so, to learn how she took it, and how far he still had a chance with her. 'I loved her, I say, I still love her, though she has shown that she puts as little faith in me, as she can ever have entertained affection for me. But I knew her as Miss Maitland, I did not know that she was your sister. Once I think she mentioned a brother; but no more, no name. For the rest. I had as little reason to expect to find her here as you had. That I swear!'

The last words hit Tom uncomfortably; her presence in this man's room was a fact hard to swallow. The brother turned on the sister. 'Is this true?' he hissed.

Sophia winced. 'It is true,' she faltered.

'Then what brought you here?' Tom cried, with brutal frankness.

The girl shivered; she never forgot the pain of that moment, never forgot the man who had caused her that humiliation. 'Ask him!' she panted. 'Or no, I will tell you, Tom. He swore that he loved me. He made me, poor silly fool that I was, believe him. He said that if I would elope with him tomorrow, he would marry me at Dr Keith's chapel; and fearing they – my sister – would marry me against my will to – to another man, I consented. Then – they were going to send me away in the morning, and it would have been too late. I came away this afternoon to tell him, and – and—'

'There you have the explanation. Sir Thomas,' Hawkesworth interposed, with an air of candid good nature. 'And in all you'll say, I think, that there is nothing of which I need be ashamed. I loved your sister, she was good enough to fancy that she was not indifferent to me. My intentions were honourable, but her friends were opposed to my suit. I had her consent to elope, and if she had not on a sudden discovered, as she apparently has discovered, that her heart is not mine, we should have been married within a few days.'

'Tomorrow, sir, tomorrow!' Sophia cried. And would have confronted him with his letter; but it was in the folds of her dress, and she would not let him see where she kept it.

'Tomorrow. certainly, if it had been your pleasure,' Hawkesworth answered smoothly. 'The sole, the only point it concerns me to show, is, Sir Tom, that I did not know my Miss Maitland to be your sister. I give you my word, Sir Tom, I did not!'

'Liar!' she cried, unable to contain herself.

He shrugged his shoulders, and smiled. 'There is but one Sir Thomas Maitland,' he said, 'but there are many Maitlands. Miss Maitland may hold what opinion she pleases, and express what view of my character commends itself to her, without fear that I shall call her natural guardians to account. But I cannot allow a gentleman to doubt my word. I repeat, Sir Tom, that I did not know that this lady was your sister.'

The boy listened, scowling and thinking. He had no lack of courage, and was as ready to fly at a man's throat as not. But he was young; he was summoned, suddenly and in conditions most perplexing, to protect the family honour; it was no wonder that he hesitated. At this, however, 'Then why the deuce were you so ready to bet,' he blurted out, 'that she would be married at Keith's?'

Before Hawkesworth could frame the answer, 'That is not all!' Sophia cried; and with a rapid movement she snatched from the table the book that had first opened her eyes. 'Here, here,' she cried, tapping it passionately. 'In his own handwriting is the plot! The plot against us both! Tom, look; find it! You will find it under my name. And then he cannot deny it.'

She held out the book to Tom; he went to take it. But Hawkesworth, who knew the importance of the evidence, was too quick for them. With an oath he sprang forward, held Tom back with one hand, and with the other seized the volume, and tried to get possession of it. But Sophia clung to it, screaming; and before he could wrest it from her hold, Tom, maddened by the insult and her cries, was at his breast like a wild cat.

The fury of the assault took the Irishman by surprise. He staggered against the wall, and alarmed by the girl's shrieks, let the book go. By that time. however, Sophia had had enough of the struggle. The sight of the two locked in furious conflict horrified her, her grasp relaxed, she let the book fall; and as Hawkesworth, recovering from his surprise, gripped her brother's throat and by main force bent him backwards – the lad never ceasing to rain blows on the taller man's face and shoulders – she fled to the door, opened it, and screamed for help.

Fortunately it was already on the road. Mr Wollenhope, crying, 'Lord, what is it? What is it?' was half-way up the stairs when she appeared, and close on his heels followed his wife, with a scared face. Sophia beckoned them to hasten, and wringing her hands, flew back. They followed.

They found Hawkesworth dragging the boy about, and striving savagely to force him to the floor. As soon as he saw Wollenhope, he cried with fury, 'Will someone take this mad dog off me? He has tried his best to murder me. If I had not been the stronger, he would have done it!'

Wollenhope, panting with the haste he had made, seized Tom from behind and held him, while Hawkesworth disengaged himself. 'You'll – you'll give me satisfaction for this!' the lad cried, gasping, and almost blubbering with rage. His wig was gone, so was his cravat; the ruffle of his shirt was torn from top to bottom.

The other was busy readjusting his dress, and staunching the blood that flowed from a cut lip. 'Satisfaction, you young booby?' he answered, with savage contempt. 'Send you back to school and whip you! Turn 'em out, Wollenhope! Turn them both out! That devil's cub sprang on me and tried to strangle me. It's lucky for you, sir, I don't send you to Hicks's Hall!'

'Oh, Lord, let's have none of that!' Wollenhope interposed hastily. 'Mine's a respectable house, and there's been noise enough already. A little more and I shall be indicted. March, young sir, if you please. And you too, miss.'

Tom swelled with fresh rage. 'Do you know who I am, fellow?' he cried. 'I'd have you to know—'

'I don't want to know!' Wollenhope rejoined, cutting him short. 'I won't know! It's march – that's all I know. And quick, if you please,' he continued, trying to edge the lad out of the room.

'But, William,' his wife protested, and timidly touched his arm, 'it's possible that they may not be in fault. I'm sure the young lady was very well spoken when she came.'

'None of your advice!' her husband retorted.

'But, William—'

'None of your advice, I say! Do you hear? Do you understand? This gentleman is our lodger. Who the others are, I don't know, nor care. And I don't want to know, that's more.'

'You'll smart for this!' Tom cried, getting in a word at last. He was almost bursting with chagrin and indignation. 'I'd have you know, my fine fellow, I am Sir—'

'I don't want to know,' Wollenhope retorted, stubbornly. 'I don't care who you are; and for smarting, perhaps I may. When you are sober, sir, we'll talk about it. In the meantime, this is my house, and you'll go, unless you want me to fetch the constable. And that mayn't be best for the young lady, who seems a young lady. I don't suppose she'll like to be taken to the Round house, nor run the risk of it. Take my advice, young sir, take my advice, and go quietly while you can.'

Tom, half-choked with rage, was for retorting; but Sophia, who had quite broken down and was weeping hysterically, clutched his arm. 'Oh, come,' she cried piteously, 'please come!' And she tried to draw him towards the door.

But the lad resisted. 'You'll answer to me for this,' he said, scowling at Hawkesworth, who remained in an attitude, eyeing the two with a smile of disdain. 'You know where to find me, and I shall be at your service until tomorrow at noon.'

'I'll find you when you are grown up,' the Irishman answered, with a mocking laugh. 'Back to your books, boy, and be whipped for playing truant!'

The taunt stung Tom to fresh fury. With a scream of rage he sprang forward, and, shaking off Wollenhope's grasp, tried to close with his enemy. But Sophia hung on him bravely, imploring him to be calm; and Wollenhope seized him again and held him back, while Mrs Wollenhope supplied, for assistance, a chorus of shrieks. Between the three he was partly led and partly dragged to the door, and got outside. From the landing he hurled a last threat at the smiling Hawkesworth, now left master of the field; and then, with a little rough persuasion, he was induced to descend.

In the passage he had a fresh fit of stubbornness, and wished to state his wrongs and who he was. But Sophia's heart was pitifuly set on escaping from the house – to her a house of bitter shame and humiliation – and the landlord's desire was to see the last of them; and in a moment the two were outside. Wollenhope lost not a moment, but slammed the door on them; they heard the chain put up, and, an instant later, the man's retreating footsteps as he went back to his lodger.

CHAPTER IX

In Clarges Row

IF TOM had been alone when he was thus ejected, it is probable that his first impulse would have been either to press his forehead against the wall and weep with rage, or to break the offender's windows – eighteen being an age at which the emotions are masters of the man. But the noise of the fracas within, though dulled by the walls, had reached the street. A window here and a window there stood open, and curious eyes, peering through the darkness, were on the two who had been put out. Tom was too angry to heed these on his own account, or care who was witness of his violence; but for Sophia's sake, whose state as she clung to his arm began to appeal to his manhood, he was willing to be gone without more.

After shaking his fist at the door, therefore, and uttering a furious word or two, he pressed the weeping girl's hand to his side. 'All right,' he said, 'we'll go. It'll not be long before I'm back again, and they'll be sorry! A houseful of cheats and bullies! There, there, child, I'll come. Don't cry,' he continued, patting her hand with an air that, after the reverse he had suffered, was not without its grandeur. 'I'll take care of you, never fear. I've rooms a little way round the corner, taken today, and you shall have my bed. It's too late to go to Arlington Street tonight.'

Sophia, sobbing and frightened, hung down her head, and did not answer; and Tom, forgetting in his wrath against Hawkesworth the cause he had to be angry with her, said nothing to increase her misery or aggravate her sense of the folly she had committed. His lodgings were in Clarges Row, a little north of Shepherd's Market, and almost within a stone's throw of Mayfair Chapel. Four minutes' walking brought the two to the house, where Tom rapped in a peculiar manner at the window-shutter; when this had been twice repeated, the door was opened grudgingly by a pale-faced, elderly man, bearing a lighted candle-end in his fingers.

He muttered his surprise on seeing Tom, but made way for him, grumbling something about the late hour. When he saw the girl about to follow, however, he started, and seemed to be going to refuse her entrance. But Tom was of those who carry off by sheer force of arrogance a difficult situation. 'My sister, Miss Maitland, is with me,' he said. 'She'll have my room to-night. Don't stare, fellow, but hold the light for the lady to go up.'

The man's reluctance was evident; but he let them enter, and barred the door after them. Then snuffing his candle with his fingers, he held it up and surveyed them. 'By gole,' he said, chuckling, 'you don't look much like bride and bridegroom!'

Tom stormed at him, but he only continued to grin. 'You've been fighting!' he said.

'Well what's that to you, you rogue!' the lad answered sharply. 'Light the lady up, do you hear?'

'To be sure! To be sure! But you'll be wanting a light in each room,' he continued with a cunning look, as he halted at the head of a narrow boarded staircase, up which he had preceded them. 'That's over and above, you'll remember. Candles here and candles there, a man's soon ruined!'

Tom bade him keep a civil tongue, and himself led the way into a quaint little three-cornered parlour, boarded like the staircase; beyond it was a bedroom of the same shape and size. The rooms had a small window apiece looking on the Row, and wore an air of snugness that would have appealed to Sophia had her eyes been opened to anything but her troubles. Against the longer wall of the little parlour stood a couple of tall clocks; a third eked out the scanty furniture of the bedroom, and others, ticking with stealthy industry in the lower part of the house, whispered that it was a clockmaker's shop.

Sophia cared not. She felt no curiosity. She put no questions, but accepted in silence the dispositions her brother made for her comfort. Bruised and broken, fatigued in body, with a sorely aching heart she took the room he gave her, sleep offering all she could now hope for or look for, sleep bounding all her ambitions. In sleep – and at that moment the girl would fain have lain down not to rise again – she hoped to find a refuge from trouble, a shelter from thought, a haven where shame could not enter. To one in suspense, in doubt, in expectation, bed is a rack, a place of torture; but when the blow has fallen, the lot been drawn, the dulled sensibilities sink to rest in it as naturally as a bird in the nest – and as quickly find respose.

She slept as one stunned, but weak is the anodyne of a single night. She awoke in the morning, cured indeed of love by a radical operation, but still bleeding; still in fancy under the cruel knife, still writhing in remembered torture. To look forward, to avert her eyes from the past, was her sole hope; and speedily her mind grew clear; the future began to take shape. She would make use of Tom's good offices, and through him she would negotiate terms with her sister. She would not, could not, go back to Arlington Street! But any penance short of that she would undergo. If it pleased them she would go to Chalkhill; or in any other way that seemed good to them, she would expiate the foolish, and worse than foolish, escapade of which she had been guilty. Life henceforth could be but a grey and joyless thing; provided she escaped the sneers and gibes of Arlington Street, she cared little where it was spent.

She was anxious to broach the subject at breakfast; but, through a natural reluctance to open it, she postponed the discussion as long as she dared. It was not like Tom to be over careful of her feelings; but he, too, appeared to be equally unwilling to revert to past unpleasantness. He fidgeted and seemed preoccupied; he rose frequently and sat down again; more than once he went to the window and looked out. At last he rose impulsively and disappeared in the bedroom.

By-and-by he returned. He was still in his morning cap and loose wrapper, but he carried a shirt over each arm. 'Which ruffles do you like the better, Sophy?' he asked; and he displayed one after the other before her eyes. 'Of course I'd like to look my best today,' he added, shamefacedly.

She stared at him, in perplexity at first, not understanding him; then in horror, as she discerned on a sudden what he meant. 'Today?' she faltered. 'Why today, Tom, more than on other days?'

His face fell. 'Is't odd,' he said, 'to want to look one's best to be married? At any rate, I never thought so. Until yesterday,' he added, with a glance at her dress.

She was sitting on the narrow window-seat; she stood up, her back to the window. 'To be married?' she exclaimed. 'Oh,

Tom! It is impossible – impossible you intend to go on with it, after all you have heard!'

His face grew darker and more sullen. 'At any rate I am not going to marry Hawkesworth!' he sneered. And then as she winced under the cruel stroke he repented it. 'I only mean,' he said hurriedly, 'that – that I don't see what he and his villainy have to do with my marriage.'

'But, oh, Tom, it is all one!' Sophia cried, clasping her hands nervously. 'He was with – with her, when you met her. I heard you say so last night. I heard you say that if it had not been for him you would never have seen her, or known her.'

'Well!' Tom answered. 'And what of that? If her chaise had not broken down, I should never have seen her or known of her. That is true, too. But what has that to do with it, I'd like to know?'

'He planned it!'

'He could not plan my falling in love,' Tom answered, stroking his chin fatuously.

'But if you had seen the book,' Sophia retorted, 'the book he snatched from me, you would have seen it written there! His plan was to procure you to be married first. You know you forfeit ten thousand pounds to me, Tom, and ten to Anne, if you marry without your guardians' consent?'

'Hang them and the ten thousand!' Tom cried grandly. 'Lord, miss, I've plenty left! You are welcome to it, and so is sister. As for their consent, they'd not give it till I was Methuselah!'

'But surely you're not that yet!' she pleaded. 'Nor near! You are only eighteen.'

'Well, and what are you?' he retorted. 'And you were for being married yesterday!'

'I was!' she cried, wringing her hands. 'And to what a fate! I am unhappy today, unhappy, indeed; but I shall be thankful all my life that I escaped that! Oh, Tom, for my sake take care! Don't do it! Don't do it! Wait, at least, until—'

'Till I am Methuselah?' he cried. 'It's likely!'

'No, but until you have taken advice!' she answered. 'Till you know more about her. Tom, don't be angry,' Sophia pleaded, as he turned away with an impatient gesture. 'Or if you will not be guided, tell me, at least, who she is. I am your sister, surely I have the right to know who is to be your wife?'

'I am sure I don't mind your knowing!'

'I have only your interests at heart,' she cried.

'I have no reason to be ashamed of her, I am sure,' he answered, colouring. 'Though I don't know that she is altogether one of your sort. She is the most beautiful woman in the world that I know! And so you will say when you see her!' he added, his eyes sparkling. 'She has as much wit in her little finger as I have in my head. And you'll find that out, too. She don't look at most people, but she took to me at once. It seems wonderful to me now,' he continued rapturously. 'Wonderful! But you should see her! You must see her! You can't fancy what she is until you see her!'

It was on the tip of Sophia's tongue to ask, 'But is she good?' Like a wise girl, however, she refrained; or rather she put the question in another form. 'Her name,' she said timidly; 'is it by any chance – Oriana?'

Tom was pacing the room, his back to her, his thoughts occupied with his mistress's charms. He whirled about so rapidly that the tassels of his morning wrapper – at that period the only wear of a gentleman until he dressed for the day – flew out level with the horizon. 'How did you know?' he cried, his face flushed, his eyes reading her suspiciously. 'Who told you?'

'Because I read that name in the book,' Sophia answered, her worst fears confirmed. 'Because—'

'Did you see Oriana only, or her full name?'

'What is her full name?'

'You don't know? Then you cannot have seen it in the book!' Tom retorted triumphantly. 'But I am not ashamed of it. Her name is Clark.'

'Clark? Oriana Clark?' Sophia repeated. And she wondered where she had heard the name. Why did it seem familiar to her?

'What does her name matter?' Tom answered irritably. 'It will be Lady Maitland by night.'

'She's a widow?' Sophia asked. She did not know how she knew.

Tom scowled. 'Well, and what if she is?' he cried.

'What was her huband, Tom? I suppose she had a husband?'

'Look here, take care what you are saying!' Tom returned,

with an ugly look. 'Don't be too free with your tongue, miss. Her husband, if you must know, was a – a Captain Clark of – of Sabine's foot, I think it was. He was a man of the first fashion, so that's all you know about it! But he treated her badly, spent all her money, you know. and – and when he died,' Tom added vaguely. 'she had to look out for herself, you understand.'

'But she must be years and years older than you!' Sophia answered, opening her eyes. 'And a widow! Oh, Tom, think of it! Think of it again! And be guided! Wait at least until you know more about it,' she pleaded earnestly, 'and have learned what life she has led, and—'

But Tom would hear no more. 'Wait?' he cried rudely. 'You're a nice person to give that advice! You were waiting, of course, and doing what you were told. And what life she has led? I tell you what it is, miss; I kept my mouth shut last night, but I might have said a good deal! Who got us into the trouble? What were you doing in his room? The less you say. and the quieter you keep, the better for all, I think! A man's one thing but a girl's another, and she should do what she's bid, and take care of herself, and not run the risk of shaming her family!'

'Oh, Tom!'

'Oh, it's every word true!' the lad answered cruelly. 'And less than you deserve, ma'am! Wait till sister sees you, and you'll hear more. Now, cry, cry, that's like a girl!' he continued contemptuously. 'All the same a little plain truth will do you good, miss, and teach you not to meddle. But I suppose women will scratch women as long as the world lasts!'

'Oh, Tom, it is not that!' Sophia cried between her sobs. 'I've behaved badly, if you please. As badly as you please! But take me for a warning. I thought – I thought him all you think her!'

'Oh, d—n!' Tom cried, and flung away in a rage, went into the bedroom, and slammed the door. Sophia heard him turn the key, and a minute later, when she had a little recovered herself, she heard him moving to and fro in the room. He was dressing. He had not, then, changed his mind.

She waited awhile, trying to believe that her words might still produce some effect. But he made no sign, he did not emerge. Presently she caught the rustle of his garments as he changed his clothes; and in a fever of anxiety she began to pace the room. Nature has provided no cure for trouble more wholesome or more powerful than a generous interest in another's fate. Gone was the apathy, gone were the dullness of soul and the greyness of outlook with which Sophia had risen from her bed. Convinced of the villainy of the man who had nearly snared her, she foresaw nothing but ruin in an alliance between her brother and a person who was connected ever so remotely with *him*. Nor did the case rest on this only; or on Tom's youth; or on the secrecy of the marriage. Oriana was the name she had spelt in the book, the name of one of the women suggested in Hawkesworth's sordid calculations. No wonder Sophia shrank from thinking what manner of woman she was, or what her qualifications for a part in the play. It was enough that she knew Hawkesworth, and was known by him.

The cruel lesson which she had learned in her own person, the glimpse she had had of the abyss into which her levity had all but cast her, even the gratitude in which she held the brother who had protected her, rendered her feelings trebly poignant now; her view of the case trebly serious. To see the one relation she loved falling into the pit which she had escaped. and to be unable to save him; to know him committed to this fatal step, and to foresee that his whole life would be blasted by it, these prospects awoke no less pity in her breast, because her eyes were open today to her madness of yesterday. Something, something must be done for him; something, but what?

Often through the gloom of reflections, alien from them, shoot strange flashes of memory. 'Oriana? Oriana Clark?' Sophia muttered, and she stood still, remembered. Oriana Clark! Surely that was the name of the woman in whose stead she had been arrested, the woman whose name the bailiff had read from the writ in Lane's shop. Sophia had only heard the name once, and the press of after events and crowding emotions had driven it for the time into a side cell of the brain, whence it now as suddenly emerged. Her eyes sparkled with hope. Here, at last, was a fact, here was something on which she could go. She stepped to Tom's door, and rapped sharply on it.

'Well?' he called sourly. 'What is it?'

'Please, come out!' she cried eagerly. 'I have something to tell you. I have indeed!'

'Can't come now,' he answered. 'I'm in a hurry.'

It seemed he was; or he wished to avoid further discussion, for when he appeared a few minutes later – long minutes to Sophia, waiting and listening in the outer room – he snatched up his hat and malacca and made for the door. 'I can't stop now,' he cried, and he waved her off as he raised the latch. 'I shall be back in an hour – in an hour, and if you like to behave yourself, you – you may be at it. Though you're not very fine, I'm bound to say!' he concluded with a grudging glance. Doubtless he was comparing her draggled sacque and unpowdered hair with the anticipated splendours of his bride. He was so fine himself, he seemed to fill the little room with light.

'Oh, but, Tom, one minute!' she cried, following him and seizing his arm. 'Have a little patience, I only want to tell you one thing.'

'Well, be quick about it,' he answered ungraciously, his hand still on the latch. 'And whatever you do, miss, keep your tongue off her, or it will be the worse for you. I'll not have my wife miscalled,' he continued, looking grand, and a trifle sulky, 'as you'll have to learn, my lady.'

'But she is not your wife yet,' Sophia protested earnestly. 'And, Tom, she only wants you to pay her debts. She only wants a husband to pay her debts. She was arrested yesterday.'

'Arrested!' he exclaimed.

'Yes,' Sophia answered; and then, beginning to flounder, 'at least, I mean,' she stammered, 'I was arrested – in her place. This is to say, on a writ against her.'

'You were arrested on a writ against her!' Tom cried again. 'On a writ against Oriana? You must be mad! Mad, girl! Why, you've never seen her in your life. You did not know her name!' He had not heard, it will be remembered, a word of her adventures on the way to Davies Street, and the statement she had just made seemed to him the wanton falsehood of a foolish girl bent on mischief. 'Oh, this is too bad!' he continued, shaking her off in a rage. 'How dare you, you little vixen? You cowardly little liar!' he added, pale with anger. And he raised his hand as if he would strike her.

She recoiled. 'Don't hurt me, Tom,' she cried.

'I'll not! but – but you deserve it, you little snake!' he retorted. 'You are bad! You are bad right through!' he continued from a height of righteous indignation. 'What you did yesterday was nothing in comparison of this! You let me hear another word against her, make up another of your lies, and you are no sister of mine! That's all! So now you know, and if you are wise you will not try it again!'

As he uttered the last word Tom jerked up the latch, and strode out; but only to come into violent collision, at the head of the stairs, with his landlord, who appeared to be getting up from his knees. 'Hang you, Grocott, what the deuce are you doing here?' the lad cried, backing from him in a rage.

'Cleaning the stairs, your honour,' the man pleaded.

'You rascal. I believe you were listening!' Tom retorted. 'Is the room below stairs ready? We go at noon, mark me, and shall be back to dine at one.'

'To be sure, sir, all will be ready. Does the lady come here first?'

'Yes. Have the cold meats come from the White Horse?'

'Yes, sir!'

'And the Burgundy from Pontack's?'

'Yes, your honour.'

Tom nodded his satisfaction, and, his temper a little improved, stalked down the stairs. Sophia, who had heard every word, ran to the window and saw him cross Clarges Row in the direction of Shepherd's Market. Probably he was gone to assure himself that the clergyman was at home, and ready to perform the ceremony.

The girl watched him out of sight; then she dried her tears. 'I mustn't cry!' she murmured. 'I must do something! I must do something!'

But there was only one thing she could do, and that was a thing that would cost her dear. Only by returning to Arlington Street, at once, that moment, and giving information, could she prevent the marriage. Mr Northey was Tom's guardian; he had the power, and though he had shirked his duty while the thing was *in nubibus,* he would not dare to stand by when time and place, the house and the hour were pointed out to him. In less than ten minutes she could be with him; in half as many the facts could be made known. Long before the hour elapsed Mr

Northey might be in Clarges Row, or, if he preferred it, at Dr Keith's chapel, ready to forbid the marriage.

The thing was possible, nay it was easy; and it would withhold Tom from a step which he must repent all his life. But it entailed the one penance from which she was anxious to be saved, the one penalty from which her wounded pride shrank, as the bleeding stump shrinks from the cautery. To execute it she must return to Arlington Street; she must return into her sister's power, to the domination of Mrs Martha, and the daily endurance, not only of many an ignoble slight, but of coarse jests and gibes and worse insinuations. An hour earlier she had conceived the hope of escaping this, either through Tom's mediation, or by a voluntary retreat to Chalkhill. Now she had to choose this or his ruin.

She did not hesitate. Even in her folly of the previous day, even in her reckless self-abandonment to a silly passion, Sophia had not lacked the qualities that make for sacrifice – courage, generosity, staunchness. Here was room for their display in a better cause, and without a moment's delay, undeterred by the reflection that far from earning Tom's gratitude, she would alienate her only friend, she hurried into the bedroom and donned Lady Betty's laced jacket and Tuscan. With a moan on her own account, a pitiful smile on his, she put them on; and then paused, remembering with horror that she must pass through the streets in that guise. It had done well enough at night, but in the day the misfit was frightful. Not even for Tom could she walk through Berkeley Square and Portugal Street, the figure it made her. She must have a chair.

She opened the door and was overjoyed to find that the landlord was still on the stairs. 'Will you please to get me a chair,' she said eagerly. 'At once, without the loss of a minute.'

The man looked at her stupidly, his heavy lower lip dropped and flaccid; his fat, whitish face evinced a sort of consternation. 'A chair?' he repeated slowly. 'Certainly. But if your ladyship is going any distance, would not a coach be better?'

'No, I am only going as far as Arlington Street,' Sophia answered, off her guard for the moment. 'Still, a coach will do if you cannot get a chair. I have not a moment to lose.'

'To be sure, ma'am, to be sure.' he answered, staring at her heavily. 'A chair you'll have then?'

'Yes, and at once! At once, you understand.'

'If you are in a hurry, maybe there is one below,' he said, making as if he would enter the room and look from the windows. 'Sometimes there is.'

'If there were,' she retorted, irritated by his slowness, 'I should not have asked you to get one. I suppose you know what a chair is?' she continued. For the man stood looking at her so dully and strangely that she began to think he was a natural.

'Oh, yes,' he answered, his eyes twinkling with sudden intelligence, as if at the notion. 'I know a chair, and I'd have had one for you by now. But, by gole, I've no one to leave with the child, in case it awakes.'

'The child?' Sophia cried, quite startled. The presence of a child in a house is no secret as a rule.

''Tis here,' he said, indicating a door that stood ajar at his elbow. 'On the bed in the inner room, ma'am. I'm doing the stairs to be near it.'

'Is it a baby?' Sophia cried.

'To be sure. What else?'

'I'll stay with it, then,' she said. 'May I look at it? And will you get the chair for me, while I watch it?'

'To be sure, ma'am! 'Tis here,' he continued, as he pushed the door open, and led the way through a tiny room; the outer of two that, looking to the back, corresponded with Tom's apartments at the front. He pushed open the door of the inner room, the floor of which was a step higher. 'If you'll see to it while I am away, ma'am, and not be out of hearing?'

'I will,' Sophia said softly. 'Is it yours?'

'No, my daughter's.'

Sophia tip-toed across the floor to the bed side. The room was poorly lighted by a window, which was partially blocked by a water-cistern; the bed stood in the dark corner beside the window; Sophia, turning up her nose at the close air of the room, hesitated for an instant to touch the dirty, tumbled bedclothes. She could not see the child. 'Where is it?' she asked, stooping to look more closely.

The answer was the dull jar of the door as it closed behind her; a sound that was followed by the click of a bolt driven home in the socket. She turned swiftly, her heart standing still, her brain already apprised of treachery. The man was gone.

Sophia made but one bound to the threshold, lifted the latch, and threw her weight against the door. It was fastened.

'Open!' she cried, enraged at the trick which had been played her. 'Do you hear me? Open the door this minute!' She repeated, striking it furiously with her hands. 'What do you mean? How dare you shut me in?'

This time the only response was the low chuckling laugh of the clock-maker as he turned away. She heard the stealthy fall of his footsteps as he went through the outer room; then the grating of the key, as he locked the farther door behind him. Then – silence.

'Tom!' Sophia shrieked, kicking the door, and pounding it with her little fists. 'Tom, help! help, Tom!' And then, as she realized how she had been trapped, 'Oh, poor Tom!' she sobbed. 'Poor Tom! I can do nothing now!'

While Grocott, listening on the stairs, chuckled grimly. 'You thought you were going to stop my girl's marriage, did you?' he muttered, shaking his fist in the direction of the sounds. 'You thought you'd stop her being my lady, did you? Stop her now if you can, my little madam. I have you like a mouse in a trap; and when you are cooler, my Lady Maitland shall let you out. My lady, ha! ha! What a sound it has. My Lady Maitland!'

Then reflecting that Hawkesworth, whom he hated, and had cause to hate, had placed this triumph in his grasp – and would now, as things had turned out, get nothing by it – he shook with savage laughter. 'Lady Maitland!' he chuckled. 'Ho! ho! And he gets – the shells! The shells, ho! ho!'

CHAPTER X

Sir Hervey Takes the Field

In his rooms at the corner house between Portugal Street and Bolton Street, so placed that by glancing a trifle on one side of the oval mirror before him he could see the Queen's Walk and the sloping pastures of the Green Park, Sir Hervey Coke was being shaved. A pile of loose gold which lay on the dressing-table indicated that the evening at White's had not been unpropitious. An empty chocolate cup and half-eaten roll stood beside the money, and, with Sir Henry's turban-cap and embroidered gown, indicated that the baronet, who in the country broke his fast on beef and small beer, and began the day booted, followed, in town, town fashions. Today, however, early as it was – barely ten – his wig hung freshly curled on the stand, and a snuff-coloured coat and long-flapped waistcoat, plainly laced, were airing at the fire; signs that he intended to be abroad betimes, and on business.

Perhaps the business had to do with an open letter in his lap, at which the man who was shaving him cocked his eye inquisitively between strokes. Or perhaps not, for Sir Hervey did not seem to heed this curiosity; but the valet had before had reason – and was presently to have fresh reason – to know that his taciturn master saw more than he had the air of seeing.

Suddenly Sir Hervey raised his hand. Watkyns, the valet, stood back. 'Bring it me!' Coke said.

The man had heard without hearing, as he now understood without explanation. He went softly to the door, received a note, and brought it to his master.

'An answer?'

'No, sir.'

'Then finish.'

The valet did so. When he had removed the napkin, Sir Hervey broke the seal, and, after reading three or four lines of the letter, raised his eyes to the mirror. He met the servant's prying gaze, and abruptly crumpled the paper in his hand. Then, 'Watkyns,' he said, in his quietest tone.

'Sir?'

'About the two guineas you – stole this morning. For this time you may keep them; but in the future kindly remember two things.'

The razor the man was cleaning fell to the floor. His face was a sickly white; his knees shook under him. He tried to frame words, to deny, to say something, but in vain. He was speechless.

'Firstly,' Coke continued blandly, 'that I count the money I bring home – at irregular intervals. Secondly, that two guineas is a larger sum than forty shillings. Another time, Watkyns, I would take less than forty shillings. You will understand why. That is all.'

The man, still pale and trembling, found his tongue. 'Oh, sir!' he cried, 'I swear, if you'll – if you'll forgive me—'

Coke stopped him. 'That is all,' he said, 'that is all. The matter is at an end. Pick that up, go downstairs, and return in five minutes.'

When the man was gone, Sir Hervey smoothed the paper, and, with a face that grew darker and darker as he proceeded, read the contents of the letter from beginning to end. They were these:

'DEAR SIR,

'The honour you intended my family by an alliance with a person so nearly related to us as Miss Maitland renders it incumbent on me to inform you with the least possible delay of the unfortunate event which has happened in our household, an event which, I need not say, I regret on no account more than because it must deprive us of the advantage we rightly looked to derive from that connection. At a late hour last evening the misguided (and I fear I must call her the unfortunate) girl, whom you distinguished by so particularly a mark of your esteem, left the shelter of her home, it is now certain, to seek the protection of a lover.

'While the least doubt on this point remained, I believed myself justified in keeping the matter even from you, but I have this morning learned from a sure source – Lane, the mercer, in Piccadilly – that she was set down about nine o'clock last night at a house in Davies Street, kept by a man of the name of Wollenhope, and the residence – alas, that I should have to say it! – of the infamous Irishman whose attentions to her at one time attracted your notice.

'You will readily understand that from the moment we were certified of this we ceased to regard her as a part of our family; a choice so ill-regulated can proceed only from a mind naturally inclined to vice. Resentment on your account no less than a proper care of our household, dictates this course, nor will any repentance on her part, nor any of those misfortunes to which as I apprehend her misconduct will surely expose her, prevail on us to depart from it.

'Forgive me, dear sir, if, under the crushing weight of this deplorable matter, I confine myself to the bare fact and its consequence, adding only the expression of our profound regret and consideration.

'I have the honour to remain,

'Dear sir,

'Your most obedient, humble servant,

'J. NORTHEY.'

'A d—d cold-blooded fish!' Sir Hervey muttered when he had finished, and he cast the letter on the table with a gesture of disgust. Then he sat motionless for several minutes, gazing at nothing, with a strange expression of pain in his eyes. Perhaps he was thinking of the old mansion in Sussex, standing silent and lonely in its widespread park, awaiting – still awaiting, a mistress. Perhaps of plans late made, soon wrecked, yet no less cherished. Perhaps of a pale young face wide-browed and wilful, with eyes more swift to blame than praise; eyes which he had seen seeking – seeking pathetically they knew not what. Or perhaps he was thinking of the notorious Lady Vane – of what she had been once, of what Sophia might be some day. For he swore softly, and the look of pain deepened in his eyes. And then Watkyns returned.

Sir Hervey stood up. 'You'll go to Wollenhope's,' he said without preface. 'Wollenhope's, in Davies Street, and learn – you'll know how – whether the young lady who alighted there last night from a chair or coach is still there. And whether a person of the name of Hawkesworth is there. And whether he is at home. You will not tell my name. You understand?'

'Yes, sir.'

'You've half an hour.'

The man slid out of the room, his face wearing a look of relief, almost of elation. It was true then. He was forgiven!

After that Coke walked up and down, his watch in his hand, until the valet returned. In the interval he spoke once only. 'She is but a child!' he muttered. 'she's but a child!' and he followed it with a second oath. When his man returned, 'Well?' he said, without looking round.

'The young lady is not there, sir,' Watkyns replied. 'She arrived at eight last evening in a chair, and left a little after nine with a young gentleman.'

'The person Hawkesworth?'

'No, sir.'

'No?' Sir Hervey turned as he spoke, and looked at him.

'No, sir. Who it was the landlord of the house did not know or would not tell me. He was not in the best of tempers, and I could get no more from him. He told me that the young gentleman came in with his lodger about a quarter to nine.'

'With Hawkesworth?'

'Yes, sir, and found the young lady waiting for them. That the two gentlemen quarrelled almost immediately, and that the young lady went off with the young gentleman. Who was very young, sir, not much more than a boy.'

'What address?'

'I could not learn, sir.'

'Watkyns!'

'Yes, sir.'

'You may take two guineas.'

The man hesitated, his face scarlet. 'If you please, sir,' he muttered, 'I'll consider I have them.'

'Very good. I understand you. Now dress me.'

It took about five minutes, as London then lay, to walk from Bolton Street to Davies Street, by way of Bolton Row and Berkeley Square. At that hour, it was too early for fine gentlemen of Sir Hervey's stamp to be abroad, and fine ladies were still abed, so that he fell in with no acquaintances. He had ascertained from Watkyns in what part of the street Wollenhope's house was situate, and, well within the prescribed space of time, he found himself knocking at the door. It was opened pretty promptly by Mrs Wollenhope.

'Does Mr Hawksworth lodge here?' Sir Hervey asked, without preamble.

'Yes, sir, he does,' the good woman answered, curtseying low at the sight of his feathered hat and laced waistcoat; and instinctively she looked up and down the street in search of his chair or coach. 'But he is out at present,' she continued, her eyes returning to him. 'He left the house about half an hour ago, your honour.'

'Can you tell me where he may be found?'

'No, sir, I have no notion,' Mrs Wollenhope answered, wiping her hands on her apron.

'Still,' Sir Hervey rejoined, 'you can, perhaps, tell me the name of the young gentleman who was here last evening and took a lady away.'

Mrs Wollenhope raised her hands. 'There!' she exclaimed. 'I said we should hear of it again! Not that we are to blame, no, sir, no! Except in the way of saving bloodshed! And as for the name, I don't know it. But the address now,' dropping her voice and looking nervously behind her, 'the young gentleman did give an address, and—' with a sudden change of manner. 'Are these with you, sir?'

Coke, following the direction of her gaze, turned about, and found two rough-looking men standing at his elbow. 'No,' he said, 'they are not. What do you want, my men?'

'Lord, your honour, no hurry, we can wait till you've done,' the foremost answered, tugging obsequiously at the uncocked flap of his hat; while his companion sucked his stick and stared. 'Or after all, what's the odds? Time's money, and there's many go in front of us would rather see our backs! Is the lady that came last night in the house, mistress?'

Sir Hervey stared, while Mrs Wollenhope eyed the speaker with great disfavour. 'No,' she said, 'if that's what you want, she is not!'

The man slowly expectorated on the ground. 'Oh,' he said, 'that being the case, when did she leave? No harm in telling that, mistress!'

'She left within the hour,' Mrs Wollenhope snapped. 'And that's all I'll tell you about her, so there! And take yourself off, please!'

'If the matter of half a crown, now—?'

Mrs Wollenhope shook her head vigorously. 'No!' she cried. 'No! I don't sell my lodgers. I know your trade, my man, and you'll get nothing from me.'

The bailiff grinned and nodded. 'All right,' he said. 'No need to grow warm! Easy does it. She gave us the slip yesterday, but we're bound to nab her by-and-by. We knew she was coming here, and if we'd waited here yesterday instead of at the coach office, we'd have took her. Come, Trigg, we'll to the Blue Posts;

if she's had a coach or a chair we'll hear of it there!' And with a 'No offence, your honour!' and a clumsy salute, the two catchpolls lounged away, the one a pace behind the other, his knobby stick still in his mouth, and his sharp eyes everywhere.

Coke watched them go, and a more talkative man would have expressed his astonishment. He fancied that he knew all that was to be known of Sophia's mode of life. She might have spent a little more than her allowance at Margam's or Lane's, might have been tempted by lace at Doiley's, or ribbons at the New Exchange. But a writ and bailiffs? The thing was absurd, and for a good reason. Mr Northey was rich, yet not so rich as he was penurious; the tradesman did not exist who would not trust, to the extent of his purse, any member of that family. Coke was certain of this; and that there was something here which he did not understand. But all he said was 'They are bailiffs, are they?'

'For sure, sir,' Mrs Wollenhope answered. 'I've a neighbour knows one by sight. All day yesterday they were hanging about the door, probing if the young lady was come. 'Twas on that account she surprised me, for I'd been led to look for a fine spendthrift madam. and when she came – Lord ha' mercy, my husband's coming down! If you want the address,' she continued in a lower tone, as Wollenhope appeared at the foot of the stairs, ''twas in Clarges Row, at Grocott's.'

'Thank you,' Coke said.

'Grocott's,' she repeated in a whisper. Then in a louder tone, 'No, sir, I can't say when he will be at home.'

'Thank you,' Sir Hervey said; and having got what he wanted he did not stay to waste time with the man, but made the best of his way to Charles Street, into which the north end of Clarges Row, now Clarges Street, opened at that date. Deeply engaged with the paramount question in his mind, the identity of the young man in whose company Sophia had left Hawkesworth's lodgings, he forgot the bailiffs; and it was with some annoyance that, on reaching the Row, he espied one of them lurking in a doorway in Charles Street. It was so plain that they were watching him that Sir Hervey lost patience, turned, and made towards the man to question him. But the fellow also turned on his heel, and retreating with an eye over his shoulder, disappeared in the square. To follow was to be led from the scent; Coke wheeled again, therefore, and meeting a pot-boy who knew the street, he was directed to Grocott's. The house the lad pointed out was one of the oldest in the Row; a small house of brick, the last on the east side going north. Sir Hervey scanned the five windows that faced the street, but they told him nothing. He knocked – and waited. And presently, getting no answer, he knocked again. And again – the pot-boy looking on from a little distance.

After that Coke stood back, saw that the windows were still without sign of life, and would have gone away – thinking to return in an hour or two – but a woman came to the door of the next house, and told him, 'the old man is at home, your honour; it is not ten minutes since he was at the door.' On which he knocked again more loudly and insistently. Suspicions were taking shape in his mind. The house seemed too quiet to be innocent.

He had his hand raised to repeat the summons once more, when he heard a dragging, pottering step moving along the passage towards him. A chain was put up, a key turned, the door was opened a little, a very little way. A pale, fat face, with small cunning eyes, peered out at him. Unless he was mistaken, it was the face of a frightened man.

'I want to see Miss Maitland,' Sir Hervey said.

'To be sure, sir,' the man answered, while his small eyes scanned the visitor sharply. 'Is it about a clock?'

'No,' Coke answered. 'Are you deaf, man? I wish to see the young lady who is here; who came last night.'

'You're very welcome, I am sure, but there is no young lady here, your honour.'

Sir Hervey did not believe it. The man's sly face, masking fear under a smirk, inspired no confidence; this talking over a chain, at that hour, in the daylight, of itself imported something strange. Apparently Grocott – for he it was – read the last thought in his visitor's eyes, for he dropped the chain and opened the door. 'Was it about a clock,' he asked, the hand that held the door trembling visibly, 'that the lady came?'

'No,' Sir Hervey answered curtly; he was not deceived by this apparent obtuseness. 'I wish, I tell you, to see the young lady who came here with a gentleman last night. She came here from Davies Street.'

'There is a lady here,' the clock-maker answered, slowly. 'But I don't know that she will see anyone.'

'She will see me,' Coke replied with decision. 'You don't want me to summon her friends, and cause a scandal, I suppose?'

'Well, sir, for her friends,' Grocott answered, smiling unpleasantly, 'I know nothing about them, begging your honour's pardon. And, it is all one to me whom she sees. If you'll give me your name, sir, I'll take it to her.'

'Sir Hervey Coke.'

'Dear, dear, I big your honour's pardon, I am sure,' Grocott exclaimed, bowing and wriggling obsequiously. 'It's not to be thought that she'll not see a gentleman of your honour's condition. But I'll take her pleasure if you'll be so good as to wait a minute.'

He left Coke standing on the threshold, and retreated up the passage to the door of a room on the left. Here he went in, closing the door after him. Sir Hervey waited until he was out of sight, then in three strides he reached the same door, lifted the latch, and entered.

''Twill take him finely, Sal!'

The words were in the air – they were all he caught, then silence; and he stood staring. Abrupt as had been his entrance, he was the most completely surprised of the three. For the third in the room, the lady to whom Grocott's words were addressed, was not Sophia, but a stranger; a tall, handsome woman, with big black eyes, fashionably dressed and fashionably painted. The surprise drew from her a hasty exclamation; she rose, her eyes sparkling with anger. Then, as Sir Hervey, recovering from his astonishment, bowed politely, she sat down again with an assumption of fineness and languor. And, taking a fan, she began to fan herself.

'A thousand pardons, madam,' Coke said. 'I owe you every apology. I came in under a misapprehension. I expected to find a friend here.'

'That's very evident, I think, sir!' madam replied, tossing her head. 'And one you were in a hurry to see, I should fancy.'

'Yes,' Sir Hervey answered. He noted that the table, laid with more elegance than was to be expected from Grocott's appearance, displayed a couple of chickens, pigeons, and a galantine, besides a pretty supply of bottles and flasks. 'I trust you will pardon my mistake. I was informed that a young lady came here last evening with a gentleman.'

Madam flamed up. 'And what, sir, is it to you if I did!' she cried. And she rose sharply.

'Your pardon! I did not mean—'

'I say, sir, what is it to you if I did?' she repeated in a tone of the utmost resentment. 'If I did come from Davies Street, and come here? I don't remember to have met you before, and I fail to see what ground you had for following me or for watching my movements. I am sure I never gave you any, and I am not used to impertinence. For the rest, I am expecting some friends – Grocott!'

'Yes, ma'am.'

'Show this gentleman out. Or – or perhaps I am hasty,' she continued, in a lower tone and with an abrupt return of good nature. 'The last thing I should wish to be to any gentleman,' with a glance from a pair of handsome eyes. 'If I have met you at any time – at my Lady Bellamy's perhaps, sir?'

'No, ma'am, I think not.'

'Or at that good-natured creature, Conyers' – dear delightful woman; you know her, I am sure?'

'No,' Coke said, bluntly, 'I have not the honour of her ladyship's acquaintance; and I don't think I need trouble you farther. If there is no one else in the house, it is evident I have made a mistake. I offer my apologies, ma'am, regretting extremely that I trespassed on you.'

'I occupy the only rooms,' she answered drily. 'And – Grocott, if the gentleman is quite satisfied – the door please! And send my woman to me.'

Sir Hervey bowed, muttered a last word of apology, and with a look round the room, which brought to light nothing new except a handsome mail that stood packed and strapped in a corner, he passed out. After all, his discovery explained the appearance of the bailiffs outside Wollenhope's. The overdressed air and easy manners of the lady he had seen were those of one not given to economy, nor, probably, too particular as to ways and means. It accounted, also, for the lady's departure from Davies Street immediately after her arrival. Clearly Lane had misinformed the Northeys. It was not Sophia who had gone to the house in Davies Street; nor Sophia who had left that house in a gentleman's company. Then where was she?

As he paused in the passage revolving the question and seeking half a crown to give to the man whom he had suspected without reason, a dull sound as of a muffled hammer beating wood caught his ear. He had heard it indistinctly in the parlour – it appeared to come from the upper floor; but he had given no heed to it. 'What's that?' he asked, idly, as he drew out a coin.

'That noise, your honour?'

'Yes.'

'My journeyman. Perhaps you'd like to see him,' Grocott continued with a malicious grin. 'May be he's the young lady you're looking for. Oh, make yourself at home, sir,' he added bitterly. 'A poor man mustn't grumble if his house isn't his own and his lodgers are insulted.'

'Here,' Coke said, and dropping the half-crown into the dirty hand extended for it, he passed out. Instantly the door clanged behind him, the chain was put up, a bolt was shot; but although Sir Hervey stood a moment uncertain which way he should go, or what he should do next, he did not notice these extreme precautions, nor the pale, ugly face of triumph that watched him from the window as he turned south to go to Arlington Street.

CHAPTER XI

The Tug of War

At the corner of Bolton Row Sir Hervey paused. He felt, to be candid, a trifle awkward in the *rôle* of knight-errant, a part reserved in those days for Lord Peterborough. The Northeys' heartless cynicism, and their instant and cruel desertion of the girl, had stirred the chivalry that underlay his cold exterior. But from the first he had been aware that his status in the matter was ill-defined; he now began to see it in a worse, an absurd light. He had taken the field in the belief that Sophia had not stayed in Davies Street; that Hawkesworth, therefore, was beside the question; and that whatever folly she had committed, she had not altogether compromised herself; he now found the data on which he had acted painfully erroneous. She had not stayed in Davies Street, because she had not gone to Davies Street. But she might have joined Hawkesworth elsewhere; she might by this time be his wife; she might be gone with him never to return!

In that event Coke began to see that his part in the matter would prove to be worse than ridiculous; and he paused at the corner of Bolton Row, uncertain whether he should not go home and erase with a sore heart a foolish child's face from his memory. His was a day of coarse things; of duchesses who talked as fishwives talk now, of madcap maids of honour, such as she—

Who, as down the stairs she jumps,
Sings over the hills and far away,
Despising doleful dumps!

of bishops seen at strange levées, of clergy bribed with livings to take strange wives; of hoyden Lady Kitties, whose talk was a jumble of homely saws and taproom mock-modesties; of old men still swearing as they had sworn in Flanders in their youth. At the best it was not an age of ideals; but neither was it an age of hypocrisy, and women were plentiful. Why, then, all this trouble for one? And for one who had showed him plainly what she thought of him.

For a moment, at the corner of Bolton Row, Sophia's fate hung in the balance. Hung so nicely, that if Coke had not paused there, but had proceeded straight through Bolton Street, to Piccadilly, and so to Arlington Street, her lot would have been very different. But the debate kept him standing long enough to bring to a point – not many yards from the corner – two figures, which had just detached themselves from the crowd about Shepherd's Market. In the act of stepping across the gutter, he saw them, glanced carelessly at them, and stood. As the two, one behind the other, came up, almost brushing him, and turned to enter Clarges Row, he reached out his cane and touched the foremost.

'Why, Tom!' he cried, 'is it you, lad? Well met!'

Tom – for it was he – turned at the sound of his name, and seeing who it was recoiled, as if the cane that touched him had been red hot. The colour mounted to his wig; he stood, grinning in his finery, unable to say a word. 'Why, Tom!' Sir Hervey repeated, as he held out his hand, 'what is it, lad? Have you bad news? You are on the same business as I am, I take it?'

Tom blushed redder and redder, and shifted his feet uneasily. 'I don't know, Sir Hervey,' he stammered. 'I don't know what your business is, you see.'

'Well, you can easily guess,' Coke answered, never doubting that Tom had heard what was forward, and had posted from Cambridge in pursuit of his sister. 'Have you news? That's the point.'

Tom had only his own affair in mind. He wondered how much the other knew, and more than half suspected that he was being roasted. So 'News?' he faltered. 'What sort of news, sir?' He had known Sir Hervey all his life, and still felt for him the respect which a lad feels for the man of experience and fashion.

Coke stared at him. 'What sort of news?' he exclaimed. 'It isn't possible you don't know what has happened, boy?' Then, seeing that the person who had come up with Tom was at his elbow, listening, 'Is this fellow with you?' he cried angrily. 'If so, bid him stand back a little.'

'Yes, he's with me,' Tom answered, sheepishly; and turning to the lad, who was laden with a great nosegay of flowers as well as a paper parcel from which some white Spitalfields ribbons protruded, he bade him go on. 'Go on,' he said, 'I'll follow you. The last house on the right.'

Sir Hervey heard, and stared afresh. 'What?' he cried. 'Grocott's?'

Tom winced, and changed his feet uneasily, cursing his folly in letting out so much. 'It's only something that – that he's taking there,' he muttered.

'But you know about your sister?'

'Sophia?' Tom blurted out. 'Oh, she's all right. She's all right, I tell you. You need not trouble about her.'

'Indeed? Then where is she? Where is she, man? Out with it.'

'She's with me.'

'With you?' Sir Hervey cried, his cynicism quite gone. 'With you?'

'Yes.'

'Was it you who – who took her from Davies Street, then?'

'To be sure,' Tom said. In his preoccupation with his own affairs his sister's position had been forgotten. Now he began to recover himself; he began, too, to see that he had done rather a clever thing. 'Yes, I was there when she met that fellow,' he continued. 'Hawkesworth, you know, and I brought her away. I tell you what, Sir Hervey, that fellow's low. He should be in the Clink. She found him out sharp, before he had time to sit down, and it's lucky I was there to bring her away, or Lord knows what would have happened. For he's a monstrous rascal, and the people of the house are none too good!'

'Last night was it?'

'Yes.'

'And you took her to Grocott's?' Sir Hervey could not make the tales agree.

'Ye – es,' Tom faltered; but the word died on his lips, and he grew hot again. He saw too late that he had put his foot in a hobble from which he would find it hard to extricate himself, with all his skill. For it wanted only a few minutes of noon, and at Grocott's, a hundred paces away, his bride was expecting him. Presently Keith, the Mayfair parson, from whom he had just come after making the last arrangements, would be expecting both! Even now he ought to be at Grocott's; even now he ought to be on his way to the chapel in Curzon Street. And Grocott's was in sight; from where he stood he could see the boy with the flowers and wedding favours waiting at the door. But Coke – Coke the inopportune – had hold of his elbow, and if he went to Grocott's, would wish to go with him – would wish to see his sister, and from her would hear all about the marriage. Aye, and hearing, would interfere!

The cup of Tantalus was a little thing beside this, and Tom's cheeks burned; the wildest projects flashed through his brain. Should he take Sir Hervey to Grocott's, inveigle him into a bedroom and lock him up till the wedding was over? Or should he turn that instant, and take to his heels like any common pickpocket, without word or explanation, and so lead him from the place? He might do that, and return by coach himself, and—

Coke broke the tangled thread of thought. 'There is something amiss, here,' he said with decision. 'She is not at Grocott's. Or they lied to me.'

'She's not?' Tom cried, with a sigh of relief. 'You've been there? Then you may be sure she has gone to Arlington Street. That is it, you may be sure!'

'Aye, but they said at Grocott's that she had not been there,' Coke retorted, looking more closely at Tom, and beginning to discern something odd in his manner. 'If she's been there at all, how do you explain that, my boy?'

'She's been there all right,' Tom answered eagerly. 'I'm bail she has! I tell you it is so! And you may be sure she has gone to Arlington Street. Go there and you'll find her.'

'I don't know about that. You don't think that when your back was turned—'

'What?'

'She went off again!'

'With Hawkesworth?' Tom cried impatiently. 'I tell you she's found him out! He's poison to her! She's there, I tell you. Or she was.'

'But Grocott denied her!'

'Oh, nonsense!' Tom said – he was as red as fire with asking himself whom Sir Hervey had seen. 'Oh, nonsense,' he repeated, hurriedly; he felt he could bear it no longer. 'She was there, and she has gone to Arlington Street.'

'Very good,' Sir Hervey replied. 'Then we'll ask again. The man at the house lied to me, and I'll have an explanation, or I'll lay my cane across his shoulders, old as he is! There was some one I did see— But come along! Come along. We'll look into this, Tom.'

It was in vain Tom hung back, feebly protesting that she had gone – there was no doubt that she had gone to Arlington Street. Will-he, nill-he, he was dragged along. A moment and the two, Coke swinging his cane ominously, were half-way up the Row. In the midst of his agony Tom got a notion that his companion was taking sidelong looks at his clothes; and he grew hot and hotter, fearing what was to come. When they were within a few yards of the door, a hackney coach passed them, and, turning, came to a stand before the house.

'There! What did I say?' Sir Hervey muttered. 'I take it, we are only just in time.'

'Perhaps it's the coach that took her away,' Tom suggested, trying to restrain his companion. 'Shall I go in – I know the people – and – and inquire? Yes, you'd better let me do that,' he continued eagerly, buttonholing Sir Hervey, 'perhaps they did not know you. I really think you had better leave it to me, Sir Hervey. I—'

'No, thank you,' Coke answered drily. 'There's a shorter way. Are you here to take up, my man?'

'To be sure, your honour,' the coachman answered readily. 'And long life to her!'

'Eh?'

'Long life to the bride, your honour!'

'Ah!' Sir Hervey said, his face growing dark. 'I thought so. I think, my lad,' he continued to Tom as he knocked at the door, 'she and somebody have made a fool of you!'

'No, no,' Tom said, distractedly. 'It's not for her.'

'We shall soon learn!' Coke answered. And he rapped again imperatively.

Tom tried to tell him the facts; but his throat was dry, his head whirled, he could not get out a word. And by-and-by Grocott's dragging steps were heard in the passage, the latch was raised, and the door opened.

'Now, sir!' Coke cried, addressing him sharply. 'What did you mean by lying to me just now? Here is the gentleman who brought Miss Maitland to your house. And if you don't tell me, and tell me quickly, where she is, I'll – I'll send for the constable!'

Grocott was pale, but his face did not lose its sneering expression. 'She's gone,' he said.

'You said she had not been here.'

'Well, it was her order. I suppose,' with a touch of insolence, 'a lady can be private, sir, if she chooses.'

'What time did she go?'

'Ten minutes gone.'

Tom heaved a sigh of relief. 'I told you so,' he muttered. 'She's gone to Arlington Street. It's what I told you.'

'I don't believe it,' Coke answered. 'This coach is for her. It is here to take her to the rascal we know of; and I'll not leave till I've seen her. Why, man,' he continued, incensed as well as perplexed by Tom's easiness, 'have you no blood in your body that you're ready to stand by while your sister's fooled by a scoundrel?'

Tom smiled pitifully, and passed his tongue over his lips; he looked guiltily at Grocott, and Grocott at him. The lad's face was on fire, the sweat stood out in beads on Grocott's forehead. Neither knew with precision the other's position nor how much he had told. And while the two stood thus, Sir Hervey looking suspiciously from one to the other, the same dull sound Coke had heard before – a sound as of the drumming of heels on the floor – continued in the upper part of the house. The hackney coachman, an interested spectator of the scene, heard it, and looked at the higher windows in annoyance. The sound drowned the speaker's words.

'Are you going to let me search?' Coke said at last.

Grocott shook his head. He could not speak. He was wondering what they would call the offence at the Old Bailey or Hicks's Hall. He saw himself in the dock with the tall spikes and bunches of herbs before him, and the gross crimson face of the Red Judge glowering at him through horn-rimmed spectacles – glowering death. Should he confess and bring her down, and with that put an end to his daughter's hopes? Or should he stand it out, defy them all, gain time, perhaps go scot free at last?

'Well?' Coke repeated sternly; 'have you made up your mind? Am I to send for the constable?'

Still Grocott found no answer. His wits were so jumbled by fear and the predicament in which he found himself, that he could not decide what to do. And while he hesitated, gaping, the matter was taken out of his hands. The door behind him opened, and the lady whom Sir Hervey had seen before came out of the room.

She looked at the group with a mixture of weariness and impatience. 'Is the gentleman not satisfied yet?' she said. 'What is all this?'

'I am satisfied, madam,' Sir Hervey retorted, 'that I did not hear the truth before.'

'Well, you are too late now,' she answered, 'for she's gone. She didn't wish to see you, and there's an end.'

'I shall not believe, ma'am—'

'Not believe?' she cried, opening her eyes with sudden fire. 'I thought you were a gentleman, sir. I suppose you will take a lady's word?'

'If the lady will tell me for whom the coach at the door is waiting,' Sir Hervey answered quietly; and as he spoke he made good his footing by crossing the threshold. He could not see the hot, foolish face that followed him into the passage, or he might have been enlightened sooner.

'The coach?' she said. 'It is for me.'

'It is for a bride.'

'I am the bride.'

'And the bridegroom?'

Her eyes sparkled. 'Come!' she cried. 'How is that your affair? We poor women must have impertinences enough to suffer on these occasions; but it is new to me that the question of chance visitors are part of them! Room's more than company, sometimes,' she added, tossing her head, her accent not quite so genteel as it had been when she was less moved. 'And I'll be glad to see your back.'

'I beg your pardon a thousand times, ma'am,' Coke replied unmoved. 'But I see no impertinence in my question – unless, indeed, you are ashamed of your bridegroom.'

'That I'm not!' she cried. 'That I'm not! And' – snapping her fingers in his face – 'that for you. You are impertinent! Ashamed? No, sir, I am not!'

'And God forbid I should be ashamed of my bride!' cried a husky voice behind Sir Hervey; who turned as if he had been pinched. 'No, I'll be silent no longer,' Tom continued, his face the colour of a beet, albeit his eyes overflowed with honest devotion. 'I've played coward too long!' he went on, stretching out his arms as if he were throwing off a weight. 'Let go, man' – this to Grocott, as the latter stealthily plucked his sleeve. 'Sir Hervey, I didn't tell you before, but it wasn't because I was ashamed of my bride. Not I!' poor Tom cried bravely. 'It was because I – I thought you might do something to thwart me.

This lady has done me the honour of entrusting her happiness to me, and before one o'clock we shall be married. Now you know.'

'Indeed!' Sir Hervey said. And great as was his amazement, he managed to cloak it after a fashion. In the first burst of Tom's confession he had glanced from him to the lady, and had surprised a black – a very black look. That same look he caught on Grocott's face; and in a wonderfully short space of time he had drawn his conclusions. 'Indeed!' he repeated. 'And whom have I – perhaps we might step into this room, we shall be more of a family party, eh? – whom have I to felicitate on the possession of Sir Thomas Maitland's heart?'

He bowed so low before madam that she was almost deceived; but not quite. She did not answer.

'Oriana, tell him,' Tom cried humbly. He *was* deceived. His eyes were shining with honest pride.

Coke caught at the name. 'Oriana!' he repeated, bowing still lower. 'Mistress Oriana—'

'Clark,' she said drily. And then, 'You are not much wiser now.'

'My loss, ma'am,' Sir Hervey answered politely. 'One of Sir Robert Clark of Snailwell's charming daughters, perchance? Until now I had only the pleasure of knowing the elder, but—'

'You know no more now,' she retorted, with an air of low breeding that must have opened any eyes but a lover's. 'I don't know your Sir Robert.'

'Indeed!' Sir Hervey said. 'One of the Leicestershire Clarks, of Lawnd Abbey, perhaps?'

'No,' madam answered sullenly, hating him more and more, yet not daring to show it. How she cursed her booby for his indiscretion!

'Surely not a daughter of my old friend, Dean Clark of Salisbury? You don't say so?'

She bit her lip with mortification. 'No,' she said, 'I don't say so. I ain't that either.'

Tom intervened hurriedly. 'You are under a misapprehension, Sir Hervey,' he said. 'Clark was Oriana's – her husband's name. Captain Clark, of Sabine's Foot. He did not treat her well,' poor Tom continued, leaning forward, his hands resting on the table – they were all in the room now. 'But I hope to make the rest of her life more happy than the early part.'

'Oh, I beg pardon,' Sir Hervey said, a trifle drily. 'A widow! Your humble servant, ma'am, to command. You will excuse me, I am sure. You are waiting for Mrs Northey, I suppose?' he continued, looking from one to the other in seeming innocence.

Tom's face flamed. It was in vain Grocott from the doorway made signs to him to be silent. 'They don't know,' he blurted out.

Sir Hervey looked grave. 'I am sorry for that,' he said. 'I am sure this lady would not wish you, Sir Tom, to do anything – anything underhand. You have your guardians' consent, of course?'

'No,' Tom said flatly; 'and I am not going to ask for it.'

Outwardly, Sir Hervey raised his eyebrows in protest; inwardly, he saw that argument would be thrown away, and wondered what on earth he should do. He had no authority over the boy, and it was not likely that Dr Keith, an irregular parson, would pay heed to him.

Madam Oriana, scared for a moment, discerned that he was at a loss, and smiled in triumph.

'Well, sir, have you anything more to say?' she cried.

'Not to Tom,' Sir Hervey answered.

'And to me?'

'Only, ma'am, that a marriage is not valid if a false name be used.'

The shot was not fired quite at large, for he had surprised Grocott calling her not Oriana, but Sallie. And, fired at large or not, her face showed that it reached the mark. Whether Captain Clark of Sabine's Foot still lived, or there had never been a Clark; whether she had foreseen the difficulty and made up her mind to run the risk, or had not thought of it at all, her scowling, beautiful face betrayed dismay as well as rage.

'What have you to do with my name?' she hissed.

'Nothing,' he said politely. 'But my friend here, much. I hope he knows it, and knows it correctly. That is all.'

But Tom was at the end of his patience.

'I do,' he cried hotly, 'I do know it! And I'll trouble you, Sir Hervey, to let it alone. Oriana, don't think that anything he can say can move me. I see, Sir Hervey, that you are no true friend to us. I might have known it,' he continued bitterly. 'You have lived all your life where – where marriage is a bargain, and women are sold, and – you don't believe in anything else. You can't; you can't believe in anything else. But I am only sorry for you! Only – only you'll please to remember that this lady is as good as my wife, and I expect her to be treated as such. She'll not need a defender as long as I live,' poor Tom continued, gallantly, though his voice shook. 'Come, Oriana, the coach is waiting. In a few minutes I shall have a better right to protect you; and then let anyone say a word!'

'Tom,' Sir Hervey said gravely, 'don't do this.'

Madam marked his altered tone, and laughed derisively. 'Now he's in his true colours!' she cried. 'What will you do, Sir Thomas? La! they shall never say that I dragged a man to church against his will. I've more pride than that, though I may not be a dean's daughter.'

Tom raised her hand and kissed it, his boyish face aglow with love. 'Come, dear,' he said. 'What is his opinion to us? A little room, if you please, Sir Hervey. We are going.'

'No,' Coke answered. 'You are not going! I'll not have this on my head. Hear sense, boy. If this lady be one whom you may honestly make your wife you cannot lose, and she must gain, by waiting to be married in a proper fashion.'

'And at a nice expense, too!' she cried, with a sneer.

'She is right,' Tom said manfully. 'I'm not going to waste my life waiting on the pleasure of a set of old fogies. Make way, Sir Hervey.'

'I shall not,' Coke returned, maintaining his position between the two and the door. 'And if you come near me, boy—'

'Don't push me too far,' Tom cried. From no one else in the world would he have endured so much. 'Sir Hervey, make way!'

'If he does not, we will have him put out!' madam cried, pale with rage. 'This is my room, sir! and I order you to leave it. If you are a gentleman you will go.'

'I shall not,' Coke said. He was really at his wits' end to know what to do. 'And if the boy comes near me,' he continued, 'I will knock him down and hold him. He's only fit for Bedlam!'

Tom would have flown at his throat, but madam restrained him. 'Grocott,' she cried, 'call in a couple of chairmen, and put this person out. Give them a guinea apiece, and let them throw him into the street.'

Grocott hung a moment in the doorway, pale, perspiring, irresolute. He could not see the end of this.

'Do you hear, man?' madam repeated, and stamped her foot on the floor. 'Call in two men. A guinea apiece if they turn him out. Go at once. I'll know whether the room is mine or his,' she continued, in a fury.

'Yours, ma'am,' Sir Hervey answered coolly, as Grocott shambled out. 'I ask nothing better than to leave it, if Sir Thomas Maitland goes with me.'

'You'll leave it without him!' she retorted contemptuously. And, as Tom made forward movement, 'Sir Thomas, you'll not interfere in this. I've had to do with nasty rogues like him before,' she continued, with growing excitement and freedom, 'and know the way. You're mighty fine, sir, and think to tread on me. Oh, for all your bowing, I saw you look at me when you came in as if I was so much dirt! But I'll not be put upon, and I'll let you know it. You are a jackanapes and a finicky fool, that's what you are! Aye, you are! But here they come. Now we'll see. Grocott!'

'They are coming,' the clock-maker muttered, cringing in the doorway. The line of action adopted was too violent for his taste. 'But I hope the gentleman will go out quietly,' he rejoined. 'He must see he has no right here.'

It was no question of courage; Sir Hervey had plenty of that. But he had no stomach for a low brawl; and at this moment he wished very heartily that he had let the young scapegrace go his own way. He had put his foot down, however wisely or unwisely; and he could not now retreat.

'I shall not go,' he said firmly. And as heavy, lumbering footsteps were heard coming along the passage, he turned to face the door.

'We'll see about that,' Mrs Clark cried spitefully. 'Come in, men; come in! This is your gentleman.'

CHAPTER XII

Don Quixote

COKE HAD spent a dozen seasons in London; and naturally to those who lived about town his figure was almost as familiar as that of Sir Hanbury Williams, the beau of the last generation, or that of Lord Lincoln, the pride and hope of the golden youth of '42. The chairman who had never left the rank in St James's Street in obedience to his nod was as likely as not to ask the way to Mrs Cornely's rooms; the hackney-coachman who did not know his face and liveries was a stranger also to the front of White's, and to the cry of 'Who goes home?' that on foggy evenings drew a hundred link-boys to New Palace Yard. In his present difficulty his principal, and almost his only hope of escaping from a degrading shuffle lay in this notoriety.

It bade fair to be justified. The two men who slouched into the room in obedience to Mrs Clark's excited cry had scarcely crossed the threshold when they turned to him and grinned, and the foremost made him a sort of bow. Sir Hervey stared, and wondered where he had seen the men before; but in a twinkling his doubt, as well as the half-smothered cry that at the same instant burst from madam's lips, were explained.

'Mrs Oriana Clark, otherwise Grocott?' the elder man muttered, and, stepping forward briskly, he laid a slip of paper on the table before her. 'At suit of Margam's, of Paul's Churchyard, for forty-seven, six, eight, debt and costs. Here's the *capias*. And there's a detainer lodged.' So much said, he seemed to feel the official part of his duty accomplished, and he turned with a wink to Grocott. 'Much obliged to the old gentleman for letting us in. As pretty a capture as I ever made! Trigg, mind the door.'

The miser who sees his hoarded all sink beneath the waves; the leader who, in the flush of victory, falls into the deadly ambush and knows all lost; the bride widowed on her wedding morn – these may in some degree serve to image madam at that moment. White to the lips, her eyes staring, she plucked at the front of her dress with one hand, and, leaning with the other against the wall, seemed to struggle for speech.

It was Tom who stepped forward, Tom who instinctively, like the brave soul he was, screened her from their eyes. 'What is it?' he said hoarsely. 'Have a care, man, whom you speak to! What do you mean, and who are you?'

'Easy asked and soon answered,' the fellow replied, civilly enough. 'I'm a sworn bailiff, it's a *capias* forty-seven, six, eight, debt and costs – that's what it is. And there's a detainer lodged, so it's no use to pay till you know where you are. The lady is here, and I am bound to take her.'

'It's a mistake,' Tom muttered, his voice indistinct. 'There's some mistake, man. What is the name?'

'Well, it's Clark, *alias* Grocott on the writ; and it's Clark, *alias* Hawkesworth—'

'Hawkesworth?'

'Yes, Hawkesworth, on the detainer,' the bailiff answered, smiling. 'I don't take on myself to say which is right, but the old gentleman here should know.'

At that word the unhappy woman, thwarted in the moment of success, roused herself from the first stunning effects of the blow. With a cry she tore her handkerchief into two or three pieces, and, thrusting one end into her mouth, bit on it. Then, 'Silence!' she shrieked. 'Silence, you dirty dog!' she continued coarsely. 'How dare you lay your tongue to me? Do you hear me?'

But Tom interfered. 'No, one moment,' he said grimly. That word, Hawkesworth, had chilled his blood. 'Let us hear what he has to say. Listen to me, man. Why should the old gentleman know?'

The man hesitated, looking from one to the other. 'Well, they say he's her father,' he answered at last. 'At any rate he brought her up; that is, until – well, I suppose you know.'

She shrieked out a denial; but Tom, without taking his eyes from the bailiff's face, put out his hand, and, gripping her arm, held her back. 'Yes man, until what?' he said hoarsely. 'Speak out. Until what?'

'Well, until she went to live with Hawkesworth, your honour.'

'Ah!' Tom said, his face white; only that word. But, dropping his hand from her arm, he stood back.

She should have known that all was lost then; that the game

was played out. But, womanlike, she could not accept defeat. 'It's a lie!' she shrieked. 'A dirty, cowardly lie! It's not true! I swear it is not true! It's not true!' And breathless, panting, furious, she turned first to one and then to another, stretching out her hands, heaping senseless denial on denial. At last, when she read no relenting in the boy's face, but only the quivering of pain as he winced under the lash of her loosened tongue, she cast the mask – that had already slipped – completely away, and, turning on the old man, 'You fool! oh, you fool!' she cried. 'Have you nothing to say now that you have ruined me? Pay the beast, do you hear? Pay him, or I'll ruin you!'

But the clock-maker, terrified as he was, clung sullenly to his money. 'There's a detainer,' he muttered. 'It's no good, Bess. It's no good, I tell you!'

'Well, pay the detainer! Pay that, too!' she retorted. 'Pay it, you old skinflint, or I'll swear to you for gold clipping! and you'll hang at Tyburn, as your friend Jonathan Thomas did! Have a care, will you, or I'll do it, so help me!'

The old man screamed a palsied curse at her. Sir Hervey touched the lad's arm. 'Come,' he said sternly. And he turned to the door.

Tom shuddered, but followed at his heels as a beaten hound follows. The woman saw her last chance passing from her, sprang forward, and tried to seize his arm; tried to detain him, tried to gain his ear for a final appeal. But the bailiff interfered. 'Softly, mistress, softly,' he said. 'You know the rules. Get the old 'un to pay, and you may do as you please.'

He held her while Tom was got out, dizzy and shaking, his eyes opened to the abyss from which he had been plucked back. But, though Coke closed the door behind them, the woman's voice still followed them, and shocked and horrified them with its shrill clamour. Tom shuddered at the dreadful sound; yet lingered.

'I must get something,' he muttered, avoiding his companion's eyes. 'It is upstairs.'

'What is it?' Coke answered impatiently. And, anxious to get the lad out of hearing, he took his arm, and urged him towards the street. 'Whatever it is, I'll send my man for it.'

But Tom hung back. 'No,' he said. 'It's money. I must get it.'

'For goodness' sake don't stay now,' Sir Hervey protested.

But Tom, instead of complying, averted his face. 'I want to pay this,' he muttered. 'I shall never see her again. But I would rather she – she were not taken now. That's all.'

Coke stared. 'Oh Lord!' he said; and he wondered. But he let Tom go upstairs; and he waited himself in the passage to cover his retreat. He heard the lad go up and push open the door of the little three-cornered room, which had been his abode for a week; the little room where he had tasted to the full of anticipation, and whence he had gone aglow with fire and joy an hour before. Coke heard him no farther, but continued to listen, and 'What is that?' he muttered presently. A moment, and he followed his companion up the stairs, at the head of the flight he caught again the sound he had heard below; the sound of a muffled cry deadened by distance and obstacles, but still almost articulate. He looked after Tom; but the door of the room in which he had disappeared was half open. The sound did not issue thence. Then he thought it came from the room below; and he was on the point of turning when he saw a door close beside him in the angle of the stairs, and he listened at that. For the moment all was silent, yet Sir Hervey had his doubts. The key was in the lock, he turned it softly, and stepped into an untidy little bedroom. sordid and dull; the same, in fact, through which Sophia had been decoyed. He noticed the door at the farther end, and was crossing the floor towards it, with an unpleasant light in his eyes – for he began to guess what he should find – when the door of the room below opened, and a man came out, and came heavily up the stairs. Sir Hervey paused and looked back; another moment and Grocott reaching the open door stood glaring in.

Sir Hervey spoke only one word. 'Open!' he said; and he pointed with his cane to the door of the inner room. The key was not in the lock.

The clock-maker, cringing almost to the boards, crept across the floor, and, producing the key from his pocket, set it in the lock. As he did so Coke gripped him on a sudden by the nape of the neck, and irresistibly but silently forced him to his knees. And that was what Sophia saw when the door opened. Grocott kneeling, his dirty, flabby face quivering with fear, and Sir Hervey standing over him.

'Oh!' she exclaimed, and stepped back in amazement; but, so

much thought given to herself, her next was for Tom. She had been a prisoner nearly two hours, in fear as well as in suspense, assailed at one time by the fancy that those who had snared her had left her to starve, at another by the dread of ill-treatment if they returned. But the affection for her brother, which had roused her from her own troubles, was still strong, and her second thought was of Tom.

She seized Sir Hervey's arm. 'Thank Heaven you have come!' she cried. 'Did he send you? Where is he?'

'Tom?' Coke answered cheerily. 'He is all right. He is here.'

'Here? And he is not married?'

'No, he is not married,' Sir Hervey answered; 'nor is he going to be yet awhile.'

'Thank God!' she exclaimed. And then, as their eyes met, she remembered herself, and quailed, the blushes burning in her cheeks. She had not seen him since the evening at Vauxhall, when he had laboured to open her eyes to Hawkesworth's true character. The things that had happened, the things she had done since that evening crowded into her mind; she could have sunk into the floor for very shame. She did not know how much he knew or how much worse than she was he might be thinking her; and in an agony of recollection she covered her face and shrank from him.

'Come, child, come, you are safe now,' he said hurriedly; he understood her feelings. 'I suppose they locked you here that you might not interfere? Eh, was that it?' he continued, seizing Grocott's ear and twisting it until the old rogue grovelled on the floor. 'Eh, was that it.'

'Oh, yes, yes,' the clock-maker cried. 'That was it! I'll beg the lady's pardon. I'll do anything. I'll—'

'You'll hang – some day!' Sir Hervey answered, releasing him with a final twist. 'Begone for this time, and thank your lucky stars I don't haul you to the nearest justice! And do you, child, come to your brother. He is in the next room.'

But when Sophia had so far conquered her agitation as to be able to comply, they found no Tom there; only a scrap of paper, bearing a line or two of writing, lay on the table.

'I'm gone to enlist, or something. I don't care what. It doesn't matter,' it ran. 'Don't come after me, for I shan't come back. Let Sophy have my setter pup, it's at the hall. I see it now; it was a trap. If I meet H. I shall kill him. – T.M.'

'He has found her out, then?' Sophia said tearfully.

'Yes,' Sir Hervey answered, standing at the table and drumming on it with his fingers, while he looked at her and wondered what was to be done next. 'He has found her out. In a year he will be none the worse and a little wiser.'

'But if he enlists?' she murmured.

'We shall hear of it,' Coke answered, 'and can buy him out.' And then there was silence again. And he wondered again what was to be done next.

Below, the house was quiet. Either the bailiffs had removed their prisoner, or she had been released, and she and they had gone their ways. Even Grocott, it would seem, terrified by the position in which he found himself, had taken himself off for a while, for not a sound save the measured ticking of clocks broke the silence of the house, above stairs or below. After a time, as Sophia said nothing, Sir Hervey moved to the window and looked into the Row. The coach that had waited so long was gone. A thin rain was beginning to fall, and through it a pastrycook's boy with a tray on his head was approaching the next house. Otherwise the street was empty.

'Did – did my sister send you?' she faltered at last.

'No.'

'How did you find me?'

'I heard from your brother-in-law,' he answered, his face still averted.

'What?'

'That you had gone to Davies Street.'

'He knew?' she muttered.

'Yes.'

She caught her breath. 'Is it public?' she whispered. 'I suppose everybody – knows.'

'Well, some do, I've no doubt,' he answered bluntly. 'Women will worry something, and, of course, there is a – sort of a bone in it.'

She shivered, humiliated by the necessity that lay upon her. She must clear herself. It had come to this, she had brought it to this, that she must clear herself even in his eyes. 'My brother was there,' she said indistinctly, her face covered from his gaze.

'I know.' he answered.

'Do they know?'

He understood that she meant the Northeys. 'No,' he answered. 'Not yet.'

She was silent a moment. Then – 'What am I to do?' she asked faintly.

She had gone through so many strange things in the last twenty-four hours that this which should have seemed the strangest of all – that she should consult *him* – passed with her for ordinary. But not with Coke. It showed him more clearly than before her friendlessness, her isolation, her forlornness, and these things moved him. He knew what the world would think of her escapade, what sharp-tongued gossips like Lady Harrington would make of it, what easy dames like Lady Walpole and Lady Townshend would proclaim her; and his heart was full of pity for her. He knew her innocent; he had the word of that other innocent, Tom, for it; but who would believe it? The Northeys had cast her off; perhaps when they knew all they would still cast her off. Her brother, her only witness, had taken himself away, and was a boy at most. Had he been older, he might have given the gossips the lie and forced the world to believe him, at the point of the small sword. As it was she had no one. Her aunt's misfortune was being repeated in a later generation. The penalty must be the same.

Must it? In the silence Sir Hervey heard her sigh. and his heart beat quickly. Was there no way to save her? Yes, there was one. He saw it, and with the coolness of the old gamester he took it.

'What are you to do?' he repeated thoughtfully; and turning, he sat down, and looked at her across the table, his face, voice, manner all businesslike. 'Well, it depends, child. I suppose you have no feeling left for – for that person?'

She shook her head, her face hidden.

'None at all?' he persisted, toying with his snuff-box, while he looked at her keenly. 'Pardon me, I wish to have this clear because – because it's important.'

'I would rather die,' she cried passionately, 'than be his wife.'

He nodded. 'Good,' he said. 'It was to be expected. Well, we must make that clear, quite clear, and – and I can hardly think your sister will still refuse to receive you.'

Sophia started; her face flamed. 'Has she said anything?' she muttered.

'Nothing,' Coke answered. 'But you left her yesterday – to join him; and you return today. Still – still, child, I think if we make all clear to her, quite clear, and to your brother Northey, they will be willing to overlook the matter and find you a home.'

She shuddered. 'You speak very plainly,' she murmured faintly.

'I fear,' he said, 'you will hear plainer things from her. But,' he continued, speaking slowly now, and in a different tone, 'there is another way, child, if you are willing to take it. One other way. That way you need not see her unless you choose, you need see none of them, you need hear no plain truths. That way you may laugh at them, and what they say will be no concern of yours, nor need trouble you. But 'tisn't to be supposed that with all this you will take it.'

'You mean I may go to Chalkhill?' she cried, rising impetuously. 'I will, I will go gladly, I will go thankfully! I will indeed!'

'No,' he said, rising also, so that only the table stood between them. 'I did not mean that. There is still another way. But you are young, child, and it isn't to be supposed that you will take it.'

'Young!' she exclaimed in bitter self-contempt. And then, 'What way is it?' she asked. 'And why should I not take it, take it gladly if I can escape – all that?'

'Because – I am not very young,' he said grimly.

'You?' she exclaimed in astonishment. And then, as her eyes met his across the table, the colour rose in her cheeks. She began to understand; and she began to tremble.

'Yes,' he said bluntly, 'I. It shocks you, does it? But, courage, child; you understand a little, you do not understand all. Suppose for a moment that you return to Arlington Street today as Lady Coke; the demands of the most exacting will be satisfied. Lady Harrington herself will have nothing to say. You left yesterday, you return today – my wife. Those who have borne my mother's name have been wont to meet with respect; and, I doubt not, will continue to meet with it.'

'And you – would do that?' she cried aghast.

'I would.'

'You would marry me?'

'I would.'

'After all that has passed? Here? Today?'

'Here, today.'

For a moment she was silent. Then, 'And you imagine I could consent?' she cried. 'You imagine I could do that? Never! Never! I think you good, I think you noble, I thank you for your offer, Sir Hervey; I believe it to be one the world would deem you mad to make, and me mad to refuse! But,' and suddenly she covered her face with her hands, as if his eyes burned her, 'from what a height you must look down on me.'

'I look down?' he said lamely. 'Not at all. I don't understand you.'

'You do not understand?' she cried, dropping her hands and meeting his eyes as suddenly as she had avoided them. 'You think it possible, then, that I, who yesterday left my home, poor fool that I was, to marry one man, can give myself a few hours later to another man? You think I hold love so light a thing I can take it and give it again as I take or give a kerchief or a riband? You think I put so small a price on myself – and on you? Oh, no, no, I do not. I see, if you do not, or will not, that your offer, noble, generous, magnanimous as it is, is the sharpest taunt of all that you have it in your power to fling at me.'

'That,' Sir Hervey said, placidly, 'is because you don't understand.'

'It is impossible!' she repeated. 'It is impossible!'

'What you have in your mind may be impossible,' he retorted; 'but not what I have in mine. I should have thought, child, that on your side, also, you had had enough of romance.'

She looked at him in astonishment.

'While I,' he continued, raising his eyebrows, 'have outgrown it. There is no question, at least, in my offer there was no question of love. For one thing it is out of fashion, my dear; for another, at the age I have reached, not quite the age of Methuselah, perhaps,' with a smile, 'but an age, as you once reminded me, at which I might be your father, I need only a lady to sit at the head of my table, to see that the maids don't rob me, or burn the Hall, and to show a pretty face to my guests when they come from town. My wife will have her own wing of the house, I mine; we need meet only at meals. To the world we shall be husband and wife; to one another, I hope, good friends. Of course,' Sir Hervey continued, with a slight yawn, 'there was a time when I should not have thought this an ideal marriage; when I might have looked for more. Nor should I then have – you might almost call it – insulted you, *ma chère*, by proposing it. But I am old enough to be content with it; and you are in an awkward position from which my name may extricate you; while you have probably had enough of what children call love. So, in fine, what do you say?'

After a long pause, 'Do you mean,' she asked in a low voice. 'that we should be only – friends?'

'Precisely,' he said. 'That is just what I do mean. And nothing more.'

'But have you considered,' she asked, her tone still low, her voice trembling with agitation. 'Have you thought of – of yourself? Why should you be sacrificed to save me from the punishment of my folly? Why should you do out of pity what you may repent all your life? Oh, it cannot, it cannot be!' she continued more rapidly and with growing excitement. 'I thank you, I thank you from my heart, Sir Hervey, I believe you mean it generously, nobly, but—'

'Let us consider the question – without fudge!' he retorted, stolidly forestalling her. 'Pity has little to do with it. Your folly, child, has much; because apart from that I should not have made the suggestion. For the rest, put me out of the question. The point is, will it suit you? Of course you might wish to marry someone else. You might wish to marry in fact and not in name—'

'Oh, no, no!' she cried, shuddering; and, shaken by the cruel awakening through which she had gone, she fancied that she spoke the truth.

'You are sure?'

'Quite, quite sure.'

'Then I think it lies between Chalkhill and Coke Hall,' he said, cheerfully. 'Read that, child.' And drawing from his pocket the letter in which Mr Northey had announced her flight, he laid it before her. 'If I thought you were returning to your sister I would not show it to you,' he continued, watching her as she read. And then, after an interval, 'Well, shall it be Coke Hall?' he asked.

'Yes,' she said, shivering under the cruel, heartless phrases of the letter as under a douche of cold water. 'If you really are in earnest, if you mean what you say?'

'I do.'

'And you will be satisfied with – that?' she murmured, averting her eyes. 'With my friendship?'

'I will,' he answered. 'You have my word for it.'

'Then, I thank you,' she muttered faintly.

And that was all, absolutely all. He opened the door, and in her sacque and Lady Betty's Tuscan, as she stood – for she had no change to make – she passed down the stairs before him, and walked beside him through the rain across a corner of Shepherd's Market. Thence they passed along Curzon Street in the direction of the little chapel with the country church porch – over against Mayfair Chapel, and conveniently near the Hercules Pillars – in which the Rev Alexander Keith held himself ready to marry all comers, at all hours, without notice or licence.

It was the common dinner time, and the streets were quiet; they met no one whom they knew. Sophia, dazed and shaken, had scarcely power to think; she walked beside him mechanically, as in a dream, and could never remember in after days the way she went to be married, or whether she travelled the route on foot or in a chair. The famous Dr Keith, baulked of one couple and one guinea – for that was his fee, and it included the clerk and a stamped certificate – welcomed the pair with effusion. Accustomed to unite at one hour a peer of the realm to a reigning toast, at another an apprentice to his master's daughter, he betrayed no surprise even when he recognized Sir Hervey Coke; but at once he led the way to the chapel, set the kneelers, called the witnesses, and did his part. He wondered a little, it is true, when he noticed Sophia's pallor and strange dress; but the reasons people had for marrying were nothing to him; the fee was everything, and in ten minutes the tie was tied.

Then only, as they stood waiting in the parlour while the certificate was being written, fear seized her, and a great horror, and she knew what she had done. She turned to Sir Hervey and held out her shaking hands to him, her face white and piteous. 'You will be good to me?' she cried. 'You will be good to me? You will keep your word?'

'While I live,' he said quietly. 'Why not, child?'

But, calmly as he spoke, his face, as they went out together, wore the look it wore at White's when he played deep; when, round the shaded candles, oaks, noted in Domesday, crashed down, and long-descended halls shook, and the honour of great names hung on the turn of a die. For, deep as he had played, much as he had risked, even to his home, even to his line, he had made today the maddest bet of all. And he knew it.

CHAPTER XIII

The Welcome Home

'YOUR GRACE is very good to call,' Mrs Northey said, working her fan with a violence that betrayed something of the restraint which she was putting on her feelings. 'But, of course, the mischief is done now, the girl is gone, and—'

'I know, my dear, I know,' the duchess answered soothingly. 'Believe me, I am almost as sorry as if she were one of my own daughters.'

'La, for the matter of that, it may be yet!' Mrs Northey answered, unable to behave herself longer. 'Begging your Grace's pardon. Of course, I hope not,' she continued sourly, 'but, indeed and in truth, young ladies who show the road are very apt to follow it themselves.'

'Indeed, I fear that is so; too often,' her Grace answered patiently. 'Too often!' She had come prepared to eat humble pie, and was not going to refuse the dish.

'I hope, at any rate, that the young lady will take the lesson to heart!' Mrs Northey continued, with a venomous glance at Lady Betty; who, much subdued, sat half-sullen and half-frightened on a stool beside and a little behind her mother. 'I hope so for her own sake.'

'It is for that reason I brought her,' the duchess said with dignity. 'She has behaved naughtily, very naughtily. His Grace is so angry that he will not see her. Tomorrow she goes into the country, where she will return to the schoolroom until we leave town. I hope that that and the scandal she has brought upon us may teach her to be more discreet in future.'

'And more steady! I trust it may,' Mrs Northey said, biting her lip and looking daggers at the culprit. 'I am sure she has done mischief enough. But it is easier to do than to undo, as she would find to her sorrow if it were her own case.'

'Very true! Very true, indeed! Do you hear, miss?' the duchess asked, turning and sharply addressing her daughter.

'Yes, ma'am,' Lady Betty whispered meekly. Quick of fence as she was with men, or with girls of her own age, she knew better than to contradict her mother.

'Go and sit in the window, then. No, miss, with your back to it. And now,' the duchess continued when Lady Betty had withdrawn out of earshot, 'tell me what you wish to be known, my dear. Anything I can do for the foolish child – she is very young, you know – I will do. And if I make the best of it, I have friends, and they will also make the best of it.'

But Mrs Northey's face was hard as stone. 'There is no best to it,' she said.

'Oh, but surely in your sister's interest?' the duchess expostulated.

'Your Grace was misinformed. I have no sister,' Mrs Northey replied, her voice a trifle high, and her thin nostrils more pinched than usual. 'From the moment Miss Maitland left this house in such a way as to bring scandal on my husband's name, she ceased to be my sister. Lord Northey has claims upon us. We acknowledge them.'

The duchess stared, but did not answer.

'My husband has claims upon me, I acknowledge them,' Mrs Northey continued with majesty.

The duchess still stared; her manner betrayed that she was startled.

'Well, of course,' she said at last, 'that is what we all wish other people to do in these cases; for the sake of example, you know, and to warn the – the young. But, dear me,' rubbing her nose reflectively with the corner of her snuff-box. 'it's very sad! I don't know, I really don't know that I should have the courage to do it – in Betty's case now. His Grace would – would expect it, of course. But really I don't know!'

'Your Grace is the best judge in your own case,' Mrs Northey said, her breath coming a little quickly 'For our part,' she added, looking upward with an air of self-denial, 'Mr Northey and I have determined to give no sanction to a connection so discreditable!'

The duchess had a vision of her own spoiled daughter laid ill in a six-shilling lodging, of a mother stealing to her under cover of darkness, and in his Grace's teeth; of a tiny baby the image of Betty at that age. And she clutched her snuff-box tightly. 'I suppose the man is – is impossible?' she said impulsively.

'He is quite impossible.'

'Mr Northey has not seen him?'

'Certainly not,' Mrs Northey exclaimed, with a virtuous shudder.

'But if she – if she were brought to see what she has done in its true light?' the duchess asked weakly, her motherly instinct still impelling her to fight the young thing's battle.

'Not even then,' Mrs Northey replied with Roman firmness. 'Under no circumstances, no circumstances whatever, could Mr Northey and I countenance conduct such as hers.'

'You are sure that there's – there's no mistake, my dear?'

'Not a shadow of a mistake!' madam answered with acrimony. 'We have traced her to the man's lodging. She reached it after dark, and under – under the most disgraceful circumstances.'

Mrs Northey referred to the arrest by bailiffs, the news of which had reached Arlington Street through Lane the mercer. But the duchess took her to mean something quite different; and her Grace was shocked.

'Dear, dear,' she said in a tone of horror; and looking instinctively at her daughter, she wished that Lady Betty had not seen so much of the girl, wished still more fervently that she had not mixed herself up with her flight. 'I am infinitely sorry to hear it,' she said. 'Infinitely sorry! I confess I did not think her that kind of girl. My dear, you have indeed my sympathy.'

Mrs Northey, though she knew quite well what the duchess was thinking, shook her head as if she could add much more, but would not; and the duchess, her apologies made, rose to take leave; resolved to give her daughter such a wigging by the way as that young lady had never experienced. But while they stood in the act of making their adieux, Mr Northey entered; and his dolorous head shaking, which would have done credit to a father's funeral, detained her so long, that she was still where he found her, when an exclamation from Lady Betty, who had profited by her mother's engrossment to look out of the window, startled the party.

'Oh, la, ma'am, here she is!' the girl cried. 'I vow and declare she is!'

'Betty!' her Grace cried sharply. 'Remember yourself. What do you mean? Come, we must be going.'

'But, ma'am, she's at the door,' Lady Betty replied with a giggle. And turning and thrusting her muff into her mouth – as one well understanding the crisis – she looked over it at the party, her eyes bright with mischief.

Mrs Northey's face turned quite white. 'If this – if your daughter means that the misguided girl is returning here,' she cried, 'I will not have it.'

'It is not to be thought of!' Mr Northey chimed in. 'She would not have the audacity,' he added more pompously, 'after her behaviour.' And he was moving to the window – while the kind-hearted duchess wished herself anywhere else – when the door opened, and the servant announced, 'Sir Hervey Coke!'

The duchess gave vent to a sigh of relief, while the Northeys looked daggers at Lady Betty, the author of the false alarm. Meantime Coke advanced, his hat under his arm. 'I am really no more than an ambassador,' he said gaily. 'My principal is downstairs waiting leave to ascend. Duchess, your humble servant! Lady Betty, yours – you grow prettier every day. Mrs Northey, I have good news for you. You will be glad to hear that you were misinformed as to the object of your sister's departure from the house – about which you wrote to me.'

'Misinformed!' Mrs Northey exclaimed with a freezing look. 'I was misinformed, sir?'

'Completely, at the time you wrote to me,' Sir Hervey

answered, smiling on the party. 'As you will acknowledge in one moment.'

'On whose authority, pray?' with a sniff.

'On mine,' Coke replied. ''Twas an odd coincidence that you wrote to me, of all people.'

'Why, sir, pray?'

'Because—' he began; and there he broke off and turned to the duchess, who had made a movement as if she would withdraw. 'No,' he said, 'I hope your Grace will not go. The matter is not private.'

'Private?' Mrs Northey cried shrilly – she could control her feelings no longer. 'The hussy has taken good care it shall not be that! Private, indeed? It is not her fault if there is a man in the town who is ignorant of her disgrace!'

'Nay, ma'am, softly, if you please,' Sir Hervey interposed, with the least touch of sternness in his tone. 'You go too far.'

Mrs Northey glared at him; she was pale with anger. 'What?' she cried. 'Hoity-toity! do you think I shall not say what I like about my own sister?'

'But not about my wife!' he answered firmly.

She stepped back as if he had aimed a blow at her, so great was her surprise. 'What?' she shrieked. 'Your wife?' While the others looked at him, thunderstruck; and Lady Betty, who, on the fringe of the group, was taking in all with childish dilated eyes, uttered a scream of delight.

'Your wife?' Mr Northey gasped.

'Precisely,' Coke answered. 'My wife.'

But Mrs Northey could not, would not, believe it. She thought that he was lending himself to some cunning scheme; some plan for bringing about a reconciliation. 'Your wife?' she repeated. 'Do you mean that Sophia, my sister—'

'Preferred a quiet wedding *à deux*,' he answered, helping himself to a pinch of snuff, and smiling slightly, as at the recollection. 'Your Grace will understand,' he continued, turning with easy politeness to the duchess, 'how it amused me to read Mrs Northey's letter under such circumstances.'

But Mrs Northey was furious. 'If this be true,' she said hoarsely, 'but I do not believe it is, why did you do it? Tell me that? Until I know that I shall not believe it!'

Sir Hervey shrugged his shoulders. 'Mr Northey will believe

it, I am sure,' he said, with a look in that gentleman's direction. 'For the rest, ma'am, it was rather Lady Coke's doing than mine. She heard that her brother was about to make a ruinous marriage, and discovered that he was actually in the company and under the influence of the Irishman, Hawkesworth, whom you know. There were those who should more properly have made the effort to save him, but these failed him; and the result of it was, thanks to her, he was saved. Thanks to her, and to her only,' Sir Hervey repeated with a look, beneath which Mr Northey quailed, and his wife turned green with rage, 'since, as I said, those who should have interfered did not. But this effected, and Keith, who should have married her brother, being in attendance – well, we thought it better to avail ourselves of his services. 'Twould have been a pity, your Grace, to lose a guinea,' Coke added, his eyes twinkling, as he turned to the duchess. 'It was the best instance I've ever known of "a guinea in time saves ninety!"'

The duchess laughed heartily. ''Twas cheap at any rate, Sir Hervey,' she said. 'I am sure for my part I congratulate you.'

'I don't!' Mrs Northey cried before he could answer. 'She has behaved abominably! Abominably!' she repeated, her voice quivering with spite. For, strange human nature! here was the match made, on making which she had set her heart; yet so far was she from being pleased, or even satisfied, she could have cried with mortification. 'She has behaved infamously!'

'Tut, tut!' Sir Hervey cried.

But the angry woman was not to be silenced. 'I shall say it!' she persisted. 'I think it, and I shall say it.'

'Of Miss Maitland, as often as you please,' he retorted, bowing. 'Of Lady Coke only at your husband's peril. Of course, if you do not wish to receive her, ma'am, that is another matter.'

But on this Mr Northey interposed. 'No, no,' he cried, fussily. 'Mrs Northey is vexed, if I may say so, not unnaturally vexed by the lack of confidence in her, which Sophia has shown. But that – that is quite another thing from – from disowning her. No, no, let me be the first to wish you happiness, Coke!' And with an awkward essay at heartiness, and an automaton-like grin, he shook Sir Hervey by the hand. 'I'll fetch her up,' he continued, 'I'll fetch her up! My dear, ahem! Congratulate Sir

Hervey. It is what we wanted from the first, and though it has not come about quite as we expected, nothing could give us greater pleasure. It's an alliance welcome in every respect. Yes, yes, I'll bring her up.'

He hurried away, while the duchess hastened to add a few words of further congratulation, and Mrs Northey stood silent and waiting, her face now red, now pale. She had every reason to be satisfied, for except in the matter of Tom – and there Sophia had thwarted her selfish plans – all had turned out as she wished. But not through her, there was the rub! On the contrary, she had been duped, she felt it. She had been tricked into betraying how little heart she had, how little affection for her sister; and bitterly she resented the exposure.

But even her face cleared in a degree when Sophia appeared. As the girl moved forward on Sir Hervey's arm – who went gallantly to the door to meet her – so far from exhibiting the blushing pride of a woman vain of her conquest, glorying in the trick she had played the world, she showed but the timid, frightened face of a shrinking child. Her eyes sought the floor, nervously; her bearing was the farthest removed from exultation it was possible to conceive. So different, indeed, was she from all they had looked to see in the new Lady Coke, the heroine of this odd romance, that even Mrs Northey found the cold reconciliation on which her husband was bent more feasible, the frigid kiss more possible than she had thought; while to the duchess the bride's aspect seemed so unnatural, that she drew Sir Hervey aside and questioned him keenly.

'What have you done to her?' she said. 'That a runaway bride? Why, if she had been dragged to the altar and sold to a Jew broker she could hardly look worse, or more downhearted! Sho, man, what is it?'

'She's troubled about her brother,' Coke explained elaborately. 'She's saved him from a wretched match, but he's taken himself off, and we don't know where to look for him.'

The good-natured duchess struck him on the shoulder with her fan. 'Fudge!' she cried. 'Her brother? I don't believe it.'

'My dear duchess,' Coke remonstrated. 'Half a dozen witnesses are prepared to swear to it.'

'I don't believe it any the more for that!'

'You think she's unhappy?'

'I am sure of it.'

'Well,' Sir Hervey answered, and for a moment a gleam which the duchess could not interpret shone in his eyes, 'wait six months! If she is not happy then – I mean,' he added, hastily correcting himself, 'if she does not look happy then, I have made a mistake.'

The duchess stared. 'Or she?'

'No, I,' he answered, almost in a whisper 'I only, duchess.'

She nodded, understanding somewhat; not all. 'Oh!' she said; and looked him over, considering what kind of a lover she would have thought him in the old days when all men presented themselves in that capacity, and were measured by maiden eyes. She found him satisfactory. 'What are your plans?' she said.

'I am going to Coke Hall tonight, to give the necessary orders. There are changes to be made.'

'Quick work!' she said, smiling. 'Leaving her?'

'Yes.'

'You are not killing her with kindness then, my friend?'

'She will follow in two or three days.'

'In the meantime – does she stay here?' she asked; with a glance round the room that said much.

'Well, no,' Sir Hervey answered slowly, his face growing hard. 'I don't quite know – it has all been very sudden, you know.'

'I'll take her if you like,' the duchess said impulsively.

Sir Hervey's face grew pink 'You dear, good, great lady!' he said. 'Will you do that?'

'For you, I will,' she said, 'if it will help you?'

'Will it not,' he cried; and, stooping over her hand, he kissed it after the fashion of the day; but a little more warmly – we were going to say, a little more warmly than the duke would have approved.

While they talked, Mrs Northey had left the room, to take order for 'my lady's' packing; and Mr Northey, who was dying for a word with her on the astonishing event, had followed, after murmuring an apology and an indistinct word about a carriage. Sophia was thus left *tête-à-tête* with the one person in the room who had not approached her, or offered felicitation or compliment; but who now, after assuring herself by a hurried glance that the duchess was out of hearing, hastened to deliver her mind.

'Wait till you want to elope again, miss,' Lady Betty hissed, in a fierce whisper. 'And see if I'll help you! Oh, you deceitful cat, you! To trick me with a long story of your lover and your wrongs, and your dear, dear Irishman! And then to come back "my lady," and we're all to bow down to you. Oh, you false, humdrum creature!'

Sophia, in spite of her depression, could not refrain from a smile. 'My dear Lady Betty,' she whispered gratefully, 'I shall ever remember your kindness.'

'Don't Lady Betty me, miss!' the girl retorted, thrusting her pretty, eager face close to the other's. 'Do you know that I am to go into the country, ma'am? and be put to school again, and the backboard; and lose the Ridotto on the 17th, and the frolic at the King's House Miss Ham had arranged – and all for helping you? All for helping you, ma'am! See if I ever do a good-natured thing again, as long as I live!'

'My poor Lady Betty! I am so sorry!'

'But that's not all,' the angry little beauty cried. 'Didn't you lead me to think, ma'am – oh, yes, madam, you are now,' with a swift little curtsey – 'to think that 'twas all for love and the world lost! That 'twas a dear delicious elopement, almost as good as running away myself! And that all the town would be wild to hear of it, and every girl envy me for being in it! Romance? And the world well lost! Oh, you deceitful madam! But see if I ever speak to you again! That's all, my lady!'

Sophia, with a smile that trembled on the brink of tears, was about to crave her pardon, when the approach of the duchess and Sir Hervey closed her mouth. 'Your sister has gone up-stairs?' her Grace said.

'Only to take order for my packing,' Sophia answered.

'I have just been talking to your husband,' the duchess continued, and smiled faintly at the hot blush that at the word rose to Sophia's brow. 'If you are willing, my dear, you shall keep Lady Betty company until he returns.'

'Returns?' Sophia exclaimed.

'From Coke Hall,' Sir Hervey interposed glibly, 'whither I must go tonight, sweet, to give orders for our reception. In the meantime the duchess has most kindly offered to take care of you, and has also promised that, when you go into the country, Lady Betty shall go with you and keep you company until the duke leaves town.'

The tears rose in Sophia's eyes at this double, this wonderful proof of his thought for her; and through her tears her eyes thanked him though it was only by a swift glance, averted as soon as perceived. In a tremulous voice she made her acknowledgements to the duchess. It was most kind of her Grace. And any – any arrangement that Sir Hervey thought fit to make for her – would be to her liking.

'Dear me,' the duchess said, laughing, 'a most obedient wife. My dear, how long do you think you will play the patient Grizel?'

Poor Sophia drooped, blushing under the question, but was quickly relieved by Lady Betty. 'Oh la!' the young lady cried, 'am I really, really, to go with her? When, ma'am? When?'

'When I choose,' the duchess answered sharply. 'That's enough for you. Thank your stars, and Sir Hervey, miss, that it's not back to the schoolroom, as it was to be.'

'Yes, ma'am,' Lady Betty murmured obediently.

But a little later, when they were alone together in her room, she fell upon Sophia, and pinched and tweaked her in a way that implied a full pardon. 'Oh, you double-faced madam!' she cried. 'You sly thing! But I'll be even with you! I'll make love to him before your eyes, see if I don't! After all I like him better than O'Rourke! You remember:

" 'O'Rourke's noble fare
Will ne'er be forgot,
By those who were there
And those who were not!'

For Coke, he's as grave as grave! But he's a dear for all that!'

'A dear!' Sophia repeated, opening her eyes

'Yes, a dear! Not that you need be proud, my lady! I'll soon have his heart from you, see if I don't. What'll you say to that?'

But Lady Coke, from whom Sir Hervey had parted gravely a few minutes before, did not answer. She sat silent, conjuring up his face – in a new light. She did not acknowledge that he was a dear. She felt the same shrinking from him, the same fear of him, that had depressed her from the moment she knew the knot tied, the thing done. But she began to see him in a new light. The duchess liked him, and Lady Betty thought him a dear? Would Lady Betty – even Lady Betty have taken him?

At that moment, in the little house at the end of Clarges Row, three persons sat vowing vengeance over Tom's wedding feast. One with the rage of a gamester baffled by an abnormal run of the cards, beaten by the devil's own luck, breathed naught but flames and fury, pistols, and nose-slitting. The second, who stormed and wept by turns, broke things with her hands and gnawed them, in futile passion, with her strong white teeth, could have kissed him for that last word. The third, mulcted in purse, and uncertain on whom to turn, chattered impotent, senile curses. 'I shall die a beggar!' he cried; and cursed his companions. 'I shall die in a ditch! But I'll not die alone, I'll not be the only one to suffer!'

'By G—d, I'll show you better than that!' the Irishman answered between oaths. 'They are three and we are three Wait! I'll have them watched every minute of the day, and by-and-by it'll be our turn. A little money—'

'Money!' old Grocott shrieked, clawing the air. And he got up hurriedly, and sat down again. 'Always money! More money! But you'll have none of mine! Not a farthing! Not a farthing more!'

'Why not, fool, if it will bring in a thousand per cent,' Hawkesworth growled. The thin veneer of fashion that had duped poor Sophia was gone. With the loss of the venture, on which he had staked his all, the man stood forth a plain unmitigated ruffian. 'Why not?' he continued, bending his brows. 'D'you think anything is to be done without money? And I shall risk more than money, old skinflint!'

The woman looked at the man, her eyes gleaming; her face under the red that splashed it, was livid. 'What'll you do?' she muttered, 'what'll you do?' She had been – almost a lady. The chance would never, never, never recur! When she thought of what she had lost, and how nearly she had won it, she was frantic. 'What'll you do?' she repeated.

'Hark, I hear the sound of coaches
The hour of attack approaches,
And turns our lead to gold!'

Hawkesworth hummed for answer. 'Gold is good, but I'll wait my opportunity, and I'll have gold and – a pound of flesh!'

'Ah!' she said thirstily And then to her father: 'Do you hear, old man? You'll give him what he wants.'

'I'll not!' he screamed. 'I shall die a beggar! I shall die in a ditch! I tell you I—' his voice suddenly quavered off as he met his daughter's eyes. He was silent.

'I think you will,' she said.

'I think so,' the Irishman murmured grimly.

CHAPTER XIV

The First Stage

A WEEK later the sun of a bright May morning shone on King's Square, once known as Monmouth, now as Soho, Square. Before the duke's town house on the east side of the Square – on the left of the King's Statue which then, and for many years to come, faced Monmouth House – a travelling carriage waited, attended by a pair of mounted grooms, and watched at a respectful distance by a half-circle of idle loungers. It was in readiness to convey Lady Coke and Lady Betty Cochrane into Sussex. On the steps of the house lounged no less a person than the duke himself; who, unlike his proud Grace of Petworth, was at no pains to play a part. On the contrary. he sunned himself where he pleased, nor thought it beneath him to display the anxiety on his daughter's account which would have become a meaner man. He knew, too, what he was about in the present matter; neither the four sturdy big-boned horses, tossing their tasselled heads, nor the pair of armed outriders, nor Watkyns, Sir Hervey's valet, waiting hat in hand at the door of the chariot, escaped his scrutiny. He had the tongue of a buckle secured here and a horse's hoof lifted there – and his

Grace was right, there was a stone in it. He inquired if the relay at Croydon was ordered, he demanded whether it was certain that Sir Hervey's horses would meet them at Lewes. Finally – for he knew that part of the country – he asked what was the state of the roads beyond Grinstead, and whether the Ouse was out.

'Not to hurt, your Grace,' Watkyns who had come up with the carriage answered. 'The roads will be good if no more rain falls, if your Grace pleases.'

'You will make East Grinstead about five, my man?'

''Tween four and five, your Grace, we should.'

'And Lewes – by two tomorrow?'

The servant was about to answer when the duchess and the two young ladies, followed by Lady Betty's woman, appeared at the duke's elbow. The duchess holding a fan between her eyes and the sun, looked anxiously at the horses. 'I don't like them to be on the road alone,' she said. 'Coke should have come for them. My dear,' she continued, turning to Sophia, 'your husband should have come for you instead of sending. I don't understand such manners, and a week married.'

Sophia, blushing deeply, did not answer. She knew quite well why Sir Hervey had not come, and she was thankful when Lady Betty took the word.

'Oh, ma'am,' she child cried. 'I am sure we shall do well enough; 'tis the charmingest thing in the world to be going a journey, and this morning the most delicious of all mornings. We are going to drive all day, and at night lie at an inn, and tell one another a world of secrets. I declare I could jump out of my skin! I never was so happy in my life!'

'And leaving us!' her Grace said in a tone of reproach.

Lady Betty looked a trifle dashed at that, but her father pinched her ear. 'Leaving town, too, Bet,' he said good-naturedly. 'That's more serious, isn't it?'

'I am sure, sir, I – if my mother wishes me to stay!'

'No, go, child, and enjoy yourself,' the duchess answered kindly. 'And I hope Lady Coke may put some sense into that feather brain of yours. My dear,' she continued, embracing Sophia, 'you'll take care of her?'

'I will, I will indeed!' Sophia cried, clinging to her. 'And thank you a thousand times, ma'am, for your kindness to me.'

'Pooh, pooh, 'tis nothing,' her Grace said. 'But all the same,' she added, her anxiety returning, 'I wish Sir Hervey were with you, or you had not those jewels.'

'Coke should have thought of it,' the duke answered. 'But there, kiss Bet, my love, and tell her to be a good puss. The sooner they are gone, the sooner they will be there.'

'You have your cordial, Betty?' the duchess asked anxiously.

'Yes, ma'am.'

'And the saffron drops, and your "Holy Living"? Pettitt,' to the woman; 'you'll see her Ladyship uses the face wash every morning, and wears her warm nightrail. And see that the flowered chintz is aired before she puts it on'

'Yes, sure, your Grace.'

'And I hope you'll come back safe, and won't be robbed!'

'Pooh, pooh!' the duke said. 'Since Cook was hanged last year – and he was ten times out of eleven at Mimms and Finchley – there has been nothing done on the Lewes Road. And they are too strong to be stopped by one man. You have been reading Johnson's *Lives*, and are frightening yourself for nothing, my dear. There, let them go, and they'll be in Lewes two hours before nightfall. A good journey, my lady, and my service to Sir Hervey.'

'I should not mind if it were not for the child's jewels,' her Grace muttered in a low tone.

'Pooh, the carriage might be robbed twenty times,' the duke answered, 'and they would not be found – where they are. Goodbye, Bet. Goodbye! Be a good girl, and say your prayers!'

'And mind you use the almond wash,' her Grace cried.

Lady Betty cried 'yes' to everything, and, amid a fire of similar advices, the two were shut into the chariot. From the window Lady Betty continued to wave her handkerchief, until, Watkyns and the woman having taken their seats, outside, the postboys cracked their whips and the heavy vehicle moved forward. A moment, and the house and the kind wistful faces on the steps disappeared, the travellers swung right-handed into Sutton Street, and, rolling briskly through St Giles's and Holborn, were presently on London Bridge, at that time the only link connecting London and Southwark.

Lady Betty was in a humour that matched the sparkle of the bright May morning She was leaving the delights of town, but she had a journey before her, a thing exhilarating in youth; and at the end of that she had a vision of lordlings, knights, and country squires, waiting in troops to be reduced to despair by her charms. The dazzling surface of the stream, as the tide running up from the pool sparkled and glittered in the sun, was not brighter than her eyes – that now were here, now there, now everywhere. Now she stuck her head out of one window, now out of the other; now she flashed a smile at a passing apprentice, and left him gasping; now she cast a flower at an astonished teemster, or tilted her pretty nose at the odours that pervaded the Borough. The grooms rode more briskly for her presence, the postboys looked grinning over their shoulders; even the gibbet that marked the turn to Tooting failed to depress her airy spirits.

And Sophia? Sophia sat fighting for contentment. By turns the better and the worse mood possessed her. In the better, she thought with gratitude of her lot – a lot happy in comparison of the fate which she had so narrowly escaped; happy, even in comparison of that fate which would have been hers, if, after escaping from Hawkesworth, she had been forced to return to her sister's house. If it was goodbye to love, if the glow of passion could never be hers, she was not alone. She had a friend from whose kindness she had all to expect that any save a lover could give; a firm and true friend whose generosity and thoughtfulness touched her every hour, and must have touched her more deeply, but for that other mood which in its turn possessed her.

In that mood she lived the past again, she thirsted for that which had not been hers. She regretted, not her dear Irishman – for he had never existed save in her fancy, and she knew it now – but the delicious thrill, the warm emotion which the thought of him, the sight of him, the sound even of his voice, had been wont to arouse. In this mood she could not patiently give up love; she could not willingly resign the woman's dream. In this mood she cried out on the prudence that, to save her from the talk of a week, had deprived her of love for a life. She saw in her husband's kindness, calculation; in his thoughtfulness, the wisdom of the serpent. She shook with resentment, and burnt with shame

And then, even while she thought of him most harshly, her

conscience pricked her, and in a moment she was in the melting temper; while Lady Betty chattered by her side, and town changed to country, and, leaving Brixton Causey, they rattled by the busy inns of Streatham. with the church on their right and the hills rolling upward leftwise to the blue.

Four and a half miles to Croydon and then dinner. 'Now let me see them,' Lady Betty urged. 'Do, that's a dear creature! Here we are quite safe!'

Sophia pleaded that it was too near town. 'Wait until we are through Croydon,' she said. 'They say, you know, the nearer town, the greater the danger!'

'Then, as soon as we are out of Croydon?' Lady Betty cried, hugging her. 'You promise?'

'Yes, I promise.'

'Oh, I know if they were mine I should be looking at them all day!' Lady Betty rejoined; and then shrieked and threw herself back in the carriage as they passed Croydon gibbet that stood at the ninth milestone, opposite the turn to Wallington. The empty irons swaying in the wind provided her with shudders until the carriage drew up in Croydon Street, where with recovered cheerfulness, the ladies alighted and dined at the Crown, under the eye and protection of Watkyns. After a stay of an hour, they took the road again up Banstead Downs, where they walked a little at the steeper part of the way, but presently outstripping the carriage above the turn to Reigate, grew frightened in that solitude, and were glad to step in again. So down and up, and down again through the woods about Coulsdon, where the rabbits peered at them through the bracken, and raising their white scuts, loped away at leisure to their burrows.

'Now!' Lady Betty cried, when they were again in the full glare of the afternoon sun. 'Now is the time! There is no one within a mile of us. The grooms,' she continued, after putting out her head and looking back, 'are half a mile behind.'

Sophia nodded reluctantly. 'You must get up, then,' she said.

Lady Betty did so, and Sophia, to whom the secret had been committed the day before, lifted the leather valance that hung before the seat. Touching a spring she drew from the apparently solid woodwork of the seat – which was no more than three inches thick, so that a mail could be placed beneath it – a shallow covered drawer about twenty inches wide. She held this until Lady Betty had dropped the valance, and the two could take their seats again. Then she inserted a tiny key which she took from her bodice, into a keyhole cunningly placed at the side of the drawer – so that when the latter was in its place the keyhole was invisible. She turned the key, but before she raised the lid, bade Lady Betty look out of the window again, and assure herself that the grooms were at a distance.

'You provoking creature!' Lady Betty cried. 'They are where they were – a good half-mile behind. And – yes, one of them has dismounted, and is doing something to his saddle. Oh! let me look, I am dying to see them!'

Sophia raised the lid, and her companion gasped, then screamed with delight. Over the white Genoa of the jewel case shone, and rippled, and sparkled in rills of liquid fire, a necklace, tiara, and bracelet of perfect stones, perfectly matched. Lady Betty had expected much; her mother had told her that, at the coronation of '27, Lady Coke's jewels had taken the world by storm; and that no one under the rank of a peeress had worn any like them But reality exceeded imagination; she could not control her delight, admiration, envy. She hung over the tray, her eyes bright as the stones they reflected, her cheeks catching the soft lustre of the jewels.

'Oh, ma'am, now I know you are married!' she cried. 'Things like these are not for poor lambkins! I vow I grow afraid of you. My Lady Brook will have nothing like them, and couldn't carry them if she had! She'd sink under them, the wee thing! And my Lady Carteret won't do better, though she is naught but airs and graces, and he's fifty-five if he's a day! When you go to the Drawing-Room, they'll die of envy. And to think the dear things lie under that dingy valance! I declare, I wonder they don't shine through!'

'Sir Hervey's father planned the drawer,' Sophia explained, 'for the carriage he built for his wife's foreign tour. And when Sir Hervey had a new carriage about six years ago, the drawer was repeated as a matter of course. Once his mother was stopped and robbed when she had the diamonds with her, but they were not found.'

'And had you never seen them until yesterday?'

'Never.'

'And he'd never told you about them until they sent them from the bank, with that note?'

Sophia sighed as she glanced at the jewels. 'He had not mentioned them,' she said.

Lady Betty hugged her ecstatically: 'The dear devoted man!' she cried. 'I vow you are the luckiest woman in the world! There's not a girl in town would not give her two eyes for them! And mighty few would not be ready to sell themselves body and soul for them! And he sends them to you with scarce a word, but "Lady Coke from her husband!" – and where they are to be hidden to travel. I vow,' Lady Betty continued gaily, 'if I were in your shoes, my dear, I should jump out of my skin with joy! I – why— what's the matter, are you ill?'

For Sophia had suddenly burst into violent weeping; and now, with the diamonds lying in her lap, was sobbing on the other's shoulder as if her heart would break. 'If you knew!' was all she could say: 'If you knew!'

The young girl, amazed and frightened, patted her shoulder, tried to soothe her, asked her again and again: What? If she only knew what?'

'The sight of them kills me!' Sophia cried, struggling in vain with her emotion. 'They are not mine! I have no – no right to them!'

Lady Betty raised her pretty eyebrows in despair. 'But they *are* yours.' she said. 'Your husband has given them to you.'

'I would rather he killed me!' Sophia cried; her feelings, overwrought for a week past, finding sudden vent.

Lady Betty gasped. 'Oh!' she said. 'I don't understand, I am afraid. Doesn't he' – in an awe-struck tone – 'doesn't he love you, then?'

'He?' Sophia cried bitterly. 'Oh, yes, I suppose he does. He pities me at any rate. It's I—'

'You don't love him?'

Sophia shook her head.

The younger girl shivered. 'That must be – horrible,' she whispered.

Her tone was so grave that Sophia raised her head, and smiled drearily through her tears. 'You don't understand yet,' she said. 'It's only a form, our marriage. He offered to marry me to save me from scandal. And I agreed. But since he gave me the jewels that were his mother's, I – I am frightened, child. I know now that I have done wrong. I should not have let him persuade me.'

'Why did you?' Lady Betty asked softly.

Sophia told her, with all the circumstances of Hawkesworth's villainy, Tom's infatuation, her own dilemma, Sir Hervey's offer, and the terms of it.

After a brief silence, 'It was generous,' Lady Betty said, her eyes shining. 'I think I should – I think I could love him, my Lady Coke. And since that, you have only seen him one day?'

'That is all.'

'And he kept his word? I mean – he wasn't silly?'

'No.'

'He has been kind too. There is no denying that?'

'It is that which is killing me!' Sophia cried with returning excitement. 'It is his kindness kills me, girl! Cannot you understand that?'

Lady Betty declined to say she could. And for quite a long time she was silent. She sat gazing from the carriage, her eyes busied, to all appearance, with the distant view of Godstone Church; but a person watching her closely might have detected a gleam of mischief, a sudden flash of amusement that leapt into them as she looked; and that could scarcely have had to do with this church. She seemed at a loss, however, for matter of comfort; or she was singularly unfortunate in the choice of it. For when she spoke again she could hit on no better topic to compose Sophia's mind than a long story, which the naughty girl had no right to know, of Sir Hervey's dealings with his old flames. It is true, nods and winks formed so large a part of the tale, and the rest was so involved, that Sophia could not even arrive at the ladies' names. 'But,' as Lady Betty concluded mysteriously, 'it may serve to ease your mind, my dear. You may be sure he won't trouble you long. La! child, the things I've heard of him – but there, I mustn't tell you.'

'No,' Sophia answered primly. 'Certainly not, if you please.'

'Of course not. But you may take it from me, the first pretty face he sees – why, Sophy! what is it? What is it?'

No wonder she screamed. Sophia had gripped her arm with one hand; with the other she was striving to cover the treasure that lay forgotten on her lap. 'What is it?' Betty repeated frantically. There is nothing more terrifying than a silent alarm ill-understood.

The next moment she saw – and understood. Beside Sophia's window, riding abreast of the carriage, in such a position that only his horse's head, by forging an instant to the front, had betrayed his presence, was a cloaked stranger. Lady Betty caught no more than a glimpse of him, but that was enough. Apart from the doubt how long he had ridden there, inspecting the jewels at his leisure, his appearance was calculated to scare less nervous travellers. Though the day was mild, he wore a heavy riding cloak, the collar of which rose to the height of his cheek bone, where it very nearly met the uncocked leaf of his hat. Between the two, and eye bright and threatening gleamed forth. The rest of his features were lost in the depths of a fierce black riding wig; but his great holsters, and long swinging sword, seemed to show that his errand was anything but peaceful.

The moment his one eye met Lady Betty's gaze, he fell back; and that instant Sophia used to close the jewel case, and turn the key. To lower the drawer to the floor of the carriage, and cover it with her skirts was the work of a second, then still trembling, she put out her head, and looked back along the road. The man had pulled his horse into a walk, and was now a hundred paces behind them. Even at that distance, his cloaked figure as he lounged along the turf beside the track, loomed a dark blot on the road.

Sophia drew in her head. 'Quick!' she cried. 'Do you stand up and watch him, Betty, while I put the case away. Tell me in a moment if he comes on or is likely to overtake us.'

Lady Betty complied. 'He is walking still,' she said, her head out on one side. 'Now the grooms – lazy beasts, they should have been here – are passing him. La, what a turn it gave me. He had an eye – I hope to goodness we shall never meet the wretch again.'

'I hope we may never meet him after nightfall,' Sophia answered with a shudder. And she clicked the drawer home, dropped the valance in front of the seat, and rose from her knees.

'I noticed one thing, the left-hand corner of his cloak was

patched,' Lady Betty said, as she drew in her head. 'And I should know his horse among a hundred: chestnut, with white forelegs, and a scarred knee.'

'He saw them, he must have seen them!' Sophia cried in great distress. 'Oh, why did I take them out!'

'But if he meant mischief he would have stopped us then,' Lady Betty replied. 'The grooms were half a mile behind, and I'll be bound Watkyns was asleep.'

'He dared not here, because of these houses,' Sophia moaned, as they rolled by a small inn, the outpost of the little hamlet of Sew Chapel Green, between Lingfield and Turner's Heath. 'He will wait until we are in some lonely spot, in a wood, or crossing a common, or—'

'Sho!' Lady Betty cried contemptuously – the jewels were not hers, and weighed less heavily on her mind. 'We are only five miles from Grinstead, see, there is the milestone, and it is early in the afternoon. He'll not rob us here if he be Turpin himself.'

'All the same,' Sophia cried, 'I wish the diamonds were safe at Lewes.'

'Why, child, they are your own!' Lady Betty answered. 'If you lose them, whose is the loss?'

But Sophia, whether she agreed or had her own views of the fact, appeared to draw little comfort from it. As the horses slowly climbed the hill and again descended the slope to Felbridge, her head was more often out of the window than in the carriage. She beckoned to the grooms to come on; she prayed Watkyns, who, sure enough, was asleep, to be on the alert; she bade the post-boys whip on. Nor did she show herself at ease, or heave a sigh of relief, until the gibbet at the twenty-ninth milestone was safely passed, and the carriage rattled over the pavement of East Grinstead.

CHAPTER XV

A Squire of Dames

TO ONE of the travellers the bustle of the town was more than welcome. It was Thursday, market day at East Grinstead, and the post-boys pushed their way with difficulty through the streets teeming with chapmen and butter women, and here bleating with home-going sheep, there alive with the squeaking of pigs. Outside the White Lion a jovial half-dozen of graziers were starting home in company; for the roads were less safe on market evenings than on other days. In front of the Dorset Arms, where our party was to lie, a clumsy carrier's wain, drawn by oxen, stood waiting. The horse-block was beset by country bucks mounting after the ordinary; and in the yard a post-chaise was being wheeled into place for the night by the united efforts of two or three stable-boys. Apparently it had just arrived, for the horses, still smoking, were being led to the stable, through the press of beasts and helpers.

Sophia heaved a sigh of relief as the stir of the crowd sank into her mind. When Lady Betty, after they had washed and refreshed themselves, suggested that, until the disorder in the house abated, they would be as well strolling through the town, she made no demur; and, followed at a distance by one of the grooms, they sallied forth. The first thing they visited was the half-ruined church. After this they sat awhile in the churchyard, and then from the Sackville Almshouses watched the sun go down behind the heights of Worth Forest. They were both pleased with the novel scene, and Lady Betty, darting her arch glances hither and thither, and counting a score of conquests, drew more than one smile from her grave companion. True, these were but interludes, and poor Sophia, brooding on the future, looked sad twice for once she looked merry; but their fright in the carriage had no part in her depression. She had forgotten it in the sights of this strange place, when, almost at the inn door, it was forced on her attention.

She happened to look back to see if the groom was following, and to her horror caught sight, not of the groom, but of the cloaked stranger. It was evident he was dogging them, for the moment his eyes met hers he vanished from sight. There were still many abroad, belated riders exchanging last words before they parted, or topers cracking jokes through open windows; and the man was lost among these before Lady Betty had even seen him.

But Sophia had seen him; and she felt all her terrors return upon her. Trembling at every shadow – and the shadows were thickening, the streets were growing dark – she hurried her companion into the inn, nor rested until she had assured herself that the carriage was under lock and key in the chaise-house. Even then she was in two minds; apprehending everything, seeing danger in either course. Should she withdraw the diamonds from their hiding-place and conceal them about her person, or in the chamber which she shared with Lady Betty? Or should she leave them where they were in accordance with Sir Hervey's directions?

She decided on the last course in the end, but with misgivings. The fate of the jewels had come in her mind to be one with her fate. To lose them while they were in her care seemed to her one with appropriating them; and from that she shrank with an instinctive, overmastering delicacy, that spoke more strongly than any word of the mistake she had made in her marriage. They were his family jewels, his mother's jewels, the jewels of the women of his house; and she panted to restore them to his hands. She felt that only by restoring them to him safe, unaccepted, unworn, could she retain her self-respect, or her independence.

Naturally, Lady Betty found her anxiety excessive; and at supper, seeing her start at every sound, rallied her on her timidity. Their bedroom was at the back of the house, and looked through one window on the inn-yard and the door of the chaise-house. 'I see clearly you would have been happier supping upstairs,' Lady Betty whispered, taking advantage of an instant when the servants were out of earshot. 'You do nothing but listen. Shall I go up, as if for my handkerchief, and see that all is right?'

'Oh, no, no!' Sophia cried.

'Oh, yes, yes, is what you mean,' the other retorted good-naturedly; and was half-way across the room before Sophia could protest. 'I am going upstairs for something I've forgotten, Watkyns,' Lady Betty cried, as she passed the servant.

Sophia, listening and balancing her spoon in her hands, awaited her return; and the moments passed, and passed, and still Lady Betty did not come back. Sophia grew nervous and more nervous; rose at last to follow her, and sat down again, ashamed of the impulse. At length, when the waiter had gone out to hasten the second course, and Watkyns' back was turned, she could bear it no longer. She jumped up and slipped out of the room, passed two gaping servants at the foot of the stairs, and in a moment had darted up. Without waiting for a light, she groped her way along the narrow passage that led to the room she shared with Lady Betty. A window on the left looked into the inn-yard and admitted a glimmer of reflected light; but it was not this, it was something she heard as she passed it, that brought her to a sudden stand beside the casement. From the room she was seeking came the sound of a low voice and a stifled laugh. An instant Sophia fancied that Lady Betty was lingering there talking to her woman; and she felt a spark of annoyance. Then – what she thought she could never remember. For her eyes, looking mechanically through the panes beside her, saw, a little short of the fatal chaise-house, a patch of bright light, proceeding doubtless from the unshuttered window of the bedroom, and erect in the full of it the cloaked figure of the strange rider – of the man who had dogged them!

He was looking upwards at the illuminated window, his hat raised a little from his head, the arm that held it interposed between Sophia's eyes and his face. Still she knew him. She had not a doubt of his identity. The candle-rays fell brightly on the thick black wig, on the patched corner of the cloak, raised by the pose of his arm; and in a whirl of confused thoughts and fears, Sophia felt her knees shake under her.

A fresh whisper in the room was the signal for a low giggle. The man bowed and moved a step nearer, still bowing; which brought his knees against the sloping shaft of a cart that was set conveniently beneath the window. Sophia – a shiver running down her back as she saw how easily he could ascend – began to understand. The villain was tampering with Lady Betty's maid! Probably he was already in league with the woman; certainly, to judge by the sounds that reached the listener's ear – for again she caught a suppressed titter – he was on terms with her.

Sophia felt all a woman's rage against a woman, and wasted no further time on thought. She had courage and to spare, her fears for the jewels notwithstanding. In a twinkling she was at the door, had flung it open, and, burning with indignation, had bounced into the middle of the room, prepared to annihilate the offender. Yet not prepared for what she was. In the room was only Lady Betty; who, as she entered, sprang from the window and stood confronting her with crimson cheeks.

'Betty!' Sophia gasped. 'Betty?' And stood as if turned to stone; her face growing harder and harder, and harder. At last – 'Lady Betty, what does this mean?' she asked in icy accents.

The girl giggled and shook her hair over her flushed face and wilful eyes; but did not answer.

'What does it mean?' Sophia repeated. 'I insist on an answer.'

Lady Betty pouted and half turned her back. 'Oh, la!' she cried, at last, pettishly shrugging her shoulders. 'Don't talk like that! You frighten me out of my wits! Instead of talking, we'd better close the window, unless you want him to be as wise as we are.'

'Him!' Sophia cried, out of patience with the girl's audacity. 'Him? Am I to understand, then, that you have been talking through the window? You, a young lady in my company to a man whom you never saw until today? A strange man met on the road, and of whose designs you have been warned? I cannot, I cannot believe it! I cannot believe my eyes, Lady Betty!' she continued warmly. 'You, at this window, at this hour, talking to a common stranger? A stranger of whose designs I have warned you? Why, if your woman, miss, if your woman were to be guilty of such conduct, I could hardly believe it! I could hardly believe that I saw aright!'

And honestly Sophia was horrified; shocked, as well as puzzled. So that it seemed to her no more than fitting, no more than a late awakening to decency when the culprit, who had accomplished – but with trembling fingers – the closing of the window, pressed her handkerchief to her eyes, and flung herself on the bed. Sophia saw her shoulders heave with emotion, and hoped that at last she understood what she had done; that at last she appreciated what others would think of such reckless, such inexplicable conduct. And my lady prepared to drive home the lesson. Judge of her surprise, when Lady Betty cut her first words short by springing up as hastily as she had thrown herself down, and disclosed a face convulsed not with sorrow, but with laughter.

'Oh, you silly, silly thing!' she cried; and before Sophia could prevent her, she had cast her arms round her neck, and was hugging her in a paroxysm of mirth. 'Oh, you dear, silly old thing! And it's only a week since you eloped yourself!'

'I!' Sophia cried, enraged by the ungenerous taunt. And she tried fiercely but vainly to extricate herself.

'Yes, you! You! And were married at Dr Keith's chapel! And now how you talk! Mercy, ma'am, butter won't melt in your mouth now!'

'Lady Betty!' Sophia cried, in a cold rage, 'let me go! Do you hear? Let me go! How dare you talk to me like that? How dare you?' she continued, trembling with indignation. 'What has my conduct to do with yours? Or how can you presume to mention it in the same breath? I may have been foolish, I may have been indiscreet, but I never, never, stooped to—'

'Call it the highway at once,' said the unrepentant one,' for I know that is what you have in your mind.'

Sophia gasped. 'If you can put it so clearly,' she said, 'I hope you have more sense than appears from the – the—'

'Lightness of my conduct!' Lady Betty cried, with a fresh peal of laughter. 'Oh, you dear, silly old thing, I would not be your daughter for something!'

'Lady Betty?'

'You dear, don't you Lady Betty me! A highwayman? Oh, it is too delicious! Too diverting! Are you sure it isn't Turpin come to life again? Or Cook of Barnet? Or the gallant Macheath from the Opera? Why, you old dear, the man is nothing better nor worse than a – lover!'

'A lover?' Sophia cried.

'Well, yes – a lover,' Lady Betty repeated, lightly enough; but to her credit be it said, she did blush at last – a little, and folded her handkerchief into a hard square, and looked at it with an air of – of comparative bashfulness. 'Dear me, yes – a lover. He followed us from London; and to make the deeper impression, I suppose, made a Guy Fawkes of himself! That's all!'

'All?' Sophia said in amazement.

'Yes, all, all, all!' Lady Betty retorted, ridding herself in an instant of her penitent air. 'All! And aren't you glad, my dear, to find that you were frightening yourself for nothing!'

'But who is he – the gentleman?' Sophia asked faintly.

'Oh, he is not a gentleman,' the little flirt answered, tossing her head with pretty but cruel contempt. 'He's' – with a giggle – 'at least he calls himself – Mr Fanshaw.'

'Mr Fanshaw?' Sophia repeated; and first wondered and then remembered where she had heard the name. 'Can it be the same?' she exclaimed, reddening in spite of herself as she met Lady Betty's eye. 'Is he a small, foppish man, full of monstrous airs and graces, and – and rather underbred?'

Lady Betty clapped her hands. 'Yes,' she cried. 'Drawn to the life! Where did you see him? But I'll tell you if you like. 'Twas at Lane's, ma'am!'

'Yes, it was,' Sophia answered a trifle sternly. 'But how do you know, miss?'

'Well, I do know,' Lady Betty answered. And again she had the grace to blush and look down. 'At least – I thought it likely. Because, you old dear, don't you remember a note you picked up at Vauxhall gardens, that was meant for me? Yes, I vow you do. Well, 'twas from him.'

'But that doesn't explain,' Sophia said keenly, 'why you guessed that I saw him at Lane's shop?'

'Oh,' Lady Betty answered, wincing a little. 'To be sure, no, it doesn't. But he's – he's just Lane's son. There, now you know it!'

'Mr Fanshaw?'

Lady Betty nodded, a little shamefacedly. ''Tis so,' she said. 'For the name, it's his vanity. He's the vainest creature, he thinks every lady is in love with him. Never was such a sport as to lead him on. I am sure I thought I should have died of laughing before you came in and frightened me out of my wits!'

Sophia looked at her gravely. 'I am sure of something else,' she said.

'Now you are going to preach!' Lady Betty cried; and tried to stop her mouth.

'No, I am not, but you gave me a promise, in my room in Arlington Street, Betty, that you would have nothing more to do with the writer of that note.'

Lady Betty sat down on the bed and looked piteously at her companion. 'Oh, I didn't, did I?' she said; and at last she seemed to be really troubled. 'I didn't, did I? 'Twas only that I would not correspond with him. I protest it was only that. And I have not. I've not indeed,' she protested. 'But when I found him under the window, and heard that he was Mohocking about the country in that monstrous cloak and hat, for all the world like the Beggar's Opera on Horseback, and all for the love of me, it was not in flesh and blood not to divert oneself with him! He's such a creature! You've no notion what a creature it is!'

'I've this notion,' Sophia answered seriously. 'If you did not promise, you will promise. What is more, I shall send for him, and I shall tell him, in your presence, that this ridiculous pursuit must cease.'

'But if he will not?' Lady Betty asked, with an arch look. 'I am supposed – to have charms, you know?'

'I shall tell your father.'

'La, ma'am,' the child retorted, with a curtsey, 'you are married! There is no doubt about that!'

Sophia reddened, but did not answer; and for a moment Betty sat on the bed, picking the coverlet with her fingers and looking sulky. On a sudden she leapt up and threw her arms round Sophia's neck. 'Well, do as you like,' she cried effusively. 'After all, 'twill be a charming scene, and do him good, the fright! Don't think,' the little minx continued, tossing her head disdainfully, 'that I ever wish to see him again, or would let him touch me with his little finger! Not I! But – one does not like to—'

'We'll have no *but*, if you please,' Sophia said gently but firmly. She had grown wondrous wise in the space of a short month. 'Whatever he is, he is no fit mate for Lady Betty Cochrane. and shall not get her into trouble! I'll call your woman, and bid her go find him.'

Fortunately the maid knocked at the door at that moment. She came, anxious to learn if anything ailed them, and why they did not return to finish their supper. They declined to do so, bade her have it removed, and a pot of tea brought; then Sophia told her what she wanted, and having instructed her, dispatched her on her errand.

As assignation, through her woman, was the guise in which the affair appeared to Mr Fanshaw's eyes when he got the message. And great was his joy, not less his triumph. Was ever lover, he asked himself, more completely or more quickly favoured? Could Rochester or Bellamour, Tom Hervey or my Lord Lincoln have made a speedier conquest? No wonder his thoughts, always on the sanguine side, ran riot as he mounted the stairs; or that his pulses beat to the tune of—

But he so teased me,
And he so pleased me,
What I did, you must have done!

as he followed the maid along the passage.

The only sour in his cup, indeed, arose from his costume. That he knew to be better fitted for the road than for a lady's chamber; to be calculated rather to strike the youthful eye and captivate the romantic imagination at a distance than to become a somewhat puny person at short range. As he passed an old Dutch mirror, that stood in an angle of the stairs, he made a desperate attempt to reduce the wig, and control the cloak, but in vain, it was only to accentuate the boots. Worse, his guide looked to see why he lingered, caught him in the act, and tittered; after which he was forced to affect a haughty contempt and follow. But what would he not have given at that moment for his olive and silver, a copy of Mr Walpole's birth-night suit? Or for his French grey and Mechlin, and the new tie-wig that had cost his foolish father seven guineas at Protin, the French perruquier's? Much, yet what mattered it, since he had conquered? Since even while he thought of these drawbacks, he paused on the threshold of his lady's chamber, and saw before him his divinity – pouting, mutinous, charming. She was standing by the table waiting for him with downcast eyes, and the most ravishing air in the world.

Strange to say he felt no doubt. It was his firm belief, born of Wycherley and fostered on Crêbillon that all women were alike, and from the three beauty Fitzroys to Oxford Kate, were wax in the hands of a pretty fellow. It was this belief that had spurred him to great enterprises, if not as yet to great conquests; and yet so powerfully does virtue impress even the sceptics, that he faltered as he entered the room. Besides that ladyship of hers dashed him! He could not deny that his heart bounced painfully. But courage! As he recalled the invitation he had received, he recovered himself. He advanced, simpering; he was ready at a word, to fall at her feet. 'Oh, ma'am, 'tis a happiness beyond my desert,' he babbled – in his heart damning his boots, and trying to remember M. Siras' first position. 'Only to be allowed to wait on your ladyship places me in the seventh heaven! Only to be allowed to worship at the shrine of beauty is – is a great privilege, ma'am. But to be permitted to hope – that I am not altogether – I mean, my lady,' he amended, growing a little flustered, 'that I am not entirely—'

'What?' Lady Betty asked, eyeing him archly, her finger in her mouth, her head on one side.

'Indifferent to your ladyship! Oh, I assure your ladyship never in all my life have I felt so profound a—'

'Really?'

'A – an admiration of anyone, never have I—'

'Said so much to a lady! That, sir, I can believe!'

This time the voice was not Betty's, and he started as if he had been pricked. He spun round, and saw Sophia standing beside the fire, a little behind the door through which he had entered. He had thought himself alone with his inamorata; and his face of dismay was ludicrous. 'Oh!' he faltered, bowing hurriedly, 'I beg your pardon, ma'am, I – I did not see you.'

'So I suppose,' she answered coldly, 'or you would not have presumed to say such words to a lady.'

He cringed. 'I am sure,' he stammered, 'if I have been wanting in respect, I beg her ladyship's pardon! I am sure, I know—'

'Are you sure – you know who you are?' Sophia asked with directness.

He was all colours at once, but strove to mask the wound under a pretty sentence. 'I trust a gentleman may aspire to – to all that beauty has to give,' he snapped. 'I may not, ma'am, be of her ladyship's rank.'

'No, it is clear that you are not!' Sophia answered.

'But I am a gentleman.'

'The question is, are you?' she retorted. 'There are gentlemen and gentlemen. What is your claim to that name, sir?'

'S'help me, ma'am!' he exclaimed, affecting the utmost surprise and indignation. 'The Fanshaws of Warwickshire have been commonly taken for such.'

'The Fanshaws of Warwickshire?'

'Yes, my lady.'

'Perhaps so. It may be so. I do not know them. But the Fanshaws of nowhere in particular? Or shall I say the Lanes of Piccadilly?'

His face flamed scarlet below the black wig. His tongue stuck to the roof of his mouth. His eyes flickered as if she had threatened to strike him. For a moment he was a pitiable sight. Then with a prodigious effort, 'I – I don't know what you are talking about,' he muttered hoarsely. 'I don't understand you, ma'am.' But his smile was sickly, and his eye betrayed his misery.

'Don't lie, sir,' Sophia said sternly; and, poor little wretch, found out and exposed, he writhed under her look of scorn. 'We know who you are, a tradesman's son, parading in borrowed plumes. What we do not know, what we cannot understand,' she continued with ineffable disdain, 'is how you can think to find favour in a lady's eyes. In a lady's eyes – you! An under-bred, over-dressed apprentice, who have never done anything to raise yourself from the rank in which you were born! Do you know, have you an idea, sir, what you are in our eyes? Do you know that a lady would rather marry her footman; for, at least, he is a man. If you do not, you must be taught, sir, as the puppy is taught with the whip. Do you understand me?'

In his deserved degradation, his eyes sought Lady Betty's face. She was looking at him gravely; he read no hope in her eyes. What the other woman told him then was true; and, ah, how he hated her! Ah, how he hated her! He did not know that she scourged in him another's offence. He did not know that of her scorn a measure fell on her own shoulders; that she had been deluded by such an one as he was himself. Above all, he did not know that she was resolved that the child with her should not suffer as she had suffered!

He thought that she was moved by sheer wanton brutality; and cringing, smarting under the lash of her tongue, seeing himself for the moment as others saw him – a mean little jackanapes mimicking his betters – he could have strangled her. But he was dumb.

'You had the audacity,' Sophia continued, gravely, 'to attend me once, I remember, and ply me with your foolish compliments! And you have written to this lady, you, a shopman—'

'I am not a – a shopman!' he stuttered, writhing.

'In grade you are; it were more honour to you were you one in reality!' she retorted. 'But I repeat it, you have written to this lady, who, the better to teach you a lesson, did not at once betray what she thought you. For the future, however, understand, sir. If you pester her with attentions, or even cross her path, I will find those who will cane you into behaviour. And in such a way that you will not forget it! For the rest, let me advise you to get rid of those preposterous clothes. change that sword for an ell-wand, and go back to your counter. You may retire now. Or no! Pettitt!' Sophia continued, as she opened the door, 'Pettitt!' to Lady Betty's woman, 'show this person downstairs.'

He sneaked out, dumb. For what was he to say? They were great ladies, and he a person, fit company for the steward's room, a little above the servants' hall. He bent his head under the maid's scornful eye, hurried, stumbling in his boots, down the narrow stairs, nor did he breathe until he reached the dark street, where his little chest beginning to heave, he burst into scalding tears of rage.

He suffered horribly in his tenderest part – his conceit. He burned miserably, impotently, poor weakling, to be revenged. If he could bring those proud women to their knees! If he could see them humbled, as they had humbled him! If he could show them that he was not the poor creature they deemed him! If he could sear their insolent faces – the smallpox seize them! If he could – aye, the smallpox seize them!

Presently he slunk back to the White Lion, where he had his bed; and, finding a fire still burning in the empty taproom – for the evening was chilly – he took refuge there, and, laying his head on the beer-stained table, wept anew. The next time he looked up he found that a man and woman had entered the room, and were standing on the hearth, gazing curiously at him.

CHAPTER XVI

The Paved Ford

If Lady Betty's sprightliness ever deserted her, it returned with the morning as regularly as the light. But by Sophia the depressing influence of a strange place, viewed through sheets of rain, was felt to the full next day. The mind must be strong that does not tinge the future with the colours which the eye presents at the moment; and hers was nowise superior to the temptation. Her spirits, as she rose amid the discomforts of a Sussex inn – and Sussex inns and Sussex roads were then reputed among the worst in England – and prepared to continue the journey, were at their lowest ebb. She dreaded the meeting, now so imminent, with Sir Hervey. She shrank as the bather on the verge of the stream shrinks, from the new sphere, the new home, the new duties on which the day must see her enter; and enter unsupported by love. She was cold, she shook, her knees quaked under her; she had golden visions of what might have been, and her heart sobbed as she plucked herself from them. To Lady Betty's eye, and in the phrase of the day, she had the vapours; alas, she suffered with better reason than the fine ladies who had lately made them the fashion.

When they had once set forth, however, the motion and the change of outlook, even though it was but a change from dripping eaves to woods thrashing in the wet wind, gave something of a fillip to her spirits. Moreover, the nearer we come to a dreaded event, the more important loom the brief stages that divide us from it. We count by months, then by days; at length, when hours only remain, the last meal is an epoch on the hither side of which we sit almost content. It was so with Sophia when she had once started. They were to dine at Lewes; until Lewes was reached she put away the future, and strove to enjoy the hours that intervened.

The weather was so foul that at starting they took Lady Betty's maid into the carriage, and pitied Watkyns, who had no choice but to sit outside, with his hat pulled down to his collar, and the rain running out of his pockets. The wild hilly road through Ashdown Forest, that on a fine day charms the modern eye, presented to them only dreary misty tops and deep sloughy bottoms; the latter so delaying them – for twice in the first six miles they stuck fast – that it was noon when they reached Sheffield Green. Dane Hill was slowly climbed, the horses straining and the wheels creaking; but, this difficulty surmounted, they had a view of flatter country ahead, though spread out under heavy rains; and they became more hopeful. 'We cannot be far from Lewes, now,' Lady Betty said cheerfully. 'I wonder what Watkyns thinks. Pettitt, put your head out and ask him.'

Pettitt did so, not very willingly, and after exchanging a few words with the man drew in a scared face. 'He says, my lady, we shan't be there till half after two at the best,' she announced. 'Nor then if the water is out. He says if it goes on raining another hour, he does not know if we shall ever reach it.' It will be noticed that Watkyns, with the rain running down his back, was a pessimist.

'Ever reach it?' Lady Betty retorted. 'What rubbish! But, la, suppose we are stopped, and have to lie in the fields? Pettitt, did you ever sleep in a field?'

Pettitt fairly jumped with indignation. 'Me, my lady!' she cried. 'I should think I knew better! And was brought up better. Not *I*, indeed!'

'Well,' Betty answered mischievously, 'if we have to sleep in the carriage, I give you notice, Pettitt, there'll not be room for you! But I daresay you'll be dry enough – underneath, if we choose a nice place.'

Pettitt's eyes were wide with horror. 'Underneath?' she gasped.

'To be sure! Or we might find a haystack,' Lady Betty continued, with a face of the greatest seriousness. 'The men could lie on one side and you on the other—'

'Me, my lady! A haystack? Never!'

'Oh, it is no use to say never,' Lady Betty answered; 'these things often happen when one travels. And after all, you would have the one side to yourself, and it would be quite nice and proper. And if there were no mice or rats in the stack—'

The maid shrieked feebly.

'As there often are in haystacks, I am sure you would do as

well as we should in the carriage. And – oh, la!' in a different tone, 'who is that? How he scared me!'

A horseman going the same way had come up with the carriage; as she spoke, he passed it at a rapid trot. The two ladies poked their heads forward, and followed him with their eyes. 'It's Mr Fanshaw,' Sophia muttered in great surprise.

'Fanshaw?' Lady Betty cried, springing up in excitement, and as quickly sitting down again. 'La, so it is! You don't think the stupid is going to follow us after what you said? If he does' – with a giggle – 'I don't know what they'll say at Coke Hall. How he does bump, to be sure! And how hot he is!'

'He ought to have returned to London!'

'Well, I'm sure I thought you'd frightened him!' Lady Betty answered demurely.

Sophia said nothing, but thought the more. What did the man mean? He had collapsed so easily the night before, he had been so completely prostrated by her hard words, she had taken it for certain he would abandon the pursuit. Yet here he was, still with his back to London, still in attendance on them. Was it possible that he had some hold over Lady Betty? She asked Pettitt, whose face, as she sat clutching a basket and looking nervously out of the window, was a picture of misery, where he had lain at East Grinstead.

'At the other inn,' Pettitt answered tearfully. 'I saw him in the street this morning, my lady. talking to two men. I'm sure I little thought then that I might have to lie in – oh, Lord ha' mercy, we're over!'

She squealed, the ladies clutched one another, the carriage lurched heavily. It jolted forward a yard or two at a dangerous slant, and came to a sudden stand. The road, undermined by the heavy rain, had given way; and the near wheels had sunk into the hole, while those on the other side stood on solid ground. A little more and the carriage must have turned over. While Watkyns climbed down in haste, and the grooms dismounted, the three inside skipped out, to find themselves standing in the rain, in a little valley between two softly-rounded hills, that sloped upwards until they were lost in the fog. There was nothing else for it; they had to wait with what patience they might, until the three servants with a couple of bars, which travellers in those days carried for the purpose, had lifted the vehicle by sheer strength from the pit into which it had settled. Then word was passed to the horses, the postboys cracked their whips, and, with a bound, the carriage stood again on firm ground.

So far good; but in surmounting the difficulty, half an hour had been wasted. It was nearly two o'clock; they were barely half-way to Lewes. The patient Watkyns, holding the door for them to enter, advised that they could not now be in before four. 'If then,' he added ominously. 'I fear, my lady, the ford on this side of Chayley is like to be deep. I don't know how 'twill be, my lady, but we'll do our best.'

'You must not drown us!' Lady Betty cried gaily; but had better have held her tongue, for her woman, between damp and fright, began to cry, and was hardly scolded into silence.

So, half-past two, which should have seen them at Lewes, found them ploughing through heavy mud at a foot's pace behind sobbing horses; the rain, the roads, and the desolate landscape, all bearing out the evil repute of Sussex highways. Abreast of the windmill at Plumpton by-road they found dry going, which lasted for half a mile, and the increase of speed cheered even the despairing Pettitt. But at the foot of the descent they stuck fast once more, in a hole ill-mended with faggots; and for a fair hundred yards the men had to push and pull. They lost another half-hour here, so that it wanted little of half-past three when they came, weary and despondent, to the ford below Chayley, about six miles short of Lewes. The grooms were mired to the knees, Watkyns was little better, all were in a poor humour. Lady Betty's woman clung and screeched on the least alarm; and on all the steady drizzle and the heavy road had wrought depressingly.

'Shall we have difficulty in crossing?' Sophia asked nervously, as they drew towards the ford, and saw a brown line of water swirling athwart the road. A horseman and two or three country folk were on the bank, gauging the stream with their eyes.

Watkyns shook his head. 'I doubt it's not to be done at all, my lady,' he said. 'Here's one stopped already, unless I am mistaken.'

'But we can't stay here,' Sophia protested, looking with longing at the roofs and spire that rose above the trees beyond the stream. On the bank on which they stood was a single hovel of mud, fast melting under the steady downpour.

'I'll see what they say, my lady,' Watkyns answered, and leaving the carriage thirty paces from the water, he went forward and joined the little group that conferred on the brink. The grooms moved on also, while the leading postboy, standing up in his stirrups. scanned the current with evident misgiving.

' 'Tis Fanshaw on the horse,' Sophia said in a low tone.

'So it is!' Lady Betty answered. 'He's afraid to cross, it is clear! You don't think we shall have to spend the night here?'

The horses hanging their heads in the rain, the dripping postboys, the splashed carriage, the three faces peering anxiously at the flood, through which they must pass to gain shelter – a more desolate group it were hard to conceive; unless it was that which talked and argued on the bank, and from which Watkyns presently detached himself. He came back to the carriage.

'It's not to be done, my lady,' he said, his face troubled. 'There's but one opinion of that. It's a mud bottom, they tell me, and if the horses dragged the carriage in, they could never pull it through. Most likely they wouldn't face the water. It must fall a foot. they say, before it'll be safe to try it.'

The maid shrieked. Even Sophia looked scared. 'But what are we to do?' she said. 'We cannot spend the night here.'

'Well, my lady, the gentleman says if we keep down the water this side, there's a paved ford a mile lower that should be passable. It's not far from Fletching, and we could very likely cross there or get shelter in Fletching, if your ladyship should not choose to risk it.'

'But how does the gentleman know?' Sophia asked sharply.

'He's of this country,' Watkyns answered. 'Leastwise bred here, my lady, this side of Lewes, and says he knows the roads. It's what he's going to do himself. And I don't know what else we can do, if your ladyship pleases.'

'Well,' Sophia said doubtfully. 'if you think so?'

'Oh, yes,' Lady Betty cried impulsively. 'Let us go! We can't sit here all night. It must be nearly four now.'

'It's all that, my lady.'

'And we shall have it dark, if we stay here. And shall really have to lie under a haystack. Besides, you may be sure *he'll* not lead us into much danger!' she continued, with a contemptuous look at Mr Fanshaw. 'If we take care to go only where he goes we shall not run much risk.'

As if he heard what she was saying, Mr Fanshaw at that moment turned his horse, and passed the carriage; he was on his way to take the lane that ran down stream. A countryman plodded at his stirrup, and Sir Hervey's grooms followed. After them came a second countryman with a sack drawn over his shoulders. As this man passed the carriage Sophia leaned from the window and called on him.

'Does this lane lead to a better ford, my man?' she asked.

The fellow stared at Lady Betty's pretty face and eager eyes. 'Aye, there's a ford,' he answered, the rain dripping off his nose.

'A better ford than this?'

'Ay, 'tis paved.'

'And how far from here is it?'

'A mile, or may be a mile and a bit.'

Sophia gave him a shilling. She nodded to Watkyns. 'I think we had better go,' she said. 'But I hope it may not be a long round,' she continued with a sort of foreboding. 'I shall be glad when we are in the main road again.'

The horses' heads once turned, however, things seemed to go better. The sky grew lighter, the rain ceased, the lane, willow-lined, and in places invaded by the swollen stream that ran beside it, proved to be passable. Even the mile and a bit turned out to be no more than two miles, and in half an hour, the cavalcade, to which Mr Fanshaw, moving in front, had the air of belonging, reached the ford.

The stream was wide here, but so full that the brown water swept swiftly and silently over the shallows. Nevertheless it was evident that Lane knew his ground for, to Lady Betty's astonishment, he rode in gallantly, and spurred his horse to the other side, the water barely reaching its knees. Encouraged, the postboys cracked their whips and followed, the carriage swayed, Pettitt screamed; for a moment the water seemed rising all round them, the next they were across and jolting up the farther bank.

'There!' Lady Betty cried with a laugh of triumph. 'I'd have bet that would be all right! When I saw him go through I knew that there was not much danger. Six miles more and we shall be in Lewes.'

Suddenly, on the bank they had left, a man appeared, waving his arms to them. The carriage had turned to the left after crossing, and the movement brought the man full into view from the window. 'What is it?' Sophia asked anxiously. 'What is he shouting?' And she called to Watkyns to learn what it was.

'I think he wants help to come over, my lady,' Watkyns answered. 'But I'll ask, if your ladyship pleases.' And he went back and exchanged shouts with the stranger, while the carriage plodded up the ascent. By-and-by Watkyns overtook them. 'It was only to tell me, my lady, that there was a second ford we should have to pass,' he explained.

'A second ford?'

'Yes, but the gentleman in front had told me so already, and that it was no worse than this, or not much; and a farm close to it, with men and a team of oxen, if we had need. I told the man that, my lady, and all he answered was, that they had only one small ox at the farm, and he kept shouting that, and nothing else. But I could not make much of him. And anyway we must go on now,' Watkyns continued, with just so much sullenness as showed he had his doubts. 'We came through that grandly; and with luck, my lady, we should be in Lewes before dark.'

'At any rate let us go as fast as we can,' Sophia answered. This late mention of a second ford disturbed her, and she looked ahead with increasing anxiety.

It was soon plain that to travel quickly in the country in which they now found themselves was impossible. The road followed a shallow valley which wound among low hills, crowned with trees. Now the carriage climbed slowly over a shoulder, now plunged into a roughly wooded bottom, now dragged painfully up the other side, the ladies walking. In places the road was so narrow that the wheels barely passed. It was in vain Sophia fretted, in vain Lady Betty ceased to jest, that Pettitt cast eyes to heaven in token of speechless misery, Watkyns swore and sweated to think what Sir Hervey would say of it. There was no place where the carriage could be turned; and if there had been, to go back seemed as bad as to go forward.

By way of compensation the sky had grown clear; a flood of pale evening sunshine gilded the western slopes of the hills. The clumps that here and there crowned the summits rose black against an evening sky, calm and serene. But far as the eye could reach not a sign of man appeared; the country seemed without population. Once indeed through an opening on the left, they made out a village spire peeping above a distant shoulder; but it was two miles away, and far from their direction. The road, at the moment the sun set, wound round a hill and began to descend following the bottom of a valley. By-and-by they saw before them a row of trees running athwart the way, and marking water. Here, then. was the second ford.

The two grooms had ridden for a time with Lane – to give Fanshaw his proper name – a couple of hundred yards ahead of the carriage. The countrymen had dropped off by tracks invisible to the strange eye, and gone to homes as invisible. Watkyns alone was beside the carriage, which was still a hundred yards short of the crossing, when one of the grooms was seen riding back to it.

He waved his hand in the air as he reigned up. 'It won't do!' he cried loudly. 'We can never get over. You can see for yourself, Mr Watkyns.'

'I can see a fool for myself!' the valet answered sharply. 'What do you mean by frightening the ladies?'

The groom – Sophia noticed that his face was flushed – fell sullenly behind the carriage without saying more; but the mischief was done. Pettitt was in tears, even Sophia and Lady Betty were shaken. They insisted on alighting, and joined Lane and the other groom who stood silenced by the prospect.

The stream that barred the way was a dozen yards wide from bank to bank, the water running strong and turbid with ugly eddies, and a greedy swirl. Nor was this the worst. The road on the side on which they stood sloped gently into the stream. But on the farther side the bank was high and precipitous, and the road rose so steeply out of the water that the little hamlet which crowned the ridge beyond hung high above their heads. It needed no experience to see that tired horses, fagged by a journey and by the labour of wading through the deep ford, would never drag the carriage up so steep a pitch.

Sophia took it all in. She took in also the late evening light, and the desolate valley, strewn with sparse thorn trees, down which they had come – and from which this was their exit; and her eyes flashed with anger. Hitherto, in her desire to have no dealings with Lane, but to ignore, if she must bear, his company, she had refrained from questioning him; though with each mile of the lengthening distance the temptation had grown. Now she turned to him.

'What do you mean, sir,' she cried harshly, 'by bringing us to such a place as this? Is this your good ford?'

He did not look at her, but continued to stare at the water. 'It's generally low enough,' he muttered sulkily.

'Did you expect to find it low today? After the rain?'

He did not answer, and Watkyns took the word. 'If we had oxen and some ropes, or even half a dozen men,' he said, 'we could get the carriage across.'

'Then where is this farm? And the team of oxen of which you told us?' Sophia continued, addressing Lane again. 'Explain, sir, explain! Why have you brought us to this place? You must have had some motive.'

'The farm is there,' he answered sulkily, pointing to the buildings on the ridge across the water. 'And it would be all right, but – but it has changed hands since I was here. And the people are – they tell me that the place has a bad nam.'

She fancied that he exchanged a look with the groom who stood nearest; at any rate the man hastened to corroborate him. 'That's true enough!' he cried with a hiccough. 'It's dangerous, my lady, so they tell me.'

Sophia stared. The servant's manner was odd and free. And how did he know? 'Who told you?' she asked sharply.

'The men who came part of the way with us, my lady.'

Sophia turned to Watkyns. 'It's a pity you did not learn this before,' she said severely. 'You should not have allowed this person to decoy us from the road. For you, sir,' she continued addressing Lane, 'I cannot conceive why you have done this, or why you have brought us here, but of one thing you may be sure. If there be roguery in this you will pay a sharp reckoning for it.'

He stood by his horse's head, looking doggedly at the stream, and avoiding their eyes. In the silence Lady Betty's woman began to sob, until her mistress bade her be quiet for a fool. Yet there was excuse for her. With the fading of the light the valley behind them had taken on a sinister look. The gnarled thorn trees of the upper part, the coarse marsh-grass of the lower, through which a small stream trickled, forming sullen pools among stunted alders, spoke of desolation and the coming of night. On the steep slopes above them no life moved; from the silent hamlet beyond the water came no sound or shout of challenge.

Suddenly one of the postboys found a voice. 'We could get two of the horses through,' he said, 'and fetch help from Lewes. It cannot be more than four or five miles from here, and we could get a fresh team there, and with ropes and half a dozen men we could cross well enough!'

Sophia turned to him. 'You are a man,' she said. 'A guinea apiece, my lads, if you are back with fresh horses in two hours.'

'We'll do our best, my lady,' the lad answered, touching his cap. ''Twill be no fault of ours, if we are not back. We'll try the house first. We're six men,' he continued, looking round, 'and need not be afraid of one or two, if they ben't of the best.'

But as he turned the nearest groom whispered something in his ear, and his face fell. His eyes travelled to the little cluster of buildings that crowned the opposite ridge. On the left of the steep road stood two cottages; on the right the gable end of a larger house rose heavily from the hillside, and from the sparse gorse bushes that bestrewed it.

None of the chimneys emitted smoke; but Sophia following the man's eye, saw that, early as it was, and barely inclining to dusk, a small window in the gable end showed a light. 'Why,' she exclaimed, 'they have a light! Let us all shout, and they must hear. Why should we be afraid? Shout!' she continued, turning to Watkyns. 'Do you hear, man? What are you afraid of?'

'Nothing, my lady,' Watkyns stammered; and he hastened to shout 'Halloa! Halloa there! House!' But his pale face, and the quaver in his voice, betrayed that, in spite of his boast, he was afraid; while the faces of the other men, as they stood waiting for an answer, their eyes riveted on the house, seemed to show that they shared the feeling.

Sophia noticed this, and was puzzled. But the next moment the postboys began to free the leaders from the harness, and to mount and ride them into the water; and in the excitement of the scene she forgot her suspicions. One of the horses refused to cross, and, wheeling round in the stream, came near to unseating its rider. But the postboy persisted gamely, the beast was driven in again, and, after hesitating awhile, snorting in the shallows, it went through with a rush, and plunged up the bank amid an avalanche of mud and stones. The summit of the ridge gained, the postboys rose in their stirrups and looked back, waving a farewell. The next moment they passed between the cottages and the house, and disappeared.

The group, left below, strained their eyes after them. But nothing rewarded expectation. No cry came back, no hurrying band appeared, laden with help, and shouting encouragement. From the buildings, that each moment loomed darker and darker, came no sign of life. Only, as the dusk grew, and minute by minute night fell in the valley, the light in the window of the gable end waxed brighter and brighter, until it shone a single mysterious spark in a wall of blackness.

CHAPTER XVII

In the Valley

WHEN SOPHIA at last lowered her eyes, and with a sigh of disappointment turned to her companions – when she awoke, as it were, and saw how fast the dusk had gathered round them, and what strides towards shutting them in night had made in those few minutes, she had much ado to maintain her composure. Lady Betty, little more than a child, and but one remove from a child's fear of the dark, clung to her; the girl, though a natural high spirit forbade her to expose her fears, was fairly daunted by the gloom and eeriness of the scene. Pettitt seated on a step of the carriage, weeping at a word and shrieking on the least alarm, was worse than useless; while the men, now reduced to four, had withdrawn to a distance, whence their voices, subdued in earnest colloquy, came at intervals to her ears.

What was to be done? Surely something? Surely they were not going to sit there, perhaps through the whole night, doing nothing to help themselves, wholly depending on the success of the postboys? That could not be; and impatiently Sophia summoned Watkyns. 'Are you going to do nothing,' she asked sharply, 'until they come back? Cannot one of the grooms return the way we came? There was the man at the mill – who warned us? He may know what to do. Send one of the servants to him.'

'I did ask the gentleman to go,' Watkyns answered with a sniff of contempt, 'or else to ride on with the postboys and guide them. He's got us into this scrape, begging your ladyship's pardon, and he ought to get us out! But he's all for not separating; says that it isn't safe, and he won't leave the ladies. He'll do nothing. He's turned kind of stupid like,' the valet added with a snort of temper.

Sophia's lip curled. 'Then let one of the grooms go,' she said, 'if he's afraid.'

Watkyns hesitated. 'Well, the truth is, my lady,' he said, speaking low, and looking warily behind him, 'they are fuddled with drink, and that's all about it. Where they got the stuff I don't know, but I've suspicions.'

Sophia stared.

'I think I can guess what is in the gentleman's holsters,' Watkyns continued, nodding mysteriously. 'And I've a notion they had a share of it, when my back was turned. But why I cannot say. Only they are not to be trusted. I'd go back myself, for it is well to have two strings; and I could take one of their horses. But I don't like to leave you with him, my lady.'

'With the gentleman?'

'Yes, my lady. Seeing he has given the men drink.'

Sophia laughed in scorn. 'You need not trouble yourself about him,' she said. 'We are not afraid of him. Besides it is not as if I were alone. There are three of us. As to the house opposite, however, that's another matter.'

He was off his guard. 'Oh, there's no fear of that!' he said.

'No? But I thought you said there was.'

'This side of the water, my lady – I mean,' he answered hurriedly. 'There are stepping-stones you see a little above there; but they are covered now, and the people can't come over.'

'You are sure of that?'

'Quite sure, my lady.'

'Then you had better go,' Sophia said with decision. 'We've had nothing to eat since midday, and we are half famished. We cannot stay here all night.'

Watkyns hesitated. 'Your ladyship is right,' he said, 'it is not as if you were alone. And the moon will be up in an hour. Still, my lady, I don't know as Sir Hervey would like me to leave you?'

But in the end he gave way and went; and was scarcely out of hearing before she was sorry that she had sent him, and would fain, had it been possible, have recalled him.

Still the darkness was not yet Egyptian; night had not yet completely fallen. She could see the figures of Lane and the two servants, seated a score of paces away on a fallen thorn tree, to which they had tethered their horses. She could dimly make out Lady Betty's face, as the girl sat beside her in the carriage, getting what comfort she could from squeezing her hand; and Pettitt's, who sat with them, for it would have been cruel to exclude her in her state of terror. But the knowledge that by-and-by she would lose all this, the knowledge that by-and-by they must sit in that gloomy hollow, ignorant of what was passing near them, and at the mercy of the first comer, began to fill even Sophia with dread. She began to fear even Lane. She remembered that he had cause to dislike her; that he might harbour thoughts of revenge. If it were true that he had made the men drunk—

'It's absurd,' Lady Betty whispered, pressing her hand, 'He would not dare! He's just a clothes peg! You're not afraid of him?'

'No,' Sophia answered bravely, 'I don't know that I am afraid of anyone. Only—'

'Only you wish you had not let Watkyns go?'

'Yes.'

'So do I!' Lady Betty whispered eagerly. 'But I did not like to say so. I was afraid you would think me afraid. What I can't make out is, why some of the men don't go over and get help where the light is, instead of riding miles and miles for it.'

'They seem to think that the people are not to be trusted.'

'But why? What do they think that they are?' Lady Betty asked nervously.

'I don't know! Watkyns said something of smugglers from Goudhurst.'

'And how does he know?'

'From Lane, I suppose.'

'Who brought us here, the little wretch! There!' Betty exclaimed, clutching her companion, 'what is that? Oh, they have got a candle.'

Lane had produced one from his holsters; the men had lighted it. By-and-by, he brought it to the carriage, shading it with his hat; with a sheepish air he prayed the ladies to make use of it. Sophia added distrust to her former contempt of him, and would have declined the gift; but Lady Betty's trembling hand prayed mutely for the indulgence, and she let him place it in the lanthorn in the carriage. It conferred a kind of protection; at least they could now see one another's faces.

She soon regretted her easiness, however, for instead of withdrawing when he had performed the office, Lane lingered beside the door. He asked Lady Betty the time, he went away a little, returned, a flitting shadow on the fringe of light; finally he stood irresolute watching them, at a distance of a couple of yards. Sophia bore this as long as she could, at last, out of patience, she asked him coldly if he had not another candle. It was now quite dark.

'No, my lady,' he said humbly, 'I've no other.'

She wished that she had bitten her tongue off before she put the question, for now it appeared barbarous to send him into the darkness. He seemed, too, to see the advantage he had gained, and by-and-by he ventured to take his seat on a log beside the carriage. He cast a timid look at Lady Betty, and heaved an audible sigh.

If he hoped to move that hard little heart by sighing, however, he was much mistaken. Cheered by the light, Lady Betty was herself again. Sophia felt her begin to shake, and knew that in a moment the laugh, half hysterical, half mirthful, would break all bounds; and she sought to save the situation. 'Where are the men?' she said hurriedly. 'Will you be good enough to ask one of them to come to me?'

Lane rose, and went reluctantly; soon he came stumbling back into the circle of light.

'I cannot find them,' he stammered, standing by the carriage.

'Not find them?' Sophia answered, staring at him. 'Are they not there?'

'No, my lady,' he returned, glancing nervously over his shoulder and back again. 'At least I – I can't find them, ma'am. It is very dark. You don't think,' he continued – and for the first time she discerned by the poor light of the candle that he was trembling, 'that – that they can have fallen into the river?'

His tone alarmed her, even while she thought his fears preposterous. 'Fallen into the river?' she exclaimed contemptuously. 'Nonsense, sir! Are you trying to frighten us?' And without waiting for an answer, she raised her voice and called 'George! George!'

No answer. She stepped quickly from the carriage. 'Take me,' she said imperiously, 'to where you left them.'

Lady Betty protested; Pettitt clutched at her habit, begged her to stay. But Sophia persisted, and groped her way after Lane until he came to a stand, his hand on the bark of the fallen blackthorn, beside which she had last seen the men. 'They were here,' he said, in the tone of one half dazed. 'They were. They were just here.'

'Yes, I remember,' she answered. And undeterred by Pettitt's frantic appeals to her to return, she called the man again and again; still she got no answer.

At length, fear of she knew not what came on her, and shaken by the silence of the valley through which her voice rang mournfully, she hurried back to the carriage, and sprang into it in a panic; the man Lane following close at her elbow. It was only when she had taken her seat, and found him clutching the door of the carriage and pressing as near as he could come, that she saw he was ashake with fear; that his eyes were staring, his hair almost on end.

'They've fallen into the river,' he cried wildly, his teeth

chattering. 'I never thought of that! They have fallen in, and are drowned!'

'Don't be a fool, man!' Sophia answered sharply. She was striving to keep fear at bay, while Lady Betty awe-stricken, clung to her arm. 'We should have heard a cry or something.'

'They were drunk,' he whispered. 'They were drunk! And now they are dead! They are dead! Dead!'

Pettitt shrieked at the word; and Sophia, between fear and rage, uncertain whether he was frightened or was trying to frighten them, bade him be silent. 'If you can do nothing, at least be still,' she cried wrathfully. 'You are worse than a woman. And do you, Pettitt, behave yourself. You should be taking care of your mistress, instead of scaring her.'

The man so far obeyed that he sank on the step of the carriage, and was silent. But she heard him moan; and despite her courage she shuddered. Fear is infectious; it was in vain she strove against the uneasy feelings communicated by his alarm. She caught herself looking over her shoulder, starting at a sound; trembling when the candle flickered in the lanthorn or the feeble ring of light in which they sat, in that hollow of blackness, wavered or varied. By-and-by the candle would go out; there was but an inch of it now. Then they would be in the dark; three women and this craven, with the hidden river running silent, bankful beside them, and she knew not what, prowling, hovering, groping at their backs.

On a sudden Lane sprang up. 'What is that?' he cried, cowering against the door, and clutching it as if he would drag it open and force himself in among them. 'See, what is it? What is it?'

But it was only the first shaft of light, shot by the rising moon through a notch in the hills, that had scared him. It struck the thorn tree where the men had sat, and slowly the slender ray widened and grew until all the upper valley through which they had come lay bathed in solemn radiance. Gradually it flooded the bottom, and dimmed the yellow, ineffectual light of their taper; at length only the ridge beyond the water remained dark, pierced by the one brooding spark that seemed to keep grave vigil in the hill of shadow.

The women breathed more freely; even Pettitt ceased to bewail herself. 'They will be back soon, with the horses,' Sophia said, gazing with hopeful eyes into the darkness beyond the ford. 'They must have left us an hour and more.'

'An hour?' Lady Betty answered with a shiver. 'Three, I vow! But what is the man doing?' she continued, directing Sophia's attention to Lane. 'I declare he's a greater coward than any of us!'

He was, if the fact that the light which had relieved their fears had not removed his, stood for anything. He seemed afraid to move a yard from them; yet he seldom looked at them, save when a gust of terror shook him, and he turned as if to grip their garments. His hand on the door of the carriage, he gazed now along the valley down which they had come, now towards the solitary light beyond the stream; and it was impossible to say which prospect alarmed him the more. Sophia, whom his restlessness filled with apprehension, noticed that he listened; and that more than once, when Lady Betty spoke or Pettitt complained, he raised his hand, as if he took the interruption ill. And the longer she watched him, the more she was infected with his uneasiness.

On a sudden he turned to her. 'Do you hear anything?' he asked.

She listened. 'No,' she answered, 'I hear nothing but the wind passing through the trees.'

'Not horses?'

She listened again, inclining her head to catch any sound that might come from the other side of the stream. 'No,' she replied, 'I don't.'

He touched her shoulder. 'Not that way!' he exclaimed. 'Not that way! Behind us!'

Suddenly Lady Betty spoke. 'I do!' she said. 'But they are a long way off. It's Watkyns coming back. He must have found horses, for I hear more than one!'

'It's not Watkyns!' Lane answered and he took two steps from the carriage, then came back. 'Get out!' he cried hoarsely. 'Do you hear? Get out! Or don't say I didn't warn you. Do you hear?' he repeated, when no one stirred; for Sophia, her worst suspicions confirmed, was speechless with surprise, and the others cowered in their places, thinking him gone mad. 'Get out, get out, and hide if you can. They are coming!' he continued wildly. 'I tell you they are coming.

And it is off my shoulders. In ten minutes they'll be here, and if you're not hidden, it'll be the worse for you. I've told you!'

'Who are coming?' Sophia said her lips forming the words with difficulty.

'Hawkesworth!' he answered. 'Hawkesworth! He and two more, as big devils as himself. If you don't want to be robbed, and worse, hide, hide! Do you hear me?' he continued, pulling frantically at Sophia's habit. 'I've told you! I've done all I can! It's not on my head!'

For an instant she sat, turned to stone; deaf to the cries, to the prayers, to the lamentations of the others. Hawkesworth? The mere name of him, with whom she had once fancied herself in love, whom now she feared and loathed, as she feared and loathed no other man, stopped the current of her blood. 'Hawkesworth!' she whispered. 'Hawkesworth? Here? Following us? Do you mean it?'

'Haven't I told you?' Lane answered with angry energy. 'He was at Grinstead, at the White Lion, last night. I saw him, and – and the woman. You'd made me mad, you know, and – and they tempted me! They tempted me!' he whined. 'And they're coming. Can't you hear them now? They are coming!'

Yes, she could hear them now. In the far distance up the valley the steady fall of horses' hoofs broke the night silence. Steadily, steadily, the hoof-beats drew nearer and nearer. Now they were hushed; the riders were crossing a spongy bit, where a spring soaked the road – Sophia could remember the very place. Now the sound rose louder, nearer, more fateful. Trot-trot, trot-trot, trot-trot! Yes, they were coming. They were coming! In five minutes, in ten minutes at most they would be here!

It was a crisis to try the bravest. Round them the moonlight flooded the low wide mouth of the valley. As far as the eye reached, all was bare and shelterless. A few scattered thorn trees, standing singly and apart, mocked the eye with a promise of safety, which a second glance showed to be futile. The only salient object was the carriage stranded beside the ford, a huge dark blot, betraying their presence to eyes a furlong away. Yet if they left its shelter, whither were they to turn, where to hide themselves? Sophia, her heart beating as if it would suffocate her, tried to think, tried to remember; while Lady Betty clung to her convulsively, asking what they were to do, and Pettitt, utterly overcome, sobbed at the bottom of the carriage, as if she were safer there.

And all the time the tramp of the approaching horses, borne on the night breeze, came clearer and sharper, clearer and sharper to the ear; until she could distinguish the ring of bit and bridle as the men descended the valley. She looked at Lane. The craven was panic-stricken, caught hither and thither, by gusts of cowardice; there was no help there. Her eye passed to the river, and her heart leapt, for in the shadowed bank on the other side she read hope and a chance. There in the darkness they could hide; there – if only they could find the stepping-stones which Watkyns had said were upstream.

Quick as thought she had Lady Betty out, and seizing her woman by the shoulder, shook her impatiently. 'Come,' she cried, 'come, we must run. We must run! Come, or we shall leave you.'

But Pettitt only grovelled lower on the floor, deaf to prayers, orders, threats. At last, 'We must leave her,' Sophia cried, when she had wasted a precious minute in vain appeals. 'Come! We must find the stepping-stones. It is the only chance.'

'But is the danger – so great?' the child panted.

'It's – oh, come! Come!' Sophia groaned. 'You don't understand.' And seizing Lady Betty by the hand she ran with her to the water's edge, and in breathless haste turned up the stream. They had gone twenty yards along the bank, the elder's eyes searching the dark full current, when Sophia stopped as if she had been shot. 'The jewels!' she gasped.

'The jewels?'

'Yes, I've left them.'

'Oh, never mind them now!' Betty wailed, 'never mind them now!' and she caught at her to stay her, but in vain. Already Sophia was half-way back to the carriage. She vanished inside it; in an incredibly short space – though it seemed long to Betty, trembling with impatience and searching the valley with eyes of dread – she was out again with the jewel-case in her hand, and flying back to her companion. 'They are his!' she muttered, as she urged her on again. 'I couldn't leave them.

Now, the stones! The stepping-stones! Oh, child, use your eyes! Find them, or we are lost!'

The fear of Hawkesworth lay heavy on her; she felt that she should die if his hand touched her. It was unfortunate that all the bank on which they stood was light; it was in their favour that the moon had now risen high enough to shine on the stream. They ran fifty yards without seeing a sign of what they sought. Then – at the very moment when the pursuers' voices broke on their ears, and they realized that in a minute or two they must be espied – they came to a couple of thorn trees, standing not far apart, that afforded a momentary shelter. A yard further, and Lady Betty stumbled over something that lay in the shadow of the trees. She recoiled with a cry. 'It's a man!' she murmured.

'The grooms!' Sophia answered, her wits sharpened by necessity; and she felt for and shook one of the sleepers, tugged at his clothes, even buffeted him in a frenzy of impatience. 'George! George!' she muttered; and again she shook him. But in vain; and as quickly as she had knelt she was on foot again, and had drawn the child on. 'Drugged!' she muttered. 'They are drugged! We must cross! We must cross! It's our one chance!'

She hurried her on, bending low; for beyond the two thorn trees all lay bare and open. Suddenly a cry rent the night; an oath, and a woman's scream followed and told them that their flight was known. Their hands clasped, their knees shaking under them, they pressed on, reckless now, expecting every moment to hear footsteps behind them. And joy! Sophia nearly swooned, as she saw not five yards ahead of them a ripple of broken water that ran slantwise across the silver; and in a line with it a foot above the surface, a rope stretched taut from bank to bank.

The stones were covered, all save one; but the rope promised a passage, more easy than she had dared to expect. 'Will you go first, or shall I?' was on the tip of her tongue; but Lady Betty, wasted no time on words. She was already in the water, and wading across, her hands sliding along the rope, her petticoats floating out on the surface of the current. The water was cold, and though it rose no higher than her knees, ran with a force that but for the rope must have swept her off her feet. She reached the middle in safety, however, and Sophia who dared not throw the weight of two on the rope, was tingling to follow, when the dreaded sound of feet on the bank warned her of danger. She turned her head sharply. A man stood within five paces of her.

A pace nearer, and Sophia would have flung herself into the stream! heedless of the rope, heedless of all but the necessity of escape. In the nick of time, however, she saw that it was not Hawkesworth who had found her, but Lane the poor rogue who had ruined them. In a low harsh voice, she bade him keep his distance.

'I don't know what to do!' he faltered, wringing his hands and looking back in terror. 'They'll murder me! I know they will! But there's smallpox the other side! You're going into it! There are three dead in the house, and everybody's fled. I don't know what to do,' he whined.

Sophia answered nothing, but slid into the stream and waded across. As she drew her wet skirts out of the water, and, helped by Lady Betty, climbed the bank, she heard the chase come down the side she had left; and thankful for the deep shadow in which they stood, she pressed the girl's hand to enjoin silence, as step by step they groped their way from the place. To go as far as possible from the crossing was her object; her fear that a stumble or a rolling stone – for the side of the ridge below the houses was steep and rough – would discover their position. Fortunately the darkness which lay there was deepened by contrast with the moonlit country on the farther side; and they crept some forty yards along the hill before they were brought up short by a wattled fence. They would have climbed this, but as they laid hands on it they heard men shouting, and saw two figures hurry along the opposite bank, and come to a stand, at the point where they had crossed. A moment Sophia hung in suspense; then Hawkesworth's voice thrilled her with terror. 'Over!' he cried. 'Over, fool, and watch the top!' And she heard the splashing of a horse as it crossed the ford, and the thud of its hoofs as it dashed up the road.

The two fugitives had turned instinctively downstream, in the direction of the road and the houses. The rider's movement up the road therefore tended to cut off their farther retreat; while the distance they had been able to put between themselves and the stepping-stones was so short that they dared not move again, much less make the attempt to repass their landing-place, and go up stream. For the moment, close as they were to their enemies, the darkness shielded them; but Sophia's heart beat thickly, and she crouched lower against the wattle as she heard Hawkesworth step into the stream and splash his way across, swearing at the coldness of the water.

CHAPTER XVIII

King Smallpox

HE DREW himself out on their side and shook himself; then for a time it seemed that the earth had swallowed him, so still was he. But Sophia knew that he was listening, standing in the dark a few paces from them, in the hope of hearing the rustle of their skirts or their footseps as they stole away. Disappointed in this, he began to move to and fro, beating the bushes this way and that; now loudly threatening them with horrid penalties if they did not show themselves, now asserting that he saw them, and now calling to his fellow who kept guard on the farther bank to know if he heard them. It was clear that he knew, probably from Pettitt, that they had not had time to go far from the carriage.

Fortunately, the trend of his search was from them, and as he receded up stream they breathed more freely. But when the sound of his movements was beginning to grow faint, and Sophia to think of continuing their flight, he turned, and she heard him come back on his tracks. This time, if the ear could be trusted, he was making directly for the place where they cowered beside the wattle fence.

Yes, he was drawing nearer – and nearer; now a stick snapped under his foot, now he stumbled and swore, as he recovered himself. Sophia felt the younger girl shake under her hand, and instinctively drew the child's face against her shoulder that she might not see. Presently she could make out his head and shoulders dark against the sky; and still she watched him, fascinated. Three more steps and he would be on them! Two more – the impulse to shriek, to spring up and fly at all risks was scarcely to be controlled. One more – there was a sudden rustle, a fathom below them, he sprang that way, something whisked from a gorse-bush, and he stood.

'What was it?' cried the man on the other side.

'A rabbit!' he answered with an oath. 'So they're not this way. I don't believe they crossed. Are you sure they're not in that thorn tree behind you? One of them might hide in it.'

Apparently the man went to see, for half a minute later, a shriek, followed by a thud, as of a heavy body brought hurriedly to earth, proved the success of his search. Hawkesworth sprang towards the stepping-stones.

'Which is it?' he cried.

'Neither,' the fellow answered. 'It's the whipper-snapper you sent for a decoy.'

'D—n it!' Hawkesworth exclaimed, and he came to a stand. 'But if you've got him, they are not far off. We'll wring his neck if he does not say where they are! Prick him, man, prick him with your knife.'

But the poor fop's squeals showed that little cruelty would be needed to draw from him all he knew. 'Don't! Don't!' he screamed. 'They're on the other side! I swear they are!'

'None of your lies now, or I'll slit your throat!' the ruffian growled. He appeared to be kneeling on Lane's breast.

'It's the truth! I swear it is! They were just across when you came!' Lane cried. 'They can't be fifty yards from the bank! If they'd moved I should have seen them. Let me up, and I'll help you to find them.'

'Tie him up,' Hawkesworth cried. 'Tie him up. And if he's lied to us, we'll shall soon know. If we don't find them, we'll drop him in the water. Tell him that, and ask him again.'

'They're by you!' Lane cried. 'I swear they are!'

Sophia felt, she could not see, that Hawkesworth was peering round him. Even now he was not more than ten or twelve paces from them; but the gorse-bush from which the rabbit had darted, formed a black blurr against the fence, and deepened the obscurity in which they lay. Unless he came on them they were safe; but at any moment he might discover the fence, and guess it had brought them up, and beat along it. And

– and while she thought of this she heard him chuckle.

'Be still, man,' he cried to the other, 'and keep your ears open. The moon will be over the hill in five minutes, and we'll have them safe, if they are here. Meantime, stand and listen, will you? or they may creep off.'

Sophia swallowed a sob. It seemed so hard – so hard after all they had done to escape – that nature itself should turn against them. Yet, it was so; the man was right. Already the moonlight touched the crest of a gorse-bush that grew a little higher than its neighbours; and overhead the sky was growing bright where the ridge line cut it. In five minutes the disc of the moon, sailing high, would rise above that spot, and all the hill side, that now lay veiled in shadow, would be flooded with light. Then—

She shuddered, watching paralysed the oncoming of this new and inexorable foe. Slowly the light was creeping down the gorse-bush. Minute by minute, sure as the tide that surges to the lips of the stranded mariner, the pale rays silvered this spray and that spray, dark before; touched the fence, and now lay a narrow streak along the nearer margin of the stream. And the streak widened; not slowly now but quickly. Even while she watched it, from the shelter of the fence, feeling her heart beat sickening bumps against her side, the light crept nearer and nearer. In three or four minutes it would be upon them.

Sophia was brave, but there was something in the sure and stealthy approach of this danger that sapped her will, and robbed her limbs of strength. Unable to think, unable to act, she crouched panic-stricken where she was; as the hare surprised on her form awaits the hunter's hand. Until only a minute remained; then with a groan she shook off the spell. To run, even to be caught running, was better than to be taken so. But whither could they run with the least chance of escape? She turned her head to see, and her eyes, despairing, climbed the slope behind her until they rested on the faint yellow spark that, solemn and unchanged, shone from the window of the dark house on the crest.

That way lay some chance, a desperate chance. She warned Lady Betty by a touch. 'We must run!' she breathed in the girl's ear. 'Look at the fence, and when I tap your shoulder, climb over and run to the house!'

Lady Betty disengaged herself softly and nodded. Then, as if she was granted some new insight into the character of the woman whose arms were round her, as if she saw more clearly than before the other's courage, and understood the self-denial that gave her the first and better chance, she drew Sophia's face to her, and clinging to her, kissed it. Then she crouched, waiting, waiting, her eyes on the fence.

Very, very gently Sophia lifted her head, saw that Hawkesworth was looking the other way, and gave the signal. Betty, nimble and active, was over in a moment, unseen, unheard. Sophia followed, but the fence creaked under her, and Hawkesworth heard it and turned. He saw her poised on the fence, in the full moonlight, so that not a line of her figure escaped him; with a yell of triumph he darted towards her. But directly in his path lay a low gorse-bush, still in shadow. He did not see it, tripped over it, and fell all his length on the grass. By the time he was up again, the two were dim flying shadows, all but lost in the darkness that lay beyond the fence.

All but lost; not quite. In three seconds he was at the fence, he was over it, he was beginning to gain on them. They strained every nerve, but they had to breast the steep side of the hill, and though fear and the horror of his hand upon their shoulders gave them wings, breath was lacking. Then Betty fell, and lost a precious yard; and though she was up again, and panting onwards gallantly, for a few seconds he thought that he would catch them with ease. Then the ascent began to tell on him also. The fall had shaken him. He began to pant and labour; he saw that he was not gaining on them, but rather losing ground, and he slackened his pace, and shouted to the man on guard in the road above, bidding him to stop them.

The man with an answering shout reined back his horse to the narrow pass where the road ran between the house and the cottages. There, peering forward, he made ready to intercept them. Fortunately, the moon, above and a little behind him, showed his figure in silhouette in the gap; and Sophia, clutching Betty's hand, dragged her back at the moment she was stepping into the moonlit road. An instant the two listened, trembling, palpitating, staring, like game driven into the middle of the field. But behind them Hawkesworth's scrambling footsteps and heavy breathing still came on; they could not wait. A moment's sickening doubt, and Sophia pressed Betty's hand, and the two darted together across the road, and took cover in a space still dark, between the two cottages that flanked it on the farther side.

The man in the gap gave the alarm, shouting that they had crossed the road; and Hawkesworth, coming up out of breath, asked with a volley of curses why he had not stopped them.

'Because they did not come my way!' the fellow answered bluntly. 'Why didn't you catch 'em, captain?'

'Where are they?' Hawkesworth panted fiercely.

'Straight over they went. No! Between the hovels here.'

But Hawkesworth had a little recovered his breath, and with it his cunning. Instead of following his prey into the dark space between the buildings, he darted round the other side of the lower cottage, and in a twinkling was on the open slope beyond. Here the moonlight fell evenly, the hillside was clear of gorse, he could see a hundred yards. But he caught no glimpse of fleeing figures, he heard no sound of retiring footsteps; and quick as thought he turned up the hill, and learned the reason.

A high wall ran from cottage to cottage, rendering exit that way impossible. Sophia had trapped herself and her companion; they were in a *cul de sac*! With a cry of triumph he turned to go back; as he ran he heard the horseman he had left call to him. Opportunely, as he gained the road, he was joined by the third of the band, the rogue he had left at the stepping-stones.

'Have you nabbed them?' the fellow panted.

'They're here!' Hawkesworth answered. 'I think he's got them.'

'And the sparklers?'

Hawkesworth nodded; but the next instant he swore and stood. The man on the horse, who should have been guarding the mouth of the dark entry, where the girls lay trapped, was a dozen yards farther up the road, his back to the cottages, and his face to the house with the gable end.

'What the devil are you doing?' Hawkesworth roared. 'They are here, man!'

'They have bolted!' the fellow answered sullenly. 'Or one of them has. She shook a shawl in this brute's face, and he reared. Before I could get him round—'

'She got off?' the Irishman shrieked.

'No! She's here, in the house! Burn her, when I get hold of her I'll make her smart for it!'

'She? Then where's the other?'

'She's where she was, for all I know,' the man answered. 'I've seen nothing of her.'

But he lied in that. While he had been marking down the woman who had frightened his horse with her shawl – and who then had glided coolly into the house, the door of which stood ajar – he had seen with the tail of his eye a flying skirt vanish down the road behind him. He had a notion that one had got clear, but he was not sure; and if he said anything he would be blamed. So he stood while Hawkesworth and the other searched the dark space between the cottages.

A few seconds sufficed to show that there was no one there, and Hawkesworth turned and swore at him.

'Well, there's one left!' the offender answered sulkily. 'We've got her in the house, and there's no back door. Take your change out of her.'

'Aye, but who's going in to fetch her?' Hawkesworth snarled. 'I've not had the smallpox. Perhaps you have. In that case, in you go, man. You run no risk, or but little.'

The rogue's face fell. 'Oh Lord!' he said. 'I'd not thought of that! What a vixen it is!'

'In you go, man, and have her out!'

'I'm hanged if I do!' was the answer; and the fellow reined back his horse in a hurry. 'Faugh! I can smell the vinegar from here!' he cried. And he spat on the ground.

'Will you go, Clipper? Come, man, you're not afraid?'

But Clipper, the third of the band, so called because he had once lain in the condemned hold for the offence of reducing His Majesty's gold coin, declined in terms not doubtful; and for a few seconds the three glared at one another, rage in the greater villain's eyes, a dogged resolution, not unmingled with shame, in his hirelings'. To be baffled, and by a girl! To have her at bay, and fear the encounter! To be outwitted, outdared, and by a woman! The moonlight that lay on the lovely countryside, the night wind that stirred the willows by the stream, the height of blue above them with its myriad watching eyes, these things had no awe for them, touched no chord in their dulled consciences; but the smoky yellow gleam that shone from the window of the dark gable, and was visible where two of them stood – that and the dread terror that lay behind it scared even these hardened men.

'Will you let all go?' Hawkesworth cried in rage. 'We have the girl, and not a soul within four miles to interfere! We've jewels to the tune of thousands! And you'll let them go when it's only to pick them up!'

'Aye, and the smallpox with them!' Clipper retorted grimly. 'I've seen a man that died of that,' with a shudder, 'and I don't want to see another. Go yourself, captain,' he sneered; 'it's your business.'

The thrust went home. 'So I will, by—!' the Irishman cried passionately. 'I'll have her out, and the stuff! But I'll think twice before I pay you, you lily-livers! You chicken hearts. Give me a light!'

'There's light enough upstairs!' the Clipper answered mockingly. But the other man, more amenable, produced a flint and steel and a candle end, and lighting the one from the other handed it to Hawkesworth. 'Likely enough you'll find her behind the door, captain,' he said civilly. ''Twon't be much risk after all.'

'Then go yourself, you cur,' Hawkesworth answered brutally. He was torn this way and that; between fear and rage, cupidity and cowardice. The ardour of the chase grew cool in this atmosphere of disease; the courage of the man failed before this house given up to the fell plague, that in those days took pitiless toll of rich and poor, of old and young, of withered cheeks and bright eyes, of kings' and joiners' daughters. His gorge rose at the sharp scent of vinegar, at the duller odour of burnt rags with which the air was laden, they were the rough disinfectants of the time, used before the panic-stricken survivors fled the place. In face of the danger he had to confront, women have ever been bolder than men, though they have more to lose. He was no exception.

Yet he would go. To flinch was to be lessened for ever in the eyes of the meaner villains, his hirelings; to dare was to confirm the evil pre-eminence he claimed. Bitter black rage in his heart – rage in especial against the woman who laid this necessity upon him – he thrust the door wide open, and shielding the candle, of which the light but feebly irradiated the black cavern before him, he crossed the threshold.

The place he entered seemed all dark to eyes fresh from the moonbeams; but some light there was beside that which he carried. From the open door of a narrow staircase that led to the upper rooms a faint reflection of the candles that burned above issued; by aid of which he saw that he stood in the great kitchen of the farm. But the black pot that tenanted the vast gloomy recess of the fireplace hung over dead, white ashes – cold relics of the cheer that had once reigned there. The cradle in the corner was still and shrouded. In the middle of the stone floor a bench, a mere slab on four straddling legs, lay overturned, upset by the panic-stricken survivors in their hurried flight; and beside it, stiff and grinning, sprawled the body of a black cat, killed in some frenzy of fear or superstition ere the living left the house to the care of the dead. A brooding odour of disease filled the gaunt, wide-raftered room, infected the shadowy hanging flitches, and grew stronger and more sickly towards the staircase at the farther end.

Yet it was there he saw her, as he paused uncertain, his heart like water. She was standing on the lowest step of the stair as if she had retreated thither on his entrance. Her one hand held her skirt a little from the floor, and close to her; the other hung by her side. Her eyes shone large in her white face; and in her look and in her attitude was something solemn and unearthly, that for a moment awed him.

He stared spell-bound. She was the first to speak. 'What do you want?' she whispered – as if the dead in the room above could hear her.

'The jewels!' he muttered, his voice subdued to the pitch of hers. 'The jewels! Give me the jewels, and I will go!'

'They are not here,' she said. 'They are far away. Here is only death. Death is here, death is above,' she continued solemnly. 'The air is full of death. If you would not die, go! Go before it be too late.'

He battled with the dark fear which her words fluttered before him; the fear that was in the air of the room, the fear that made his light burn more dimly than was natural. He battled with it, and hated her for it, and for his cowardice. 'You she-devil!' he cried, 'where are the jewels?'

'Gone,' she answered solemnly.

'Where?'

'Where you will never find them.'

'And you think to get off with that?' he hissed; and advanced a step towards her. 'You lie!' he cried furiously. 'You have them. And if you do not give them up—'

'I have them not!' she answered firmly; and little did he suspect how wildly her heart was leaping behind the bold front she showed him. Little did he suspect the deadly terror she had had to surmount before she penetrated so far into this loathsome house. 'I have them not,' she repeated. 'Nor have I any fear of you. There is that here is your master and mine. Come up, come up,' she continued, a touch of wildness in her manner, and she mounted a step or two of the narrow staircase, and beckoned him to follow her. 'Come up and you will see him.'

'You drab!' he cried, 'do you come down, or it will be the worse for you! Do you hear me? Come down, you slut, or when I fetch you I will have no mercy. You don't know what I shall do to you; I do, and—'

He stood, he was silent, he choked with rage; for as if he had not spoken, her figure first and then her feet, mounting without pause or hesitation, vanished from sight. He was left, scared and baffled, alone in the great desolate kitchen where his light shone a mere spark, making visible the darkness that canopied him. A rat moving in the dim fringe between light and shadow startled him. A rope of onions swayed by the draught of air that blew through the open door, brought the sweat to his brow. He took two steps forward and one backward; the shroud on the cradle fluttered, and but for the men waiting outside, he would have fled at once and given up woman and booty. But fear of ridicule still conquered fear of death; conquered even the superstition that lay dormant in his Irish blood; he forced himself onward. His eyes fixed balefully, his hands withheld from contact with the wall – as if he had been a woman with skirts – he crept upwards till his gaze rose above the level of the upper floor; then for a moment the light of two thick candles, half-burned, gave him back his courage. His brow relaxed, he sprang with a cry up the upper stairs, set his foot in the room and stood!

On the huge low wooden bed from which the coarse blue and white bedding protruded, two bodies lay sheeted. At their feet the candles burned dull before the window that should have been open, but was shut; as the thick noisome air of the room, that turned him sick and faint, told him. Near the bed, on the farther side, stood that he sought; Sophia, her eyes burning, her face like paper. His prey then was there, there, within his reach; but she had not spoken without reason. Death, death in its most loathsome aspect lay between them; and the man's heart was as water, his feet like lead.

'If you come near me,' she whispered, 'if you come a step nearer, I will snatch this sheet from them, and I will wrap you in it! And you will die! In eight days you will be dead! Will you see them? Will you see what you will be?' And she lowered her hand to raise the sheet.

He stepped back a pace, livid and shaking. 'You she-devil!' he muttered. 'You witch!'

'Go!' she answered, in the same low tone. 'Go! Or I will bring your death to you! And you will die! As you have lived, foul, noisome, corrupt, you will die! In eight days you will die – if you come one step nearer!'

She took a step forward herself. The man turned and fled.

CHAPTER XIX

Lady Betty's Fate

LADY BETTY had left the house on the hill a mile behind, her breath came in heavy gasps, her heart seemed to be bursting through her bodice; still she panted bravely along the road that stretched before her, white under the moonbeams. Sophia had bidden her run, the moment the man's back was turned. 'Give the alarm, get help,' she had whispered as she thrust the diamonds into the child's hand; and acting on that instinct of obedience, prompt and unquestioning, which the imminence of peril teaches, Betty had fled on the word. She had slipped behind the man's back, passed between the houses, and escaped into the open, unseen, as she fancied.

For a time she had sped along the road, looking this way and that, expecting at each turn to discover a house, a light, the help she sought. At length, coming on none of these, she began to suspect the truth, and that Sophia had saved her at her own cost; and she paused and turned, and even in her distraction made as if she would go back. But in the end, with a sob of grief, she hurried on, seeing in this their only chance.

At length her strength began to fail. Presently she could go no farther, and with a cry of anguish came to a stand in a dark part of the road. She alone, in an unknown country, with the night before her, with the sounds of the night around her; and commonly she was afraid of the night. But now all the child's thought was for Sophia; her heart was breaking for her friend. And by-and-by she pressed on again, her breath fluttering between sobs and exhaustion. She turned a corner – and oh, sweet, she saw a light before her!

She struggled towards it. The spark grew larger and larger; finally it became the open doorway of an alehouse, from which the company were departing. The goodman and two or three topers were on their feet having a last crack, the goodwife from her bed above was demanding lustily why they lingered, when the girl, breathless and dishevelled, her hair hanging about her face, appeared on the threshold. For a moment she could not speak; her face was white, her eyes stared wildly. The men fell back from her, as a flock of sheep crowd away from the dog.

'What beest 'ee?' the landlord bleated faintly. 'Lord save us and help us! Be 'ee mortal?'

'Help!' she muttered, as she leaned almost swooning, against the doorpost. 'Help! Come quickly! They'll – they'll murder her – if you don't!' And she stretched out her hands to them.

But the men only shuddered. 'Lord save us!' one of them stammered. 'It's mostly for murder they come.'

She saw that no one moved, and she could have screamed with impatience. 'Don't you hear me?' she cried hoarsely. 'Come, or they'll kill her! They'll kill her! I've left her with them. Come, if you are men!'

They began to see that the girl was flesh and blood; but their minds were rustic, and none of the quickest, and they might have continued to gape at her for some time longer, if the goodwife, who had heard every word, had not looked through the trap in the ceiling. She saw the girl. 'Lord's sake!' she cried, struck with amazement. 'What is it?'

'Help!' Betty answered, clasping her hands, and turning her eyes in that direction. 'For pity's sake send them with me! There's murder being done on the road! Tell them to come with me.'

'What is it? Footpads?' the woman asked sharply.

'Yes, oh yes! They have stopped Lady Coke's carriage—'

The woman waited to hear no more. 'Quick, you fools!' she cried. 'Get sticks, and go! Lady Coke's carriage, eh? You'll be her woman, I expect. They'll come, they'll come. But where is't? Speak up, and don't be afraid!'

'At a house on a hill,' Lady Betty answered rapidly. 'She's there, hiding from them. And oh, be quick! be quick, if you please!'

But at that word the goodman, who had snatched up a thatching stake, paused on the threshold. 'A house on a hill?' he said. 'Do you mean Beamond's farm?'

'I don't know,' she answered. 'It's on a hill about a mile or more – oh, more from here – on the way I came! You must know it!'

'This side of a ford?'

'Yes, yes.'

'They've the smallpox there?'

'Yes, I think so!'

The man flung down the stake. 'No,' he said. 'It's no! I don't go there. Devil take me if I do. And she don't come here. If you are of my mind,' he continued, looking darkly at his fellows, 'you'll leave this alone!'

The men were evidently of that mind; they threw down their weapons, some with a curse, some with a shiver. Betty saw, and frantic, could not believe her eyes. 'Cowards!' she cried. 'You cowards!'

The woman alone looked at her uncertainly. 'I've children, you see,' she said. 'I've to think of them. But there's Crabbe could go. He's neither chick nor child.'

But the lout she named backed into a corner, sullen and resolute; as if he feared they would force him to go. 'Not I,' he said. 'I don't go near it, neither. There's three there dead and stiff, and three's enough.'

'You cowards!' Betty repeated, sobbing with passion.

The woman, too, looked at them with no great favour. 'Will none of you go?' she said. 'Mind you, if you go I'll be bound you'll be paid! Or perhaps the young sir there will go!'

She turned as she spoke, and Betty, looking in the same direction, saw a young man seated on the side of a box bed in the darkest part of the kitchen. Apparently her entrance had roused him from sleep, for his hair was rough, and he was in his shirt and breeches. His boots, clay-stained to the knees, stood beside the bed; his coat and cravat, which were drying in the chimney corner showed that he had been out in bad weather. The clothes he retained bore traces of wear and usage; but, though plain, they seemed to denote a higher station than that of the rustics in his company. As his eyes met Lady Betty's, 'I'll come,' he said gruffly. And he reached for his boots and began to put them on; but with a yawn.

Still she was thankful. 'Oh, will you!' she cried. 'You're a man. And the only one here!'

'He won't be one long!' the nearest boor cried spitefully.

But the lad, dropping for a moment his listless manner, took a step in the speaker's direction; and the clown recoiled. The young fellow laughed, and, snatching up a stout stick that rested against his truckle bed, said he was ready. 'You know the way?' he said; and then, as he read exhaustion written on her face, 'Quick, mother,' he cried in an altered tone, 'have you naught you can give her? She will drop before she has gone a mile!'

The woman hurried up the ladder and fetched a little spirit in a mug. She handed it to the girl at arm's length, telling her to drink it, it would do her good. Then cutting a slice from a loaf of coarse bread that lay on the table, she pushed it over to her. 'Take that in your hand,' she said, 'and God keep you.'

Betty did as she was bidden, though she was nearly sick with surprise. Then she thanked the woman, turned, and, deaf to the boors' gibes, passed into the road with her new protector. She showed him the way she had come, and the two set off walking at the top of her pace.

She swallowed a morsel of bread, then ran a little, the tears rising in her eyes as she thought of Sophia. A moment of this feverish haste, and the lad bade her walk. 'If we've a mile to go,' he said wisely, 'you cannot run all the way. Slow and steady kills the hare, my dear. How many are there of these gentry?'

'Three,' she answered; and as she pictured Sophia and those three a lump rose in her throat.

'Any servants? I mean had your mistress any men with her?'

Betty told him, but incoherently. The postboys, the grooms, Watkyns, Pettitt, all were mixed up in her narrative. He tried to follow it, then gave up the attempt. 'Anyway, they have all fled,' he said. 'It comes to that.'

She admitted with a sob that it was so; that Sophia was alone.

The moonlight lay on the road; as she tripped by his side, he turned and scanned her. He took her for my lady's woman, as the mistress at the alehouse had taken her. He had caught the name of Coke, but he knew no Lady Coke; he had not heard of Sir Hervey's marriage, and, to be truthful, his mind was more concerned for the maid than the mistress. Through the disorder of Betty's hair and dress, her youth and something of her beauty peeped out; it struck him how brave she had been to come for help, through the night, alone; how much more brave she was to be willing to return, seeing that he was but one to three, and there was smallpox to face. As he considered this he felt a warmth at his heart which he had not felt for days. And he sighed.

Presently her steps began to lag; she stood. 'Where are we?' she cried, fear in her voice. 'We should be there!'

'We've come about a mile,' he said, peering forward through the moonlight. 'Is it on a hill, did you say?'

'Yes, and I see no hill.'

'No,' he answered, 'but perhaps the fall this way is gentle.'

She muttered a word of relief. 'That is so,' she said. 'It's above the water, on the farther side, that it is steep. Come on, please come on! I think I see a house.'

But the house she saw proved to be only a deserted barn, at the junction of two roads; and they stood dismayed. 'Did you pass this?' he asked.

'I don't know,' she cried. 'Yes, I think so.'

'On your right or your left?'

She wrung her hands. 'I think it was on my right,' she said.

He took the right-hand turn without more ado, and they hurried along the road for some minutes. At length her steps began to flag. 'I must be wrong,' she faltered. 'I must be wrong! Oh, why,' she cried, 'why did I leave her?' And she stood.

'Courage!' he answered. 'I see a rising ground on the left. And there's a house on it. We ought to have taken the other turning. Now we are here we had better cross the open. Shall I lift you over the ditch, child? Or shall I leave you and go on?'

But she scrambled into the ditch and out again; on the other side the two set off running with one accord, across an open field, dim and shadowy, that stretched away to the foot of the ascent. Soon he outpaced her, and she fell to walking. 'Go on!' she panted bravely. 'On, on, I will follow!'

He nodded, and clutching his stick by the middle, he lengthened his stride. She saw him come to a blurred line at the foot of the hill, and heard him break through the fence. Then the darkness that lay on the hither slope of the hill – for the moon was beginning to decline – swallowed him; and she walked on more slowly. Each moment she expected to hear a cry, an oath, the sudden clash of arms would break the silence of the night.

But the silence held; and still silence. And now the fence brought her up also; and she stood waiting, trembling, listening, in a prolongation of suspense, almost intolerable. At length, unable to bear it longer, she pushed her way into the hedge, and struggled, panting, through it; and was starting to clamber up the ascent on the other side when a dark form loomed beside her.

It was her companion. What had happened?

'We were wrong,' he muttered. 'It's a clump of trees, not a house. And there are clouds coming up to cover the moon. Let us return to the road while we can, my girl.'

But this was too much. At this, the last of many disappointments, the girl's courage snapped, as a rush snaps. With a wild outburst of weeping, she flung herself down on the sloping ground, and rubbed her face in the grass, and tore the soil with her fingers in an agony of abandonment. 'Oh, I left her! I left her!' she wailed, when sobs allowed words to pass. 'I left her, and saved myself. And she's dead! Oh, why didn't I stay with her? Why didn't I stay with her?'

The young man listened awhile, awkward, perturbed; when he spoke his voice was husky. ''Tis no use,' he said peevishly. 'No use, child! Don't – don't go on like this! See here, you'll have a fever if you lie there. You will, I know,' he repeated.

'I wish I had!' she cried with passion, and beat her hands on the ground. 'Oh why did I leave her?'

He cleared his throat. 'It's folly this!' he urged. 'It's – it's of no use to anyone. No good! And there, now it's dark. I told you so – and we shall have fine work getting to the road again!'

She did not answer, but little by little his meaning reached her brain, and after a minute or two she sat up, her crying less violent. 'That's better,' he said. 'But you are too tired to go farther. Let me help you to climb the fence. There's a log the other side – I stumbled over it. You can sit on it until you are rested.'

She did not assent, but she suffered him to help her through the hedge, and seat her on the fallen tree. The tide of grief had ebbed; she was regaining her self-control, though now and again a sob shook her. But he saw that an interval must pass before she could travel, and he stood, shy and silent, seeing her dimly by the light which the moon still shed through a flying wrack of clouds. Round and below them lay the country, still, shadowy, mysterious; stretching away into unknown infinities, framing them in a solitude perfect and complete. They might have been the only persons in the world.

By-and-by, whether he was tired, or really had a desire to comfort her at closer quarters, he sat down on the tree; and by chance his hand touched her hand. She sprang a foot away, and uttered a cry. He laughed softly.

'You need not be afraid,' he said. 'I've seen enough of women to last me my life. If you were the only woman in the world, and the most beautiful, you would be safe enough for me. You may be quite easy, my dear.'

She ceased to sob, but her voice was a little broken and husky when she spoke. 'I'm very sorry,' she said humbly. 'I am afraid I have given you a vast deal of trouble, sir.'

'Not so much as a woman has given me before this,' he answered.

She looked at him furtively out of the tail of her eye, as a woman at that would be likely to look. And if the truth be told she felt, amid all her grief, an inclination to laugh. But with feminine tact she suppressed this. 'And yet – and yet you came to help me?' she muttered.

He shrugged his shoulders. 'One has to do certain things,' he said.

'I am afraid somebody has – has behaved badly to you,' she murmured; and she sighed.

Somehow the sigh flattered him. 'As women generally behave,' he replied with a sneer. 'She lied to me, she cheated me, she robbed me, and she would have ruined me.'

'And men don't do those things,' she answered meekly, 'to women.' And she sighed again.

He started. It could not be that she was laughing at him. 'Anyway, I have done with women,' he said brusquely.

'And you'll never marry, sir?'

'Marry? Oh, I say nothing as to that,' he answered contemptuously. 'Marry I may, but it won't be for love. And 'twill be a lady anyway; I'll see to that. I'll know her father and her mother, and her grandfather and her grandmother,' Tom continued. For poor Tom it was, much battered and weathered by a week spent on the verge of 'listing. 'I'll have her pedigree by heart, and she shall bring her old nurse with her to speak for her, if marry I must. But no more ladies in distress for me. No more ladies picked up off the road, I thank you. That's all.'

'You are frank, sir, at any rate,' she said: and she laughed in a sort of wonder, taking it to herself.

At the sound, Tom, who had meant nothing personal, felt ashamed of himself. 'I beg your pardon, my dear,' he answered. 'But – but I wished to put you at your ease. I wished to show you, you were safe with me; as your mistress would be.'

'Oh, thank you,' Betty answered. 'For the matter of that, sir, I've had a lover myself, and said no to him, as well as my betters. But it wasn't before he asked me,' she continued ironically. And she tossed her head again.

'I didn't mean – I mean I thought you were afraid of me,' Tom stammered, wondering she took it so ill.

'No more than my mistress would be,' she retorted sharply. 'And I'm just as particular as she is – in one thing.'

'What's that?' he asked.

'I don't take gentlemen off the road, either.'

He laughed, seeing himself hit; and as if that recalled her to herself, she sprang up with a sob of remorse. 'Oh,' she said, wringing her hands, 'we sit here and play, while she suffers! We don't think of her! Do something! do something if you are a man!'

'But we don't know where we are, or where she is.'

'Then let us find her,' she cried; 'let us find her!'

'We can do nothing in the dark,' he urged. 'It is dark as the pit now. If we can find our way to the road again, it will be as much as we can do.'

'Let us try! let us try!' she answered, growing frantic. 'I shall go mad if I stay here.'

He gave way at that, and consented to try. But they had not gone fifty yards before she tripped and fell, and he heard her gasp for breath.

'Are you hurt?' he asked, stooping anxiously over her.

'No,' she said. But she rose with difficulty, and he knew by her voice that she was shaken.

'It's of no use to go on,' he said. 'I told you so. We must stay here. It is after midnight now. In an hour, or a little more, dawn will appear. If we find the road now we can do no good.'

She shivered. 'Take me back,' she said miserably. 'I – I don't know where we are.'

He took her hand, and with a little judgement found the tree again. 'If you could sleep awhile,' he said, 'the time would pass.'

'I cannot,' she cried, 'I cannot.' And then, 'Oh Sophy! Sophy!' she wailed, 'why did I leave you? Why did I leave you?'

He let her weep a minute or two, and then as much to distract her as for any other reason, he asked her if she had been brought up with her mistress.

She ceased to sob. 'Why?' she asked, startled.

'Because – you called her by her name,' he said. 'I noticed because I've a sister of that name.'

'Sophia?'

'Yes. If I had listened to her – but there, what is the use of talking?' And he broke off brusquely.

Lady Betty was silent awhile, only betraying her impatience by sighing or beating the trunk with her heels. By-and-by, the hours before the dawn came, and it grew cold. He heard her teeth chatter, and after fumbling with his coat, he took it off, and, in spite of her remonstrances, wrapped her in it.

'Don't,' she said, feebly struggling with him. 'Don't! You're a gentleman, and I am only—'

'You're a woman as much as your mistress,' he answered roughly.

'But – you hate women!' she cried.

'You don't belong to me,' he answered with disdain, 'and you'll not die on my hands! Do as you are bidden, child!'

After that he walked up and down before the tree; until at last the day broke, and the grey light, spreading and growing stronger, showed them a sea of mist, covering the whole world – save the little eminence on which they sat – and flowing to their very feet. It showed them also two haggard faces – his weary, hers beautiful in spite of its pallor and her long vigil. For in some mysterious way she had knotted up her hair and tied her kerchief. As she gave him back his coat, and their eyes me, he started and grew red.

'Good heavens, child!' he cried, 'you are too handsome to be wandering the country alone; and too young.'

She had nothing to say to that, but her cheeks flamed, and she begged him to come quickly – quickly; and together they went down into the mist. At that hour the birds sing in chorus as they never sing in the day; and, by the time the two reached the road the sun was up and the world round them was joyous with warmth and light and beauty. The dew besprinkled every bush with jewels as bright as those which Betty carried in her bosom – for she had thrown away the case – and from the pines on the hill came the perfume of a hundred Arabys. Tom wondered why his heart beat so lightly, why he felt an exhilaration to which he had been long a stranger. Heartbroken, a woman-hater, a cynic, it could not be because a pair of beautiful eyes had looked kindly into his? because a waiting-maid had for a moment smiled on him? That was absurd.

For her, left to herself, she would have pursued the old plan, and gone wildly, frantically up and down, seeking at random the place where she had left Sophia. But he would not suffer it. He led her to the nearest cottage, and learning from the staring inhabitants the exact position of Beamond's Farm, got his companion milk and bread, and saw her eat it. Then he announced his purpose.

'I shall leave you here,' he said. 'In two hours at the most I shall be back with news.'

'And you think I'll stay?' she cried.

'I think you will, for I shall not take you,' he answered coolly. 'Do you want the smallpox, silly child? Do you think your ladics will be as ready to hire you when you have lost your looks? Stay here, and in two hours I shall be back.'

She cried that she would not stay; she would not stay! 'I shall not!' she cried a third time. 'Do you hear me? I shall go with you!'

'You will not!' Tom said. 'And for a good reason, my girl. You heard that woman ask us whether we came from Beamond's and you saw the way she looked at us. If it's known we've been there, there's not a house within ten miles will take us in, nor a coach will give us a lift. You have had one night out, you'll not bear another. Now, with me it is different.'

'It is not,' she cried. 'I shall go.'

'You will not,' he said; and their eyes met. And presently hers dropped. 'You will not,' he repeated masterfully; 'because I am the stronger, and I will tie you to a gate before you shall go. And you, little fool, will be thankful to me tomorrow. It's for your own good.'

She gave way at that, crying feebly, for the night had shaken her. 'Sit here in sight of the cottage,' he continued, thrusting aside the brambles and making a place for her beside a tree, 'and if you can sleep a little, so much the better. In two hours at the farthest I will be back.'

She obeyed, watched him go, and saw his figure grow smaller and smaller, until it vanished at a turn of the road. She watched the woman of the cottage pass in and out with pail and pattens, and by-and-by she had to parry her questions. She saw the sun climb higher and higher in the sky, and heard the hum of the bees grow loud and louder, and felt the heat of the day take hold; and yet he did not return. And while she watched for him most keenly, as she imagined, she fell asleep.

When she awoke he was standing over her, and his face told her all. She sprang up. 'You've not found her!' she cried, clasping her hands, and holding them out to him.

'No,' he said, 'There's no one in the house. No one but the dead.'

CHAPTER XX

A Friend in Need

SOPHIA'S KNEES shook under her, her flesh shuddered in revolt, but she held her ground until Hawkesworth's footsteps and the murmur of his companions' jeering voices sank and died in the distance. Then, with eyes averted from the bed, she crept to the head of the stairs and descended, her skirts gathered jealously about her. She reached the kitchen. Here, in the twilight that veiled the shrouded cradle, and mercifully hid worse things, she listened awhile; peering with scared eyes into the corners, and prepared to flee at the least alarm. Satisfied at last that those she feared had really withdrawn, she passed out into the open, and under the night sky, with the fresh breeze cooling her fevered face, she drank in with ecstasy a first deep breath of relief. Oh, the pureness of that draught! Oh, the freedom and the immensity of the vault above her – after that charnel-house!

She felt sure that the men had retired the way they had come, and after a moment's hesitation she turned in the other direction, and venturing into the moonlight, took the road that Betty had taken. Now she paused to listen, now on some alarm effaced herself in the shadow cast by a tree. By-and-by, when she had left the plague-stricken house two or three hundred paces behind her, her ear caught the pleasant ripple of water.

Her throat was parched, and she stopped, and traced the sound to a spring that, bubbling from a rock, filled a mossy caldron sunk in the earth, then ran to waste in a tiny rill beside the road. The hint was enough; in a second she had dragged off her outer garment, a green riding-coat, and shuddering, flung it from her; in another she had thrown off her shoes and loosened her hair. A moment she listened; then, having assured herself that she was not pursued, she plunged head and hair and hands in the fountain, let the cool water run over her fevered arms and neck, revelled in the purifying touch that promised to remove from her the loathsome infection of the house. She was a woman, she had not only death, but disfigurement to fear. One of the happy few who, under the early Georges, when even inoculation was in its infancy, had escaped the disease, she clung to her immunity with a nervous dread.

When she had done all she could, she rose to her feet and knotted up her hair. She had Betty on her mind; she must follow the girl. But midnight was some time past, the moon was declining, and her strength, sapped by the intense excitement under which she had laboured, was nearly spent. The chances that she would alight on Betty were slight, while it was certain that the girl would eventually return, or would send to the place where they had parted company. Sophia determined to remain where she was; and with the music of the rill for company, and a large stone that stood beside it for a seat, hard but dry, the worst discomfort which she had to fear was cold; and this, in her fervent gratitude for rescue from greater perils, she bore without complaint.

The solemnity of the night, as it wore slowly to morning, the depth of silence – as of death – that preceded the dawn, the stir of thanksgiving that greeted the birth of another day, these working on a nature stirred by strange experiences and now subject to a strange solitude, awoke in her thoughts deeper than ordinary. She saw in Betty's recklessness the mirror of her own; she shuddered at Hawkesworth, disclosed to her in his true colours; and considered Sir Hervey's patience with new wonder. Near neighbour to death, she viewed life as a thing detached and whole; with its end as well as its beginning. And she informed resolutions, humble at the least.

By-and-by she had to rise and be walking to keep herself

warm; for she would not resume her riding-coat, and her arms were bare. A little later, however, the sun rose high enough to reach her. In the great oak that overhung the spring, the birds began to flit like moving shadows; a squirrel ran down the bark and looked at her. And in her veins a strange exhilaration began to stir. She was alive! She was safe! And then, on a sudden, she heard a footstep close at hand.

She cowered low, seized with terror. It might be Hawkesworth! The villain might have repented of his fears, have gathered courage with the light, have returned more ruthless than he had gone. Fortunately, the panic which the thought bred in her was short-lived. An asthmatic cough, followed by the noise of heavy breathing, put an end to her suspense. Next moment an elderly man wearing a rusty gown and a shabby hat decked with a rosette, came in sight. He leant on a stout stick, and carried a cloak on his arm. He had white hair and a benevolent aspect, with features that seemed formed by nature for mirth, and compelled by circumstances to sober uses.

Aware of the oddity of her appearance – bare-armed and in her stockinged feet – Sophia hung back, hesitating to address him; he was quite close to her when he lifted his eyes and saw her. The good man's surprise could scarcely have been greater had he come upon the nymph of the spring. He started, dropped his stick and cloak, and stared, his jaw fallen; it even seemed to her that a little of the colour left his face.

At last, 'My child,' he cried, 'what are you doing here, of all places? D'you come from the house above?'

'I have been there,' she answered.

He stared. 'But they have the smallpox!' he exclaimed. 'Did you know it?'

'I went there to avoid worse things,' she cried; and fell to trembling. 'Do you live here, sir?'

'Here? No; but I live in the valley below,' he answered, still contemplating her with astonishment. 'I am only here,' he continued, with a touch of sternness which she did not understand, 'because my duty leads me here, I am told – God grant it be not true – that there are three dead at the farm, and that the living are fled.'

'It is true,' she answered briefly. And against the verdure, framed in the beauty of this morning world, with its freshness, its dancing sunlight, and its flitting birds, she saw the death-room, the foetid mist about the smoking, guttering candles, the sheeted form. She shuddered.

'You are sure?' he said.

'I have seen them,' she answered.

'Then I need go no farther now,' he replied in a tone of relief. 'I can do no good. I must return and get help to bury them. It will be no easy task; my parishioners are stricken with panic, they think only of their wives and families. Even in my own household – but I am forgetting, child. You are a stranger here? And, Lord bless me, what has become of your gown?'

She pointed to the place where it lay a little apart, in a heap on the ground. 'I've taken it off,' she explained, colouring slightly. 'I fear it carries the infection. I was attacked in my carriage on the other side of the ford. And robbed. And to avoid worse things I took refuge in the house above.'

'Lord save us!' he cried, lifting his hands in astonishment. 'I never heard of such a thing! Never! We have had no such doings in these parts these twenty years!'

'Perhaps you could lend me your cloak, sir?' she said. 'Until I can get something.'

He handed it to her. 'To be sure, to be sure,' he answered. And then, 'In your carriage?' he continued. 'Dear, dear, and had you anyone with you, ma'am?'

'My friend escaped,' she explained, 'with – with some jewels I had. The postboys had been sent ahead to Lewes to get fresh horses. Watkyns, one of the servants, had returned towards Fletching, to see if he could get help in that quarter. My woman was so frightened that she was useless, and the two grooms had been made drunk on the road, and were useless also!'

She did not notice, that with each item in her catalogue, the old clergyman's eyes grew wider and wider; nor that towards the end surprise began to give place to incredulity. This talk of horses, and grooms, and servants, and maids, and postboys in the mouth of a girl found hatless and shoeless by the roadside – a creature with tumbled hair, without a gown, and in petticoats soaked with water and stained with dust and dirt, overstepped the bounds of reason. Unfortunately, a little before this a young woman had appeared in a town not far off, in the guise of a countess; and with all the apparatus of the rank had taken in no less worshipful a body than the mayor and corporation of the place, who in the issue had been left to bewail their credulity. The tale was rife along the country-side; the old clergyman knew it, and being by nature a simple soul – as his wife often told him – had the cunning of simplicity. He bade himself be cautious – be cautious; and as he listened bethought him of a test. 'Your carriage should be there, then?' he said. 'Where you left it, ma'am?'

'I have not dared to return and see,' she answered. 'We might do so now, if you will be kind enough to accompany me.'

'To be sure, to be sure. Let us go, child.'

But when they had crossed the ridge – keeping as far as they could from the door of the plague-stricken house – he was no whit surprised to find no carriage, no servant, no maid! From the brow of the hill they could trace with their eyes the desolate valley and the road by which she had come; but nowhere on the road, or beside it, was any sign of life. Sophia had been so much shaken by the events of the night that she had forgotten the possibility of rescue at the hands of her own people. Now that the notion was suggested to her, she found the absence of the carriage, of Watkyns, of the grooms, inexplicable. And she said so; but the very expression of her astonishment, following abruptly on his suggestion that the carriage should be there, did but deepen the good parson's doubts. She had spun her tale, he thought, without providing for this point, and now sought to cover the blot by exclamations of surprise.

He had not the heart, however, good honest soul as he was, to unmask her; on the contrary, he suffered as great embarrassment as if the deceit had been his own. He found himself constrained to ask in what way he could help her; and when she suggested that she should rest at his house, he assented. But with little spirit.

'If it be not too far?' she said, struck by his tone, and with a thought also for her unshod feet.

'It's – it's about a mile,' he answered.

'Well, I must walk it.'

'You don't think – I could send,' he suggested weakly, 'and – and make inquiries – for your people, ma'am?'

'If you please, when I am there,' she said; and that left him no recourse but to start with her. But as they went amid all the care she was forced to give to her steps, she noticed that he regarded her oddly; that he looked askance at her when he thought her eyes elsewhere, and looked away guiltily when she caught him in the act.

They plodded some half-mile, then turned to the right, and a trifle farther came in sight of a little hamlet that nestled among chestnut trees in a dimple of the hill-face. As they approached this, his uneasiness became more marked; nor was Sophia left in ignorance of its cause. The first house to which they came was a neat thatched cottage beside the church. A low wicket-gate gave access to the garden, and over this appeared for a moment an angry woman's face, turned in the direction whence they came. It was gone as soon as seen; but Sophia, from a faltered word which dropped from her companion, learned to whom it belonged; and when he tried the wicket-gate she was not surprised to see it was fastened. He tried it nervously, his face grown red; then he raised his voice. 'My love,' he cried, 'I have come back. I think you did not see us. Will you please to open the gate?'

An ominous silence was the only answer. He tried the gate a second time, in a shamefaced way. 'My dear,' he cried aloud, a quaver in his patient tone, 'I have come back.'

'And more shame to you,' a shrill voice answered, the speaker remaining unseen. 'Do you hear me, Michieson? More shame to you, you unnatural father! Didn't you hear me say I would not have you going to that place? And didn't I tell you if you went you would not come here again! You thought yourself mighty clever, I'll be bound,' the termagant continued, 'to go off while I was asleep, my man! But you'll sleep in the garden house, for in here you don't come! Who's that with you?'

'A – a young lady in trouble,' he stammered.

'Where did you find her?'

'On the road, my love! In great trouble.'

'Then on the road you may leave her,' the shrew retorted. 'No, my man, you don't come over me that way. You brought the hussy from that house. Tell me she's not been in it, if you dare? And you'd bring her among your innocent, lawful children, would you, and give 'em their deaths! Fie,' with rising indignation, 'you silly old fool! If you weren't a natural, in place of such rubbish, you'd have been over to Sir Hervey's and complimented madam this fine morning, and been 'pointed chaplain. But 'tis like you. Instead of providing for your wife and children, as a man should, you're trying to give 'em their deaths, among a lot of dead people that'll never find you in a bit of bread to put in their bellies, or a bit of stuff to put on their backs! I tell you, Michieson, I've no patience with you.'

'But, my dear—'

'Now send her packing. Do you hear me, Michieson?'

He was going to remonstrate, but Sophia intervened. Spent with fatigue, her feet sore and blistered, she felt that she could not go a yard farther. Moreover, to eyes dazed by the horrors of the night, the thatched house among the rosebriars, with its hum of bees and scent of woodbine and honey-suckle, seemed a haven of peace. She raised her voice. 'Mrs Michieson,' she said, 'your husband need not go to Sir Hervey's. I am Lady Coke.'

With a cry of amazement a thin, red-faced woman, scantily dressed in an old soiled wrapper that had known a richer wearer – for Mrs Michieson had been a lady's maid – pushed through the bushes. She stared a moment with all her eyes; then she burst into a rude laugh. 'You mean her woman, I should think,' she said. 'Why, you saucy piece, you must think us fine simpletons to try for to come over us with that story. Lady Coke in her stockinged feet, indeed!'

'I have been robbed,' Sophia faltered, trying not to break down. 'You are a woman. Surely you have some pity for another woman in trouble?'

'Aye, you are like enough to have been in trouble! That I can see!' the parson's lady answered with a sneer. 'But I'll trouble you not to call me a woman!' she continued, tossing her head. 'Woman, indeed! A pretty piece you are to call names, trapesing the country like a guy, and – why, whose cloak have you there? *Michieson!*' in a voice like vinegar. 'What does this mean?'

'My dear,' he said humbly – Sophia, on the verge of tears, could say no more lest she should break down, 'the – the lady was robbed on the road. She was travelling in her carriage—'

'In her carriage?'

'And her servants ran away – as I understand,' he explained, rubbing his hands, and smiling in a sickly way, 'and the post-boys did not return, and – and her woman—'

'Her woman!'

'Well, yes, my dear, so she tells me, was so frightened she stayed with the carriage. And her friend, a – another lady, escaped in the dark with some jewels – and—'

'Michieson!' madam cried, in her most awful voice, 'did you believe this – this cock and bull story that you dare to repeat to me?'

He glanced from one to the other. 'Well, my dear,' he answered in confusion, 'I – at least, the lady told me—'

'Did you believe it? Yes or no! Did you believe it?'

'Well, I—'

'Did you go to look for the carriage?'

'Yes, my dear, I did.'

'And did you find it?'

'Well, no,' the clergyman confessed. 'I did not.'

'Nor the servants?'

'No, but—'

She did not let him explain. 'Now,' she cried, with shrill triumph, 'you see what a fool you are! And where you'd be if it were not for me. Did she say a word about being Lady Coke until she heard her name from me? Eh? Answer me that, did she?'

Very miserable, he glanced at Sophia. 'Well, no, my dear, I don't think she did!' he admitted.

'So I thought!' madam cried. And then with a cruel gesture, 'Off with it, you baggage! Off with it!' she continued. 'Do you think I don't know that the moment my back is turned you'll be gone, and a good cloak with you! No, off with it, my ragged madam, and thank your stars I don't send you to the stocks!'

But her husband plucked up spirit at that.

'No,' he said firmly. 'No, she shall keep the cloak till she can get a covering. For shame, wife, for shame,' he continued with a smack of dignity. 'Do you never think that a daughter of yours may some day stand in her shoes?'

'You fool, she has got none!' his wife snarled. 'And you'll give her that cloak at your peril.'

'She shall keep it, till she gets a covering,' he answered.

'Then she'll keep it somewhere else, not here!' the termagant answered in a fury. 'Do you call yourself a parson and go trapesing the country with a slut like that? And your lawful wife left at home!'

Sophia, white with exhaustion, could scarcely keep her feet, but at that she plucked up spirit. 'The cloak I shall keep, for it is your husband's,' she said. 'For yourself, ma'am, you will bitterly repent before the day is out that you have treated me in this way.'

'Hoity-toity! you'd threaten me, would you?' the other cried viciously. 'Here, Tom, Bill! Ha' you no stones. Here's a besom ill-speaking your mother. Ah, I thought you'd be going, ma'am,' she continued, leaning over the gate, with a grin of satisfaction. 'It'll be in the stocks you'll sit before the day is out, I'm thinking.'

But Sophia was out of hearing; rage and indignation gave her strength. But not for long. The reception with which she had met, in a place where, of all places, peace and charity and a seat for the wretched should have been found, broke down the last remains of endurance. As soon as the turn in the road hid her from the other woman's eyes, she sank on a bank, unable to go farther. She must eat and drink and rest, or she must die.

Fortunately, the poor vicar, worthy of a better mate, had not quite abandoned her cause. After standing a moment divided between indignation and fear, he allowed the more generous impulse to have way; he followed and found her. Shocked to read exhaustion plainly written on her face, horrified by the thought that she might die at his door, that door which day and night should have been open to the distressed, he half led and half carried her to the little garden house to which his wife had exiled him; and which by good fortune stood in an orchard, beyond, but close to the curtilage of the house. Here he left her a moment, and procuring the drudge of a servant to hand him a little bread and milk over the fence, he fed her with his own hands, and waited patiently beside her until the colour returned to her face.

Relieved by the sight, and satisfied that she was no longer in danger, he began to be troubled; glancing furtively at her and away again, and often moving to the door of the shed, which looked out on a pleasant plot of grass dappled with sunlight and overhung by drooping boughs on which the late blossom lingered. Finally, seeing her remain languid and spiritless, he blurted out what was in his mind. 'I daren't keep you here,' he muttered, with a flush of shame. 'If my wife discovers you, she may do you a mischief. And the fear of the smallpox is such, they'd stone you out of the parish if they knew you have been at Beamond's – God forgive them!'

Sophia looked at him in astonishment. 'But I have told you who I am,' she said. 'I am Lady Coke. Surely you believe me.'

'Child!' he said in a tone of gentle reproof. 'Let be. You don't know what you say. There's not an acre in this parish is not Sir Hervey's, nor a house, nor a barn. Is it likely his honour's lady would be wandering shoeless in the roads?'

She laughed hysterically. Tragedy and comedy were strangely mingled this morning. 'Yet it is so,' she said. 'It is so.'

He shook his head in reproof, but did not answer.

'You don't believe me?' she cried. 'How far is it to Coke Hall?'

'About three miles,' he answered unwillingly.

'Then the doubt is solved. Go thither! Go thither at once!' she continued, the power to think returning, and with it the remembrance of Lady Betty's danger. 'At once!' she repeated, rising in her impatience, while a flood of colour swept over her face. 'You must see Sir Hervey, and tell him that Lady Coke is here, and that Lady Betty Cochrane is missing; that we have been robbed, and he must instantly, instantly before he comes here, make search for her.'

The old parson stared. 'For whom?' he stammered.

'For Lady Betty Cochrane, who was with me.'

He continued to stare; with the beginnings of doubt in his eyes. 'Child,' he said, 'are you sure you are not bubbling me? 'Twill be a poor victory over a simple old man.'

'I am not! I am not!' she cried. And suddenly bethinking her of the pocket that commonly hung between the gown and petticoat, she felt for it. She had placed her rings as well as her purse in it. Alas, it was gone! The strings had yielded to rough usage.

None the less, the action went some way with him. He saw her countenance fall, he read the disappointment it expressed, he told himself that if she acted, she was the best actress in the world. 'Enough,' he said, almost persuaded of the truth of her story. 'I will go, ma'am. If 'tis a cheat, I forgive you beforehand. And if it is the cloak you want, take it honestly. I give it you.'

But she looked at him so wrathfully at that, that he said no more, but went. He took up his stick, and as he passed out of sight among the trees he waved his hand in token of forgiveness – if after all she was fooling him.

CHAPTER XXI

The Strolling Players

HE PUSHED on sturdily until he came to the high road, and the turn that led to Beamond's farm. There his heart began to misgive him. The impression which Sophia's manner had made on his mind was growing weak; the improbability of her story rose more clearly before him. That a woman tramping the roads in her petticoats could be Lady Coke, the young bride of the owner of all the country side, seemed, now that he weighed it in cold blood, impossible. And from misgiving he was not slow in passing to repentance. How much better it would have been, he thought, had he pursued his duty to the dead and the parish with a single eye, instead of starting on this wild-goose chase. How much better – and even now it was not too late. He paused; he was as good as turned. But in the end he remembered that he had given the girl his word, and, turning his back on Beamond's farm, he walked in the opposite direction.

He had not gone far when he saw a young man of a strange raffish appearance coming along the road to meet him. The man swung a stick as he walked, and looked about him with a devil-may-care air which on the instant led the good parson to set him down for a strolling player. As such he was for passing him with a good day, and no more. But the other, who had also marked him from a distance, stopped when they came to close quarters.

'Well met, Master Parson!' he cried. 'And how far may you have come?'

'A mile or a little less,' the vicar answered mildly. And seeing, now that they were face to face, that the stranger was little more than a lad, he went on to ask him if he could be of service to him.

'Have you seen a lady on the road?'

The clergyman started. 'Dear, dear!' he said. ''Tis well met, indeed, sir, and a mercy you stayed me. To be sure I have! She is no farther away than my house at this moment!'

'The devil she is!' the young man answered heartily. 'That's to the purpose then. I was beginning to think – but never mind! Come on, and tell her woman where she is.'

'Certainly I will. Is she here?'

'She's sitting in the hedge at the next corner. It's on your way. Lord!' with a sigh of relief, not unmixed with pride, 'what a night I have had of it!'

'Indeed, sir,' his reverence said with sympathy; and as they turned to proceed side by side, he eyed his neighbour curiously.

'Aye, indeed, and indeed!' Tom answered. 'You'd say so if you'd been called out of bed the moment you were in it, and after a long day's tramp too! And been dragged up and down the country the whole living night, my friend.'

'Dear me; is it so, sir? And you were in her ladyship's company when she was stopped, I suppose, sir?'

'I? Not at all, or it would not have happened. I've never set eyes on her.'

'Her servants fetched you then?'

'Her woman did! I've seen no more of them.'

The vicar pricked up his ears. 'Nor the carriage?' he ventured.

'Not I. Hasn't she got the carriage with her?'

Mr Michieson rubbed his head. 'No,' he said slowly; 'no, she has not. Do I understand then, sir, that – that you are yourself a complete stranger to the parties?'

'I? Totally. But here's her woman. She can tell you about it. Oh, you need not look at me,' Tom continued with a grin, as the vicar, startled by the sight of the handsome gipsy-like girl, looked at him dubiously. 'She's a pretty piece, I know, to be straying the country, but I'm not in fault. I never set eyes on the little witch until last night.' And then, 'Here, child,' he cried, waving his hat to her, 'I've news! Your lady is at the parson's, and all's well! Now you can thank me that I did not let you go into the smallpox.'

Lady Betty clasped her hands. Her face was radiant. 'Are you sure? Are you quite sure?' she cried, her voice trembling. 'Are you sure she is safe?'

'She is quite safe,' Mr Michieson answered slowly; and he looked in wonder from one to the other. There was something suspiciously alike in their tumbled finery, their dishevelled appearance. 'I was even now on my way,' he continued, 'to Coke Hall to convey the news to Sir Hervey.'

It was Tom's turn to utter a cry of astonishment. 'To Sir Hervey?' he said. 'To Sir Hervey Coke, do you mean?'

'To be sure, sir.'

'But – why, to be sure, I might have known,' Tom cried. 'Was she going there?'

'She is his wife, sir.'

Tom laughed with a knowing air. 'Oh, but that's a flam at any rate!' he said. 'Sir Hervey's not married. I saw him myself, ten days ago.'

The girl stood up. 'Where?' she said.

'Where?'

'Aye, where, sir, where, since you are so free with his name.'

'In Clarges Row, in London, if you must know,' Tom answered, his face reddening at the reminiscence. 'And if he'd been married, or had thoughts of being married then, he'd have told me.'

Lady Betty stared at him, her breath coming quickly; something began to dawn in her eyes. 'Told you, would he?' she said slowly. 'He'd have told you? And who may you be, if you please?'

'Well,' Tom answered a trifle sharply, 'my name is Maitland, and for the matter of that, my girl, you need not judge me by my clothes. I know Sir Hervey, and—'

He did not finish. To his indignation, to the clergyman's astonishment, the girl went into a fit of laughter; laughing till she cried, and drying her eyes only that she might laugh again. Sir Tom stared and fumed and swore; while the vicar looked from one to the other, and asked himself – not for the first time – whether they were acting together, or the man was as innocent as he appeared to be.

One thing he could make clear, and he hastened to do it. 'I don't know why you laugh, child,' he said patiently. 'At the same time, the gentleman is certainly wrong in the fact. Sir Hervey Coke is married, for I had it from the steward some days ago, and I am to go with the tenants to the Hall to see her ladyship.'

Tom stared. 'Sir Hervey Coke married!' he cried in amazement, and forgot the girl's rudeness. 'Since I saw him? Married? Impossible! Whom do you say he has married?'

The vicar coughed. 'Well, 'tis odd, sir, but it's a lady of the same name – as yourself.'

'Maitland?'

'Yes, sir! A Miss Maitland, a sister of Sir Thomas Maitland, of Cuckfield.'

Sir Tom's eyes grew wide. 'Good Lord!' he cried; 'Sophia!'

'A relation, sir? Do I understand you that she's of your family?'

'My sister, sir; my sister.'

The clergyman stared a moment, and then without comment he walked aside and looked over the hedge. He smiled feebly at the well-known prospect. Was it possible, he asked himself, that they thought he could swallow this? That they deemed him so simple, so rustic, that such a piece of play-acting as this could impose upon him? Beyond a doubt they were in league together; with their fine story and their apt surprise, and 'my lady' in his garden. The only point on which he felt doubt was the advantage they looked to draw from it, since the moment he reached the Hall the bubble must burst.

He turned by-and by, thinking in his honest cunning to resolve that doubt. He found Tom in a sort of maze staring at the ground, and the girl watching him with a strange smile. For the first time the good vicar had recourse to the wisdom of the serpent. 'Had I not better go to the Hall at once,' he said blandly, 'and send a carriage for my lady?'

'Go to the Hall without seeing her?' Tom cried, awakening from his reverie. 'Not I! I go to her straight. Sophia? Sophia? Good Lord!'

'And so do I, sir, by your leave,' the girl cried pertly. 'And at once. I know my duty.'

'And you're the man to show us the way,' Tom continued heartily, slapping his reverence on the back. 'No more going up and down at random for me! Let's to her at once! We can find a messenger to go to the Hall, when we have seen her. But Lord! I can't get over it! When was she married, my girl?'

'Well,' Betty answered demurely, ''twas the same day, I believe, as your honour was to have been married.'

Tom winced and looked at her askance. 'You know that, you baggage, do you?' he cried.

'So it went in the steward's room, sir!'

But the vicar, his suspicions confirmed by their decision not to go to the Hall, hung back. 'I think I had better go on,' he said. 'I think Sir Hervey should be warned.'

'Oh, hang Sir Hervey!' Tom answered handsomely. 'Why is he not looking after his wife? Lead on! Lead on, do you hear, man? How far is it?'

'About a mile,' the vicar faltered; 'I should say a – a long mile,' he added, as he reluctantly obeyed the pressure of Tom's hand.

'Well, I am glad it's no farther!' the young man answered. 'For I'm so sharp set I could eat my sister. You've parson's fare, I suppose? Bacon and eggs and small beer?' he continued, clapping the unfortunate clergyman on the back with the utmost good humour. 'Well, sir, you shall entertain us! And while we are dining, the messenger can be going to the Hall. Soap and a jack-towel will serve my turn, but the girl – what's your name, child?'

'Betty, sir.'

'Will be the better for the loan of your wife's shoes and a cap! And Sophy is married? Where was it, my girl?'

'At Dr Keith's, sir.'

'The deuce it was!' Tom cried ruefully. 'Then that's two hundred out of my pocket! Were you with her, child?'

'No, sir, her ladyship hired me after she was married.'

Tom looked at her. 'But – but I thought,' he said, 'that you told me last night that you had been brought up with your mistress?'

Betty bit her lip, unable to remember if she had told him so.

'Oh, yes, sir,' she said hastily, 'but that was another mistress.'

'Also of the name of Sophia?'

'Yes, sir.'

'And for which Sophia – were you weeping last night?' Tom asked with irony.

Betty's face flamed; her fingers tingled also, though the slip was her own. It would have been the easiest thing in the world to throw off the mask, and tell the young man who she was. But for a reason, Betty did not choose to adopt this course. Instead, she stooped, pretending that her shoe-buckle was unfastened; when she rose there were tears in her eyes.

'You are very unkind, sir,' she said in a low voice. 'I took a – a liberty with my mistress in calling her by her name, and I – I had to account for it, and didn't tell quite the truth.'

Tom was melted, yet his eyes twinkled. 'Last night or today?' he said.

'Both, sir.' she whispered demurely. 'And I'm afraid, sir, I took a liberty with you, too, talking nonsense and such like. But I'm sure, sir – I am very sorry, and I hope you won't tell my mistress.'

The girl looked so pretty, so absurdly pretty in her penitence, and there was something so captivating in her manner, that Tom was seized with an inordinate desire to reassure her. 'Tell, child? Not I!' he cried generously. 'But I'll have a kiss for a forfeit. You owe me that,' he continued, with one eye on the vicar, who had gone on while she tied her shoe. 'Will you pay it now, my dear, or tomorrow with interest?'

'A kiss? Oh, fie, sir!'

'Why, what is the harm in a kiss?' Tom asked; and the rogue drew a little nearer.

'Oh, fie, sir!' Betty retorted, tossing her head, and moving farther from him. 'What harm indeed? And you told me last night I should be as safe with you as my mistress need be!'

'Well?' Tom exclaimed triumphantly. 'And shouldn't I kiss your mistress? Isn't she my sister? And – pooh, child, don't be silly. Was ever waiting-maid afraid of a kiss. And in daylight?'

But Betty continued to give him a wide berth. 'No, sir, I'll not suffer it!' she cried tartly. 'It's you who are taking the liberty now! And you told me last night you had seen enough of women to last you your life!

'That was before I saw you, my dear!' Tom answered with impudence. But he desisted from the pursuit, and resuming a sober course along the middle of the road, became thoughtful almost to moodiness; as if he were not quite so sure of some things as he had been. At intervals he glanced at Betty; who walked by his side primly conscious of his regards, and now blushing a little, and now pouting, and now when he was not looking, with a laughing imp dancing in her eyes that must have effected his downfall in a moment, if he had met her gaze. As it was he lost himself in thinking how pretty she was, and how fresh; how sweet her voice, and how dainty her walk; how trim her figure, and—

And then he groaned; calling himself a fool, a double, treble, deepest-dyed fool! After the lesson he had learned, after the experience through which he had passed, was he really, really going to fall in love again? And with his sister's maid? With a girl picked up – his vows, his oaths, his resolutions notwithstanding – in the road! It was too much!

And Lady Betty walking beside him, knowing all and telling nothing, Betty the flirt? 'He put his coat on me; I have worn his coat. He said he would tie me to the gate and he would have tied me,' with a furtive look at him out of the tail of her eye – that was the air that ran in her mind as she walked in the sunshine. A kiss? Well, perhaps; sometime. Who knew? And Lady Betty blushed at her thoughts. And they came to a corner where the garden-house lay off the road. The vicarage was not yet in sight.

At the gate of the orchard the poor parson waited for them, smiling feebly, but not meeting their eyes. He was in a state of piteous embarrassment. Persuaded that they were cheats and adventurers, hedge-players, if nothing worse, he knew that another man in his place would have told them half as much, and sent them about their business. But in the kindness of his heart he could no more do this than he could fly. On the other hand, his hair rose on end when he pictured his wife, and what she would say when he presented them to her. What she would do were he to demand the good fare they expected, he failed to conceive; but at the thought, the dense holly hedge that screened the house seemed all too thin. Alas, the thickest hedge is pervious to a woman's tongue!

In the others' ease and unconsciousness he found something pitiful; or he would have done so, if their doom had not involved his own punishment. 'She is here, is she?' Tom said, his hand on the gate.

The vicar nodded, speechless; he pointed in the direction of the garden house.

Betty slipped through deftly. 'Then, if you please, sir, I'll go first,' she said. 'Her ladyship may need something before she sees you – by your leave, sir!' And dropping a smiling curtsey, she coolly closed the gate on them, and flew down the path in the direction the vicar had indicated.

'Well, there's impudence!' Tom exclaimed. 'Hang me if I know why she should go first!' And then, as a joyful cry rang through the trees, he looked at the vicar.

But Michieson looked elsewhere. He was listening, he was shivering with anticipation. If that cry reached her! Tom, however, failed to notice this; innocent and unconscious, he opened the gate and passed through; and, thinking of his sister and his last parting from her, went slowly across the sunlit grass until the low-hanging boughs of the apple-trees hid him.

The parson looked up and down the road with a hunted eye. The position was terrible. Should he go to his wife, confess and prepare her? Or should he wait until his unwelcome guests returned to share the brunt. Or – or should he go? Go about his business – was there not sad, pressing business at Beamond's farm? – until the storm was overpast.

He was a good man, but he was weak. A few seconds of hesitation, and he skulked down the road, his head bent, his eyes glancing backwards. He fancied that he heard his wife's voice, and hurried faster and faster from the dreaded sound. At length he reached the main road and stood, his face hot with shame. He considered what he should do.

Beamond's? Yes, he must go about that. He must, to save his self-respect, go about business of some kind. At a large farm two miles away his churchwarden lived; there he could get help. The farmer and his wife had had the disease, and were in less terror of it than some. At any rate he could consult them: in a Christian parish people could not lie unburied. In vital matters he was no coward, and he knew that if no one would help him

– which was possible, so great was the panic – he would do all himself, if his strength held out.

In turning this over he tried to forget the foolish imbroglio of the morning; yet now and again he winced, pricked in his conscience and his manhood. After all, they had come to him for help, for food and shelter; and who so proper to afford these as God's minister in that place. At worst he should have sent them to one of the farms, and allowed it out of the tithe, and taken the chance when Easter came, and Peg discovered it. Passing the branch-road on his left which Tom and Betty had taken in the night, he had a distant view of a horseman riding that way at speed: and wondered a little, the sight being unusual. Three minutes later he came to the roadside ale-house which Betty had visited. The goodwife was at the door, and watched him come up. As he passed she cried out to learn if his reverence had news.

'None that's good, Nanny,' he answered; never doubting but she had the illness at Beamond's on her mind. And declining her offer of a mug of ale he went on, and half a mile farther turned off the road by a lane that led to the churchwarden's farm. He crossed the farm-yard, and found Mrs Benacre sitting within the kitchen door, picking over gooseberries. He begged her not to move, and asked if the goodman was at home.

'No, your reverence, he's at the Hall,' she answered. 'He was leading hay in the Furlongs, and was fetched all in a minute this hour past, and took the team with him. The little lad came home and told me.'

The vicar started, and looked a little odd. 'I wanted to see him about poor Beamond,' he said.

' 'Tis true, then, your reverence?'

'Too true. There's nothing like it happened in the parish in my time.'

'Dear, dear, it gives one the creeps! After all, when you've got a good husband, what's a little marking, and be safe? There should be something done, your reverence. 'Tis these gipsies bring it about.'

The vicar set back the fine gooseberry he had selected. 'What time did her ladyship arrive yesterday?' he asked.

Mrs Benacre lifted up her hands in astonishment. 'La, didn't you hear?' she cried. 'But to be sure, you're off the road a good bit, and all your people so taken up with they poor Beamonds too! No time at all, your reverence? She didn't come. I take it, it's about that, Sir Hervey has sent for Benacre. He thinks a deal of him, as his father before him did of the old gaffer! I remember a cocking was at the Hall,' Mrs Benacre continued, 'when I was a girl – 'twas a match between the gentlemen of Sussex and the gentlemen of Essex – and the old squire would have Benacre's father to dine with them, and made so much of him as never was!'

The vicar had listened without hearing. 'She stopped the night in Lewes, I suppose?' he said, his eyes on the gooseberries, his heart bumping.

' 'Twasn't known, the squire being at Lewes to meet her. And today I've had more to do than to go fetching and carrying, and never a soul to speak to but they two hussies and the lad, since Benacre went on the land. There, your reverence, there's a berry should take a prize so far away as Croydon.'

'Very fine,' the parson muttered. 'But I think I'll walk to the Hall and inquire.'

' 'Twould be very becoming,' Mrs Benacre allowed; and made him promise he would bring back the news.

As he went down the lane, he saw two horsemen pass the end of it at a quick trot. When he reached the road, the riders were out of sight; but his heart misgave him at this sign of unusual bustle. A quarter of an hour's walking along a hot road brought him to the park gate; it was open, and in the road was the lodge-keeper's wife, a child clinging to her skirts. Before he could speak, 'Has your reverence any news?' she cried.

He shook his head.

'Well, was ever such a thing?' she exclaimed, lifting up her hands. 'They're gone, to be sure, as if the ground had swallowed them. It's that, or the rogues ha' drowned them in the Ouse!'

He felt himself shrinking in his clothes. 'How – how did it happen?' he muttered faintly. What had he done? What had he done?

'The postboys left them in the carriage the other side of Beamond's,' the woman answered, delighted to gain a listener. 'And went back with fresh horses, I suppose it would be about seven this morning; they could not get them in the night. They found the carriage gone, and tracked it back so far almost as Chayley, and there found it, and the woman and the two grooms with it; but not one of them could give any account, except that their ladyships had been carried off by a gang of men, and they three had harnessed up and escaped. The post-boys came back with the news, and about the same time Mr Watkyns came by the main road through Lewes, and knew naught till he was here! He was fit to kill himself when he found her ladyship was gone,' the woman continued with zest, 'and Sir Hervey was fit to kill 'em all, and serve 'em right; and now they are searching the country, and a score with them; but it's tolerable sure the villains ha' got away with my lady, some think by Newhaven and foreign parts! What? Isn't your reverence going to the house?'

'No,' his reverence muttered, with a sickly smile. 'No.' And he turned from the cool shadows of the chestnut avenue, that led to the Hall, and setting his face the way he had come, hastened through the heat. He might still prevent the worst! He might still – but he must get home. He must get home. He had walked three miles in forty minutes in old days; he must do it now. True, the sun was midsummer high, the time an hour after noon, the road straight and hot, and unshaded, his throat was parched, and he was fasting. But he must press on. He must press on, though his legs begin to tremble under him – and he was not so young as he had been. There was the end of Benacre's Lane! He had done a mile; but his knees were shaky, he must sit a moment on the bank. He did so, and found the trees begin to dance before his eyes, his thoughts to grow confused; frightened he tried to rise, but instead he sank in a swoon, and lay inert at the foot of the bank.

CHAPTER XXII

'Tis Go or Swim

IT WAS a strange meeting between brother and sister. Tom, mindful how they had parted in Clarges Row, and with what loyalty she had striven to save him from himself – at a time when he stood in the utmost need of such efforts – was softened and touched beyond the ordinary. While Sophia, laughing and crying at once in the joy of a meeting as unexpected as it was welcome, experienced as she held Tom in her arms something nearer akin to happiness than had been hers since her marriage. The gratitude she owed to Providence for preservation amid the dangers of the night strengthened this feeling; the sunshine that flooded the orchard, the verdure under foot, the laden sprays of blossom overhead, the songs of the birds, the very strangeness of the retreat in which they met, all spoke to a heart peculiarly open at that moment to receive impressions. Tom recovered, Tom kind, formed part of the world which welcomed her back, and shamed her repining; while her brother, sheepish and affectionate, marvelled to see the little sister whom he had patronized all his life, suddenly and wonderfully transmogrified into Lady Coke.

He asked how she came to be so oddly dressed, learned that she also had fallen in with the vicar; and, when he had heard: 'Well,' he exclaimed, ' 'tis the luckiest thing your woman met me I ever knew!'

'You might have been in any part of England!' she answered, smiling through her tears. 'Where were you going, Tom?'

'Why, to Coke's to be sure,' he replied; 'and wanted only two or three miles of it!'

'Not – not knowing?' she asked. And she blushed.

'Not the least in life! I was on the point of enlisting,' he explained, colouring in his turn, 'at Reading, in Tatton's foot, when a man he had sent in search of me, found me, and gave me a note.'

'From Sir Hervey?'

'Of course,' Tom answered, 'telling me I could stay at the Hall until things blew over. And – and not to make a fool of myself,' he added ingenuously. ' 'Twas like him and I knew it was best to come, but when I was nearly there – that was last night, you know – I thought I would wait until morning and hear who were in the house before I showed myself. That is why Mistress Betty found me where she did.'

Sophia could not hide her feelings on learning what Sir Hervey had done for Tom and for her; what he had done silently, without boasting, without telling her. Tom saw her tremble, saw that for some reason she was on the verge of tears, and he wondered.

'Why,' he said, 'what is the matter, Sophy? What is it now?'

'It's nothing, nothing,' she answered hurriedly.

'I know what it is!' he replied. 'You've been up all night, and had nothing to eat. You will be all right when you have had a meal. The old parson said he'd give us bacon and eggs. It should be ready by this time.'

Sophia laughed hysterically. 'I fear it doesn't lie with him,' she said. 'His wife would not let me into the house. She's afraid of the smallpox.'

'Pooh!' Tom said contemptuously. 'When she knows who we are she'll sing another tune.'

'She won't believe,' Sophia answered.

'She'll believe me,' Tom said. 'So let us go.'

'Do you go first, sir, if you please,' Lady Betty cried pertly, intervening for the first time. She had stood a little apart to allow the brother and sister to be private. 'I'm sure her ladyship's not fit to be seen. And I'm not much better,' she added; and then a sudden bubble of laughter rising to the surface, she buried her face in Sophia's skirts, and affected to be engaged in repairing the disorder. Tom saw his sister's face relax in a smile, and he eyed the maid suspiciously; but before he could speak, Sophia also begged him to go, and see what reception the old clergyman had secured for them. He turned and went.

At the gate he looked back, but a wealth of apple blossom intervened; he did not see that the girls had flown into one another's arms, nor did he hear them laughing, crying, asking, answering, all at once, and out of the fullness of thankful hearts. Tom's wholesome appetite began to cry cupboard. He turned briskly up the road, discovered the wicket-gate of the parsonage, and marching to it, found to his surprise that it was locked. The obstacle was not formidable to youth, but the welcome was cold at best; and where was his friend the parson? In wonder he rattled the gate, thinking someone would come; but no one came, and out of patience he vaulted over the post, and passing round a mass of rose bushes that grew in a tangle about the pot-herb garden, he saw the door of the house standing ajar before him.

One moment; the next and before he could reach it, a boy about twelve years old, with a shock of hair and sullen eyes, looked out, saw him, and hastened to slam the door in his face. The action was unmistakable, the meaning plain; Sir Tom stood, stared, and after a moment swore. Then in a rage he advanced and kicked the door. 'What do you mean?' he cried. 'Open, sirrah, do you hear? Are these your manners?'

For a few seconds there was silence in the sunny herb garden with its laden air and perfumed hedges. Then a casement above creaked open, and two heads peered cautiously over the window-ledge. 'Do you hear?' Tom cried, quickly espying them. 'Come down and open the door, or you'll get a whipping.'

But the boys, the one he had seen at the door, and another, a year or two older preserved a sulky silence; eyeing him with evident dread and at the same time with a kind of morbid curiosity. Tom threatened, stormed, even took up a stone; they answered nothing, and it was only when he had begun to retreat, fuming, towards the gate that one of them found his voice.

'You'd better be gone!' he cried shrilly. 'They are coming for you.'

Sir Tom turned at the sound, and went back at a white heat. 'What do you mean, you young cubs?' he cried, looking up 'Who are coming for me?'

But they were dumb again, staring at him over the ledge with sombre interest. Tom repeated his question, scolded, even raised his stone, but without effect. At last he turned his back on them, and in a rage flung out of the garden.

He went out as he had entered, by vaulting the gate. As he did so, he heard a woman's shrill voice raised in anger; and he looked in the direction whence it came. He saw a knot of people coming down the road. It consisted of three or four women, and a rough-looking labourer; but while he stood eyeing them a second party, largely made up of men and boys, came in sight, following the other; and tailing behind these again came a couple of women, and last of all two or three lads. The women speaking loudly, with excited gestures, appeared to be scolding the men; those on the outside of each rank hurrying a step in advance of the others, and addressing them with turned heads. Tom watched them a moment, thinking that they might be a search party sent by Coke; then he reflected that the noise would alarm his sister, and turning in at the gate he crossed the orchard.

Sophia came to meet him. 'What is it?' she asked anxiously. 'What is the matter, Tom?' The clamour of strident voices, the scolding of the women had preceded him. 'Have you seen the clergyman? Why, they are coming here!'

'The deuce they are!' Tom answered. He looked back, and seeing through the trees that the man with the first gang had opened the gate of the orchard, he went to meet him.

'What is it?' he asked. 'What are you doing here? Has Sir Hervey sent you?'

'We want no sending!' one of the women cried sharply. ''Tis enough to send us of ourselves.'

'Aye, so it is!' a second chimed in with violence. 'And do you keep your distance if you be one of them! Let's have no nonsense, master, for we won't stand it!'

'No, no nonsense!' cried another, as the larger party arrived and raised the number to something like a score. 'She's got to go, and you with her if you be one of her company! Ain't that so?' the speaker continued, turning to her backers.

'Aye, she must go!' cried one. 'We'll ha' no smallpox here!' cried another. 'She'll go or swim! Out of the parish, I say!' shrieked a third.

Tom looked along the line of excited faces, faces stupid and cruel; at the best of a low type, and now brutalized by selfish panic. And his heart sank. But for the present he neither blenched nor lost his temper.

'Why, you fools,' he said, thinking to reason with them, 'don't you know who the lady is?'

'No, nor care!' was the shrill retort. 'Nor care, do you understand that?'

And then a man stepped forward. 'She's got to go,' he said, 'whoever she be. That's all.'

'I tell you, you don't know who she is,' Tom answered stubbornly. 'Whose tenant are you, my man?'

'Sir Hervey's, to be sure,' the fellow answered, surprised at the question.

'Well, she's his wife,' Tom answered. 'Do you hear? Do you

understand?' he repeated, with growing indignation. 'She is Lady Coke, Sir Hervey's wife. Lady Coke, Sir Hervey's wife! Get that into your heads, will you! His wife, I tell you. And if you raise a finger or wag a tongue against her, you'll repent it all your lives.'

The man stared, doubting, hesitating, in part daunted. But a woman behind him – a lean vixen, her shoulders barely covered by a meagre kerchief, pushed herself to the front, and snapped her fingers in Tom's face. 'That my lady?' she cried. 'That for the lie. You be a liar, my lad, that's what you be! A liar, and ought to swim with her. Neighbours,' the shrew continued volubly, 'she be no more my lady than I be. Madam told me she faked for to be it, but was a gipsy wench as had laid the night at Beamond's and now was for 'fecting us.'

'Anyway she don't go another step into this parish,' pronounced an elderly man, something better off than the others. 'We don't want to swim her, and we don't want to stone her, but she must go, or worse come of it. And you, my lad, if you be with her and the other.' For Lady Betty had crept timidly out of the garden-shed and joined the pair.

Tom was bursting with passion. 'I!' he cried. 'You clod, do you know who I am? I am Sir Thomas Maitland, of Cuckfield.'

'Sir, or no sir, you'll ha' to go,' the man retorted stubbornly. He was a dull fellow, and an unknown Sir Thomas was no more to him than plain Tom or Dick. 'And 'tis best, with no more words,' he continued heavily.

Tom, enraged, was for answering in the same strain, but Sophia plucked his sleeve, and took the word herself. 'I am quite willing to go,' she said, holding her head up bravely. 'If you let me pass safely to the Hall, that is all I ask.'

'To the Hall?'

'Yes, to my husband.'

'To the Hall indeed! No! No! That's likely,' cried the crowd; and were not to be silenced till the elderly farmer who had spoken before raised his hand for a hearing.

' 'Tis no wonder they shout,' he said, with a smile half-cunning, half-stupid. 'The Hall? No, no. Back by Beamond's and over the water, my girl, you'll go, same as Beamond's folk did. There's few live the other side, and so the fewer to take it, d'ye see? Besides, 'tis every one for himself.'

'Aye! aye!' the crowd cried. 'He's right; that way, no other! Hall indeed?' And at the back they began to jeer.

'You've no law for this!' Tom cried, furious and panting.

'Then we'll make a law,' they answered, and jeered again, with some words that were not very fit for the ladies to hear.

Tom, at that, would have sprung at the nearest and punished him; but Sophia held him back. 'No, no,' she said in a low tone. 'We had better go. Sir Hervey is surely searching for us. We may meet him, and they will learn their mistake. Please let us go. Let us go quickly, or they may – I don't know what they may do.'

Tom suffered himself to be convinced; but he made the mistake of doing with a bad grace that which he had to do whether he would or no.

'Out of the way, you clods!' he cried, advancing on them with his stick raised. 'You'll sing another tune before night! Do you hear, I say? Out of the way!'

Moving sullenly, they left his front open; and he marched proudly through the gate of the orchard, Sophia and Betty beside him. But his challenge had raised the devil that lies dormant in the most peaceful crowd. He had no sooner passed than the women closed in upon his rear, and followed him with taunts and laughter. And presently a boy threw a stone.

It fell short of the mark; but another stone followed, and another; and the third struck Tom on the leg. He wheeled round in a towering passion, caught sight of the offender, and made for him. The boy tripped in trying to escape, and fell, shrieking. Tom got home two cuts; then a virago, her tongue spitting venom, her nails in the air, confronted him over the body of the fallen, and he returned sullenly to his charges, and resumed his retreat.

But the boy's screams had exasperated the rabble. Groans took the place of laughter, curses succeeded jeers. The bolder threw dirt, the more timid hooted and booed, while all pressed more and more closely on his heels, threatening every moment to jostle him. Tom had to turn and brandish his stick to drive them back, and finding that even so he could scarcely secure the briefest respite, he began to grow hot and confused, and looked about for a way of escape in something between rage and terror.

To run, he knew, would only precipitate the disaster. To defend himself was scarcely possible, for Sophia, fearing he would attempt reprisals, hampered him, on one side, while Betty, in pure fear, clung to him on the other. Both were sinking with apprehension, while his ears tingled under the coarse jeers and coarser epithets that were hurled at them. Yet he dared not suffer them to move a pace from him. Cries of 'Roll them! Duck them! To the pond!' began to be heard; and once he barely checked an ugly rush by facing about at the last moment. At last he espied a little before him the turning into the main road, and whispering the women to keep up their courage, he pressed sullenly towards it.

He had as good as reached it, when a stone more weighty and better aimed than those which had preceded it, struck Lady Betty fairly between the shoulders. The girl stumbled forward with a gasp, and Sophia, horror-stricken and uncertain how much she was hurt, sprang to her side to hold her up. The movement freed Tom's arm; his sister's furious cry, 'You cowards! Oh, you cowards!' burned up the last shred of his self-control.

In a tempest of rage he rushed on the nearest hobbledehoy, and felling him with his stick, rained blows upon him. In an instant he was engaged, hand to hand, with half a dozen combatants.

Unfortunately the charge had carried him a dozen yards from his companions; the more timid of the rascals, who were not eager to encounter him or his stick, saw their opportunity. In a twinkling they cut off the two girls, and hemmed them in. Beginning with pushing and jostling them they would soon have gone on to further insults if Sophia had not flown at them in her turn, and repelled them with a rage that for a few seconds daunted them. Tom, too, heard the girls' cries, and turned to relieve them: but as he sprang forward a boy tripped him up, and he fell prone on the road.

That gave the last impulse to the evil instincts of the crowd. The louts darted on him with a savage yell, and began to pommel him; and ill it must have gone with Tom as well as with his womenfolk if the crowd had had their way with them for many seconds.

But at that critical instant, without warning, or any at least that the victors regarded, the long lash of a hunting-whip flickered in the air, and fell as by magic between the girls and their assailants; it seared, as with a red-hot iron, the hand which a sturdy young clown, half-boy, half-man, was brandishing under Sophia's nose; it stung with the sharpness of a dozen wasps the mocking face that menaced Betty on the other side. The lads who had flung themselves on Tom, awoke with yells of pain to find the same whip curling about their shoulders, and to see behind it, set in grim rage, the face of their landlord.

That instant, the harpies, who had been hounding them on, vanished as by magic, scuttling all ways like frightened hens. And Sir Hervey let them go – for the time; but behind the lads and louts, fleeing and panting and racing and sweating down the road, and aiming fruitlessly at gates and gaps, the lash fell ever and mercilessly on sturdy backs and fleshy legs. The horse he rode was an old hunter, known in the district, quick and cunning, broken to all turns of the hare; and that day it carried fate, and punishment with no halting foot followed hard upon the sin!

Sobbing with exhaustion, with labouring chests that at intervals shot forth cries of pain, as the flickering thong licked their hams, and they bounded like deer under the sting, the bullies came at last to the vicarage gate. There Sir Hervey left them, free at last to rub their weals and curse their folly; sorer, but it is to be hoped wiser men.

Sophia, supporting herself by a gate, and now laughing hysterically, now repressing with difficulty the inclination to weep, watched him return. She saw him through a mist of smiles and tears. For the moment she forgot that he was her husband, forgot that this was the meeting so long and greatly dreaded.

He sprang from his horse.

'You're not hurt?' he cried. 'Child—' and then, with astonishment she saw that he was speechless.

Her own words came easily; even her manner was eager and unembarrassed. 'No,' she cried, 'nor Lady Betty! You came just in time, Sir Hervey.'

'Thank God, I did,' he answered; 'thank God! And you are sure, child, you are none the worse? You are not hurt?'

'No,' she answered, laughing, as people laugh in moments of

agitation. 'Not a whit! You are looking at my dress? Oh, we have had adventures, a vast lot of adventures, Sir Hervey! It would take a day to tell them, wouldn't it, Betty? Betty's my maid, Sir Hervey.' She was above herself. She spoke gaily and archly, as Betty might have spoken.

'Lady Betty your maid?' he exclaimed, turning to Betty, who blushed and laughed. 'What do you mean?'

'Mean? Why only – hush, where is Tom? Oh, repairing himself! Why, only a frolic, Sir Hervey! Tom took her for my woman, and we want to keep him in it! So not a word, if you please. This is Betty the maid, you'll remember?'

'I obey,' Sir Hervey answered. 'But to tell the truth,' he continued soberly, 'my head turns. Where did you meet Tom, my dear? What has happened to you? And why are you wearing – that queer cloak? And where are your shoes?'

'It's not very becoming, is it?' she cried, and she looked at him. Never before in her life had she played the coquette, never; now in this moment of unrestrained feeling, her eyes, provocative as Lady Betty's, challenged the compliment. And she wondered at herself.

'You are always – the same to me,' he said simply. And then: 'You are really all of you unhurt? Well, thank God for it! And, Tom, my lad, you know, I suppose, how you came to be in this? I am sure I don't; but I thought it was you when I came up.'

'I hope you flayed them!' Tom growled, as they gripped hands. 'See, she's barefoot! They hunted us half a mile, I should think.'

Sir Hervey looked and grew red. 'I did!' he answered. 'I think they have learned a lesson. And they have not heard the last of it!' Then the post-chaise, which he had escorted to Beamond's Farm on a fruitless search, came up, and behind it a couple of mounted servants, whose training scarce enabled them to conceal their surprise, when they saw the condition of their new mistress.

Sir Hervey postponed further inquiry. He hurried the two ladies into the carriage, set Tom on a servant's horse, and gave the word. A moment later the party were travelling rapidly in the direction of the Hall. Coke rode on the side next to his wife, Tom by Lady Betty. But the noise of the wheels made conversation difficult, and no one spoke.

Presently Sophia stole a glance at Sir Hervey; and whether his country costume and the flush of colour which exercise had brought to his cheek became him, or he had a better air, as some men have, on horseback, it is certain that she wondered she had ever thought him old. The moment in which he had appeared, towering on his horse above the snarling, spitting rabble, and driven them along the road as a man drives sheep, remained in her memory. He had wielded, and grimly and ably wielded, the whip of authority. He had ridden as if horse and man were one; he had disdained weapons, and had flogged the hounds into submission and flight. Now in repose his strong figure in its plain dress wore in her eyes a new air of distinction.

She looked away and looked again, wondering if it really was so. And slowly a vivid blush spread over her pale face. The man who rode beside the wheel, the man whose figure she was appraising was – her husband. At the thought she turned with a guilty start to Lady Betty; but the poor girl, worn out by excitement and the night's vigil, had fallen asleep. Sophia's eyes went slowly back to her husband, and the carriage, leaving the road, swept through the gates into the park.

CHAPTER XXIII

Two Portraits

TOM RUBBED his hands in cruel anticipation. 'They are coming to the Hall at four o'clock,' he said. 'And I wouldn't be in their shoes for a mug and a crust. Coke will swinge them,' he continued with zest. 'He must swinge them, like it or not! It'll be go, bag and baggage, for most of them, and some, I'm told have been on the land time out of mind!

He had seated himself on the broad balustrade of the terrace, with his back to the park, and his eyes on the windows of the house. Sophia, on a stone bench not far from him, gazed thoughtfully over the park as if she found refreshment merely in contemplating the far stretch of fern and sward, that, set with huge oak trees, fell away into half-seen dells of bracken and fox-gloves. Recreated by a long night's rest, her youth set off, her freshness heightened by the dainty Tuscan and chintz sacque she had put on that morning, she was not to be known for the draggled miss who had arrived in so grievous a plight the day before. From time to time she recalled her gaze to fix it dreamily on her left hand; now reviewing the fingers, bent or straight, now laying them palm downwards on the moss-stained coping. She was so employed when the meaning of her brother's last words came tardily home to her and roused her from her reverie.

'Do you mean,' she cried, 'that hc will will put them out of their farms?'

'I should rather think he would!' said Tom. 'Wouldn't you? And serve them right, the brutes!'

'But what will they do?'

'Starve, for all I care!' Tom answered callously; and he flipped a pebble from the balustrade with his forefinger. He was not at his best a soft-hearted young gentleman. 'And teach them to know better!' he added presently.

Sophia's face betrayed her trouble. 'I don't think he would do that,' she said, slowly.

'Coke?' Tom answered. 'He won't have much choice, my dear. For the sake of your *beaux yeux* he will have to swinge them, and lustily. To let them off would be to slight you; and 'twouldn't look very well, and a fortnight married. No, no, my girl. And that reminds me. Where is he? And where has he been since yesterday?'

Sophia reddened. 'He has some business,' she said, 'which took him away at once.'

'I don't think you know.'

Sophia blushed more warmly, but added nothing; and fortunately Tom caught sight of a certain petticoat disappearing down the steps at the end of the terrace. It is not impossible that he had been expecting it, for he rose on the instant, muttered an unintelligible word, and went in pursuit.

Sophia sat awhile, pondering on what he had said. It was right that the offenders of yesterday should be punished; their conduct had been cruel, inhuman, barbarous. But that her home-coming should mean to any man the loss of home, shocked her. Yet she thought it possible that her brother was right; that pride, if not love, the wish to do his duty by her, if not the desire to commend himself to her, would move Sir Hervey to especial severity. What bridegroom indeed, what lover, could afford to neglet so obvious a flattery? And if in her case Coke counted neither for lover nor bridegroom, what husband?

She rose. She must go at once and seek him, intercede with him, convince him that it would not pleasure her. But two steps taken she paused, her pride in arms. After she had changed her dress and repaired her disorder the day before, she had waited, expecting that he would come to her. But he had not done so, he had not come near her; at length she had asked for him. Then she had learned with astonishment, with humiliation, that immediately after her arrival he had left the house on business.

If he could slight her in that fashion, was there any danger that out of regard to her he would do injustice to others? She laughed at the thought – yet believed all the same that there was, for men were inconsistent. But the position made intercession difficult, and instead of calling a servant and asking if he had returned she wandered into the house. She remembered that the housekeeper had begged to know when her ladyship would see the drawing-rooms; and she sent for Mrs Stokes.

That good lady found her young mistress waiting for her in the larger of the two rooms. It was scantily furnished after the fashion of the early part of the century, with heavy chairs and a table, set at wide intervals on a parquet floor, with a couple of box-like settees, and as many buhl tables, the latter bought by Sir Hervey's mother on her wedding tour, and preserved as the apple of her eye. On either side of the open blue-tiled fireplace a round-headed alcove exhibited shelves of Oriental china, and on the walls were half a dozen copies of Titians and Raphaels, large pictures at large intervals. All was stately, proper, a little out of fashion, but decently so. Sophia admired, yawned, said a pleasant word to Mrs Stokes, and passed into the smaller room.

There she stood, suddenly engrossed. On each side of the fireplace hung a full-length portrait. The one on the right hand, immediately before her, represented a girl in the first bloom of youth, lovely as a rose-bud, graceful as a spray of jessamine, with eyes that charmed and chained the spectator by their pure maidenliness. A great painter in his happiest vein had caught the beauty and innocence of a chosen model; as she smiled from the canvas, the dull room – for the windows were curtained – grew brighter and lighter. The visitor, as he entered, saw only that sweet face, and saw it ever more clearly; as the playgoer sees only the limited space above the footlights, and sees that grow larger the longer he looks.

It was with an effort and a sigh Sophia turned to the other picture; she looked at it, and stood surprised, uncertain, faintly embarrassed. She turned to the housekeeper, 'It is Sir Hervey, is it not?' she said.

'Yes, my lady,' the woman answered. 'At the age of twenty-one. But he is not much changed to my eyes,' she added jealously.

'Of course, I did not know him then,' Sophia murmured apologetically; and after a long thoughtful look she went to the other picture. 'What a very, very lovely face!' she said, 'I did not know that Sir Hervey had ever had a sister. She is dead, I suppose?'

'Yes, my lady, she is dead.'

'It is his sister?' with a look at the other.

The housekeeper gave back the look uncomfortably. 'No, my lady,' she said at last.

'No!' Sophia exclaimed, raising her eyebrows. 'Then who is it, pray?'

'Well, my lady, it – it should have been removed,' Mrs Stokes explained, her embarrassment evident. 'At one time it was to go to Sir Hervey's library, but 'twas thought it might be particular there. And so nothing was done about it. Sir Hervey wouldn't let it go anywhere else. But I was afraid that your ladyship might not be pleased.'

Sophia stared coldly at her. 'I don't understand,' she said stiffly. 'You have not told me who it is.'

'It's Lady Anne, my lady.'

'What Lady Anne?'

'Lady Anne Thoresby. I thought,' the housekeeper added in a faltering tone, 'your ladyship would have heard of her.'

Sophia looked at the lovely young face, looked at the other

portrait – of Sir Hervey in his gallant hunting-dress, gay, laughing, debonair – and she understood. 'She was to have married Sir Hervey?' she said.

'Yes, my lady.'

'And she died?'

'Yes, my lady, two days before their wedding-day,' Mrs Stokes answered, her garrulity beginning to get the better of her fears. 'Sir Hervey was never the same again – that is to say, in the old days, my lady,' she added hurriedly. 'He grew that silent it was wonderful, and no gentleman more pleasant before. He went abroad, and 'tis said he lost twenty thousand pounds in one night in Paris. And before that he had played no more than a gentleman should.'

Sophia's eyes were full of tears.

'How did she die?' she whispered.

'Of the smallpox, my lady. And that is why Sir Hervey is so particular about it.'

'How do you mean? Is he afraid of it?'

'Oh, no, my lady, far from it! He had it years ago himself. But wherever it is, he's for giving help. That's why we kept it from him that 'twas at Beamond's Farm, thinking that as your ladyship was coming, he would not wish to be in the way of it. But he was wonderful angry when he learned about it, and went off as soon as news came from his reverence; who would have sent sooner, but he was took ill yesterday. I can pretty well guess what Sir Hervey's gone about,' she added sagaciously.

'What?' Sophia asked.

Mrs Stokes hesitated, but decided to speak.

'Well, it happened once before, my lady,' she said, 'that they could get no one to help bury; and Sir Hervey went and set the example. You may be sure there were plenty then, as had had it, and had no cause to fear, ready to come forward to do the work. And I've not much doubt, my lady, it's for that he's gone this time. He'd stay away a night at the keeper's cottage, I expect,' Mrs Stokes continued, nodding her head sagely, 'just to see to his clothes being destroyed and the like. For there's no one more careful to carry no risks, I will say that for his honour.'

Sophia stared.

'But do you mean,' she cried, her heart beating strangely, 'that Sir Hervey would do the work with his own hands?'

'Well, it's what he did once, I know, my lady,' the housekeeper answered apologetically. 'It was not very becoming, to be sure, but he was not the less thought of about here, I assure your ladyship. You see, my lady, 'tis in the depth of the country, and the land is his own, and it's not as if it was in London. Where I know things are very different,' Mrs Stokes continued with pride, 'for I have been there myself with the family. But about here I'm sure he was not the less considered, begging your ladyship's pardon.'

'I can believe it,' Sophia said, in a voice suspiciously quiet and even. And then, 'Thank you, Mrs Stokes, you can leave me now,' she continued. 'I shall sit here a little.'

But when Mrs Stokes, feeling herself a trifle snubbed, had withdrawn and closed the door of the outer room upon her, Sophia's eyes grew moist with tears, and the nosegay that filled the open bodice of her sacque rose and fell strangely. In that age philanthrophy was not a fashion. Pope indeed had painted the Man of Ross, and there was Charitable Corporation, lately in difficulties, and there was a Society of the Sons of the Clergy, and there were other societies of a like kind; and in the country infirmaries were beginning to be founded on the patterns of Winchester and Shrewsbury, and to subscribe to such objects after dining well and drinking deeply, was already, under the Walpoles and the Pelhams, a part of a fine gentleman's life. But for a man of condition to play the Borromeo – to stoop to give practical help and run risks among the vulgar was still enough to earn for him a character as eccentric as that of the famous nobleman who had seen more kings and more postillions than any of his contemporaries.

In the eyes of the world, but not in Sophia's, or why this dimness of vision, as she gazed at Sir Hervey's picture? Why the unrest of the bodice that threatened to find vent in sobs? Why the sudden rush of self-reproach? More sharply than any kindness shown to her in the long consistent course of his dealings with her, more keenly than his forethought for her brother, this stabbed her. This was the man she had flouted, the man whose generous, whose unselfish offer she had accepted to save her reputation; but whose love she had deemed a floor-clout, not worthy the picking up! Was it wonderful that, cynical, taciturn, almost dull as the world thought him, he was not the less considered here?

At twenty-one he had been handsome, with wit and laughter and the gay insouciance of youth written on his face. Time, the lapse of thirteen years, had robbed his features of their bloom, his lips of their easy curve, his eyes of their sparkle. But something, surely, time had given in return. Something, Sophia could not say what. She could not remember; she could only recall a smile, kindly, long-suffering, a little quizzical, with which he had sometimes met her eyes. That she could recall; and as she did so, before his portrait in the stillness of this long-abandoned room, with the dead air of old pot-pourris in her nostrils, she grew frightened. What was it she had thrown away? And how would it fare with her if she could not recover it?

Twisting one hand in the other, she turned to the second portrait, and looked, and looked. At length she glanced round with a guilty air, perceived a tall, narrow mirror that stood framed between the windows, and went towards it. Furtively assuring herself that she was not watched from the terrace, she viewed herself in it.

She saw a pale grave face, barely redeemed from plainness by eloquent eyes and a wealth of hair; a face that looked sombrely into hers, and grew graver and more sombre as she looked. 'He is more like his old self than I am like her,' she thought. 'Why did he choose me? Why did he not choose Lady Betty? She is such another now as Lady Anne was then!'

She was still peering at herself when she heard his voice in the hall, and started guiltily. She would not for the world he caught her in that room, and she darted to the door, dragged it open, and was half-way across the long drawing-room when he entered. She felt that her face was on fire, but he did not seem to notice it.

'A thousand pardons that I was not with you before,' he cried pleasantly. 'I'd business, and – no, I must not touch you, my dear. I have been nearer than was pleasant to one of your friends with the smallpox.'

'You have run – no risk, I hope?' she asked faintly.

'Not a whit!' he answered, striking his boot with his whip

and looking round the room as if he seldom entered it. 'I've had it, you know. I've also had the whole story of your adventures from Betty, whom I met as I was going to my room.'

She was agitated; he was at his ease. 'I am sorry that we managed so clumsily,' she murmured.

'So bravely, I think,' he answered lightly; and then, looking round, 'This is your part of the house, you know, Sophia. You must make what changes you please here.'

'Thank you,' she said. 'You are very good.'

'These rooms have been little used since my mother's death,' he continued, again surveying them. 'So I have no doubt they want refurnishing. You must talk it over with Lady Betty. And that reminds me, I saw your brother slipping away a few minutes ago, and he had something – the air of following her.' And Sir Hervey laughed and sat down on one of the stiff-backed chairs. 'For my part, I think he ought to be told,' he continued, tapping the toe of his boot with his whip.

Sophia smiled faintly. 'You think he is taken with her?'

'Who would not be?' Sir Hervey answered bluntly. 'Maid or mistress, he'll be head over ears in love with her before twenty-four hours are out!'

Sophia sat down. 'It's her fancy that he should not know,' she said languidly. 'Of course, if you wish it, I will tell him.'

'No, no, child, have it your own way,' he answered with good humour. 'I suppose she is prepared to pay for her frolic.'

'Well – I think she likes him.'

'And 'twould do very well on both sides – in a year or two!'

'I suppose so.'

Sir Hervey rose. 'Then let be,' he said. And he wandered across the room, taking up things and setting them down again as if he did not think it quite polite to leave her, yet had nothing more to say. Sophia watched him with growing soreness. Was it fancy, or was it the fact that she had never seen him so cold, so indifferent, so little concerned for her, so well satisfied with himself as now? A change, so subtle she could not define it, had come over him. Or was it that a change had come over her?

She wondered, and at length plunged desperately into speech. 'Is it true,' she asked, 'that the people who treated us so ill yesterday are coming to see you to-day?'

'Those of them who are householders are coming,' he answered soberly. 'At four o'clock. But I do not wish you to see them.'

'You will not be – too severe with them?'

'I shall not be more severe, I hope, than the occasion required,' he answered.

But his tone was hard, and she felt that what she had heard was true. 'Will you grant me a favour?' she blurted out, her voice trembling a little.

'I would like to grant you many,' he answered, smiling at her.

'It's only that you will not send them away,' she said.

'Send them away?'

'I mean, send them off their farms,' she explained hurriedly. 'I was told – Tom told me that you were going to do so; and that some had held the land for generations, and would be heartbroken as well as ruined.'

He did not answer at once, and his silence confirmed her in her fears. 'I don't say that they have not deserved to be punished,' she urged. 'But – but I should not like my coming here to be remembered by this. And it seems out of proportion to the crime, since they did me no harm.'

'Whatever they intended?'

'Yes.'

He looked at her gravely. 'What led you to think,' he said, 'that I had it in my mind to punish them in that way?'

'Well, Tom told me,' she explained in growing confusion, 'that you might do it to – that you might think it would please me. He said that any one in your place – I mean—'

'Any one newly married?'

Sophia's face flamed. 'I suppose so,' she murmured, ' – would do it.'

'To please his bride? And you agreed with him, Sophia? You thought it was probable?'

'I thought it was possible,' she said.

He walked across the room, came back, and stood before her. He looked down at her. 'My dear,' he said soberly – but she winced under the altered tone of his voice – 'you will learn to know me better in a little while. Let me tell you at once that the purpose you have mentioned never entered my head, and that I am, I hope, incapable of it. There are people who might entertain it, and might carry it out to please a mistress or gratify a whim. There are, I know. But I am not one of that kind. I am too old to misuse power to please a woman, even the woman I have chosen. Nor,' he continued, stopping her as she tried to speak, 'is that all. In the management of an estate we do not act so hurriedly as you appear to think, my dear. Old tenants, like old wine, are the best, and, where it is possible, we keep them. I have sent, it is true, for those who were guilty yesterday, and I shall see that they are made to smart for it. But not to the extent of loss of home and livelihood.'

'I am sorry,' she muttered.

'There is no need, child,' he answered. 'And while we are on this, I may as well deal with another matter. I found your note and the jewel case on my table, and as you wish, so it shall be. I might prefer – indeed, I should prefer,' he continued prosaically, 'to see my wife properly equipped when she goes into the world. But that's a small matter. Lady Coke will always be Lady Coke, and if you will feel more free and more happy without them—'

'I shall,' she muttered hurriedly, 'if you please.'

'So be it. They shall be returned to my goldsmith's as soon as a safe conveyance can be found. I wish, my dear,' he added good-naturedly, 'I could rid you of all troubles as easily.'

'I am much obliged to you,' she muttered, and could have shrunk into the floor with shame. For on a sudden she saw herself a horrid creature, imposing all, taking nothing, casting all the burden and all the stress, and all the inconvenience of their strange relations on him. In town and on the road she had fancied that there was something fine, something of the nature of abnegation and dignity in the return of the jewels, and in her determination that she would not go decked in them. But the simplicity with which he had accepted her whim and waived his own wishes, tore away the veil of self-deception, and showed Sophia the childishness of her conduct. She would not wear his jewels; but his name and his title, his freedom and his home, she had not scrupled to take from him with scarce a word of gratitude, with scarce one thought for him!

The very distress she was feeling gave her, she knew, a sullen air, and must set her in a worse light than ever. Yet she was tongue-tied. He yielded freely, handsomely, generously; and that bare, that cold 'I am very much obliged to you' was all she could force her tongue to utter. She was beginning to feel that she was growing afraid of him; and then he spoke.

'There is one other matter,' he said, 'I wish to name. It touches Mrs Stokes. She has been here a number of years, and I dare say, like this room, smacks a little of good Queen Anne. If you think it necessary to discharge her—'

Sophia started.

'I?' she said.

'To be sure. I should at the worst pension her. But she has served us faithfully, I believe – beginning, I think,' Sir Hervey continued with a slight touch of constraint, 'by whipping me when I needed it; and she would be distressed, I fear, if she had to go. If you could contrive to do with her for a while, therefore, I should be much obliged to you.'

Sophia had risen and moved a little way from him.

'Did you think I should discharge her?' she said, without turning her head.

'Well,' he answered, 'I did not know, my dear. Young housekeepers—'

'Why did you think I should discharge her?' she cried, interrupting him sharply; and then, 'Pray forgive me,' she continued hurriedly, yet stiffly, 'I – you hurt me a little in what you said of – the tenants. I only ask you to believe that I am as incapable of dismissing an old servant for a trifle as you are of behaving unjustly to your tenants!'

He did not appear to notice her emotion.

'Thank you,' he said. 'Then we understand one another. Of course, I don't wish you to feel this an obligation. Mrs Stokes is growing old—'

'It is no obligation,' she said coldly. And then, 'I think it will be more pleasant on the terrace,' she continued; and she moved towards the door.

He held it open that she might pass through; and he followed her into the hall. He little dreamt that, as she walked before him, she was wondering, almost with terror, whether he would go out with her or leave her; whether this was all she was to see of him, day by day. The doubt was not solved; for they were interrupted. As they entered the shady hall by one door

Lady Betty darted into it from the terrace, her face scarlet, her hat crushed, her eyes sparkling with rage. They were so near her she could not escape them; nor could she hide her disorder. 'Why, Betty,' Sophia cried in astonishment, 'what is it? What in the world is the matter?'

'Don't ask me,' Betty cried, almost weeping. 'You ought to be ashamed of yourself. You – your brother has insulted me! He has held me and kissed me against my will! And he laughed at me! He laughed at me! Oh, I could kill him!'

CHAPTER XXIV

Who Plays, Pays

It must be confessed that the flicker of skirts with which Lady Betty ran down the steps when she started for her airing, still more a certain toss of the head that was its perfect complement, gave her mischievous soul huge delight; for she had watched a French maid, and knew them to be pure nature, and the very quintessence of the singing chambermaid's art. It was not impossible that as she executed them she had a person in her eye and meant him to profit by them; for by-and-by she repeated the performance at a point where two paths diverged, and where it put the fitting close to a very pretty pause of indecision. Tom was so hard on her heels that ordinary ears must have detected his tread; but that my lady heard nothing was proved by the fact that she chose the more retired track and tripped along it, humming and darting from flower to flower like some dainty insect let loose among the bracken.

She plucked at will, and buried her shapely little nose in the blossoms; she went on, she stopped, she went on again, and Tom let her go; until the path, after winding round a low spreading oak that closed the view from the house, began to descend into a sunny dell where it ran, a green ribbon of sward, through waist-high fern, leapt the brook by a single plank, and scaled the steeper side by tiny zig-zags.

On the hither side of this summer hollow, sleepy with the warm hum of bees and scent of thyme, Tom overtook her, and never sure was anyone so surprised and overwhelmed as this poor maid.

'La, sir, I declare you frightened my heart into my mouth,' she cried, pressing a white hand to her bodice and looking timidly at him from the shelter of her straw hat. 'I'm sure I beg your pardon, sir,' with a curtsey. 'I would not have come here, if I'd known, for the world.'

'No, child?'

'No, sir, indeed I would not!'

'And why not?' Tom asked pertinently. 'Why should you not come here?'

'Why?' she retorted, properly scandalized. 'What! Come where the family walk? I should hope I know my place better than that, sir. And to behave myself in it.'

'Very prettily, I am sure.' Tom declared, with a bold stare of admiration.

'As becomes me, sir, I hope,' Betty answered demurely, and to show that the stare had no effect upon her, primly turned her head away.

'Though you were brought up with your mistress? Or was it with your late mistress?' Tom asked slily. 'Or have you forgotten which it was, Betty?'

'I hope I've never forgotten anyone who was kind to me,' she whispered, her head drooping so that he could not see her face. 'There's not many think of a poor girl in service; though I come of some that ha' seen better days.'

'Indeed, Betty. Is that so?'

'So I've heard. sir.'

'Well, will you count me among your friends, Betty?'

'La, no, sir!' with vivacity, and she shot him an arch glance. 'I should think not indeed! I should like to know why, sir?' and she tossed her head disdainfully. 'But there, I've talked too long. I'm sure her ladyship would not like it, and asking your pardon, sir, I'll go on.'

'But I'm coming your way.'

'No, sir.'

'But I am,' Tom persisted. 'Why shouldn't I? You are not afraid of me, child? You were not afraid of me in the dark on the hill, when we sat on the tree together, and you wore my coat.'

Betty sighed. ' 'Twas different then, sir,' she murmured, hanging her head, and tracing a pattern on the sward with the point of her toe.

'Why?'

'I'd no choice, sir.'

'Then you would choose to leave me, would you?'

'And I didn't know that you belonged to the family,' she continued, evading the question, 'or I should not have made so free, sir. And besides, asking your pardon, you told me that you had seen enough of women to last you your life, sir. You know you did.'

'Oh, d—n!' Tom cried. The reminder was not welcome.

Betty recoiled virtuously. 'There, sir,' she cried, 'now I know what you think of me! If I were a lady, you'd not have said that to me, I'll be bound. Swearing, indeed? For shame, sir! But I'm for home, and none too soon!'

'No, no!' Tom cried. 'Don't be silly!'

'It's yes, yes, sir, by your leave,' she retorted. 'I'm none such a fool as you'd make me. That shows me what you think of me.'

And turning with an offended air, she began to retrace her steps. Tom called to her, but fruitlessly. She did not answer nor pause. He had to follow her, feeling small and smaller. A little farther, and they would be again within sight of the house.

The track was narrow, the fern on each side grew waist high; he could not intercept her without actual violence. At length, 'See here, child,' he said humbly, 'if you'll turn and chat a bit, I'll persuade you it was not meant. I'll treat you every bit as if you were a lady. I swear I will!'

'I don't know,' she cried. 'I don't know that I can trust you.' But she went more slowly.

' 'Pon honour I will,' he protested. 'I swear I will!'

She stopped at that, and turned to him. 'You will?' she said doubtfully. 'You really will? Then will you please—' with a charming shyness, 'pick me a nosegay to put in my tucker, as my lady's beaux used to do? I should like to feel like a lady for once,' she continued eagerly. ' 'Twould be such a frolic as you gentlefolk have, sir, when you pretend to be poor milk-maids and make syllabub, and will have a bandbox or a hoop-petticoat near you!'

'Your ladyship shall have a nosegay,' Tom answered gaily. 'But I must first see the colour of your eyes that I may match them.'

She clapped her hands in a rapture. 'Oh, how you act, to be sure!' she cried. ''Tis too charming. And for my eyes, sir, it's no more than matching wools.' And she looked at him shyly, dropping a curtsey the while.

'Oh, isn't it?' he retorted. 'Matching wools indeed. Wool does not change, nor shift its hues. Nor glance, nor sparkle, nor ripple like water running now on the deeps, now on the shallows. Nor mirror the clouds, nor dance like wheat in the sunshine. Nor melt like summer,' he continued rapidly, 'nor freeze like the Arctic. Nor say a thousand things in a thousand seconds.'

'La! And do my eyes do all that?' Betty cried, opening them very wide in her innocent astonishment. 'What a thing it is, to be sure, to be a lady. I declare, sir, you are quite out of breath with the fine things you've said. All the same they are blue in the main, and I'll have forget-me-nots, if you please, sir. There's plenty in the brook, and while your honour fetches them I'll sit here and do nothing, like the gentlefolks.'

The brook ran a hundred paces below them, and the sun was hot in the dell, but Tom had no fair excuse. He ran down with a good grace, and in five minutes was back again, his hands full of tiny blossoms.

'They're like a bit of the sky,' said Betty, as he pinned them in her bodice.

'Then they are like your eyes, sweet,' he answered, and he stooped to pay himself for the compliment with a kiss.

But Betty slipped from him without betraying, save by a sudden blush, that she understood.

'Now, it's my turn,' she cried gaily. 'Do you sit, and I'll make you a posy!' And humming an air she floated through the fern to a tree of wild cherry that hung low boughs to meet the fern and fox-gloves. She began to pluck the blossom while Tom watched her and told himself that never was sweeter idyll than this, nor a maid more entrancingly fair, nor eyes more blue, nor lips more inviting, nor manners more daintily sweet and naïve. He sighed prodigiously, for he swore that not for the world would he hurt her, though it was pretty plain how it would go if he choose, and he knew that

Pride lures the little warbler from the skies!
The light-enamoured bird deluded dies.

And – and then, while his thoughts were full of this, he saw her coming back, her arms full of blossom.

'Lord, child!' he cried, 'you've plucked enough for a Jack o' the Green.'

She shot an arch glance at him. 'It is for my Jack o' the Green,' she murmured.

He ogled her and she blushed. But he had his misgivings when he saw that she was making a nosegay as big as his head. Presently it was done, and she found a pin and advanced upon him.

'But you're not going to put that on me!' he cried. He had a boy's horror of the ridiculous.

She stopped, offended. 'Oh,' she said, 'if you don't wish it?' and with lips pouting and tears ill-repressed, she turned away.

He sprang up. 'My dear child, I do wish it!' he cried. ''Pon honour I do! But it's – it's immense.'

She did not answer. Already she was some way up the slope. He ran after her, and told her he would wear it, begged her to pin it for him.

She stood looking at him languidly.

'Are you sure?' she said.

He vowed he was by all his gods, and still pouting she pinned the flowers to the breast of his coat. Now, if ever, he thought was his opportunity. Alas, the nosegay was so large, the cherry twigs of which it was composed were so stiff and sharp, he might as well have kissed her over a hedge! It was provoking in the last degree, and so were her smiling slips. And yet – he could not be angry with her. The very artlessness with which she had made up this huge cabbage and fixed it on him was one charm the more.

'There,' she said, stepping back and viewing him with innocent satisfaction, 'I'm sure a real lady could not have managed that better. It does not prick your chin, does it?'

'No, child.'

'And it isn't in your way? Of course, if it is in your way, sir?'

'No, no!'

'That's well. I'm so glad.' And with a final nod of approval – with that, and no more – Betty turned, actually turned, and began to walk back towards the Hall.

Tom stood, looking after her in astonishment. 'But you are not going?' he cried.

'To be sure, sir,' she answered, looking back and smiling, 'my lady'll be waiting for me.'

'What? This minute?'

'Indeed, sir, and indeed, sir, yes, it is late already,' she said 'But you can come with me a little way, if you like,' she added modestly. And she looked back at him.

He was angry. He had even a suspicion, a small, but growing suspicion, that she was amusing herself with him! But he could not withstand her glance; and as she turned for the last time, he made after her. He overtook her in a few strides, and fell in beside her. But he sulked. His vanity was touched, and willing to show her that he was offended, he maintained a cold silence.

On a sudden he caught the tail of her eye fixed on him, saw that she was shaking with secret laughter; and felt his cheeks begin to burn. The conviction that the little hussy was making fun of him, that she had dared to put this great cabbage upon him for a purpose, burst on him in a flash. It pricked his vanity to the very quick. His heart burned as well as his face; but if she thought to have all the laughing on her side he would teach her better! He lagged a step or two behind, and stealthily tore off the hateful nosegay. The next moment his hot breath was on her neck, his arm was round her; and despite her scream of rage, despite her frantic, furious attempt to push him away, he held her to him while he kissed her twice.

'There, my girl,' he cried, as he released her with a laugh of triumph. 'That's for making fun of me.'

For answer she struck him a sounding slap on the cheek; and as he recoiled, surprised by her rage, she dealt him another on his ear.

Tom's head rung. 'You cat!' he cried. 'I've a good mind to

take another! And I will if you don't behave yourself!'

But the little madcap's face of scarlet fury, her eyes blazing with passion, daunted him. 'How dare you?' she hissed. 'How dare you touch me? You creature! You—' And then, even in the same breath and while he stared, she turned and was gone, leaving the sentence unfinished; and he watched her flee across the sward, a tumultuous raging little figure, with hanging hat, and hair half down, and ribbons that flew out and spoke her passion.

Tom was so taken by surprise he did not attempt to follow, much less to detain her. His sister's maid to take a kiss so? A waiting-woman? A chit of a servant? And after she had played for it, as it seemed to him, aye, and earned it and over-earned it by her impudent trick and her confounded laughter. He had never been so astonished in his life. The world was near its end, indeed, if there was to be this bother about a kiss. Why, his head hummed, and his cheek would show the mark for an hour to come. Nor was that the worst. If she went to the house in that state and published the thing, he would have an awkward five minutes with his sister. Hang the prude! And yet what a charming little vixen it was.

He stood awhile in the sunshine, boring the turf with his heel, uncertain what to do. At length, feeling that anything was better than sneaking there, like a boy who had played truant and feared to go home, he started for the Hall. He would not allow that he was afraid, but as he approached the terrace he had an uneasy feeling; first of the house's many windows, and then of an unnatural silence that prevailed about it, as if something had happened or was preparing. To prove his independence he whistled, but he whistled flat, and stopped.

Outside he met no one, and he plucked up a spirit. After all the girl would not be such a fool as to tell. And what was there to tell? A kiss? What was a kiss? But the moment he was out of the glare and over the threshold of the Hall, he knew that she had told. For there in the cool shadow stood Sophia waiting for him, and behind her Sir Hervey, seated on a corner of the great oak table and whistling softly.

Sophia's tone was grave, her face severe. 'Tom,' she said, 'what have you been doing?'

'I?' he cried.

'Yes, you, young man,' his brother-in-law answered sharply. 'I see no one else.'

'Why, what's the bother?' Tom asked sulkily. 'If you mean about the girl, I kissed her, and what's the harm? I'm not the first that's stolen a kiss.'

'Oh, Tom!'

'And I sha'n't be the last.'

'Nor the last that'll get his face smacked!' Sir Hervey retorted grimly.

Tom winced. 'She has told you that, has she?' he muttered.

'No,' Sir Hervey answered. 'Your cheek told me.'

Tom winced again. 'Well, we're quits then,' he said sullenly. 'She needn't have come Polly Peachuming here!'

Sophia could contain herself no longer. 'Oh, Tom, you don't know what you have done,' she cried impetuously. 'You don't indeed. You thought she was my maid. You took her for my woman that night we were out, you know – and she let you think it.'

'Well?'

'But she is not.'

'Then,' Tom cried in a rage, 'who the devil is she?'

'She's Lady Betty Cochrane, the duke's daughter.'

'And the apple of his eye,' Sir Hervey added with a nod. 'I tell you what, my lad, I would not be in your shoes for something.'

Tom stared, gasped, seemed for a moment unable to take it in. But the next, a wicked gleam shone in his eyes, and he smacked his lips.

'Well, Lady Betty or no, I've kissed her,' he cried. 'I've kissed her, and she can't wipe it off!'

'You wicked boy!' Sophia cried, with indignation. 'Do you consider that she was my guest, under my care, and you have insulted her? Grossly and outrageously insulted her, sir! She leaves tomorrow in consequence, and what am I to say to her people? What am I to tell them? Oh, Tom, it was cruel! it was cruel of you!'

'I'm afraid,' Sir Hervey said with a touch of sternness, 'you were rough with her.'

Tom's momentary jubilation died away. His face was gloomy.

'I'll say anything you like,' he muttered doggedly, 'except that I'm sorry, for I'm not. But I'll beg her pardon humbly. Of course, I should not have done it if I'd known who she was.'

'She won't see you,' Sophia answered.

'You might try her again,' Sir Hervey suggested, beginning to take the culprit's part. 'Why not? She need not see Tom or speak to him unless she wishes.'

'I'll try,' Sophia answered; and she went and presently came back. Lady Betty would stay, and, of course, 'she couldn't forbid Sir Thomas Maitland his sister's house.' But she desired that all intercourse between them should be restricted to the barest formalities.

Tom looked glum. 'Look here,' he said, 'if she'll see me alone I'll beg her pardon, and let us have done with it!'

'She won't see you alone! It is particularly that she wishes to avoid.'

'All right,' Tom answered sulkily. But he made up his mind that before many hours elapsed he would catch my lady and make her come to terms with him.

He was mistaken, however; as he was also in his expectation that when they met she would be covered with shame and confusion of face. When the time came it was he who was embarrassed. The young lady appeared, and was an icicle; stiff, pale and reserved, she made it clear that she did not desire to speak to him, did not wish to look at him, and much preferred to take things at table from any hand but his. Beyond this she did not avoid his eyes, and in hers was no shadow of consciousness. Tom's face grew hot where she had slapped it, he chafed, fretted, raged, but he got no word with her. He was shut out, he was not of the party, she made him feel that; and at the end of twenty-four hours he was her serf, her slave, watching her eye, consumed with a desire to throw himself at her feet, ready to anticipate her wishes, as a dog those of his master, anxious to abase himself no matter how low, if she would give him a word or a look.

Even Sir Hervey marvelled at her coldness and perfect self-control. 'I suppose she likes him,' he said, as he and Sophia walked on the terrace that evening.

'She did, I fancy,' Sophia answered, 'before this happened.'

'And now?'

'She does not like him. I'm sure of that.'

'But she may love him, you mean?' Sir Hervey said, interpreting her tone rather than her words.

'Yes, or hate him,' she answered. 'It is the one or the other.'

'Since he kissed her?'

'Yes, I think so,' and then on a sudden Sophia faltered. She felt the blood begin to rise to her cheeks in one of those blushes, the most trying of all, that commence uncertainly, mount slowly, but persist, and at length deepen into pain. She remembered that the man walking beside her, talking of these others' love affairs, had never kissed her! He must think, he could not but think of their own case. He might even fancy that she meant her words for a hint.

He saw her distress, understood it, and took pity on her. But the abruptness with which he changed the conversation, and by-and-by withdrew, persuaded her that he had read her thoughts, and long after he had left her, her face burned.

The whole matter, Tom's misbehaviour and the rest, had upset her; she told herself that this was what ailed her and made her restless. Nor was she quick to regain her balance. She found the house, new as all things in it were to her, dull and over-quiet; she found Lady Betty, once so lively, no company; she found Tom snappish and ill-tempered. And she blamed Tom for all; or told herself that town and the opera and the masquerade had spoiled her for a country life. She did not lay the blame elsewhere. Even to herself she did not admit that Sir Hervey, polite and considerate as he was, to the point of leaving her much to herself, would have pleased her better had he left her less. But she did think – and with soreness – that he would have been wiser had he given her more frequent opportunities of learning to be at ease with him.

She did not go further than this even in her thoughts until three days after Tom's escapade. Then, feeling dull herself, she came on Tom moping on the terrace, and undertook to rally him on his humour. 'If you would really be in her good graces again, 'tis not the way to do it, Tom; I can tell you that,' she said. 'Laugh and talk, and she'll wish you. Pluck up a spirit, and 'twill win more on her than a million sighs.'

'What's the good?' he muttered sourly.

'Well, at any rate, you do no good by moping.'

Tom sat silent awhile, his head buried between his hands, his elbows resting on the balustrade. 'I don't see that anything's any good,' he muttered at last. 'We're both in one case, I think. You know your own business, I suppose. You know, I take it, what you were doing when you married in such a hurry; but I'm d—d,' with sudden violence, 'if I understand it. Three weeks married, and put on one side for another!'

'Tom!'

'Oh, you may Tom me, you don't alter it,' he answered roughly. 'I am hanged if I understand or know what's a-foot. Here are you and I sitting at home like sick cats, and my lord and my lady up and down and in and out, as thick as thieves. That is what it comes to. 'Tis vastly pretty, isn't it?' Tom continued with a cynical laugh. 'I think you said she was under your protection. Oh, Lord.'

Hitherto, astonishment had robbed Sophia of speech. But with Tom's last word her sense of her duty to herself and to her husband awoke, and found her words.

'You wicked boy!' she cried with indignation. 'You wicked, miserable boy! How dare you even think such things, much more say them, and say them to me! Never hint at such things again if you wish to – to keep your sister. Sir Hervey and I understand one another, you may be sure of that.'

'Well, I am glad you do,' Tom muttered. 'For I don't!' But he spoke shamefacedly, and only to cover his discomfiture.

'We understand one another perfectly,' Sophia replied with pride, and drew herself to her full height. 'For my friend, she is above your suspicions, as far above them as, I thank God, is my husband. No, not another word, I have heard too much already. I don't wish to speak to you again until you are in a better mind, sir.'

She turned from him, crossed the terrace with her proudest step, and entered the house. But underneath she was panting with excitement, her head was in a whirl. She dared not think; and to avoid thought – thought that might lower her in her own eyes, thought that might wrong her husband – she hastened through the hall to the still-room; and finding that the ash-keys which she had ordered to be done with green whey had been boiled with white, was sharp with the maid, and tart with Mrs Stokes. Thence she flew in a bustle up the wide staircase, and along the corridor under portraits of dead Cokes, to her room; but there, thought seemed inevitable, it was in vain she paced the floor. And feverishly tying the strings of her hat she hurried down again, her face burning. She would walk.

At the outer door she paused. She saw that Tom was still there, and she was unwilling to pass him, lest he read in this sudden activity the sign of disturbance. The pause was fatal. A moment she stood irresolute, fighting with herself and her cowardly impulses. Then she opened the door of the grand drawing-room, and gliding like a culprit down its shadowy length, opened the door of the smaller room, and closed that too behind her. This inner room was little used in the daytime, and though the windows were open the curtains were drawn across them. Stealthily, fearing to be observed, she raised the corner of the nearest curtain and turned to look at Lady Anne's picture; the lodestone that had drawn her hither as the candle draws the moth. But she never looked; for as she turned she met her own face, pale, anxious, plain – yes, plain – staring from the mirror at her shoulder, and what use to look after that? To look would not make Lady Anne less comely or herself more fair. She let the curtain fall.

But she stood. Someone was passing the open window. A voice she knew spoke, a second voice answered. And from where she stood Sophia heard their words as if they had spoken in the room.

CHAPTER XXV

Repentance at Leisure

THE FIRST speaker was Lady Betty, and her first remark seemed to be an answer to a question. 'Well, 'tis me you like,' she said. 'But if you'll be guided by me you'll not tell her. Then, when you go, it will put the finishing touch to our – friendship' – with a sly laugh – 'if that be your wish, sir. On the other hand, if you tell madam, who is beginning to be jealous, take my word for it, there's an end of that! And there's this besides. If you tell her, it's not to be said what she will do, I warn you.'

'She might insist on going?' Sir Hervey's voice answered. 'That's what you mean?'

'If she knew she would go! I think she would, at any rate. At the best there's danger. On the other hand, say nothing to her, and here's the opportunity you said you desired. Of course, if you are weakening,' Lady Betty continued in the tone of one ready to take offence, 'and don't desire it any longer, that's another matter, sir.'

'My dear girl,' Sir Hervey cried eagerly, 'have I not done everything to show her that she is indifferent to me? Do you want any other proof? Have I omitted anything? Have not I' – and then his voice died abruptly. The two speakers had turned the corner of the house, and Sophia heard no more. But she had heard enough. She had heard too much!

It is sadly trite that that we cannot have we want. It is an old tale that it is for the sour grapes the mouth waters, and not for the bunch within reach. A thousand kindnesses, the hand ever waiting, the smile ever ready, gain no response; until a thousand rebuffs have earned their due, and the smile and the hand are another's. Then, on a sudden, the heart learns its own bitterness. Then we would give the world for the look we once flouted, for the kind word from lips grown silent. And it is too late. Too late!

In the gloom of the inner drawing-room, where she sat with fingers feverishly interlaced, Sophia remembered his longsuffering with her, his thoughtfulness for her, his watchfulness over her, proved by a hundred acts of kindness and consideration. By a word at a drum when she was strange to town, and knew few. By countenance and a jest when Madam Harrington snubbed her. By the recovery of a muff – of value and her sister's – before it was known that she had lost it. By the gift of a birthnight fan which she had never carried; and the arrangement of a party to which she had not gone. By a word of caution when her infatuation for the Irishman began to be noticed; by a second word and a third. Through all he had been patience, she had been scorn. Now, on a sudden, she was in the dust before him. The smile that had never failed her in a difficulty, nor been wanting in a strait, had its value at last; and she felt that to read it once more in those eyes she would give the world, herself, all!

But too late. She had lost his love as she deserved to lose it. It was her doing. She had but herself to thank that this was the end. Only, she whispered, if he had had a little, a very little more patience! A day even! If he had given her one day more. That, or left her to her fate!

Fearful at last of being found in that room, seated before his picture, she crept out into the hall, and stood, marking the silence that prevailed in the house; listening to the dull tick of the clock that stood in the corner; watching the motes that danced in the dusty bars of sunshine before the door. With pathetic self-pity she found in these things – and in the faint taste of dry rot that told of the generations that had walked the old floor – the echo of her thoughts. Such, so quiet, so still, so regular, so far removed from the joy of the world was her life to be henceforth. 'And I am young! I am young!' she whispered.

If he had only, when he met her in Clarges Row, left her to her fate! Nothing worse could have happened to her than this which had happened; and he might have wedded Lady Betty in innocence and honour. The fault was hers, and yet it was his too. A wild infatuation had brought her to the brink of ruin; an impulse of chivalry, scarcely less foolish, had led him to save her. The end for both must be misery. For him God knew what! For her, loneliness and this silent, empty, ordered house with its faint dead perfume, its aroma of long-stored linen, its savour of the dead and the by-gone.

As she stood in the middle of the floor, thinking these thoughts, the shadow of a bird flitted across the patch of sunshine that lay within the doorway. It startled her, and she looked up, just as Lady Betty, swinging her hat by its strings, and humming a gay air, appeared on the threshold. The girl hung an instant as in doubt, and then, whether she espied Sophia standing in the shadow and did not want to meet her, or she changed her mind for another reason, she turned and left the doorway empty.

The sight was too much for Sophia's composure. That airy, laughing figure – youthful, almost infantine – poised in sunshine – that and her own brooding face, seen lately in the glass, suggested a comparison that filled her heart to bursting. She crept to the oak side table that stood in the bayed recess behind the door, and leaning her arms upon it, hid her face in them. She did not weep, but from time to time she shivered, as if the June air chilled her.

She had sat in this position some minutes when a faint sound roused her. Ashamed of being found in that posture, she looked up, and saw Lady Betty in the act of crossing the hall on tip-toe. Apparently the girl had just entered from the terrace and thought herself alone; for when she reached the middle of the floor, she stood weighing a letter in her hand, as if she doubted what to do with it. Her eyes travelled slowly from the long oak table to an almoner; and thence to a chest that stood beside the inner door. In the end she chose the chest, and, gliding to the door, placed the letter on it, arranging its position with peculiar care. Then she turned to go out again by the terrace door, but had not taken two steps before her eyes met Sophia's. She uttered a low cry, and stood, arrested.

Sophia did not speak, but she rose, crossed the hall, and as the other, with a rapid movement, recovered the letter from the chest, she extended her hand for it.

'Give it to me,' she said.

For a moment Lady Betty confronted her, holding the letter hidden. Then, whether Sophia's pale set face cowed her, or she really had no choice, she held out the letter. 'It is for you,' she faltered. 'But—'

'But,' Sophia answered, taking her up with quiet scorn, 'I was not to know the bearer! I am obliged to you.'

Again for a moment the two women looked at one another. And Lady Betty's face grew slowly scarlet. 'You have his confidence,' Sophia continued in the same tone. 'It's fitting you wait, miss, and take the answer.'

'But he's gone,' Betty stammered.

'Then I do not think you will take the answer!' Sophia retorted. 'But you will wait, nevertheless! You will wait my pleasure.' She broke the seal as she spoke, and began to read the contents of the note. They were short. A moment and she crumpled the paper in her hand and dropped it on the floor. 'A very proper letter,' she said with a sneer. 'There's no fault to be found with it, I am sure. He is my affectionate husband, I can be no less than his dutiful wife. 'Tis no part of a dutiful wife to find fault with her husband's letter, I suppose.'

'I don't know what you would be at,' Lady Betty muttered, looking more and more frightened.

'No? That's what I'm going to explain – if you'll sit, miss? Sit, girl!'

Lady Betty shrugged her shoulders, but obeyed, an uneasy look in her eyes. Sophia sat also, on the farther side of the small oak table; but for a full minute she did not speak. When she did her voice had lost its bitterness, and was low and absent and passionless. 'There are two things to be talked about – you and I,' she said, drumming slowly on the table with her fingers. 'And by your leave I'll speak of myself first. If I could set him free I would! D'you hear me? D'you understand? If the worst that could have befallen me in Clarges Row, the worst that he had in his mind when he married me, were the price to be paid, I would pay it today. He should be free to marry whom he would; and if by raising my hand I could come between him and her I would not! Nay, if by raising my hand I could bring them together I would! And that though when he married me, he did me as great a wrong as a man can do a woman!'

Suddenly, without warning, Lady Betty burst into irrepressible sobbing. 'Oh,' she cried, 'do you hate him so!'

'Hate him?' Sophia answered. 'Hate him? No, fool, I love him so!' And then in a strain of bitterness, the more intense as she spoke in a tone little above a whisper. 'You start, miss? You think me a fool, I know, to tell you that! But see how proud I am! I will not keep from the woman he loves the least bit of her triumph! Let her enjoy it – though 'tis an empty one – for I cannot free him, do what I will. Let her know, for her pleasure, that she is fairer than I, as I know it! Let her know that she has won the heart that should be mine, and – which will be sweetest of all to her – that I would fain have won it myself and could not! Let her – but you are crying, miss? And I'd forgotten. What's all this to you?' with a change to quiet irony. 'You are too young to understand such things! And, of course, 'twas not of this that I wished to speak to you; but of yourself, and of – Tom. Of course – Tom,' with a faint laugh. 'I'm sorry that he misbehaved to you in the park. I've had it on my mind ever since. There's but one thing to be done, I am sure, and that is what your own judgement, Lady Betty—'

'Sophy!'

But Sophia continued without heeding the remonstrance – 'pointed out to you! I mean, to return to your mother without loss of time. It is best for you, and best for – Tom,' with a crooked smile. 'Best, indeed, for all of us.'

Lady Betty, her face held aloof, was busy drying her tears; her position such that it was not possible to say what her sentiments were, nor whether her emotion was real or assumed. But at that she looked up, startled; she met the other's eyes. 'Do you mean,' she muttered, 'that I am to go home?'

'To be sure,' Sophia answered coldly. ''Tis only what you wished yourself, three days ago.'

'But – but Sir Tom hasn't – hasn't troubled me again,' Betty faltered.

'Tom?' Sophia answered, in a peculiar tone. 'Ah, no. But – I doubt if he's to be trusted. Meanwhile, I gather from the letter you gave me that Sir Hervey will not return until tomorrow noon. We must act then without him. You will start at daybreak tomorrow. I shall accompany you as far as Lewes. Thence Mrs Stokes, who has been in London, and Watkyns, with sufficient attendance, will see you safe to her Grace's house. You are in my care—'

'And you send me home in disgrace!'

'Not at all!' my lady answered, with coldness. 'The fault is Tom's.'

'And I suffer! Do you mean, do you really mean—' Betty protested, in a tone of astonishment, 'that I am to go back tomorrow – at daybreak – by myself?'

'I do.'

'Before Sir Hervey returns?'

'To be sure.'

'But it is monstrous!' Betty cried, grown indignant; and in her excitement she rose and stood opposite Sophia. 'It is absurd! Why should I go? In this haste, and like a thing disgraced? I've done nothing. I don't understand.'

Sophia rose also; her face still pale, a fire smouldering in her eyes. 'Don't you?' she said. 'Don't you understand?'

'No.'

'Think again, girl. Think again!'

'N-no,' Betty repeated; but this time her voice quavered. Her eyes sank before Sophia's, and a fresh wave of colour swept over her face. There is an innocent shame as well as a guilty shame; a shame caused by that which others think us, as well as by that which we are. Betty sank under this, yet made a fight. 'Why should I go?' she repeated weakly.

'Not for my sake,' Sophia answered gravely. 'For your own. Because I have more thought for you, more mercy for you, more compassion for you than you have for yourself. You say you go in disgrace? It is not true; but were you to stay, you would stay in disgrace! From that I shall save you whether you will or no. Only—' and suddenly stretching out her hand she seized Betty's shoulder and swayed the slighter girl to and fro by it – 'only,' she cried, with sudden vehemence, 'don't think I do it to rid myself of you! To keep him, or to hold him, or to glean after you! If I could give him the woman he loves I would give her to him though you were that woman! If I could set her in my place, I would set her there, though her foot were on my breast! But I cannot. I cannot, girl. And you must go.'

She let her hand fall with the last word; but not so quickly that Betty had not time to snatch it to her lips and kiss it – kiss it with an odd strangled cry. The next instant the girl flung herself on the bench beside the table, and hiding her head on her arms – as Sophia had hidden hers a while before – she gave herself up to unrestrained weeping. For a few seconds Sophia stood watching her with a cold, grave face; then she shivered, and turning in silence, left the hall.

Strange to say, the door had barely fallen to behind her when a change came over Lady Betty. She raised her head and looked round, her eyes shining through her tears. As soon as she was certain that she was alone, she sprang to her feet, and waving her hat by its riband round her head, spun round the table in a frantic dance of triumph, her hoop sweeping the hall from end to end, yet finding it too small for the exuberance of her joy. Pausing at last, breathless and dishevelled, 'Oh, you dear! Oh, you angel!' she cried. 'You'd give him the woman he loves, would you, ma'am – if you could! You'd set her foot on your breast, if 'twould make him happy? Oh, it was better than the best play that ever was, it was better than Goodman's Fields, or Mr Quin, to hear her stab herself, and stab herself, and stab herself! If he doesn't kiss her shoes, if he does not kneel in the dust to her, I'll never believe in man again! I'll die a maid at forty and content! – but oh, la!' And Lady Betty broke off suddenly with a look of consternation, 'I'd forgotten! What am I to do? She's a dragon. She'll not let me stay till he returns, no, not if I go on my knees to her! And if I go, I lose all! Oh, la, sweet, what am I to do?'

She thought awhile with a face full of mischief. 'Coke might meet us in Lewes,' she muttered, 'and cut the knot, but that's a chance. Or I might tell her – and that's to spoil sport. I must get a note to him tonight. But she'll be giving her orders now, I expect; and it's odds the men won't carry it. There's only Tom, and that's putting my hand in very far!'

She thought awhile, then rubbed her lips with her handkerchief, and laughing and blushing looked at it. 'Well, it leaves no mark,' she muttered with a grimace, 'and if he's rude I can pay him as I paid him before.'

Apparently she would face the risk, for she set herself busily to search among the dog-leashes and powder-horns, holsters, and tattered volumes of farriery, that encumbered the great table. Presently she unearthed a pewter ink-pot and an old swan-quill; and bearing these, and a flyleaf ruthlessly torn from a number of the *Gentleman's Magazine*, to a table in the bay window, she sat down and scrawled a few lines. She folded the note into the shape of a cocked hat, bound it deftly about with a floss of silk torn from her ribands; and having succeeded so far, lacked only a postman. She had a good idea where he was to be found, and having donned her hat and tied the strings more nicely than usual, went on the terrace. There she was not long in discovering him. He was kicking his heels on the horse-block under the oak, between the terrace and the stables.

No one knew better than her ladyship how to play the innocent; but on this occasion she had neither time nor mind to be taken by surprise. She tripped down the steps, crossed the intervening turf, and pausing before him opened her fire.

'Do you wish to earn your pardon, sir?' she asked. Her

manner was as cold and formal as it had been for the last three days.

Tom rose sheepishly, his mind in a whirl. For days she had avoided him. She had drawn in her skirts if he passed near her; she had ignored his hand at table; she had looked through him when he spoke. Until she paused, until her voice sounded in his ears, he had thought she would go by him; and for a moment he could not find his tongue to answer her. Then 'I don't understand,' he muttered sullenly.

'I spoke plainly,' Lady Betty answered, in a voice clear as a bell. 'But I will say it again. Do you wish, sir, to earn your pardon?'

Tom's face flamed. Unfortunately, his ill-conditioned side was uppermost. 'I don't want another slap in the face,' he grumbled.

'And I do not want what I have found,' Lady Betty retorted with dignity, though the rebuff, which she had not expected, stung her. 'I came in search of a gentleman willing to do a lady a service, and I have not found one. After this our acquaintance is at an end, sir. You will oblige me by not speaking to me. Good evening.' And she swept away her head in the air.

Tom was not of the softest material, but at that, brute and boor were the best names he gave himself. The love that resentment had held at bay, returned in a flood and overwhelmed him. Sinking under remorse, feeling that he would now die for a glance from her eyes whom he had again and hopelessly offended, he rushed after her. Overtaking her at the foot of the steps, he implored her, with humble, incoherent prayers, to forgive him – to forgive him once more, only once more, and he would be her slave for ever!

'It's only one chance I ask,' he panted. 'Give me one more chance of – of showing that I am not the brute you think me. Oh, Lady Betty, forgive me, and – and forget what I said. You've cut me to the heart every hour for days past; you haven't looked at me; you've treated me as if I were something lower than a thief-taker. And – and when I was smarting under this, because I'd rather have a word from your lips than a kiss from another, you came to me, and I – I've misbehaved myself worse than before.'

'No, not worse,' Lady Betty said, in her cold, clear voice. 'That was impossible.'

'But as bad as I could,' Tom confessed, not over-comforted. 'Oh why, oh why,' he continued, piteously, 'am I always at my worst with you? For I think more of you than of anyone. I'm always thinking of you. I can't sleep for thinking – what you are thinking of me, Lady Betty. I'd lie down in the dust, and let you walk over me if it would give you any pleasure. If it weren't for those d—d windows I'd kneel down now and ask your pardon.'

'I don't see what difference the windows make,' Lady Betty said, in her coldest tone. 'They don't make your offence any less.'

Tom might have answered that they made his punishment the greater; but, instead, he plumped down on the lowest step, careless who saw him if only Betty forgave him. 'Oh, Lady Betty,' he cried, 'forgive me!'

'That is better,' she said, judiciously.

'Oh, Lady Betty,' he cried, 'I humbly ask you to forgive me.'

Lady Betty looked at him quietly from an upper step.

'You may get up,' she said. 'But I warn you, sir, you have yet to earn your pardon. You have promised much, I want but a little. Will you take a note from me to Lewes tonight?'

'If I live!' he cried, his eyes sparkling. 'But that's a small thing.'

'I trust in small things first,' she answered.

'And great afterwards?'

She had much ado not to laugh, he looked at her so piteously, his hands clasped. 'Perhaps,' she said. 'At any rate the future will show. Here is the note.' She passed it to him quickly, with one eye on the windows. 'You will tell no one, you will mention it to no one; but you will see that it reaches his hands tonight.'

'It shall if I live,' Tom answered fervently. 'To whom am I to deliver it?'

'To Sir Hervey.'

Tom swore outright, and turned crimson. They looked at one another, the man and the maid.

When Betty spoke again – after a long, strange pause, during which he stood holding the note loosely in his fingers as if he would drop it – it was in a tone of passion which she had not used before. 'Listen!' she said. 'Listen, sir, and understand if you can – for it behoves you! There is an offence that passes forgiveness. I believe that a moment ago you were on the point of committing it. If so, and if you have not yet repented, think, think before you do commit it. For there will be no place for repentance afterwards. It is not for me to defend my conduct, nor for you to suspect it,' the young girl continued proudly. 'That is my father's right, and my husband's when I have one. It imports no one else. But I will stoop to tell you this, sir. If you had said the words that were on your lips a moment ago, as surely as you stand there today, you would have come to me tomorrow to crave my pardon, and to crave it in shame, in comparison of which anything you have felt today is nothing. And you would have craved it in vain!' she continued vehemently. 'I would rather the lowest servant here – soiled my lips – than you!'

Her passion had so much the better of her, when she came to the last words, that she could scarcely utter them. But she recovered herself with marvellous rapidity. 'Do you take the note, sir,' she said coldly, 'or do you leave it?'

'I will take it, if it be to the devil!' he cried.

'No,' she answered quickly; and she stayed him by a haughty gesture. 'That will not do! Do you take it, thinking no evil? Do you take it, thinking me a good woman? Or do you take it thinking me something lower, infinitely lower, than the creatures you make your sport and pastime?'

'I do, I do believe!' Tom cried; and, dropping on his knees, he hid his face against her hoop-skirt, and pressed his lips to the stuff. And strange to say when he had risen and gone – without another word – there were tears in the girl's eyes. Tom had touched her.

CHAPTER XXVI

A Dragon Disarmed

IT WAS five o'clock in the morning. The low sun shone athwart the cool, green sward of the park, leaving the dells and leafy retreats of the deer in shadow. In the window recess of the hall, whence the eye had that view, and could drink in the freshness of the early morning, the small oak table was laid for breakfast. Old plate that had escaped the melting-pot and the direful year of the new coinage, dragon china imported when Queen Anne was young, linen, white as sun and dew or D'Oyley could make it, gave back the pure light of early morning, and bade welcome a guest as dainty as themselves. Yet Lady Betty, for whom the table was prepared, and who stood beside it in an attitude of expectation, tapped the floor with her foot and looked but half pleased. 'Is Lady Coke not coming?' she asked at last.

'No, my lady,' Mrs Stokes answered. 'Her ladyship is taking her meal in her room.'

'Oh!' Lady Betty rejoined drily. 'She's not ailing, I hope?'

'No, my lady. She bade me say that the chariot would be at the door at half after five.'

Betty grimaced, but took her seat in silence, and kept one eye on the clock. Had her messenger played her false? Or was Coke incredulous? Or what kept him? Even if he did not come before they set out, he might meet them on the hither side of Lewes; but that was a slender thread to which to trust, and Lady Betty had no mind to be packed home in error. As the finger of the clock in the corner moved slowly downwards, as the sun drank up the dew on leaf and bracken, and the day hardened, she listened, and more intently listened for the foot that was overdue. It wanted but five minutes of the half hour now! Now it wanted but three minutes! Two minutes! Now the rustle of my lady's skirts was on the stairs, the door was opened for her to enter and – and then at last, Betty caught the ring of spurred heels on the pavement of the terrace.

'He's come!' she cried, springing from her seat, and forgetting everything else in her relief. 'He's come!'

Sophia from the inner threshold stared coldly. 'Who?' she asked. It was the first time the two had met in the morning and had not kissed; but there are bounds to the generosity of woman, and Sophia could not stoop to kiss her rival. 'Who?' she repeated, standing stiffly aloof, near the door by which she had entered.

'You will see!' Betty cried, with a bubble of laughter. 'You will see.'

The next moment Sir Hervey's figure darkened the open doorway, and Sophia saw him and understood. For an instant surprise drove the blood from her cheeks; then, as astonishment gave place to indignation, and to all the feelings which a wife – though a wife in name only – might be expected to experience in such a position, the tide returned in double volume. She did not speak, she did not move; but she saw that they understood one another, she felt that this sudden return was concerted between them; and her eyes sparkled, her bosom rose. If she had never been beautiful before, Sophia was beautiful at that moment.

Sir Hervey smiled, as he looked at her. 'Good morning, my dear,' he said cheerily. 'I'm of the earliest, or thought I was. But you had nearly stolen a march on me.'

She did not answer him. 'Lady Betty,' she said, without turning her head or looking at the girl, 'you have better leave us.'

'Yes, Betty, away with you,' he cried, good humouredly. 'You'll find Tom outside.' And as Betty whisked away through the open door, 'You'll pardon me, my dear,' he continued quietly, but with dignity, 'I have countermanded the carriage. When you have heard what I have to say you will agree with me, I am sure, that there is no necessity for our guest to leave us today.' He laid his whip aside as he spoke, and turned to the table from which Lady Betty had lately risen. I have not broken my fast,' he said. 'Give me some tea, child.'

A wild look, as of a creature caged, and beating vain wings against bars, darkened Sophia's eyes. She was trembling with agitation, panting to resist, outraged in her pride if not in her love; and he asked for tea! Yet words did not come at once, his easy manner had its effect; as if she acknowledged that he had still a right to her service, she sat down at the little table in the window bay. He passed his legs over the bench on the other side, and sat waiting, the width of the table only – and it was narrow – between them. As she washed Betty's cup in the basin the china tinkled, and betrayed her agitation; but she managed to make his tea and pass it to him.

'Thank you,' he said quietly. 'And now for what I was saying. Lady Betty sent me a note last night, stating that she was to go today, unless I interceded for her. It was that brought me back this morning.'

Sophia's eyes burned, but she forced herself to speak with calmness. 'Did she tell you,' she asked, 'why she was to go?'

Sir Hervey shrugged his shoulders. 'Well,' he said, with a smile, 'she hinted at the reason.'

'Did she tell you what I had said to her?'

'I am afraid not,' he said politely. 'Probably space—'

'Or shame!' Sophia cried; and the next moment could have bitten her tongue. 'Pardon me,' she said in an altered tone, 'I had no right to say that. But if she has not told you, 'tis I must tell you, myself. And if is more fitting. I am aware that you have discovered – all too soon, Sir Hervey – that our marriage, if it could be called a marriage, was a mistake. I cannot – I cannot,' Sophia continued, trembling from head to foot, 'take all the blame of that to myself, though I know that the first cause was my fault, and that it was I led you to commit the error. But I cannot take all the blame, she repeated, 'I cannot! For you knew the world, you should have known yourself, and what was likely, what was certain to come of it! What has come of it?'

Sir Hervey drummed on the table with his fingers, and when he spoke, it was in a tone of apology. 'The future is hard to read,' he said. 'It is easy, child, to be wise after the event.'

Her next words seemed strangely ill-directed to the issue. 'You never told me that you had been betrothed before,' she said, 'and that she died. If you had told me, and if I had seen her face – I should have been wiser. I should have foreseen what would happen. I do not wonder that such a face seen again has' – she paused, stammering and pale – 'has recalled old times and your youth. I have no right to blame you. I do not blame you. At least, I – I try not to blame you,' she repeated, her voice sinking lower and lower. 'I have told her, and it is true, that if I could bear all the consequences of our error I would bear them. That if I could release you and set you free to marry the – the woman you have learned to love – I would, sir, willingly. That, at any rate, I would not raise a finger to prevent such a marriage.'

'And did you – mean that?' he asked in a low voice, his face averted.

'As God sees me, I did.'

'You are in earnest, Sophia?' For an instant he turned his head and looked at her.

'I am.'

'Yet – you were for sending her away,' he said. 'This morning? Before I could return? That I might not see her again.'

She looked at him with astonishment, with indignation. 'Cannot you understand,' she cried, 'that that was not on my account, but on hers?'

'It seems to have been rather on my account,' he muttered doggedly, his fingers toying with the teaspoon, his eyes on the table. He seemed strangely changed. He did not seem to be himself.

She shuddered. 'At any rate, it was not on my account,' she said.

'And you are still fixed that she must go?'

'Yes.'

'Then I'll tell you what it is,' he answered with sudden determination. 'I'll take you at your word!' He raised his cup, which was half full, and held it in front of his lips, looking at her across it as he spoke. 'You said just now that if there was a way to – to give me the woman I loved – you would take it.'

She started. For a moment she did not answer.

He waited. At last: 'You didn't mean it?' he said, his tone cold.

The room, the high window with its stained escutcheons, the dark oak walls, the dark oak table, the leafage reflected cool and green in the tall mirror opposite the door, went round with her; she swallowed something that rose in her throat, and set her teeth hard, and at length she found her voice. 'Yes,' she said, 'I meant it.'

'Well, there is a way,' he answered; and he rose from the table, and, moving to the door which led to the main hall and the staircase, he closed it. 'There is a way of doing it. But it is not quite easy to explain it to you in a moment. 'Twas a hurried marriage, as you know, and informal, and a marriage only in name. And something has happened since then.'

He paused there; she asked in a low tone, 'What?'

'Well, it is what took me to Lewes yesterday,' he answered. 'I should have told you of it then, but I was in doubt how you would take it. And Betty persuaded me not to tell it. The man Hawkesworth—'

He paused, as she rose stiffly from the table. 'Have they taken him?' she exclaimed.

'Yes,' he said gently. 'They took him in hiding near Chichester. But he was ill, dying, it was thought, when they surprised him.'

She had a strange prevision. 'Of the smallpox?' she asked.

'Yes,' he answered. And then, 'He died last night,' he continued softly. 'My dear, let me get you a little cordial.'

'No, no! Did you see him?'

'I did. And I did what I could for him. I was with him when he died.'

She sat down at the table, hiding her face in her hands. Presently she shuddered. 'Heaven forgive him!' she whispered. 'Heaven forgive him, as I do!' And again she was silent for some minutes, while he stood watching her. At last, 'Was it about him,' she asked in a low voice, 'that Lady Betty was talking to you on the terrace yesterday?'

'Yes. I asked her advice. I did not know what you might do, if you knew. And I did not wish you to see him.'

'But she had another reason,' Sophia murmured, behind her hands. 'There was another motive, which she urged for keeping it from me. What was it?'

He did not answer.

'What was it?' she repeated, and lowered her hands and looked at him, her lips parted.

He walked up the hall and back again under her eyes. 'Well,' he said, in a tone elaborately easy, 'she is but a child, you know, and does not understand things. She knew a little of the circumstances of our marriage, and she thought she knew more. She fancied that a little jealousy might foster love; and so it may, perhaps, where a spark exists. But not otherwise. That was her mistake.'

'But – but I do not understand!' Sophia cried, her hands shaking, her face bewildered. 'You said – you told her that you were perfectly indifferent to me.'

'Oh, pardon me,' Sir Hervey answered lightly. 'Never, I am sure. I said, perhaps, that I had done everything to *show* that I was indifferent to you. That was part of her foolish plan. But there is a distinction, you see?'

'Yes,' Sophia faltered, her face growing slowly scarlet. 'There is a distinction, I see.'

She wanted to cry, and she wanted to think; and she wanted to hide her face from his eyes, but had not the will to do it while he looked at her. Her head was going round. If she had misinterpreted Betty's words on the terrace, and it seemed certain now that she had, what had she done? Or, rather, what had she not done? She had fallen into Betty's trap; she had proclaimed her own folly; she had misjudged her – and him! She had done them foul, dreadful wrong; she had insulted them horribly, horribly insulted them by her suspicions! She had proved the meanness and lowness of her mind! While he had been thinking of her, and for her, still shielding her, as he had shielded her from the beginning – she had been slandering him, accusing him, wronging him, and along with him this young girl, her guest, her friend, living under her roof! It was infamous! Infamous! What had so warped her?

And then, as she sat overwhelmed by shame, a ray of light pierced the darkness. She looked at him, feeling on a sudden cold and weak. 'But you – you have not yet explained!' she muttered.

'What?'

'How I can help you to – to—' Her voice failed her. She could not finish.

'To Betty,' he said, seeing her stuck in a quagmire of perplexities. 'I do not want Betty.'

'Then what did you mean?' she stammered.

'I never said I wanted Betty,' he answered, smiling.

'But you said—'

'I said that there was a way by which you could help me to the woman I loved. And there is a way. Betty, in her note to me, will have it that you can do it at slight cost to yourself. That is for you to decide. Only remember, Sophia,' Sir Hervey continued gravely, 'you are free, free as air. I have kept my word to the letter. I shall continue to keep it. If there is to be a chance, if we are to come nearer to one another, it must come from you, not from me.'

She turned to the window; and waiting for her answer – which did not come quickly – he saw that she was shaking. 'You don't help me,' she whispered at last.

'What, child?'

'You don't help me. You don't make it easy for me.' And then she turned abruptly to him and he saw that the tears were running down her face. 'Don't you know what you ought to do?' she cried, holding out her hands and lifting her face to him. 'You ought to beat me, you ought to shake me, you ought to lock me in a dark room! You ought to tell me every hour of the day how mean, how ungrateful, how poor and despicable a thing I am – to take all and give nothing!'

'And that would help you?' he said. ''Tis a new way of making love, sweet.'

''Tis an old one,' she cried impetuously. 'You are too good to me. But if you will take me, such as I am – and – and I suppose you have not much choice,' she continued, with an odd, shy laugh, 'I shall be very much obliged to you, sir. And – and I shall thank you all my life.'

He would have taken her in his arms, but she dropped as she spoke, on the bench beside the table, and hiding her face in her hands, began to weep softly – in the same posture, and in the same place, in which she had sat the day before, but with feelings how different! Ah, how different!

Sir Hervey stood over her a moment, watching her. Her riding-cap had fallen off and lay on the table beside her. Her hair, clubbed for the journey, hung undressed and without powder on her neck. He touched it gently, almost reverently, with his hand. It was the first caress he had ever given her.

'Child,' he whispered, 'you are not unhappy?'

'Oh, no, no,' she cried. 'I am thankful, I am so thankful!'

'I said I would let you kiss me?' Lady Betty exclaimed with indignation. And her eyes scorched poor Tom. 'It's quite sure, sir, I said nothing of the kind.'

'But you said,' Tom stammered, 'that if I didn't do what you wanted, you wouldn't! And that meant that if I did, you would. Now, didn't it?'

Lady Betty shrugged her shoulders in utter disdain of such reasoning. 'Oh, la, sir, you are too clever for me!' she cried. 'I wasn't at college.' And she turned from him contemptuously.

They were at the horseblock under the oak, whither Tom had followed her, with thoughts bent on bold emprise. And at the first he had put a good face on it; but the lesson of the day before, and of the day before that, had not been lost. The spirit had gone out of him. The pout of her lips silenced him, a glance from her eyes – if they were cold or distant, harsh or contemptuous – sent his heart into his boots. He grovelled before her; it may be that he was of a nature to benefit by the experience.

Having snubbed him, she was silent awhile, that the iron might enter into his soul. Then she looked to see if he was sullen; she found that he was not. He was only heartbroken, and her majesty relented. 'I said, it is true,' she continued, 'that – that you might earn your pardon. Well, you are pardoned, sir; and we are where we were.'

'May I call you Betty, then?'

Lady Betty's eyes fell modestly on her fan. 'Well, you may,' she said. 'I think that is part of your pardon, if it gives you any pleasure to call me by my name. It seems vastly foolish to me.'

He was foolish. 'Betty!' he cried softly. 'Betty! Betty! It'll be the only name for me as long as I live. Betty! Betty! Betty!'

'What nonsense!' Lady Betty answered; but her gaze fell before his.

'Do you remember,' he ventured, 'what it was I said of your eyes?'

'Of my eyes?' she cried, recovering herself. 'No; of the maid's eyes, if you please. There was some nonsense said of them, I remember.'

'It was all true of your eyes!' Tom said, gathering courage and fluency. 'It's true of them now! And all I said to the maid, I say to you. And I wish, oh, I wish you were the maid again!'

'That you might be rude to me, I suppose?' she answered,

tracing a figure with her fan on the horseblock.

'No,' Tom cried. 'That I might show you how much I love you. That I might get nothing by you but yourself. Oh, Betty, give me a little hope! Say that – that some day I shall – I shall kiss you again.'

Betty, blushing and but half disdainful, studied the ground with a gravity that was not natural to her.

'Well, perhaps – in a year,' she faltered. 'Always supposing that you kiss no one in the meantime, sir.'

'A year, a whole year, Betty!' Tom protested.

'Yes, a year, not a day less,' she answered firmly. 'You are only a boy. You don't know your own mind. I don't know yet whether you would treat me well. And for waiting, I'll have no one kiss me,' Betty continued steadfastly, 'that cannot wait and wait, and doesn't think me worth the waiting. So, sir, if you wish to show that you are a man, you must show it by waiting.'

'A year!' Tom moaned. 'It's an age!'

'So it is to a boy,' she retorted. 'To a man it's a year. And as you don't wish to wait—'

'I will wait! I will indeed!' Tom cried.

'Remember you must kiss no one in the meantime,' Betty continued, drawing patterns on the block, 'nor write, nor speak, nor look a word of love. You will be on your honour, and – and you will wait till this day twelvemonth, sir.'

'I will,' Tom cried, 'I will, and thankfully, if you on your side, Betty—'

She sprang up. 'What?' she cried, on fire in an instant. 'You would make terms with me, would you?'

Tom, the bold, the bully, cringed. 'No,' he said. 'No, of course not. I beg your pardon, Betty.'

She was silent for a full half minute, and he thought her hopelessly offended. But when she spoke again it was hurriedly, and in a tone of strange, new shyness. 'Still, I – I don't ask what I won't give,' she said. 'You've kissed me, and you are not the same to me as – as others. I don't mind telling you that. And – and what is law for you shall be law for me. I suppose you understand,' she added, her face flaming more and more. And in her growing bashfulness she glanced at him angrily. 'I never – I never have flirted, of course,' she continued, despairing of making him understand; 'but I – I won't flirt this year if you are in earnest.'

Somehow Tom had got her hand, and was kissing it. And the two formed a pretty picture. But the time allowed them was short. Tom's ecstacy was interrupted by the sound of approaching footsteps. Sir Hervey and Sophia had descended the steps of the terrace followed by the old vicar, who looked little the worse for his fainting-fit. He bore on his arm a new gown, the gift of his patron, and the token of his own favour, if not of his wife's forgiveness. The three were so closely engaged in talk that until they came face to face with the other pair they were not conscious of their presence. Then for a moment Sophia faltered and hung back, shamed and conscience-stricken, reminded of the things she had said, and the worse things she had thought, of her friend. But in a breath the two girls were in one another's arms.

Tom looked, and groaned. 'Oh, Lord!' he said. 'A year! A whole year!'

Georgette Heyer

FARO'S DAUGHTER	25p
BEAUVALLET	25p
THE CORINTHIAN	25p
APRIL LADY	30p
BLACK SHEEP	30p
COUSIN KATE	30p
BATH TANGLE	30p
FREDERICA	30p
ARABELLA	30p
SPRIG MUSLIN	30p
THE MASQUERADERS	30p
THE TALISMAN RING	30p
THE CONVENIENT MARRIAGE	30p
THE TOLL-GATE	30p
ROYAL ESCAPE	30p
THE QUIET GENTLEMAN	30p
THE BLACK MOTH	30p
DEVIL'S CUB	30p
VENETIA	30p
REGENCY BUCK	30p
THESE OLD SHADES	30p
THE UNKNOWN AJAX	30p